Tom the Barber

CONRAD PELLETIER

A novel
by
Conrad Pelletier

Chapter 1

Jersey City could have laid claim to the name 'The Windy City,' but that moniker was unfortunately already taken by a little-known town in the mid-west. The winds are extraordinarily strong. Even though on the other side of the Hudson, in lower Manhattan, there may only be a mild breeze. The strength behind the winds in Jersey City can easily overwhelm you.

Tom's barber shop was on Grove Street. It was a single store front business inconspicuously placed in a row of eight other store fronts. Four of which were no longer occupied. The windows were large and elevated off the ground by about two feet. When the wind blew, they would rattle, and sometimes it seemed like they might come crashing in. Most were confident that would not happen based on how old the glass in the windows appeared to be. Over the years, the many layers of paint on the wood frames had become a structure unto themselves holding the glass firmly in place.

The shop used to be a haberdashery in the eighteen hundreds and was also a bakery until the twenties when Tom opened his shop. Barber shops do not really need a display window in the front like the haberdashers or bakeries do. So, Tom placed some bottles of men's hair products and photographs of different hair styles, just to fill it in. Most had been there and untouched for at least ten years. Even with all the spare time Tom had on his hands, dusting off the display products did not happen very often. None of his regulars seemed to mind.

The front steps were still made of wood, and some claimed they were likely the original steps from the previous century. That was probably true. Facing the chairs was a row of mirrors and a narrow shelf the barbers would use to place the tools they were not using at the moment. Items such as the extra combs, the neck duster brush, and the various other types of shears they would switch to as the need arose. Also, the latest electric clippers, which would hang on a hook just below the shelf.

Directly above the mirrors, was another shelf that held more items similar to what were found in the front window. In the center of the shelf was a case left open for display. It was a wooden case with a clasp on the front and the letters 'GS' on it. It held the old set of professional barber's tools Tom used when he first opened his shop. Everyone knew this case was special to him. But no one knew why for certain. Rumor was, it was a gift from some old friends.

The windows of the barber shop would let a lot of cold in. The single pane would transfer the cold and make the front of the shop too frigid to work in. During the winter months Tom would use the chair farthest away from the door to help keep warm. There were three chairs in the shop. Back in the days when things were busiest, all three would be filled. Two other barbers worked for Tom on Saturdays but only one during the week. There simply was not enough business for that now. Tom worked alone.

Some would say this city had seen its best days back when the docks were in full operation. By nineteen-fifty-eight though, things were in a sharp decline. Many of the wealthy residents had moved further west into the suburbs of New Jersey. The remaining neighborhoods were filled with people that would hold to the belief the city was better off when Frank Hague was mayor. Those were the boom years.

The Santorinis had lived in Jersey City since nineteen-oh-five when they first came over from Italy. Tom's Mamma and Papà came over first. Initially, Tom stayed with his grandparents in their hometown of Montoro Superiore in the

Province of Avellino. He would come later in nineteen-oh-nine to join them once they could afford to bring him.

Back when the docks were active, Tom was able to save enough to put his two children through school, but never had time or money to take a real vacation. There were some short stays on the Jersey shore each summer. They would go to the cottage of the owner of DiDonato's Pizza where Tom worked in the evenings to help make ends meet.

Tony DiDonato was a very generous man and a close friend. He would help his friends any way he could, especially Tom. He practically gave them the cottage for free one week each year. All the Santorinis had to do was cover the agent commission and the cottage was theirs for a few days.

Retirement was coming quickly for Tom. But being self-employed all his life, he would only be looking forward to a modest income on Social Security with a small amount in savings. Tom figured he could still cut hair part time in someone else's barber shop for a bit of extra income. He was certain though he did not want to keep his shop open.

There was some talk of moving somewhere warm to get away from the cold and the wind. One of Tom's former employees, Nick, had retired to Vallejo California and would tell him in letters he thought he had moved to get away from the winters but soon realized he had also escaped the summers. It is very dry in southern California and those hazy hot and humid summer days of the northeast had become a thing of the past for him as well. That sounded very appealing to Tom and Maria, his wife of thirty-seven years.

As business slowly diminished, Tom took up hobbies to pass the time between customers. During the week he would sometimes have several hours at a time on his hands. When his son Richard was little, Tom had taught him to make model airplanes and paint them himself.

As the years went on Tom continued doing models. He eventually worked his way up to tall ships with all the sails and rigging. He would work on them in the back room of the shop when no one was there. One Friday morning in the early spring of nineteen-fifty-nine Tom heard the front doorbell jingle from the back room. His customers knew even if he was not in the shop, he was likely out back.

Tony from the pizza shop came in with a newspaper. "Morning Tom," Tony called from the front door, "you gotta see this ad in the Times."

"What's it for?" Tom called back.

"You have to see it for yourself," Tony replied, "I'm not sure if it means anything. It says something about a veteran's pension in Italy. For guys over here who were in the Italian Army over there. I remember you were there during World War One, right?"

Most men from that war would rarely talk about their experiences during those times. It was just not to be discussed. It was a time from long ago in the past and was not to be relived if possible.

"Yeah," Tom replied, "what's it about?"

"Here read it for yourself," Tony replied, "I have to go start the gravy for this weekend."

"Okay," Tom replied, "when I can get to it."

Tony dropped the paper face down on the empty barber chair closest to the door. "See ya tonight," he said as he gave him a wave and left.

Tom worked two jobs for a long time. For years he had been with Tony flipping pizzas and preparing meals in the evening and occasionally on some weekends. Before that, he had worked with Tony's father at his restaurant. Tom glanced over at the front chair occasionally throughout the day. He was not anxious to pick up the paper since he would usually shy away from any memory of his days in the Italian Army. The paper sat there through six haircuts and two shaves. It had been an unusually busy Friday morning at the shop, but things slowed down after lunch. Later in the afternoon Tom had some time on his hands. It was about three o'clock when he finally reached for the paper.

It was chilled from the draft coming in the door, so Tom took it to the back chair and sat down to browse through the classifieds. He read other parts of the paper before going to the article Tony had mentioned. The page was folded over to mark the spot.

Finally, he turned to the page with the article and read: '*Notice to Men from Italy Who Fought in World War One.*' This was not the kind of headline that would make Tom want to read on, but since Tony had brought it to him, he decided to keep going.

'*If you were in the Italian Army in World War One and fought in the at least three Battles of the Insonso River and the Battle of Vittorio Veneto in the north mountain country from the Lower Piave to Tagliamento, the Italian government has set aside funds for a pension in honor of your service.*' That got his attention. But like most things there had to be a catch. He read a bit further and found it. '*You must apply in person at the Office for Army Affairs located in Rome within one year.*' Tom chuckled. "Right," he said under his breath. It also gave the address of the office he was to report to so he could apply.

Tom stopped for a moment and looked at himself in the mirror. "How 'bout that?" Tom said aloud "that would have been nice.......... Ah it ain't gonna happen." A trip to Italy was out of the question. He was not the type of man to let things like that bother him.

'Why couldn't we just go to the embassy here?' he thought to himself. "Huh, that would make too much sense............... All the way to Italy?" he said as he got up to greet the next customer who came in. Tom threw the paper to the floor mixed in with the hair clippings and did not pick it up again for the rest of the day.

· · · ·

FIVE O'CLOCK ROLLED around and Tom closed up the shop, so he could head over to DiDonato's for the evening. Fridays were the busiest evening for the pizzeria. It was when the young people would get their paychecks and want a night out. DiDonato's served the usual items including pizza, pasta dishes, subs, and salads.

The two went straight at it with the help of Tony's daughter Deborah who would wait on tables for whatever tips she could get. It did not pay well enough to make it worth doing all the time. But on Fridays, she knew her dad needed some help. It was an especially busy night. Probably due to the slight warming of spring, winds notwithstanding. All the tables were full by six thirty so Deborah would take the orders, and Tom would take the plates out when they were ready. Tony made the pizza up front and handled the cash register.

After the crowd left and only three tables were active, Tony finally decided to ask Tom what he thought of the advertisement. "So," Tony asked. "What did you think?"

"About what?" Tom asked, knowing full well what he meant.

"The paper Tom, the paper," he said sensing Tom was playing with him, "Did you read the ad?"

"Like most things," Tom quipped, "out of touch for most of us."

"What does that mean............out of touch," Tony asked sounding confused.

"I can't go all the way to Italy," Tom said with a tone of pessimism, "There's no money for that. Let's face it. If it cost ten cents to go clear around the world, I'd have a hard time getting out of sight."

"Tom?" Tony said sounding the way he would when orders were coming out late, "You can't do that. This could be a good thing for you." Tony knew just how long to pause. Tom shook his head and grunted.

"Look," Tony continued, "go home, tell Maria about it." He figured that might work. Maria could always help him see things differently. "Go now, I'll close up here."

"You sure?" Tom asked, "It was a tough night, and Deborah shouldn't stay late either."

"I'm sure," Tony said, "I'll send her home too. Talk about a long day, you're the ones that work two jobs. I can close up."

Tom agreed and took off his apron then washed his hands. As he was walking out the door, he thought about having thrown the paper on the floor. 'Good thing it will still be there in the morning,' he muttered to himself. Maria was sure to want to see it.

· · · ·

THE WALK HOME WAS STILL safe if he stayed on Montgomery Street where the lights were bright and there was traffic. The side streets, not so much. Tom would stay on the main streets mostly for his wife's sake, even if it took a bit longer to get home. She wanted him to be safe. These settings never frightened him though. If something came up, Tom could always handle himself. Even nearing retirement, he would walk with a sense of confidence which would make the troublemakers in the area think twice about messing with him.

Tom arrived home at about nine o'clock and walked up the front steps. He opened the door with his key and stepped in as usual. "Hi, you're home early, things slow tonight at Tony's?" Maria said as he walked into the living room. She was busy straightening up after Richard's family had left for home. "Everything all right?"

"Nothing to worry about," Tom replied, "Tony sent me home early and insisted I tell you about this ad thing he brought in this morning."

"What ad?" she asked, "somebody selling something?"

Tom chuckled, "you must have read it. Selling... sounds about right....selling something."

"Tony usually doesn't get excited about things. What was it?" she persisted.

Tom took his coat off and hung it up in the hall closet. "Something about a pension fund for vets from Italy," he said hoping she would drop it there.

"Army?" she asked, "you weren't in the Army." Then she thought for a moment, "oh right, the Italy Army. Is that what it was talking about? The Italian Army?" Maria sounded confused.

"Yeah, yeah that's it............. for the Italian Army," he said reassuring her, "you know, World War One."

"Oh, sore subject huh?" she said knowing some of the history. Or so she thought.

"Eh, that's all right," Tom continued, "I haven't really thought about it too much for years now."

Maria was not totally convinced of that. But she could tell it was a bit better for him. Usually, he would not say a word when the subject of the Great War came up. Even at family events, he tended to avoid the subject.

"Where is this ad you're talking about?" she asked.

"Left it at work in the pile of hair," Tom said sheepishly.

Maria paused and looked at Tom. This sounded just like him. "Now that makes for an interesting image in my mind," she said followed by her adorable giggle that she never lost from when she was a girl, "A pile of hair you didn't sweep up before going home. When has that ever happened?"

"I had to work tonight, remember?" Tom said.

"Slow afternoon no doubt?" she teased, "hair from the morning still on the floor?"

Tom shrugged his shoulders and grunted.

Maria could tell he did not really care. "I have to run errands near the shop tomorrow," she continued, "I'll come by and check out this ad Tony was talking about."

"Okie Dokie." he said with an expected sigh. "So, Richard and Beth came by?" Tom added desperately trying to change the subject.

"Just for a bit," she answered. "He had to go early. He has to work tomorrow."

Tom sat in his favorite chair and looked for someplace to put his feet up. "Since you're home early," Maria asked, "you want to play some cribbage?"

"Always want to play cribbage," he replied reaching for the drawer in the end table to get the cards and the old board. They sat for about an hour and ran through only one board. Tom was tired and knew he had to work in the morning. But even one run through was worth the effort.

· · · ·

BY MORNING, THE WINDS had died down some and it was a bit warmer than the day before. It was a wonderful day for running errands. It gave the feeling that everything was coming back to life after a hard winter.

While cleaning up in the morning, Tom shook off the paper and put it back on the front chair so as not to lose it for when Maria came by. He still was not convinced there was anything to all of it. They decided she would stop after her errands so she could leave some of what she bought with Tom to carry home for her. Rather than go after and have to carry things home herself.

Tom did not work for Tony most Saturday evenings unless he really had to. That had always been family time. He would work two or three evenings per week and occasionally on Sunday afternoons. But usually not on Saturday night. They continued the practice after the kids were grown.

Three doors down worked an old friend and one of his regular customers. George came mid-morning for his monthly haircut. "That today's paper?" he said as he reached for the one on the chair.

"No, yesterday's," Tom said.

"Oh, I already read that one." George said as he walked back to get into Tom's chair at the end, "Hey did you see the ad? You know that one about the Italian Army?"

"You're kidding," Tom said as he was putting the sheet over him, "It sounds like everyone saw it. So, you saw it too?"

"Yeah, thought of you when I read it," George continued, "kinda thought I might see you come in yesterday." He was a travel agent who specialized in European vacations. His business was on the same row of store fronts as the barber shop. One of the only ones left. "I could set you up."

"I know George," Tom said sadly, "It all seems simple to you. You do this all the time. But I can't go all the way to Italy. I don't want to waste the little savings I have. I have to look at retirement and all. Who knows, maybe if I retire, we can move to a warmer climate? Well, once I sell this place that is............... Hey, you wanna become a barber?"

George shook his head, "Same old Tom. There are deals out there you know," George persisted.

"Yeah, ten percent off, I've seen those in the paper too," Tom moaned, "If you go when no one else wants to go."

"No, I mean real deals," he said unwilling to let it go, "Hey, think about it. I'd love to see you enjoy yourself for a change."

"Now you're sounding like Maria," Tom said with a chuckle. They chatted a bit while Tom cut George's hair. It did not take too long, there was not much on top for George, he usually wore a hat to protect his head from the sun.

As George was leaving, Maria walked in. "Maria, talk some sense into this man," George said pointing at Tom.

"Oh, he has plenty of sense," Maria responded, "Never lacking in that. How's Angie?"

"Doing good," he said, willing to get off the subject, "She misses the boy. First one off to college and all."

"Tell her I said hi," Maria added.

"Will do, got it," he said and then with a slight humorous sneer looked at Tom and added, "Bye Tom."

"Yeah, yeah," Tom answered grumbling.

No one else was in the shop at that time. The radio on the upper shelf was playing big band music. Very softly though, Tom did not really like things to be too loud.

"Find everything you were looking for?" he said trying to avoid the obvious subject. She was in no rush, so she began to show him a few things she had bought. Like most husbands, he pretended to be interested as he looked on.

Maria really could not play the game any longer. "Is that it?" she said pointing to the paper on the front chair.

Tom realized it was inevitable at this point. "Page is folded where the ad is," he said then walked to the back almost trying to run away. Maria found the ad and started to read.

"I think I remember you told me about that Battle of Vittorio Veneto," she said, "it sounds familiar. Near the end of the war, right?"

"That's what they say," he said almost in a whisper.

"You haven't been to Italy in almost forty years. Don't you want to see it again?" she said hoping he would consider it, "Besides, you probably still have some relatives you haven't seen in forever."

"Not really," Tom said, "After two wars most are gone or spread out to who knows where."

"Well, you need to think it over. Don't give it up just yet," she said knowing where to stop, then changed the subject. "Slow afternoon?"

Tom sighed "Hmm, they're getting to be that way more and more this year. Glad I'm thinking of retiring."

Unexpectedly, Tony walked in, "Well you guys talk about this?" he asked.

Maria gave him the look that said, 'not now.' Tony tilted his head back to acknowledge but decided to keep going anyway. There was an awkward silence for a moment. "Look," Tony said not wanting to give it up, "I've been thinking and......if you go...... I'll cover your hotel while you're there. Up to two weeks. That should be enough time to have some fun and look into this pension thing. Besides, the rest of the time would be on the ocean liner. That's even more time to enjoy yourselves. Can't pass that up now, can you?" Tony paused for a moment to see how Tom would react. "That could help you get out of sight, right Tom?"

"Between you and Maria, you already have me on some ocean liner," Tom said shaking his head.

"Hey," Tony laughed, "you'd love it."

"Yeah, yeah," Tom moaned again.

"Hard to pass up an offer like that Tom," Maria jumped in seeing Tony was making some headway in getting to him.

Tony knew to leave while he was ahead. "Go talk to George and see what he's got for deals, then decide," Tony said quickly, "See ya Monday. Bye Maria, love you guys."

"Bye-bye," she replied, "Love you too."

'How did he know George was just here?' Tom thought to himself as the door closed, 'maybe they're in cahoots.' He shook his head and looked at Maria, "They're all working against me," he said.

The silent look with her head tilting just to the left spoke directly to Tom with the inescapable, 'Well?'

A short pause led him to realize the it was time to give up. "All right, probably no one's coming the rest of the afternoon anyway," he said reaching for his coat, "I'll close up."

He turned the open sign around and put the key in the lock starting to close the door, "Just leave the things you bought here, we'll get them on the way back."

• • • •

GEORGE'S SATURDAY AFTERNOONS were the same as Tom's. There was no one in his office when they came in. That was why George went to get his hair cut earlier.

"Boy, you're good," George said to Maria, "Twenty-five minutes? That's got to be some sort of record."

"Yeah, yeah," Tom grumbled.

"Tony had something to do with it too," Maria said, "he's offering to cover our hotel while we're there."

"Wow." George exclaimed, "That's a deal."

"What is it with you two and deals," Tom jabbed, "it's still a lot of money."

"Well, speaking of deals. I barely had time to look it up," George said reaching for the binder he had just put on his desk, "There is an Ocean Liner that leaves New York every six weeks for Italy. If money is the issue, I can get you a decent price in Tourist class. Not much luxury. But it'll get you there."

"You mean steerage?" Tom grumbled.

George paused, trying to grasp what Tom had said. "I haven't heard that term in a long time Tom," he replied, "they don't call it steerage anymore. It's called Tourist class."

"Same thing," Tom said, "Same cabins as before, just a new name. Still steerage."

"Ah," George moaned looking at Maria, "Work on him? Please." She just shook her head.

Tom did not want to show it, but he was starting to like the idea. As they were talking, he began to reminisce about his youth in Italy. Summers there are beautiful, especially if you could go out to vineyard country. The warm breezes though the hillsides, the sound of the farm animals as you walk down the country road. These were some very fond memories of childhood that started to sparkle in his mind. One summer, in particular when his father took him to a horse farm. That was where he learned to ride. He always wanted to do that again someday, but never did.

Then there were the four years he stayed in Italy with his grandparents when his Mamma and Papà moved to America. That was filled with a mix of emotions. Some being when he had fun with his friends and some missing his parents.

'Back to the now,' Tom thought. "How much?" he asked.

"That's what I've always like about you Tom," George said with his famous smile "right to the point.......... Ah, let's see here.......... tourist class? Okay, here," George slid the book over to Tom and Maria to show them the figures.

"Yeah?" Tom said with reservation. Even with a good deal like the one George was showing him, he was not used to spending money on himself.

George gave it a little time to settle in. "Didn't the ad say something about a pension fund?" he asked, "hey if it's a decent amount of money each month, the trip could pay for itself in a couple of years. I remember it said something like thirty thousand Lira or something, what per month?"

"Sounds right," Maria jumped in.

"So, per month?" George responded. "In dollars that's............hmmm............. hey, adds up fast, put that together with your Social Security and you could do Okay. Makes it sound worth it right?"

Tom looked at him without saying a word. However, Maria knew what was going through his mind. He was close, really close.

Chapter 2

We all have our special memories. Some are our favorites we hope we will never lose. Those moments when you wish you could stop time and live it forever. It seems that any day's experience pales in comparison. And then there are the memories that we would not even want others to have.

< < <

Gaetano had not seen his parents in nearly four years when his grandmother got word they were sending for him. His grandfather had passed away two years earlier in nineteen-oh-seven from a heart attack. His grandmother was doing well but was slowing down some. Gaetano had grown close to his grandmother during that time, and it helped him to learn to take responsibility for himself and care for others who depended on him.

He worked in a small vineyard just outside of their town after school cleaning up and doing light field work as needed. He even learned a bit about how wine is made. The owner of the vineyard Santino Rizzi taught him some important things. They would prove helpful throughout his life.

His hometown was very traditional. Most families had been living there for generations. Some had migrated there from Spain during the Spanish Inquisition and now were considered natives of the region.

Gaetano had a few friends. They were good kids from good homes. He would spend most of his time with them. There were also a couple of troublemakers around. He was able to avoid them, and they knew Gaetano well enough not to cross him.

Young Gaetano was not very tall and expectedly thin at this age. He tended to be quiet around people he did not know very well. Looking for problems was the last thing he would do. But he would face them head on whenever they came his way. There was a good school in their town as well. When his grandfather died, Gaetano had to stop going since his grandmother needed him around the house. Then, before he knew it, the time came for him to go to America.

In mid-November of nineteen-oh-nine, his grandmother and Signor Rizzi took him to Napoli to see him off. He was to board a ship for America at only fifteen years old. Gaetano and his grandmother had made this trip just four years earlier when his parents Filippo and Fabiana had departed for their chance at the American dream.

Gaetano's father was a determined man. He was committed to working as many jobs as it took to get his family established and then bring his son to be with them. Once they had landed in New York Harbor, Filippo took the first job that he could find. He was able to get a job working on the docks in Jersey City. The hours were long and strenuous. He was on the crew that loaded the ships bound for Europe. They transferred lumber and grain from the trains which came from west of New York.

The ships which would dock across the harbor in New York City would usually be loaded with textiles and other products that were manufactured in the city. Hoboken and Jersey City would see all the other things shipped to the area by train from points west.

As the ships arrived, they unloaded the stones from the decks below. At that time there were more exports from America to Europe than imports. The ships would be loaded with cobble stones in Europe as ballast to keep them from capsizing. This had been done for over one hundred years. Rather than dispose of the cobble stones, they were used to pave the streets throughout New York City and the surrounding areas.

His favorite task on the docks was to work the cranes which would unload the ships. The control compartment was at the top of the crane. From there he could see the Statue of Liberty and Ellis Island where he and his wife had first landed. Each and every time he would see them, he would think of Gaetano and how he missed him. His wife would later say that Filippo worked harder in those years than any other time in his life. He loved his family, and it broke his heart to be separated from any of them for even the shortest time. The harder he worked, the sooner he would see his son again.

• • • •

THE HARBOR IN NAPOLI was the busiest place Gaetano had ever seen. It was also a rather dangerous place. That became very evident shortly after he and his grandmother arrived early that morning.

"Stay close to us," Signor Rizzi said as they got out of the train car.

"So many people," Gaetano said with a gasp.

"Not our kind of people Gaetano," his grandmother said, "you have to be careful when you are around strangers in a place like this."

"I'll be careful Nonna," he replied.

As they were getting off the train and gathering their things, a boy around nineteen and quite a bit larger than Gaetano snatched a bag from one of the ladies nearby and started to run. She was holding it close to her and very tightly. The thief had to pull it so hard she almost fell to the ground. It was obvious from the terror in her eyes that all of what she had was in the bag he took. The tickets for her voyage, the papers she would need to enter America and all her money, as little as it may be. Gaetano was only around ten yards from them when it happened. The kid made one grave miscalculation. He ran in Gaetano's direction.

He was in full stride when he passed Gaetano. At first it would seem to anyone watching Gaetano had not noticed what just happened. However, as the kid was about to pass him, Gaetano turned and grabbed his shirt just inside of his left shoulder. With the momentum he had been running at full speed, Gaetano simply leaned back and spun him around. To make it more effective, Gaetano also put his right foot out which tripped him and caused him to lose his balance even more.

By the time, the kid realized that he was not running straight anymore, he was aiming right for the side of the train, headfirst. He struck the metal side of the train with his forehead at full speed. This quickly put him into a daze. Then Gaetano hit him four times before he realized he had been hit once.

Everyone watching must have wondered what went through his mind as he hit the ground face first. He landed so hard, he did not move muscle until the police arrived. Gaetano, Signor Rizzi, and his grandmother were long gone by then and the lady had her bag returned to her.

• • • •

THE SHIP HE WAS GOING to travel on was named The Saint Paul, an American ship. She was first launched in eighteen-ninety-five from Philadelphia to South Hampton. The capacity for passengers was three hundred and fifty first class passengers, two hundred and twenty second class passengers and eight hundred steerage passengers. It was not the largest ship to bring immigrants to their new lives. But it certainly would do for Gaetano who of course would travel in steerage.

The Santorinis understood their place and did not hold any jealousy for those who were better off. But human nature always would have one wish that someday, maybe someone in the family would get to travel first class. Gaetano realized too much thinking about things like that would ruin the trip. So, he put the thought aside for the time being. After all, getting to his parents was the only thing that really mattered.

The only thing he regretted about this trip was leaving his grandmother behind. If only she could go with him, then the whole family would be together again. He was glad though that Signor Rizzi had come with them, and he would see her home. His grandmother would not have been able to make the trip back alone.

When they had come before, back in nineteen-oh-five to bring his parents, his grandfather was still alive. Gaetano was with them then as well. For his grandmother, the trip home back then was easier. This would be harder for her especially since the last of her family was going away. It would now be just her. Signor Rizzi promised he would check in on her from time to time once they got back.

"You be a good boy on the boat," Signor Rizzi told him, "remember what I taught you."

"I will," Gaetano replied, "I'm going to tell my Papà all of the things you showed me since he left."

Signor Rizzi looked up at his grandmother and grinned, "Well," he said, "maybe not everything." These years had been very formidable for Gaetano and the things he should have learned from his father needed to come from somewhere. Signor Rizzi filled in nicely.

"You be sure to write," his grandmother said.

"Every month Nonna. Just like Mamma does," he said. But deep down hoped he actually would. He had never really had to write to anyone before on a regular basis. His grandmother did all the writing to his parents and would ask Gaetano what he wanted to say to them. He would not actually do the writing himself. This just helped to speed it along. Sometimes young boys put things off too much. His grandmother wanted to get the mail sent before Gaetano started to shave. So, as a result, he never really picked up writing letters on his own. Besides, his mother would probably take over writing things for him when sending letters home.

• • • •

THE SCENE AT THE DEPARTURE of The Saint Paul was typical with the passengers standing along the deck railings and the loved ones left behind waving with the cheers and tears. Gaetano called out to his grandmother and Signor Rizzi even though he figured they could not hear him. He was fairly sure he could see them in the crowd, but it was hard to pick out just two people from over a thousand. He waved and waved.

"Good-bye Nonna, good-bye Nonna, I love you Nonna," he kept shouting. He did not stop until the ship had pulled away from the dock and his voice was hoarse.

The process of leaving the harbor seemed long, but only took about thirty minutes. It was midday when they hit the sea. Gaetano noticed he continued to see land to the east off the starboard side. The ship did not go straight out into the Mediterranean as he would have imagined but stayed within view of Italy and France. The ship needed to go to Marseille to make another pick up of passengers that were also going to America. They passed between the mainland of Italy and the Islands of Sardegna and Corsica. Signor Rizzi had shown him on a map what it all looked like before they left.

Gaetano thought they would not see any land after an hour or so from what friends of his had told him when he talked about leaving. He just watched the coastline as the ship seemed closer at times and farther away at times. The land almost went out of sight at one point only to return a few minutes later. But the open sea was indeed ahead.

It was getting late, and Gaetano was tired from the train ride and the day's activities including his confrontation with the kid that snatched the bag, brief as it happened to be. It shook him up more than he let on. He went down the three levels to one of the decks below the water line where his cabin was located. They had allowed the third-class passengers to be on the upper decks as the ship left port but once he went down those stairs, they would not let him back up. So, he stayed up as long as he could, looking at the land going by.

He had been shown where his cabin was before he went up to wave goodbye. He shared it with five other young men. Four were heading for America like him and one was going to South Hampton, England returning from visiting the wine country of Italy on business.

This young man would make this trip three or four times a year to arrange for imports of wine to London. He worked for a distributor there. His name was Niles. The owner of the wine distributor had somewhat adopted Niles at a young age and trained him in his field. Niles was wandering the streets when he was fifteen and was nearly picked up by the police on several occasions. He would have been placed in an orphanage if caught but managed to avoid them by hiding in a tool shed behind the home of the owner of the wine company each night. One night the owner discovered him and soon took a liking to him.

At first though, the owner was going to have him hauled off for trespassing, but the young man managed to talk his way out of it. He was very clever and there was something spunky about him that this man just did not see in boys this age. He gave him a chance if he promised to work for his board.

From there, he started to teach him about the wine business. The particulars of how the wine needed to be made and what brought about a successful vintage. Niles learned these things early on.

He knew what he was to watch out for in choosing good wines. The owner of the distributorship used to make this trip himself and then started to bring Niles with him. But between aging and failing health, he needed to have someone take his place. Niles was in the right place at the right time and had no problem taking over this part of the operation.

He would make the trip to see how the crops were that year and arrange shipments that would follow on cargo ships. Niles was only twenty-four years old but acted like an old pro when it came to travel.

He spoke Italian very well but Gaetano only new a few words in English. Signor Rizzi was able to speak a little English and while working would try to help Gaetano to learn some basics. Once they knew he was going to America, Gaetano started to listen because now it mattered.

"Why do you travel third class when you're here to make money?" Gaetano asked Niles in Italian.

"Well," he started to say in English then switched to Italian, "It's not what you make it's what you keep as the saying goes. I would rather spend it at home than on a boat ride." Then he looked at the others knowing they only spoke Italian and said in English with as much cockney as he could insert, "Ain't that royt ya blokes?" They just looked at him and shrugged. Niles and Gaetano both broke into a long laugh.

"Oi let's get outta here," he said to Gaetano in English, "Come on, got some of me mates to introduce you to." He could tell Gaetano did not totally understand so he waved to follow him and then gave a slight translation in Italian, minus the slangs.

"I'm gonna help ya with your English I will," he said. Gaetano did not really understand but Niles knew it by the look on his face, "Awe, we'll work on it."

Niles knew several members of the crew due to his regular travel. He wanted to introduce Gaetano to some of them. They were mostly third-class stewards. There also was a man who worked in the dining room on their level. He was a bit older than the rest.

"Billy my boy," Niles called out to one of them as they were walking down the hallway, "Want you to meet one of me bunk mates." Gaetano did not understand a word but knew what was going on, so he put his hand out. "Billy, meet Gaetano, Gaetano, meet Billy." They shook hands and made noises that sounded like greetings but neither of them could tell. They both thought it must be in the other's language, so they smiled and nodded.

"Gaetano," Niles said faking a pondering moment, "what kind of name is that, is that Italian or something?" Niles' bantering caused Billy to bust up laughing. Gaetano did not know what they were joking about but figured it must be good.

Billy Fitzgerald was an Irish kid. He was twenty-two years old and came from New York. Billy had been working on the ship for a year and a half. They chatted with him for a few minutes and then moved on.

As they approached the stairs, they ran into one of the other stewards. "Claude, Hey Claude," Niles called out, "Bon Jour ya nubbie."

Claude turned around. "Oh no, not you again. They'll let anybody on this ship," he quipped with a thick Canadian accent.

"What's the matter Frenchie, still mad at me for dumping your sister?" Niles said with a sinister smile.

"I wouldn't let you anywhere near my sister you limey," Claude said giving Niles a punch in the arm.

"Awe now, thems fightin woyds mate. Put 'em up," Niles responded and then they started to spar. But it looked more like dancing. Gaetano was smiling and laughing. He was definitely enjoying the show.

"Hey, stop your foolin' 'round," Niles said trying to stand straight up, "This here is Gaetano. From Italy, you know......the big boot."

"I'll give you the big boot," Claude bounced back to Niles as he reached out to shake Gaetano's hand and greeted him with the four of five Italian words he knew with a little French mixed in.

Claude was twenty-four and originally from Montreal before he moved to New York. He landed the job on the steamship because he could speak fluent French. This would be his third year on the crew.

Next, they passed by one of the service rooms and Niles looked in. He saw Benjamin sitting at a table and pulled Gaetano into the room. "This one is very quiet. Got to watch out for the quiet ones," he said to Gaetano in Italian, "Benny, meet Gaetano, one of me bunk mates." He went back to English because Benny could not speak Italian. Benny nodded and shook his hand.

"So, start that family yet?" Niles said to tease him.

"Yeah, you're funny, but looks ain't everything," Benny jabbed, "Time for more wine? Bring some for me this time?"

"You ain't old enough ya bloke," Niles sneered with his characteristic smile.

"I am now," Benny replied, "Just turned twenty-one last month."

Benjamin was the youngest crewman. He was from New York. His father worked in the textile industry there. He did not approve of Benjamin working on the steamship. That was no way to start a family and a waste of his time in his father's mind. The whole idea of starting a family was something Benny was preoccupied with and would talk about constantly. Mostly because it was so important to his father.

After meeting the stewards Niles took Gaetano to the dining hall. "Now this is the guy you really want to know," Niles said, "he'll take right good care of ya where it matters." pointing to Gaetano's stomach.

This was the older man. He was about thirty-five. His name was Rocco DiDonato. "He speaks your Italian too," Niles said, "Hey Rocco, meet young Gaetano here. He's one of me bunk mates this trip. Say something to him in Italian. I think the boy's homesick already."

Gaetano's eyes lit up. They chatted a bit in Italian and exchanged the obvious 'What town are you from' questions. Niles was able to chime in from time to time, but it was like these two had always known each other. After a while, Niles gave them the high sign stating it was time to get going.

"Gaetano," Rocco said, "you make sure you come see me when you're hungry, I'll take good care of you." Gaetano nodded with a big smile. They left and went back to the cabin.

That night Gaetano had a tough time falling asleep. He had never been on a ship before. Sleeping on something that moved was a bit unnerving for him. Add that to the noise of the other five in the cabin with all the snoring and grunting. It was not a very good night's sleep. Finally, around three o'clock, he dozed off with the pillow over his head.

• • • •

BY DINNER TIME ON THE second day, they were coming up on Spain and Gaetano hoped he would see the Rock of

Gibraltar. His mother had written of her amazement at the sight in her first letter back home. She wrote it while on their voyage just four years before but did not mail until almost a month later.

She wrote five letters while on board The Republic, the ship they had sailed on, describing all the joys and wonders of the trip. She mailed them all in the same envelope to save on the cost of postage. Many of these things led Gaetano to anticipate what his next two weeks would be like. He went at it with an excitement he had never feasted on before.

Being it was mid-November, the days were shorter than when his mother had passed through the Straits of Gibraltar. She had gone in May. So, his view of the great rock was limited to moonlight and only being able to look through a port hole at that. It was still quite an incredible sight to bear though. The mountains around Montoro seemed like mounds of dirt compared. It was just as his mother had said. He would have liked to see it from the upper deck, but the restrictions on the third-class passengers were enforced now. It still impressed him, nonetheless. He realized his view was likely the same as what his mother had seen. They were booked in steerage too.

• • • •

THE ARRIVAL IN SOUTH Hampton came quickly. England was chilly and damp at that time of year, so Gaetano stayed below most of the time they were in port. He was used to the Mediterranean weather and did not do well with the cold. He met Niles at the bottom of the stairs which led to the gangway.

"Niles!" Gaetano called out to him.

"Thought I was going to leave without sayin' good-bye?" Niles said, smiling back at him.

"Look me up if you make it to New York," Gaetano said in English. The short time working on his English with Niles had paid off. He was catching on fast.

"Wut? Of course, I will, you're me mate," Niles replied with a jab to the side. Gaetano knew what that meant in English. They embraced and he was off. Niles had been around long enough to know they would never see each other again.

The change in climate was causing Gaetano to feel a bit ill with a stuffy head and sore throat. The ship was not going to leave harbor for another eight hours. He decided to go below and get some sleep. He was much more tired than he thought at first and slept though dinner. Rocco saved him some food because one of his roommates told him Gaetano was not feeling very well when he asked about him. When Gaetano woke up, he was a bit disoriented. The roommate who had told Rocco about him sleeping was there.

"What time is it?" Gaetano asked.

"Late," he replied.

"Awe, I missed......." Gaetano started to say.

"Don't worry," he interrupted, "the guy in the dining room said to go see him."

The dining hall was closed with most of the lights out. Gaetano walked in anyway and went towards the swinging doors which led to the kitchen. The lights were still on. As he poked his head in Rocco saw him. "Pensavo di vederti," Rocco said with a smile.

That evening Gaetano and Rocco spent quite a while talking about all types of things. Even though Rocco was twenty years older, he took a liking to this young man from Italy who was going to America just as he had with his parents twenty-five years earlier. Rocco saw many young men on their way to New York. Many just like Gaetano. But this one seemed different.

They spoke mostly in Italian but sometimes Rocco would switch to English. "You're going to have to learn," Rocco said, "you can talk in Italian around your family, but out there, you need to know English. That's how you make it in America."

Gaetano already knew that by what Signor Rizzi had taught him. It was commonly understood in his family as well. He remembered his Papà and Mamma practicing their English before they left some years before.

After they had been talking for about an hour, Rocco told him this was to be his last trip. "I've been doing this for over ten years," he said, "I finally saved up enough money to open my own restaurant."

"Tired of being seasick and going to all of those different countries?" Gaetano asked.

"Not so much that," Rocco replied, "My wife is going to have our first baby in six months. That will give me enough time to get things started. I have family who can help me get things going."

"That's great, a Papà? I've got a long way to go before that," Gaetano chuckled hoping it was indeed true, "Where are you thinking of having your place, your restaurant?"

"Well, you haven't been there yet so you wouldn't know what it meant if I told you," Rocco said with some hesitation.

"No, no, my Mamma has been writing letters," Gaetano jumped in, "she tells me all about it. I feel as if I already know the place."

"Okay, maybe," Rocco conceded, "I'm thinking New Jersey. It probably costs less to get started there. I want to have something I can leave to my family when I'm gone."

"See I told you I knew," Gaetano exclaimed, "My Mamma and Papà live in New Jersey."

"That's right, you did tell me," Rocco replied.

"Do you want a boy or a girl?" Gaetano asked.

Rocco didn't hesitate, "Either will be fine with me. But a boy would be my first choice. Then he can take care of his little sisters when they come along. You know from all the other boys."

"What will you name it?" Gaetano said a bit confused, "I mean him...............or her."

Rocco chuckled because he had said the same thing when his wife told him she was pregnant, "My wife says she picked out names already."

"Really?" Gaetano said, "My Mamma told me she didn't name me until the day I was born. What names did she pick?"

"She told me if it's a girl, her name would be Delanna," he said as if he hoped it would not be, "and if a boy, Anthony." That came out with much more confidence, which was about all the two of them could handle talking about babies. So, the subject was quickly changed.

Rocco paused for a moment. "That's enough for one night," he said, "we both need to get some sleep."

Gaetano agreed and they said their good nights, and each went their way.

· · · ·

ON THE FIFTH DAY OF the trip, Gaetano was walking to the dining hall when he heard someone call him.

"Gitano, hey," Billy had not pronounced his name right, but Gaetano did not really mind.

"Hi Billy," he responded best he could. His English was getting much better.

"You gotta come see something," Billy said but Gaetano did not really understand him very well. "I got something I want you to see after dinner. We'll meet right here, all right?" Billy managed to communicate the point he was trying to make. Gaetano nodded to show he understood.

After dinner they met right outside of the dining hall and Billy took him upstairs to the deck where he had been on to watch the Rock of Gibraltar. They went to the port side close to the bow this time rather than the Starboard where he had been to see the Rock.

"Wait 'til you see this," Billy said. He wanted Gaetano to see the sun set over the water. They were still on a level where they had to look through portholes. They watched for about twenty minutes and then the moment was just perfect. The sun was right at the point where it was touching the water.

"Sembra che si aprano le porte del paradiso," Gaetano said in Italian and gasped.

Billy did not understand him but figured he must really like it.

Gaetano gazed more and let out a few sounds which do not need translation. "è dove il paradiso incontra la terra," he said adding even more emotion. He could tell Billy did not understand. "It is where heaven meets earth," he said in English the best he could.

Billy nodded. He had never thought of it that way before. But could see what he meant.

Gaetano stood there in awe wondering if there was anything more beautiful. The red sky above and the seemingly still water made this a sight he would remember and treasure his whole life.

· · · ·

THE SAINT PAUL WAS scheduled to arrive late on the twenty-sixth of November. It was delayed slightly and did not pull into New York harbor until early morning on the twenty-seventh. They allowed the third-class passengers to come up to the main deck but not the upper decks. Gaetano watched with the same amazement as most of the other passengers at the sight of New York before them. Rocco told him about the Statue of Liberty and to make sure he did not miss it. Gaetano was already aware of it from his mother's letters. But still, it was a spectacular sight to see.

Seeing the New York skyline from the river was equally amazing. However, his primary desire was to see his parents. The ship docked in New York across from the Statue. Being that he was in steerage, the time for processing for him would take longer.

The first and second-class passengers only had to go through some routine questions on board by the officials and a quick medical exam. Then they would be allowed to leave the ship. All the steerage passengers would then be loaded onto ferry boats and brought to Ellis Island for further examination. They were told to go back to their rooms and stay there. It was not so simple a task considering all the languages which were being spoken.

After quite some time Gaetano could hear activity around the corner and figured something was starting to move along. A couple minutes later, Benny and Claude came through with a list and a bag. Benny had the list and Claude had the bag.

Benny would look at the list and ask each person in the room his name. After they said their name, Claude would take out a tag, write a number on it, and pin it on him. This was for identification so the officials could track the steerage passengers when they got to Ellis Island. The tag would reference the line number on the ship's manifest for each person. It was so they could be processed faster.

As they were being led to the ferry boats, one passenger jumped off the dock into the water and began to swim away. It only took a minute for a small patrol boat to pull up. He soon realized he had nowhere to go and gave up. They fished him out and were not very gentle with him.

"Probably a criminal," he heard a man behind him say in Italian. Gaetano turned and looked at the man. "They would have figured out he was a criminal once they got him over there anyway. He probably thought it was his only chance at getting into America."

Several ferries were carrying the steerage passengers. They could see others coming from a couple of docks upriver. Gaetano knew that meant things would take a long time. Once they reached Ellis Island, they had them form a line. It was a very, very long line which stretched from the dock, through the baggage room in the main building and up a very steep flight of stairs.

The passengers probably did not realize it, but they had purposely had them climb the stairs to see how many of them would be out of breath or start wheezing or coughing. This was the first phase of the health inspection. There were over sixty different symptoms they would scan for.

When they came to where the doctors were, they were instructed by finger signs to stand three across. The doctors would examine them three at a time. The one thing Gaetano disliked the most was the test for trachoma, an eye disease which would cause blindness and sometimes death. This was very contagious and one of the primary reasons people would get rejected. They reached for his eyes, and he winced. They gave him a sharp rebuke and went at it again, turning back his eyelids to see if there was any trace of the infection. His eyes were clear, so they moved him on quickly.

Fortunately, even though they were busy that day, the official who did the eye exam on Gaetano was a doctor. Some of the other people were inspected by what was known as the buttonhook men. They would use instruments like hairpins or buttonhooks to conduct the exam. This doctor was considerably more gentle with Gaetano. He saw the exam being done on others and was very thankful that a real doctor had examined him.

He noticed about two out of every ten immigrants would have either a blue or white chalk mark placed on their number tag. The blue tag stood for some type of disease and the white marks stood for a mental disorder. The blue tags also had a letter abbreviation code that the inspectors came up with. For example, Ft meant they had a problem with their feet and Pg meant the woman was pregnant.

Those with diseases were sent to the Ellis Island infirmary for further treatment and possible quarantine. If anyone was deemed not curable, they were rejected and sent back.

In order to dissuade the ocean liner companies from bringing people with real medical or mental problems, there was a law passed in nineteen-oh-three that required the liner company to return the rejected immigrant to their port of origin at the liners' expense. Plus, there was a one hundred dollar fine per rejected passenger. This deterred most, but there were still many who would be sent back.

Then came the difficult part. They entered the legal hall where they would verify identification and basic abilities. Gaetano saw a variety of tests being done to different people, sometimes based on the nationality. For example, they were testing people who were Afghanistan to see if they could even hold a pencil. Serbians would be asked to read a passage from the Bible.

Gaetano had some schooling which, compared with many others, made him appear well educated. He could read and write and solve basic arithmetic problems. They even gave him a geometric puzzle to complete, and he put it together quickly. One inspector looked to another and nodded this one could go.

There was one last stop. He walked up to the documentation desk and showed them his papers. "Gitano Santorini?" the voice called out.

"That's royt," Gaetano said trying to imply he could speak a bit of English. He thought he would impress them with the little he had learned from Niles, cockney accent, and all. These inspectors were not prone to laughter, but the sight of a fifteen-year-old Italian trying to sound like a British street kid was too much for them. Several of them broke into a hearty laugh and other inspectors who were too far to hear wondered what it was all about. As they would pass the story down the line each one would try to imitate the cockney accent Italian style, more joined the laughter. It was the high point of their day.

It did not help though. The inspector could not pronounce his first name, so he looked in a translation booklet they had handy to see which name to assign him. There was a booklet for each nationality.

"Gitano, that's too hard. From now on it will be............." he said looking through but not finding it right away, "That's it. From now on.............it will be Thomas. Next!" he shouted. In an instant they made him someone else. Gaetano, or Tom was finally finished with the examinations. They stamped his documents and wrote 'Thomas' on his papers. He looked at the papers not sure what to make of it all.

"What's the matter?" the inspector asked.

"What is this word here?" he pointed to the name Thomas.

"If you don't like that," the inspector replied, "you can go by Tom. That's your name here. It's English for what your name is............or was." The inspector looked at the papers again. "Yeah, Gaetano, that's too hard............. Better if you go by Tom."

Gaetano................ or Tom just gazed and started to walk. All he knew was he wanted to see his parents. They would explain it to him. Things on Ellis Island could have taken a week, and it would not have mattered all that much because he was finally here. Here in America, where his mother and father were. When they had approached the island from the across the river, Gaetano did not have any way to know his parents lived less than five miles from where he was standing.

There were sporadic ferry boat rides back to New York and New Jersey. His Mamma had given instructions in the letter she sent to his grandmother as to where he should go after he left Ellis Island. He showed the letter to man at the dock who had a uniform on. He pointed to one of the smaller boats at the end of the dock.

Fewer people went to New Jersey than New York, so he jumped on the one the officer pointed to and waited for about a half hour for the ferry to set out. Family members could not go out to Ellis Island to meet their loved ones, so he hoped he had the right information.

The ride was quick since Ellis Island is on the New Jersey side of the Hudson. They approached a dock just as it was getting to be sunset. He figured that was where he would finally see his Mamma and Papà. As his ferry was approaching, he saw two people who stood out to him. This was the last ferry to leave Ellis Island for the evening. They had been waiting for him all day.

Chapter 3

> > >

Sunday afternoon on the Fourth of July weekend was the best time available for the going away party. Tony knew things would be slow at the pizzeria, so he closed off the back room and invited thirty-five friends and family to wish Tom and Maria a great vacation. He did all the cooking in advance late Saturday rather than go with his family to watch fireworks in the park. Nothing was too good for Tom and Maria, and he wanted them to have a good send-off.

Tony stood up and got everyone's attention. "Hey, everybody know why we should remember this day?" he called out, "This is the day that we say, 'Bon Voyage' to two special people, who should have done this years ago I might add."

All of Tom's family and friends knew he would never put himself ahead of his family. But now that he was about to retire, they all felt it was high time. "Pop, when was the last time you took a trip? I mean a real trip," His daughter Linda asked already knowing the answer.

"I haven't left the country since I returned in nineteen-nineteen from the war," Tom replied. It did not take much to get him to say it, which surprised Maria. Ordinarily Tom would change the subject when any talk of his time in the Great War came up. This trip must have opened up something in him that he had stifled for most of his life.

"Forty years?" Linda said, "I don't even know what forty years is like. I wonder if I'll get to go to Italy when I'm ready to retire." She had her hands full with her three children and knew full well mothers never retire.

"Why wait?" Maria asked, "Come with us."

"Oh no," Linda responded, "this is your time. You don't need your kids tagging along."

Richard was also excited to see his Mom and Pop enjoy something just for themselves for a change. Like most children, Richard and Linda did not fully appreciate what their folks had done for them growing up until they had children of their own. Everyone sat around eating and making small talk.

• • • •

WEDNESDAY MORNING WAS the scheduled departure, and Tom was trying to get all his things in order at the shop the day before. It was not out of the ordinary for the Barber shop to be closed for a week at a time, but this time, they would be gone for more than four weeks. There were not any other barbers working with him, so they just decided to close up and place a sign which read 'Gone on Vacation to Italy' but everyone in the area already knew that.

Tom had told everyone who had come into the barber shop for the past three months. The other merchants in the area would keep an eye on the place. Most of them had been there for over ten years and they were all friends. It was not like anyone would steal his barber's chair anyway. Just to be safe, Tom took the case with the old tools home to keep them there. Maria never really knew the story behind them and chose not to ask. She knew it had something to do with his time in the war. The way she figured, if Tom wanted to tell her the story, he would when he was ready. The night before the trip, he sat and stared at them for over twenty minutes before putting them in the attic.

• • • •

THE ONLY CONCERN THEY had was getting their passports. They had never needed them in the past. You do not need a passport to go to the Jersey Shore. Though some might argue the point. It usually took some time to get a passport, but since they already had tickets to go out of the country, it was a bit easier. George helped by pulling some strings with his friends in the business. He would have to help his customers get their passports from time to time, so he knew just who to talk to.

Richard and Linda were able to make it on Wednesday morning to go with Tony and his wife Dotty. They all squeezed into Tony's station wagon with the suitcases in the back. It was not far to Pier Eighty-four in New York, just past the Lincoln Tunnel. The arrival time was late in the morning, so the traffic was not too bad.

Parking was a challenge though. Tony dropped everyone off at the terminal and then drove five blocks to a parking lot.

"How long you gonna be?" The attendant asked.

"Two hours max," Tony replied, "I'm dropping off my friends at the pier for a trip to Italy." This immediately got the attendant's attention.

"Ah, Italy, I went four years ago," The attendant said with a huge smile, "Saw family who I hadn't seen since childhood. What's their name?"

"Santorini," Tony replied.

"And yours?" The attendant continued.

"DiDonato," Tony said proudly, "Tony DiDonato."

"Ah, DiDonato," The attendant said as if they had been lifelong friends, "I'll put your car right here in front of my shack where I can watch it for you. You come back whenever you need. Walk around for a while after, take your time."

"What's your name?" Tony asked.

"Carbone," he replied.

"Ah, Carbone," Tony smiled.

They exchanged a few more pleasantries in Italian and Tony was off.

Walking in New York on the west side near the docks was not very safe in nineteen-fifty-nine. Someone even wrote a musical about it. It was about ten o'clock in the morning though, so it was not a problem at that hour. Tony knew how to carry himself to appear confident and not be a target. That is the key to walking in a tough area. They can tell a victim from down the street just by the way they carry themselves.

"Hard time finding a spot?" Dotty asked.

"No, just got to talking with the attendant a bit," Tony replied. It did not surprise Dotty. She knew how talkative Tony could get when he wanted to.

"I think I left my passport in the car," Tom said looking frazzled.

"Got them both here Hun," Maria said with a calming voice. Tom was not usually this nervous. But she could easily understand why.

"Send us a Telegram when you arrive and let us know how the cruise went and that you're Okay," Linda jumped in.

They had some time to kill so they went to a restaurant which was near the docks and had some late breakfast. Tom did not feel like eating. It must have been his nerves. Everyone was talking and laughing except for Tom. He just stared out the window. From there they could see the ship. The others did not really notice him, except for Maria. She knew this man inside and out. She knew it was best to leave him to his thoughts.

It was getting time for them to board, so they all gave their hugs and kisses. Linda was already crying. So was Tony, but he did not want anyone to see. Emotions were running high. What should have been just a sendoff for a vacation seemed to be much more.

The gangway was much fancier than Tom had remembered from back in the teens. A red carpet ran the entire length with brass railings. In the old days, they were lucky to have railings at all, and the gangway was bare wood. Things had certainly changed over the years.

The Christoforo Columbo, commissioned by the Italian Line, was their only ship in operation for this run to Europe. Her sister ship, the Andrea Doria, had been lost in nineteen-fifty-six when she sank after a collision with SS Stockholm off the coast of Nantucket, Massachusetts in dense fog. The Christoforo Columbo was launched in nineteen-fifty-four with its maiden voyage in nineteen-fifty-five. She was built in Genoa Italy and had a capacity of two-hundred and twenty-nine first class passengers, two-hundred and twenty-two cabin class passengers, and six-hundred and four tourist class passengers. These were fancy names for second and third class.

There were three stewards at the top of the gangway. Everyone went on board by the same entry rather than separated by class. They would direct them based on their tickets once on the ship. One other difference from years before was that people would no longer line the sides of the ship to wave as the ship departed. It was something which seemed to have lost its appeal.

The steward met Tom and Maria at the end of the gangway and directed them to where they could find their cabin. "Well at least we don't have to share the cabin with anyone else," Tom said. They were in an interior cabin two levels below the water line. It was like the type of cabin which Tom was in when he traveled as a young man. They had done a much better job of making things look nice though. It was small but clean and decorated some. When he was young, these accommodations were barely tolerable. Of course, sharing a small cabin with four or five other young men for two weeks at a time did not lend itself to comfort.

Maria did not do too well in small spaces, but they had things laid out in such a way to seem too cramped. She figured out where to put the suitcases so they would be out of the way. These ships could go much faster across the Atlantic than the ships of forty years prior. The entire trip to Italy with stops in Boston, Halifax, Lisbon, Gibraltar, and the Santorini's final stop in Naples would take just over one week. From there, the ship would go on to Cannes, Genoa and finally Trieste.

They were told the return trip would take around six hours longer to get them back to New York. It was due to winds and currents. That seemed like years away and they did not want to think about going back just yet. But it was on their tickets, so the subject was discussed briefly.

Seeing the Statue of Liberty and Ellis Island from the harbor brought back many memories for Tom. He had been to the Statue a couple of times, but it was on a small ferry boat from Jersey City. This was more reminiscent of his arrival on the first and second ocean liners.

The times he had gone to the statue, it saddened him to see Ellis Island in its current state. It had been shut down for over five years by then and was beginning to show signs of significant decay.

"Shame what happened to that place," Tom said in almost a whisper. Maria heard him though. "So many people came through there."

"Including you and your family," Maria said.

"A lot of our friends and neighbors too," Tom added, "Shame."

• • • •

DINNER WAS SERVED WHILE they were going by Long Island on route to Boston. The ship would arrive in Boston during the late evening and leave in the morning for Halifax. They spent the first night in Boston Harbor. The noises of the ship were different than Maria was used to, so she did not sleep too well that night. Tom slept like a baby. By ten o'clock in the morning the ship had left port and spent the day heading for Halifax.

Each evening thus far on the trip had them either in or approaching harbor. On the evening of the third day, Tom seemed excited for some reason. Maria could not really figure out why until after dinner. "There's something you've just got to see," he said finally opening up, "Let's go up to the deck where we can see out."

They headed up the stairs to the first available deck with portholes. Tom led them to the stern so they could see west. It was within minutes of sunset and Tom was like a kid. So excited to have Maria see this sight that he had remembered from so long ago. The sky was red, and the sea was calm just as he had seen it the first time. "I'd rather be up on deck, but this will have to do," Tom said apologetically. Tom looked through one porthole and Maria through the next one which was about six feet away. He wished that they could see it standing together rather than apart. This was important to him.

Maria switched back and forth looking at the sunset and looking at Tom's face. She could not tell which was more exciting. To see this man who she had loved for so many years finally enjoying something this much brought a smile to her. Then she remembered he had told her of this sight when they were still engaged but had forgotten all about it. The subject never really came up again until this evening.

"See?" Tom said, "It's where Heaven meets Earth." He pointed and stared out of the porthole until there was not a bit of sun left then turned to Maria. "Told you."

She looked at him and smiled. This was a side of him that she did not see very often. It was when he would let his guard down. It reminded her of what he was like when they first met. For the rest of the trip, they would return each evening of the voyage to see the sunset and each time Tom was just as excited.

Chapter 4

Naples had changed much more than Tom would have imagined. Like most American cities. There were modern buildings mixed in with the old and new docks just like New York with lights everywhere. It was amazing that things had been frozen in his memory. Deep down he assumed everything would be as he had remembered it. The train station had changed as well. It was much different than he remembered. A new station was nearly completed after nearly five years of rebuilding.

They stayed in Naples the first night and then took the train to Rome the next day. Tom had figured they should take care of the pension business right away because if the Italian bureaucracy were anything like their American counterparts, they would need to give it enough time to work out the details. That way they could see things in Rome and maybe have time to rent a car and visit his hometown of Montoro.

The hotel they chose was a short way from the train station to make it easier to get there in the morning. Maria went down to the front desk to send a Telegram back home, just to let everybody know they had arrived safely. They planned to visit more in Naples for a couple of days on the way back before they returned home.

The next morning Tom took the article Tony had given him out of his suitcase. It had the information they needed for where to apply for the pension fund. They had spent the previous three months planning this all out and making reservations through George's travel agency. George had contacts in Italy and was able to get things arranged by mail. If Tom and Maria had waited any longer to decide to go, they may not have had enough time to make all the arrangements. In nineteen-fifty-nine international telephone was very costly so, most of these types of plans were still done by mail and telegraph.

It would only take about two hours to get to Rome, so they were planning to check out of the hotel late in the morning and take the train right after they ate breakfast. In doing so they were able to check into their hotel in Rome shortly after arriving. It was too late to go to the government office once they got settled in, so they decided to catch some of the sights of Rome.

They stayed relatively close to the hotel so they would not need to take a cab everywhere. For two Italian Americans in Rome, it was not as easy to decide what they wanted to eat. What they would call Italian food back home was what the food was like when their families left Italy. The food being served in Rome was a bit different than they had expected. The dishes were pretty much called the same things but the style of fixing them, and their presentation was as modern as the cities themselves. The dinner was still wonderful but not exactly what they had in mind. They were eating rather late and noticed many other people were still in the restaurant.

"I may need to show Tony some of these dishes and try them out at home," Tom joked, "think our friends would actually like the change?"

"Based on how they felt when you guys changed the recipe for his gravy last year," Maria replied with a giggle, "I would say not a chance." Her giggle was as sweet as the day they met.

Rome was very noisy. In some ways more so than New York, as hard as that was to believe for them. There were far more car horns going off because the city did not have as many traffic lights as in America. Drivers would race though the intersections and just blow their horns. Crossing the street was out of the question where it was busy. They would plan on crossing wherever there was a traffic cop. Still though, the splendor of Rome was a joy at every turn.

The excitement of being in this glorious city was so enveloping that Tom and Maria did not get back to their room until after midnight. "It's like being a kid again," Maria giggled, "Where did all that energy come from."

Tom was definitely feeling the walking even with all he did at home each day going to the shop and to Tony's. This was a lot. They would go in short spurts to a place and then find somewhere to sit for a while. Breaking it up helped to make it easier. They had been out from four in the afternoon.

"We'll feel it tomorrow," Tom moaned. They went to bed and fell asleep very quickly.

The next morning came and by the time they opened their eyes for the first time it was ten o'clock. Tom was always up early to be at the shop by nine. Even on days off they would never stay in bed past eight. The bed they were in was the most comfortable they could ever remember sleeping in. That probably contributed to them waking up so late.

"Uh……." Tom grunted, "told you we'd feel it in the morning."

"Whoa…. you're not kidding," Maria replied. This time it was her turn to moan.

"So, what do you want to do, it's too late for breakfast…….do they have brunch in Italy?" Tom said back.

"I just want to go back to sleep," Maria continued to groan.

"Great idea," Tom said, and he closed his eyes thinking it would be for just a few minutes.

Maria's eyes opened suddenly, and she jumped up. "Eleven thirty? What are we doing? We're on vacation. We need to be out and about. The maid will be knocking on the door soon."

Tom pulled the pillow over his head, "I put the do not disturb sign out. They won't knock."

"Oh. Sorry, didn't mean to jump up like that," Maria sighed, "I don't think I've slept that long since I was a teenager." And at that moment she felt like one. "You can stay in bed if you want, I'll take a shower, and did you see the shower?"

There is a good reason so many people design their bathrooms with Italian tile. They know how to do bathrooms right in Italy. This hotel was a perfect example of it. She had never seen a shower with three shower heads before and one on a hose. Their modest home in Jersey City had a claw foot tub and a shower curtain hung by rods from the ceiling in a circle because they did not have a full shower with tiles up the wall. The walls were painted and needed to be repainted almost annually. Not only was this shower exquisite, but it was separate from the tub that had water jets in it.

'I could get used to this,' Maria thought to herself while she was enjoying the steamy shower.

Tom was up when she got out....... half an hour later. "Looks like this is going to be another great day in Rome," she said with the biggest grin he had ever seen.

"Yeah, too bad I have some business to attend to," Tom grunted referring to the pension fund.

"That's Okay, we're on vacation," Maria said, "We'll just stay out until midnight again." Her grin filled her face by now.

Tom did not take nearly as long to shower and shave, so they were out looking for lunch by twelve thirty. After lunch they took a cab to the government building which the article mentioned. The driver knew exactly where it was. "You're not the first people from out of the country to come in for that," he said, "They talked about it on the news and put out ads in every major city where they thought the veterans may have moved to over the years. New York being the first, you know? We take a lot of pride in our veterans here."

"When did this all start?" Maria asked.

"Around the first of the year," he responded, "By the way, I have relatives in New York too. In Brooklyn, do you know the Santelli's? They live pretty close to Borough Park?"

"No, sorry we live in Jersey City, two rivers between us," Maria answered, "I know what you mean though. Our area has a lot of Italian pride. Have you ever been...?"

"Wish I could," he interrupted, "not on a cab driver's income," Tom figured he was bucking for a big tip.

Tom was enjoying the sights as they passed by and making a mental note of where they may want to visit beyond what George had laid out for them. He figured it was time to save Maria from the cab driver as well. "George didn't tell us about some of these. We should look around a bit more, later when I'm done," Tom said pulling her out of the conversation.

Finally, they arrived at the government building. Tom gave the driver a good tip even though he was dropping hints and did not deserve anything but the standard. He walked in behind Maria with the ad in his hands as if he were walking into a drug store to get his prescription filled. There was a reception desk by the main entrance, so they walked up to ask where to go.

"Excuse me, we came over from America when we saw this ad," Tom said to her in Italian, "Something about a pension fund for veterans." Tom almost sounded like a kid going to the principal's office.

The young lady behind the counter reminded them a bit of Deborah back home. She knew exactly what they were referring to and directed them to the elevator across the lobby and told them to take it to the fifth floor and turn right. "Look for the sign which says 'Pensione'," she said. They saw the elevator right away and went up to the fifth floor. The room was easy to find just as the receptionist had said.

"Excuse me," Tom repeated as he did downstairs as he walked up to what appeared to be another receptionist, "I came because of this ad in the paper earlier this year. Is this the right place?"

The receptionist was an older lady in her fifties and equally as pleasant as the young lady downstairs. She looked at the ad and said, "Most certainly, you came all the way from New York?" She saw the name of the paper and could obviously read English.

"It didn't say that I could go to the embassy or the consulate in America," Tom said trying not to sound as he though was complaining "it said I had to appear in person, so my wife and I decided on taking a vacation to Italy. I haven't been back here since the war."

"We welcome you back," The receptionist said, "especially if you are one of our courageous veterans from the Great War. I was just a baby when that all happened. My father was in the war and so were his three brothers. Only one besides my father survived. He's passed on now." Tom felt like they were old friends. "What is your name Signor?"

"Gaetano Santorini," he replied, "they call me Tom in America." This was the first time Tom had referred to himself as Gaetano since he finally settled in Jersey City. His mother always called him Gaetano. She did for the rest of her life, even when he was older.

"Signor Santorini?... Gaetano Santorini?... all right," she said as if she seemed familiar with the name. Then she went back into business mode. "As you would imagine, there are forms to fill out."

"Can my wife help," Tom interrupted, "she has better handwriting than I do and..."

"Of course," she replied, "but you will have to be the one to sign the forms."

"Thank you so much, this is my wife Maria," Tom replied as he gently pulled Maria's left arm forward, "Don't know what I'd do without her." Tom was now visibly nervous.

Everyone was genuinely nice to them as they asked where, when, what and how. As expected, the forms were many and hard to fill out. Once completed, Tom and Maria went back up to the desk and the receptionist reviewed them while they sat in front of her. She had a few questions about their children in America, and she seemed especially interested in his hometown. Which seemed odd to them.

"It says here you are originally from Montoro Superiore in the Province of Avellino......is that right?" she asked almost in disbelief.

"Yes," Tom replied with a little confusion, "yes for over five generations until my parents moved to America in nineteen-oh-five. And then I moved a few years later."

"Tell me a bit about your town," she continued seeming to be cautious about asking "What is the name of the church in the center of town?"

"Hmm, haven't thought of that in years. Umm, Saint Pietro a Resicco.......... fairly sure.........I think so," Tom replied almost with apology looking back and forth between the receptionist and Maria. "Took classes there as a boy." he added, "The priest there was nice if I recall, an older man who had spent time in the Vatican in his early years. I remember my father telling me that." He could have gone on and on.

Maria was a bit troubled by the types of questions but figured whenever money was involved, they would have to be certain of the identity of the person getting the funds. Especially if they were from out of the country as they were. Italian by heritage is one thing, living there is yet another. They were still from another country as far as the Italian government was concerned.

The receptionist's demeanor settled in some once she felt she had what she was looking for. "Thank you, Signor Santorini. I think we have enough to look up your military records," she said with a sigh of relief, "As you can imagine, you will need to come back in a couple of days. Day after tomorrow should be good. There are a lot of records to go through. Fortunately, they have been filed in such a way which helps us to find people based on their hometown. Montoro Superiore is a small town and how many Santorini's can there be?" Tom laughed thinking probably none at this point. But at one time dozens.

Tom now realized why they needed to come to Rome to apply for the pension. It seemed by what she had said the records were nearby and made it manageable to verify the identities of the soldiers. It would reduce the risk of someone making a false claim. Now he did not mind as much that the Italian embassy in America was not taken into consideration. All of those records would be difficult to keep track of.

With all the forms they had to fill out, it was approaching dinnertime, so Maria asked the lady if she could recommend a restaurant. There was one just two blocks to the north. It was still light out with a couple of daylight left.

As they were leaving, she noticed the receptionist go over to one of the offices and knock on the door. She said something to the man inside and he stepped out so he could see Tom and Maria. They both looked at them as they left, almost staring. Maria could see them speaking softly to one another and almost pointing to them. It looked a bit awkward, but she brushed it off figuring they did not receive applicants for this pension fund every day. Especially not from out of the country.

• • • •

THIS RESTAURANT SERVED northern Italian food. Maria ordered the House Veal as recommended by their waiter and Tom stayed with a pasta dish with sausage which the chef handmade himself. Tom looked to see if he recognized any of the vineyards on the wine list, hoping to see if the name of the Rizzi vineyard where he worked as a boy was on it. There were none that he knew or remembered.

It was a quiet restaurant, and they welcomed the peace and solitude of their table in the back. It was a Tuesday evening. They had been in Italy since Sunday and were enjoying every moment. Even the government office visit was pleasant despite all the forms.

"Thanks for coming with me and helping with the papers," Tom said with a sigh of relief now the hard part was over, "Hope she finds everything okay."

They stayed at the restaurant for about two hours and noticed things started to pick up. They remembered they had eaten rather late the night before and the restaurant was full.

Tom asked the waiter, "we couldn't help but notice how late people eat here."

"All of the American tourists ask the same question," the waiter replied, "People here usually eat later than in your country. Especially if they eat out, sometimes things don't pick up until after ten o'clock."

"What time do they usually go to bed?" Maria asked with a sort of confused look on her face.

"Whatever time seems right," he said, "usually much past midnight."

"So based on last night, Maria, we fit right in here," Tom laughed, "I could get used to this."

Maria thought 'that's what I said this morning.' If only the kids could see how much their Pop was enjoying himself, they would be thrilled. He never put his fun ahead of theirs, even when they would vacation on the Jersey shore. He made sure they did the things the kids enjoyed.

They did not have as much energy as the night before, so they took a cab back to their hotel and settled in for the night. Maria took a bubble bath, and Tom read a local newspaper which was left at their door, happy to be able to read it in Italian. They both wished they could call home to talk to everybody. But that would be too expensive. They got wonderfully comfortable in their bed and had another good night's sleep.

Chapter 5

Wake up time on Wednesday morning came a bit earlier than the day before. They were up and about by nine o'clock. Tom preferred the early rise as pleasant as the morning before was. The restaurant at the hotel did not appeal to them so they hit the streets to see what they might find. It was a day made in heaven, a slight warm breeze, and the smell of flowers in the pots along the sidewalk made this little café the perfect spot for a leisurely breakfast outdoors.

"Wonder if Tony should have some tables on the sidewalk?" Tom joked.

"In Jersey City?" Maria chuckled, "I don't think anybody would sit out there. I don't know anyone who would want to eat outside with cars driving by."

They had prepared a list of sights to see that day and decided if they saw everything, it would be great. They did not want to bite off too much though. It would be more enjoyable if they took their time. Saint Peter's Basilica at the Vatican was high on the list as well as the Colosseum. After that, it did not really matter. There were some fountains and monuments on the list. Those were not as important. Maria definitely wanted to see Michelangelo's Pieta. That would be the first stop.

They walked by a bookstore after leaving the café and noticed there were several books on display about soldiers and the wars. "I guess the driver was right yesterday, they do care a lot about their veterans here," Tom observed out loud, "quite a few about the first war, guess that's because we were on the winning side that time."

Saint Peter's was the largest cathedral they had ever seen. "Saint Patrick's in New York is a sight to see but nothing compared to this," Maria said. Being there in Rome, in Saint

Peter's Basilica, made them feel like they were in the middle of history rather than just reading about it. Maria was surprised the Pieta here was quite a bit smaller than the stature which was at Saint Patrick's in New York. But the fact it was Michelangelo himself who sculpted this made it fascinating.

Maria found a plaque which talked about Pieta. "Tom," she said calling him over "it says that in the eighteenth century, the Madonna's left hand was broken and repaired. It doesn't say who the sculptor was. Can you imagine being the person asked to repair a Michelangelo sculpture, even more something as important as Pieta?"

"Does it say how it was broken?" Tom asked.

"No," Maria said as she hesitated while reading further, "Wonder if anybody knows?" She spent another couple of minutes reading the plaque before they moved on. They were limited on how long they could see Pieta since so many were in line and many people would spend limitless hours staring at it if they let them. That would not allow as many people to see the sculpture.

They had a brochure which showed many things to see at the Basilica as well as a booklet that gave a brief history of the current cathedral. There had been another structure there before the sixteenth century and it took several Popes and even more architects before they finally came up with a plan for this building. And of course, Michelangelo's design was key. Others would contribute, but his was the main design.

"I heard Saint Peter himself was buried here," Maria said reading the booklet, "No one really knows for certain where. It says he was crucified here as well while Nero was Emperor. I remember being taught about that when I was in grade school. The sister said he insisted on being crucified upside down because he didn't feel worthy to die in the same manner as Jesus."

Tom was not talking much at this point. His eyes were taking in everything around him and speaking would interrupt his observations.

Before they realized, it was after three o'clock and they had not eaten anything since breakfast. It did not seem obvious since they had eaten such a large breakfast. It was out of the ordinary for them. "Do you want to get a bite to eat?" Maria asked.

"Maybe   a   snack," Tom   replied,   "I'm   not   really hungry............... you?"

"Well, something small," Maria said, "and then we should head over to the Colosseum." Neither of them wanted to stop for anything as simple as eating. This was so much to absorb, and they did not want to miss a thing.

There was a small place just outside of the Basilica which obviously was there to cater to tourists from Saint Peter's. They also had a gift shop attached where you could buy posters of significant sights within and even miniature versions of Pieta so you could take it home with you. They thought for a moment about getting one, but both shook their heads at the same time...... "No."

After a quick snack they took a cab to the Colosseum. The cab had to cross the Tiber River and past the Piazza Venezia, which was one of the stops on their list. They figured if they had enough time after the Colosseum, they would go back and see it.

Once they arrived at the Colosseum, they noticed there were restrictions as to where they could go. Due to safety and preservation concerns, they were kept on strict paths. They were able to go inside to see it from the center of the arena. Walkways had been installed for tourists. Overall, this was not as impressive to them as Saint Peter's. Probably because of the history of the Colosseum as it was used in the killing of Christians and also the time of the Gladiators. It did not have the romance that Saint

Peter's had. They did not stay as long as they thought they would. Both wished they had stayed at Saint Peter's longer instead. It could have filled the day. Maybe they could go back next the week if they had some time left.

The Piazza Venezia had several interesting sights surrounding it. Primarily it is the location for the National Monument to Victor Emmanuel II who was the first king of United Italy. The area also is home to the Tomb of the Unknown Soldier from World War 1 with an eternal flame.

"Boy this really is a country filled with honor for its veterans," Tom said, "It seems to be everywhere you turn."

After climbing up all the stairs on the monument, they realized they probably did not have the energy to stay out much longer. They decided to head back to the hotel and maybe watch a movie at a nearby cinema. "I guess we can't call it a foreign film now can we," Maria chuckled at the thought, "Hope it's not in French or something else." They looked forward to just sitting for a couple of hours.

In keeping with the culture 'When in Rome......' would enter the conversation on a regular basis. They decided to stop in at their room and freshen up a bit before the movie then go out for dinner after like the locals would. As they entered their room, they noticed a note under the door. The front desk had taken a message from the pension office. 'Your records have been found, please come to the office at ten o'clock in the morning' the note read.

"Oh, that was fast," Tom said with some surprise.

"That's not too early and we know where it is, so let's stay with our plans tonight," Maria replied not wanting to be distracted by the note.

"Yeah, you're right. That's not 'til morning, the evening is young as the saying goes.............. wish I was," Tom was feeling all of the walking from the day.

Tom fell asleep in the movie theatre towards the middle of the film. Maria watched the entire movie.

He woke up and asked, "Did I miss anything good?"

"Sort of," Maria said, "it was pretty good, but you looked so tired when we came in, I didn't have the heart to wake you."

"Just as well," Tom sighed, "I was tired, wasn't I? But I am hungry now, how 'bout you?"

"Definitely," Maria perked up, "Do we want to go back where we ate the first night here or try something new?"

"I know I'm a creature of habit," Tom said rolling his eyes, "but let's not get carried away, something new."

This was more dining out than they had ever done before. They were trying to keep an eye on the cost of things. Most of what they were spending money on was eating out. It was sort of a once in a lifetime experience, so they did not want to cut it too short. They had enough money with them, but it was not like them to spend it on luxuries like fancy restaurants in Rome. Maybe this pension fund would be more than they thought. That would take some of the sting out of the cost of the trip.

It was another night on the town for the Santorini's. They found a nice restaurant which was recommended to them by the front desk. You can usually count on those being good because you will be coming back afterwards and letting them know if you liked it.

They were back to their room by eleven o'clock and went right to bed. Maria called the front desk to ask for a seven thirty wake up call. This would give them enough time in the morning to get ready and make it on time for the ten o'clock appointment.

The phone rang as planned and neither of them wanted to hear it. "I think we should come back after and take a nap, what do you think?" Tom said after he thanked the wake-up caller.

"You're right," Maria groaned, "we're not used to all of this activity."

They almost called for room service but that would be too much. There were plenty of cafés in the area and they could get something fast at one of them. A light breakfast seemed to be in order to save time. Once done they caught a cab and headed to the government office. It was just after nine and they were sure they would have enough time.

Neither of them talked much in the cab, mostly because they were still tired from the day before. It took a bit longer to get to the government building than it had two days before. This driver took a different route. The day looked as if it was becoming a bit overcast. The driver said it was not supposed to rain, but you could never really tell. The clouds just made it look a bit dreary.

Tom seemed anxious to get this over with and held open the door for Maria somewhat rushing her along without realizing it. "I don't think they're going anywhere," she said trying to slow him down some.

"I guess not," he mumbled.

They knew where to go so they went straight to the elevator and took it up to the fifth floor. As they got off the elevator Maria noticed two policemen staring at them. "I think they're looking at us," she said awkwardly.

"They know a beautiful woman when they see one," Tom quipped.

"Oh, you," she said with a slap to his right arm. That got Tom to lighten up a bit too.

"Hello, we were here on Tuesday," Tom said as he approached the lady whom he had spoken with before.

She looked at them for a moment, "You're Signor Santorini......right? We've been expecting you."

"Really?" Tom said, looking at Maria a bit surprised.

"Come with me Signor," she said, and they followed her to a small conference room in the corner. "Let me be certain............... You told us that you were Signor Gaetano Santorini from Montoro Superiore in the Province of Avellino. Is that right?"

"Yes, we got a note at the hotel saying you found his records?" Maria stepped in. Just then the man whose office the receptionist had gone to when they were leaving stepped in.

"We did find Signor Santorini's records," he said, "I recognized the name but couldn't place it until after you left."

Tom and Maria looked at each other not at all understanding how that could be. "Recognized?" Maria questioned.

The man who had entered the room was the office manager. He leaned out of the room for a moment and gestured to someone then came back in. "You do say that you are Signor Gaetano Santorini?" he repeated what the lady had asked.

"Yes, yes, that's me yes," Tom said even more confused. 'Why would they doubt this?' he thought.

"Signor, I'm sorry," The office manager said. Just then the two policemen who were standing in the hall came into the room, "We must place you under arrest."

A cold chill went down Maria's back. "What did you say? Why......What has he done?"

Tom spoke at the same time, "What.... what...what. I don't understand." Everyone was talking over one another. The room became very chaotic.

"Signor, Signor," one of the policemen said, "please stand up."

"I don't understand, why, what have I done?" Tom was trying not to raise his voice but was flustered by now and Maria was in a panic. Everyone was still talking over one another.

"Don't you touch him!" she said to the policemen knowing full well it would do no good.

The office manager said, "We love our veterans here and we don't appreciate it when someone tries to deceive us. Maybe where you come from but not here." This seemed almost cruel to Maria who was in tears by now.

Then one of the policemen took out his hand cuffs and started to place them on Tom. "You are under arrest for impersonating a war hero."

"Who's a war hero?" both Tom and Maria cried.

"And attempting to defraud the Italian government," added the office manager. "Get him out of here," he said with as much anger as one could muster.

They walked Tom out and he looked back at Maria with a total disbelief. His eyes cried out, "What is happening?'

"How could you do this.... stop............ stop!" Maria was frantic and trying to follow Tom, but the other policeman stopped her.

"You are an American citizen? Aren't you?" the receptionist said with a degree of condescension.

"Yes," Maria replied and was ready for an all-out fight.

"Then go back to your hotel and arrange for a lawyer for your husband. He will need one," The receptionist said as she pointed to the door for Maria to leave.

A silence came over the room. Maria was not certain if it was actually quite or if the intensity of the moment was too much for her to bear. She paused for a moment while they all stared at her not saying a word. With her lower jaw quivering, Maria reached for her purse and started to head to the door. Not certain if she should continue the confrontation or leave, she decided nothing else could be done there. These people were convinced Tom had done something wrong and there was no point in trying any further.

Maria stood in the main lobby downstairs for a few minutes evaluating whether she could even walk. How would she get back? Tom was carrying most of the money in his wallet with some left in the hotel safe. She had a little with her, but it was likely not enough to pay for the cab ride back. What was she supposed to do now?

She did not even know where they were taking him. Everything was turned upside down. After leaving the government building, she just stood at the street corner for a long time. She could not tell how long. The noise of the city was now an annoyance, and she was wondering why they had come all this way for this to happen. An elderly man came up to her. He spoke to her in Italian, "Are you all right? You are crying."

She answered him in English, "I don't know what to do. They've arrested my husband." He signaled he could not understand her. She shook her head and repeated in Italian.

"Who arrested him?" he asked.

"The people in there," she replied pointing to the government building, "they say he's an imposter. He is not. He's my husband, and he's the most wonderful man in the world. How could they do this?"

He was not sure if he could help her. This looked complicated and if the government were involved, he knew there was not much he could do.

"You are American?" he asked.

"Why does everybody want to know that?" she barked and then realized he was only trying to help, "I'm sorry. It's not your fault. I just don't know what to do next. They told me to get a lawyer. I don't know what to do. And......I .... I don't have enough money to get back to my hotel." She was letting it all out now sobbing uncontrollably.

"Come sit and get your strength," The elderly man said as he led her to a nearby bench. "Where are you staying?"

After sitting for a while Maria was able to regain her composure. The elderly man waved a cab and put her in. Giving the driver enough to get her to her hotel and then some, he asked the driver to see to it she got into her hotel without a problem. The cab sped away, and the elderly man shook his head wishing he could make it all go away but knowing her husband was likely in a lot of trouble.

It began to rain.

Chapter 6

Tony was getting ready to open up for eleven o'clock. He got to the shop an hour earlier at about ten. The night before had a good turnout with most tables full throughout the dinner hour and later into the evening. A baseball team came in late to get pizza after their game. They were celebrating their first victory that season. They ordered nine pies and drinks for a team of fourteen. Things were further complicated by his favorite cook being away. Deborah had offered to come to work a couple of extra days a week.

A service man was there making some adjustments to the walk-in refrigerator when Tony was surprised by the knock on the door. He went to the door and said in as pleasant a voice as he could muster, "We're closed. Open at eleven."

"Western Union sir, we have a telegram for Anthony DiDonato," the voice said from the other side of the screen door.

Curious as to what it was about and knowing telegrams were usually not a good thing, he opened the door and asked, "Who's it from?"

"Please sign here sir," the man said with an all-business demeanor. Tony signed and began to read.

TOM ARRESTED BY POLICE STOP SAY HE IS IMPOSTER STOP DO NOT KNOW WHAT TO DO STOP PLEASE HELP

MARIA

The reality did not sink in right away. It almost seemed like a prank. Then all he could think of was 'Poor Maria, what is she faced with.' He called Linda right away. She had called him Sunday night to tell him her mom had sent a telegram reporting all went well on the trip so far. Linda would also know the hotels where they were staying.

"What else did it say?" Linda asked, sounding startled by the news.

"Nothing, just that," Tony replied, "It doesn't make any sense. What do they mean by imposter? What was the hotel where they were staying? I have to call right away." Linda gave him the hotel information, and he told her he would keep her informed. He dialed zero as soon as he heard a dial tone after hanging up.

"Operator," Tony said trying not to sound anxious. "I would like to place a person to person call to Maria Santorini in Rome Italy she's staying at.........."

The service man could tell something was very wrong and came to the phone to see if he could help. "No, there's nothing you can do unless you can get me to Rome within the hour," Tony said. The service man signaled everything was working now. He mouthed he would check in with him tomorrow.

"Yes operator, Mr., and Mrs. Santorini's room....... Thank you." It seemed to take forever to make the connection. Then a familiar voice came on. "Maria? Its Tony...............What's this all about? Where's Tom?"

Maria had composed herself somewhat and had cried all the tears she had in her. "Tony? This must be costing you a fortune," she said always concerned for others.

"Never mind that," he said wanting to get to the point, "What is going on over there? Linda told me Sunday you telegrammed, and all was well." Tony's voice was shaky, but he did not want it to show.

Maria told him all she knew thus far, and that the people at the government office told her to get Tom a lawyer. "I don't know how to do that, especially here. What do I do?" she said as her voice started to quiver again.

"I'm going to call my lawyer Joe once I get off the phone," Tony answered hoping he could calm her down. "I know he has some family who lives near Rome, just a few miles out. He may be able to help. Don't worry, If I have to take a plane there myself, we'll get to the bottom of this. What time is it there?"

"Just after four," Maria said trying to calm herself down.

"In the afternoon or in the morning?" Tony asked because he could not remember if they were ahead of them or behind.

"Afternoon," she said softly.

"Okay, let me think," he continued trying to figure on what he could do to help her right away, "Have you eaten yet?"

"Not since this morning," she answered in almost a whimper, "We had a light breakfast before going to the appointment." This helped her to consider something other than Tom's predicament.

"Look," Tony added, "I don't think it's a good idea for you to step out for dinner. You should stay by the phone. Order room service, don't worry I'm paying."

"Oh, you've done enough already," Maria said.

"Never mind that, you need to be Okay. So, eat something even if it's only soup or something light. Promise me," Tony said attempting to help her get through the day.

"I...I...I will Tony," she sighed, "I hope Tom knows what kind of friend he has. I should let you go this is racking up a bill."

"Don't worry about that either," he said with a slight rebuke, "I'll call you back when I hear something and if you need anything, call me collect, you hear, I mean it, call me collect." He felt like he had to take charge in order to get ready for a fight. "We all love you guys. You hang in there. I'll call soon, maybe in the morning. Don't worry if you don't hear from me tonight. It's late over there and it will be evening soon."

• • • •

MARIA HUNG UP AND A sense of calm came over her. She did not feel alone anymore. She waited a bit and decided to go to the local store she saw to get some things for the room rather than have a meal through room service. Tony would not likely call back until morning, and she wanted to settle in. That meant having something to drink and maybe something to snack on. It might help her nerves as well. She went down to the small store which was near the hotel and picked up a variety of things that ordinarily she would not get. She was trying to process the emotions and just grabbed things which caught her eye, not completely thinking things through.

Tony was able to reach Joe at his office. Joe was a friend as well as being his lawyer. "So, do you know anything about how they do things over there?" Tony asked, speaking so fast Joe could barely understand him.

"We need to have clear heads Tony," Joe said, "I think the best thing to do is to call the Italian consulate in New York. I've done some work for someone who works there. He told me they handle legal matters between the countries. I can start there. I'll call them as soon as I get off with you. Is your friend.... Maria....is it. Is she Okay?"

"I think so," Tony said, "she's a real trooper. But she's never had to go through something like this before." Tony sounded a bit relieved Joe had a possible course of action. "Don't you have family over there?"

"Yeah," Joe answered, "but I don't know what good that will do. None of them are in the legal profession. Maybe they can look in on your friend at her hotel. I'll give them a call." Joe sounded uncertain since he was not in regular contact with them.

"I'll pay for the call," Tony said wanting to do all he could to help, "I mean it."

"I know you do. We'll work out all that stuff later. Got to go," Joe said as he hung up. They left it at that. Tony wanted to get on a plane at that very second but knew he would be more effective from there. He called Linda back to tell her he had spoken to her mom and there was a plan of action underway.

"I called Richard and he's besides himself," Linda said stumbling through the words, "he wants to fly out tonight. But he can't because he doesn't have a passport either."

"Well, if it gets to that," Tony said, "I have a passport and I can go get them. It's best if I work on it from here for now. Joe is good, he'll get results."

• • • •

THEY WERE HOLDING TOM in the same building where he was arrested. His holding cell was not the least bit comfortable. For a man of his sixty-five years, he was rather tough and could put up with almost anything. He had been that way his whole life. His main concern was for Maria. How was she holding up? She was strong, but under these circumstances, he was worried.

The rules were different there. They did not give you one free phone call when you were arrested for this type of thing. He was completely counting on Maria to make arrangements for a lawyer. It was not the kind of thing he wanted her to have to do. But he knew she would do what needed to be done.

Someone came to his door and unlocked it. "We have a meal for you," the guard said, "you will have one half hour to eat and then we will come back to get the tray. If you do not eat, you will not have anything until morning."

Tom was disheartened but understood he had to obey the rules if he were to get through this. It was just like his Army experiences when he would get into some trouble and have to work things out.

"I understand. Thank you," he said knowing that being polite was important in order to keep things from getting any worse, "Can you tell me what will happen next?" He was hoping for something which would help him to settle down. Any information was better than what he had at that moment.

"Someone from the prosecutor's office will be here in the morning to conduct an interrogation," the guard said curtly.

"What if my wife can't get a lawyer by then?" Tom asked.

"Considering the nature of the crime and your alien status, you will not be able to have a lawyer present at the interrogation," the guard continued, "your lawyer will represent you at your trial."

This did not seem to make sense. But then again, this was not America, and one cannot presume all countries do things the same way. He reminded himself it would be better to cooperate and maybe they would show him some consideration.

• • • •

JOE CALLED A FEW NUMBERS and asked some questions as to how to connect with the consulate. He was given a name and a number for the legal advisor's office in New York and started to make the call. They were willing to see him by the close of day since the matter was urgent. It also helped Joe's last name was Carracci. Joe called Tony to get some further information about Tom's identity and some of his history.

"I think we have a handle on this," Joe started off, "Don't worry. My only concern is the issue of legal counsel. We may need to apply some diplomatic pressure being that he is an American citizen and there is an obvious mix up in identity." That did not really make Tony feel better.

"Let me know as soon as you hear," Tony added, "Can I go with you? I may be able to answer some questions."

"We can't risk you saying something wrong," Joe said trying to reassure Tony it was all right for him to go by himself. "One misstep and the whole thing could be ruined. We have to be very diplomatic. Let me take it."

"All right," Tony said hesitantly, "you know best."

"If it were anything other than international, I'd say yes. We just can't risk it," Joe added concerned with the intensity of the situation. Tony knew Joe had everyone's best interest in mind.

• • • •

EARLY AFTERNOON AT the pizzeria was fortunately slow. Dotty had come over once she heard, so she could be available to help customers should Tony need to get on the phone. Richard came in at about two thirty and went over to talk to her. "I left work early. The boss understood," he said, "any word?

"Not yet," Dotty said looking towards the back to see if she could see Tony through the door, "He's very upset. I've never seen him like this."

"Tony and Pop go back a long way," Richard said, "Pop knew his father since before the war. Why did they have to go there? For some pension fund? What's that all about?"

"Don't say that in front of Tony," Dotty said looking again to see if Tony heard what Richard had said, "he feels bad enough already. He's the one who showed him the ad don't forget."

"I didn't know that," Richard said looking surprised, "I thought Pop found it himself."

"No, Tony showed him," she added, "I think that's part of why he feels so bad right now." She paused for a moment, not sure if there was much else to say. "Hungry? Want a slice? Pretty slow, I'll probably have to toss these." Dotty pointed to the pies in the display.

"Actually yeah," Richard replied properly distracted, "I worked through lunch so I could leave early. Got any pepperoni?"

"Tony sure does love your Mom and Pop," Dotty said as she put two slices in the oven. That helped to lighten things up a bit. Richard gave a half smile and a chuckle.

· · · ·

MARIA HAD DONE AS TONY suggested and ordered room service. She was exhausted but could not bring herself to close her eyes. She felt that if she did, she would in some way be abandoning Tom. Logic did not play a role in her thinking. It was all about feelings at that moment.

She left one of the lights on in the bathroom just to help her not feel so alone. She thought maybe if she did sleep, she would wake up and it would all have been a dream. Then Tom would be there with her, right next to her in the bed like the previous two mornings.

· · · ·

JOE DROVE INTO NEW York. Subway travel on the east side was not as widespread, and it would have been too long of a walk from the nearest subway station to the consulate. This did not really save time but worked better.

He introduced himself at the front desk and they showed him to one of the nearby offices. "Thank you for meeting with me Signor Nardini, "Joe started, "As you can imagine, we have some very worried people who are close to Signor Santorini." Joe wanted to stress the human element at the onset. "Were you able to find out anything since we spoke earlier?"

"No information yet," Signor Nardini said, "I have placed a call with someone in the pension office you told me about from the ad in the paper. I remember that add. It was processed through this consulate. We placed the ad based on the number of soldiers who we figured had settled in America after the Great War."

"That is very kind of you to try so hard to help," Joe added, "I realize this is short notice. Do you ever have things like this happen?" Joe was trying to see if Signor Nardini had ever had success in this type of thing.

"Usually, it is a relative who skips out on a hotel bill or something like that," Signor Nardini continued, "We are reluctant to assist in matters where it is not likely a misunderstanding. This.........this could be one of those times though. It may be a misunderstanding. We will have to see."

"Well, as we present to you who Tom Santorini is," Joe said trying now to make his case, "I'm sure you will see he is not a swindler or the type of man to impersonate someone for money."

"This is what we must look into," he replied.

"Well, I can get you the necessary papers within a day or so," Joe continued, "One of their children will have to go to the house and look through their records to get the documents which you will need." Joe knew the essence of what was at play here had to do with Tom's identity. With the proper immigration papers in hand, they could show exactly who Tom was from the perspective of the Italian government.

"Let me see if they have been able to get through to the office," Signor Nardini said "It is after hours in Rome by now and it is not likely we will hear anything until morning. But at least we have begun the process for you. The secretary has some forms for you to fill out. I will show you a place where you can work. Thank you for coming."

The meeting was brief but helpful. Joe could tell Signor Nardini did not want to commit to anything. But if he played his cards right, this man would be a real asset. Joe followed him to the conference room where he was able to spread out and fill out the several forms needed to gain assistance from the consul.

. . . .

IT WAS PAST MIDNIGHT, and Maria still had not gone to sleep. There was no television in their room, but there was a radio. She found a station which played soft classical music and left it there for something to fill the air. By two in the morning, she had dozed off with the radio playing softly. Tom could not sleep all night.

. . . .

JOE CALLED TONY TO see if he could come by and help to collect the necessary papers. He had a better idea now what they would need to verify Tom's identity. Tony planned to meet him at the Santorini's house. "Richard was at the restaurant earlier, and he says he can meet you at his folk's house this evening if you can make it," Tony said.

"I'm sorry Tony, I can't make it until morning," Joe said hoping it would not create a problem, "What is the address?" Joe had already gone above and beyond, and Tony knew it.

"I understand," Tony replied, "You really are there for us. Thanks again. Just come by my house in the morning and we can go over together. I'll call Richard and let him know." Tony realized there was not much more anybody could do that night. All he could think about was how his friends were holding up, along with them being over four thousand miles away.

Chapter 7

Being Rome was six hours ahead of New York, it gave Maria a chance to get some sleep. She woke up often during the night but would go back to sleep after an hour or so. When she finally got up, she knew it was still the middle of the night at home, so she decided to step out for coffee and pastry. It was seven o'clock and she figured the government office would not be open for some time and if she did not go now, she may not be able to later. Leaving the 'Do Not Disturb' sign out, she thought she may be able to get some rest when she returned. She ate for the sake of eating. But the pleasure the previous mornings had brought was not a possibility.

At about the same time in Jersey City, Tony was still up. He thought about calling Maria but did not have anything new to add. He figured he would call in the morning once he got up. Going to sleep did not appeal to him either. But he knew he needed to. Dotty had gone to bed by eleven and left the night light on in the bathroom for him to find his way.

Richard and Linda spent the evening together trying to make some sense of it all. But there was no sense to any of it. Countless hours of talking it through over and over did not help either. "If only I had gotten my passport when Mom and Pop got theirs, I could be halfway there by now," Richard complained. He had considered it when his folks were preparing their papers.

He left at ten and drove around for a while to try to calm down. It was not working. Linda had to get up with the kids the next morning even though it was summer vacation, so she could not afford to miss any sleep. She went to bed right after Richard left.

Joe Carracci slept just fine.

. . . .

TOM DID NOT HAVE A clock in his holding cell. His watch had been taken along with all of his personal items such as his wallet and his passport which he had taken with him to the meeting just in case he needed to use it for identification. He chuckled. 'Identification,' he thought, 'Identity is what got me here in the first place.' These held in emotions from the previous twenty-one hours finally came out in an uncontrolled laughter which soon turned to tears. He needed to let it out somehow. Better now than while he was being interrogated. They would be watching for any sign of deception. He wanted to be as straight forward as possible. The truth does set you free after all.

The sound of the door unlocking startled Tom. The same guard who had brought his meal the night before came in with another tray of food. "What time is it?" Tom asked politely.

"A little before eight," the guard replied, "You will have one half hour to eat and then we will come back to get the tray. If you do not eat, you will not have anything until lunch."

Tom almost broke out in the hardy laugh again. These were the exact words the guard had spoken the evening before. 'Didn't he remember telling me that last night? Or are they required to repeat themselves?' he thought to himself, 'Better not to use sarcasm with the guard.' "Thank you," Tom said wondering if the guard could tell he was laughing on the inside. "Is there any word on when the person from the prosecutor's office will be here?"

"No," he said curtly again.

'That's it? No?' Tom thought. He really wanted to throw out a barb or some fancy retort, but Tom knew better. "Okay, thank you," he said softly.

The breakfast was not very good. But he ate it anyway. He had been in the Army after all and in the Army, you learned to eat what you were given.

• • • •

MARIA TRIED TO CALL the government office, but that accomplished nothing. Either no one knew anything, or they were purposely avoiding her request for information about Tom. Her sincere hope was with the folks back home, but she knew the time difference was not on her side. She would just have to wait. They would likely not have any news until late in the day Rome time. That ate away at her every minute.

She jumped out of her skin when the phone rang. "Hello," she answered hoping it would be Tony or one of her kids.

"Signora Santorini?" the voice said.

"Yes?" Maria said, thinking maybe it was news of Tom.

"My name is Anna Carpello," the voice on the phone continued, "I received a call yesterday from my cousin Joe Carracci in New Jersey. He knows Tony DiDonato. He asked me to contact you to see if I can help you in anyway."

Maria began to cry because it confirmed someone was looking out for her. "Oh, Tony's friend?" she said with a shaken tone, "Tony did say he had friend with family over here. So nice of you to call.............."

• • • •

IT WAS ALMOST TEN O'CLOCK when the door was unlocked again in Tom's holding cell. He knew it was not time for lunch so it must mean it was time for the interrogation. Two guards came in and asked him to stand and turn around. They placed handcuffs on him again and led him out of the room. The interrogation room was just two doors down. They entered the room then the two guards asked Tom to turn around and they removed the handcuffs. 'For thirty feet down the hall they needed to handcuff an old man?' he thought to himself. Tom understood the tactic.

"Please be seated," one guard commanded. Tom went to sit in the chair at the head of the table. "This one," the other guard said pointing to the chair facing the mirror. Tom recognized the mirror as the standard interrogation room design. It was a two-way glass with a mirror on one side and a room on the other in which someone could observe him. Tom sat for about twenty-five minutes knowing he was most likely being watched the entire time. No one was in the room with him. He figured it was best to just sit and be patient.

'Is it called a one-way mirror,' he started to think to pass the time, 'or a two-way mirror. Hmm, heard it both ways. Or is it a one-way glass, or a two-way glass. Na, that one doesn't sound right. Doesn't matter. All I know is I can see myself. I think I'll call it a two-way mirror............... for now.' Tom's need to rationalize this detail was mostly to keep his mind occupied.

A woman came in and placed a folder on the table across from him. Whatever it was, he knew he should not look at it when she left. He could hear some talking outside the door and then the door opened again. One of the guards which had brought him in came in with a man who walked with a cane. He leaned quite heavily on it as well. This man was a bit younger than Tom, but not by much. Maybe in his early sixties. Tom suspected he was the man from the prosecutor's office.

He spoke with the guard in a whisper for a bit by the door quietly. They occasionally looked at Tom and then down the hall and then back at Tom. The guard walked over and picked up the folder and handed it to the man with the cane. He browsed through it for a bit but not with any detail. With a nod to the guard, the guard left and closed the door. Tom stayed seated while the man with cane limped over.

He struggled significantly to sit down. His cane was leaning against the table, and he was no longer using it. He pulled the chair up to align it with where he wanted it to be so he would not have to slide it forward once seated. The man with the cane placed both hands flat on the table and slowly lower himself until he reached a point where gravity took over and he flopped into the chair. He let out a minor wince. It was obviously out of habit as this was likely the way he would always sit down. He was across from Tom with his back to the mirror. Tom did not say a word and neither did the man with the cane.

He started to look through the folder in much more detail this time. The lighting was not that good in the room and Tom could tell he had a tough time reading what was on the pages. He wore glasses and seemed to be in need of a new prescription as well. He kept taking his glasses off and then putting them back on.

Tom was not in any hurry to get into this. It could just be a set up or something designed to get him to say the wrong thing and maybe incriminate himself. For what, he had no idea. Which is what made him all the more cautious. Tom's street smarts were in high gear. And he was not going to fall for anything if he could help it.

The man with the cane sat there and read everything for at least ten minutes, not saying a word. Some of the papers which were in the folder were the forms Maria had helped him with. They had spent enough time with them for Tom to recognize them right away. He went back and forth through the papers looking at one then another and then back to the first. The door opened again. It was the woman who had brought in the original folder. She had more papers and placed them in front of the man with the cane and left without saying a word.

After a few more minutes of looking at the new papers, he put everything down and made a couple of grunts and sniffs. "Signor Gaetano Santorini Eh?" Tom did not say anything. They just stared at each other for a bit. "Are you aware of what that name means here?" the man with the cane asked. It caught Tom by surprise.

"Should I be?" Tom said. He was obviously confused. The man with the cane did not say anything. He was almost waiting to see if he would get a different reaction. Tom did not say anything else either. They both continued to stare at each other.

"Maybe not............maybe yes," he replied. Then there was more staring. "Most school children here know that name. It is taught in the history books."

'History books?' Tom thought but would not say. "Signor, might that be a different man with the same name as mine?" Tom asked. There were still more stares. Then Tom added. "I wouldn't know that since I live in America and have since the war. Since nineteen-nineteen to be exact."

"Well.........that could be," he said, "but you say you were from Montoro Superiore, right? That is a small town, even today."

"Yes, that's right," Tom answered hoping it would lighten up the conversation a bit. "Most of my family had come from there or the surrounding area. But by the time my parents were around thirty or thirty-five, there were only my grandparents and my parents. So, my father decided to try to make it in America. They went first and I stayed with my grandparents until they sent for me. Except my grandfather got sick and passed away a couple of years later. My grandmother .... well, that's a long story."

There was an extended silence this time and even more staring. It was as if the man with the cane was hoping Tom would have said he was not from Montoro. That would have settled everything in his mind. But he was starting to look very troubled and almost emotional.

"Signor Gaetano Santorini. That name is known here because he was a war hero," the man stated with pride.

"Oh?" Tom sighed, "I was a soldier, but no hero," he said with such certainty the man with the cane almost felt relieved. But after a moment he seemed more determined to get to the bottom of it all.

"The forms you filled out state which divisions you served in," the man said trying to get back to business, "They also state some of the battles you fought in. Where did you get that information?" He wanted Tom to confess something, but Tom did not really know what he wanted or why. So, he figured he was always better off just staying with the truth.

"That is all accurate to my recollection Signor. I didn't get it anywhere but from my own experience in the Army," Tom replied feeling like he was almost falling into a confrontation but knew it would not be wise. "I swear to you I did not make up any of it." That was not what the man with the cane wanted to hear.

"You may have read about Gaetano Santorini and decided to capitalize on his name," the man retorted, "When did they start calling you....... Tom?" His question was almost sinister and almost implying his real name was not Gaetano.

"Have you ever known anyone who moved to America during that time and went through Ellis Island?" Tom answered softly. He could tell the name Ellis Island was not familiar. Tom figured he should explain in more detail. "Ellis Island was a clearing station for immigrants coming to America from Europe. Not just Italy but all over Europe and any country to the east." The man still did not seem to understand and shrugged his shoulders to confirm.

"When immigrants first arrived in America," Tom continued sounding just a bit frustrated, "they would stop the boat and take you by ferry to this place called Ellis Island across from New York City. We were escorted off and brought into this magnificent building with the most beautiful windows I had ever seen." Tom was trying to sound relaxed. He thought maybe some simple conversation would help the situation.

He could tell the man with the cane was paying attention, so he continued. "They would have a doctor look at you to make sure you were not sick. Some were and were kept separated from the others to see how badly. They would then have you go up to some clerks and give them your papers. If they did not like your name or thought it was too hard to pronounce, they changed it to the American version of the same name or made one up in some cases. They saw my name Gaetano and said, 'here you will be Thomas.' Ever since then, I have used Tom because it's easier and it was what they put on my papers. They must have thought the name Santorini was simple enough. I knew some who had their last names changed too." Tom's explanation seemed to get through to him.

"You said before, you went there when your parents sent for you. Was that in nineteen-nineteen?" he asked, still confused.

"No, that was the second time," Tom replied figuring he was only making things worse.

"Second time?" the man with the cane asked.

"Yeah," Tom sighed, "that's an even longer story." Now Tom knew he was definitely causing confusion. "The first time was in nineteen-oh-nine."

"Maybe you should tell me that story," the man with the cane said looking over his glasses.

"It might help if I knew why," Tom said. The staring resumed. This time it was for an even longer time.

Suddenly the man with the cane struggled to get to his feet. It took him some time and effort to rise. This time he took his cane to help him balance. With one hand on the table and one on the cane he seemed to lunge upward to get enough momentum to start the process. He reached an upright state and took a second to verify he had stability.

With a deep breath, he put all the papers into the folder and left the room. Tom did not know what to make of it. So, he resumed the posture he had while he was waiting before. 'This is going to take a while' he thought to himself. He looked at the mirror again figuring he was still being watched. 'Hmm, one-way' he thought.

A few moments later, the two guards came in. The one which had spoken with the man with the cane earlier told Tom to stand up. Tom did and began to turn around to get the handcuffs again. "That won't be necessary," The other guard said, and they escorted him back to his holding cell. Tom noticed a clock on the wall in one of the rooms as he passed by. It was after twelve o'clock.

· · · ·

TONY WAS UP AT DAWN and got ready so he could leave when Joe came to get him. Joe showed up around seven thirty. He needed to get right on this because he had to be in court by ten. Even if he could not stay to find everything, he could help them to know what to look for. A birth certificate was important. It may not exist though due to his immigration. Plus, the original method for keeping records during that time period in Italy was not considered as important in the small towns.

Other records would be his papers from Ellis Island which included the date of arrival and the ship he arrived on. Then there were the usual American documents. Joe was not sure if they would help since everything in question was about his identity while he was in Italy. He also asked if they could find out anything about Tom's parents. When they came over, did they have their immigration papers from Ellis Island? All of this could help.

Joe and Tom got to the Santorini's shortly after Richard arrived. "Let's see what we can find," Joe said, "I may have to pick these up this afternoon. I can sort through them and take them to the consulate later today. They seemed willing to help and not all that busy, I might add. It may be to our advantage."

"I'll take everything with me," Tony said, "You can pick them up at the pizzeria on your way back from court." Joe had to be in court in Hoboken so that would make it easier. The pizzeria was right on the way from the courthouse to his office. They talked over the things Joe wanted them to focus on, and he left.

• • • •

ANNA CAME TO THE HOTEL where Maria was staying. She had arranged to come by around one in the afternoon. It was a bit before that when she arrived. Maria had told her which room she was in but because she was about twenty minutes early, she called her room from the house phone in the lobby. She offered to take Maria out to lunch but Maria was hesitant. She wanted to stand by the phone in case Tony called.

"They won't likely call until late afternoon our time," Anna said, "Besides the hotel will take a message and we can get back to them." Anna was trying to help Maria get her mind off it. She also had some information about a lawyer she knew. He had taken care of some contracts her husband's company needed to process. She called him and got a referral for someone who could handle this sort of thing.

Maria agreed and went with her. She was very relieved to hear there was someone locally who could help and could even arrange for a lawyer. The only problem was this lawyer was not able to do anything until the next day. Maria thought that would be too late, but Anna assured her it would be all right.

They did not go far for lunch. One of the local cafés was just fine for both of them. "The unfortunate thing Maria," Anna said trying to console her but also tried to help her to see the reality of the situation, "this may take some time to straighten out. If there is a trial, it could take weeks, maybe months."

Mary was stunned, "No!" was all she could say.

"I didn't say that to scare you," Anna continued, "but to let you know, if you would like, you can stay with us rather than paying for an expensive hotel." The thought brought mixed feelings. It would save money but prior to three hours ago, she did not even know this woman. And as generous as she seemed, it looked as if it might be a burden on them and did not know how comfortable she would be with that type of arrangement. She decided to discuss it with Tony and hopefully Tom. She would decide from there. Ana agreed.

• • • •

THEY HAD BROUGHT TOM his lunch with the same speech about having to eat it within a half hour. This time Tom grinned a bit at the repetition. This food was a little bit better than the other meals, but he still felt like he was back in the Army. It had been over two hours when the two guards came to his door and unlocked it. "Please stand up," the guard said. The repetition was getting to him, but he was happy not to get the handcuffs again though. Maybe that part was over for good. They escorted him to the same room, and he sat in the same chair he had before and once again waited.

Twenty minutes later the man with the cane returned. This time he began to speak right away and remained standing. "So, if I understand. You say you are Gaetano Santorini from Montoro

Superiore. And you fought in the Great War," he said firmly. Tom was starting to wonder if everyone in Italy liked repeating themselves. He nodded his head. "You need to speak your answer," the man with the cane commanded. That is when Tom figured they were recording the conversation.

"Yes, that's right," Tom answered.

"And you don't understand why we have a problem with that?" the man with the cane continued to ask questions Tom obviously was not able to answer.

Tom paused and then said, "No.... I don't."

"Well Signor, Gaetano Santorini is a well know war hero here," he said as if Tom should have known.

Tom started to nod again and caught himself and answered, "That is what you say. I don't know."

"You said a couple of times it was a long story," the man with the cane said trying somewhat to be just a bit more cordial now.

"You could say that," Tom answered with a slight tilt to his head.

"Maybe you should tell me that story," the man with the cane said, "I would like to hear it."

"I really don't understand all of this," Tom sighed, "Why is this all happening? What have I done? Why won't you believe me?"

"Well, you see Signor," the man with the cane stated with pride, "Gaetano Santorini was killed near the end of the Great War and is buried in his hometown of Montoro Superiore."

Chapter 8

O nce Tom had settled into his Mamma and Papà's in Jersey City it did not take long for him to make friends. He tracked down Rocco from the ship the following year and Rocco gave him a job right away at the new restaurant he had told him about when they first met.

He worked there for a few years and could see a solid future for himself in America. It was spring of nineteen-fifteen. Tom was now twenty-one. He had Thursdays off, so he went with his friend Steven to Newark on the train. They went to get together with Steven's girlfriend Laura and unknown to Tom, the two of them wanted to introduce him to one of her friends. When they told him, at first, he thought Steven and Laura were playing an April fool's joke on him.

"I'm not falling for that one Laura," Tom chuckled thinking she was not serious. "I'm not just some kid you know. You can't pull the wool over my eyes that easy.............. she wants to meet me? Really?"

"Of course, you dummy," Laura giggled, "I told her all about you. How fabulous you are. That you're handsome and that you have a job at a restaurant in Hoboken, what's the name the place?"

"Rocco's," Tom mumbled.

"That's it," she continued, "When did we go there Stevie, last fall wasn't it?"

"Yeah, for your birthday, remember?" Steven chimed in. He did not really like being called Stevie. Steven was his name, not Steve, certainly not Stevie. All his family and teachers called him Steven. It is like some men who are named James. They do not like Jim or Jimmy, only James. But for the girl who liked him, he was okay with it.

"Birthday... that's right birthday. You just turned twenty-one didn't you Tommy?" Laura said. Now she was getting on his nerves too. Nobody called him Tommy. But, if she had a nice girlfriend who wanted to meet him, he could put up with hearing a little bit of 'Tommy' now and then. Guys are like that.

"So, what's her name?" Tom asked, "Is she good looking? How tall is she?" For a young man who did not want to seem too interested, he asked a lot of questions.

"Well, her name is Margret," Laura said, "and the rest................ you'll just have to find out for yourself when you meet her." Laura was having fun with it.

"Okay, sure," Tom said speaking very fast, "When do we do this? Does she live here in Newark near you?" Tom kept asking questions like anyone in need of a girlfriend would.

"Stevie, what do you think?" Laura said as she turned, "Two weeks from Sunday?"

Steven nodded in agreement.

"Then you can always remember you met her on Sunday April eighteenth, nineteen-fifteen, a very special day you will treasure forever," she said as she held her hands together and looked up as if she were dreaming.

Steven looked at Tom and rolled his eyes. "The great romantic," he said.

Laura snapped back with a slap to the arm. "Oh you, I'm a girl, we girls like that kind of thing."

"Glad someone does," Steven added deciding to quit while he was ahead.

"Two weeks huh?" Tom questioned. Two hours would have been more like it for Tom.

"She's away at school," Laura said, "She'll be home that weekend."

Tom's mind started going into overdrive. 'School? Wonder if she's good looking? How far way? When would I get to see her? Wonder if she's good looking?' At least he stopped asking these questions out loud.

They went out for pizza and walked around downtown Newark for the afternoon. Laura suggested a dance that night, but they both had to work the next day. Steven was only working three days a week at that time and Tom had to work on Fridays and Saturdays at Rocco's, so he had days off during the week sometimes. That was why they had gone out on a Thursday.

Later that evening Steven and Tom got back on the train and went to Hoboken station. "So, you're working in the morning too?" Steven asked as they jumped off the train at the platform.

"Not until dinner shift," Tom answered, "Rocco said I can start doing some things in the kitchen. Can't wait, I'm getting sick of just washing dishes."

"Hey, it beats my job," Steven said. He worked at a foundry, and it was hot and dirty. "At least you get to smell tasty food instead of melting metal all day."

"True," Tom said nodding his head, "See ya." They each went their separate ways.

Tom headed home to Jersey City. His parents did not live too far from Hoboken Terminal. Sometimes he would take the trolley, but this evening he decided to walk. It was still quite chilly being the first of April, but the signs of spring were upon them. He enjoyed the brisk air and the wind.

He got home about ten and noticed his mother was still awake. She would sometimes wait for his father to get home if he were working on the docks into the late evening. There had been a large shipment that day and he had an opportunity to work two shifts. It was not like him passing things up. They still needed the money.

"Hi Mamma," he said and gave her a big son to mother kiss then figured he would go right to bed.

"Gaetano?" She called out to him as he began leaving the room. The tone in her voice was a giveaway.

"Something's wrong," Tom reacted, "What is it?" Tom was always quick to show concern.

"Word from the old country," she said with a saddened tone.

"Everything all right? Is Nonna all right?" he said because he still had a special place in his heart for his grandmother.

"She's fine, for now," she said, "But I'm worried about her. She's getting weak. Don't forget she's over seventy now." His grandmother had been quite healthy for a woman of her years.

"Does Papà know?" Tom asked.

"We talked," she continued, "He worries about her too. It's not easy being apart when your Mamma is getting old. I guess that's the price we paid for moving away. We tried to get her to come with us."

"I did too," Tom added, "when you sent for me, I asked her, even begged her to come with me. She said Montoro was her home for her entire life and she didn't want to leave."

"Tomorrow, when you're Papà gets up, we need to talk about what we're going to do," Fabiana said.

"What can we do from here?" Tom asked, "We don't really have much money."

"No, but your Papà and I have an idea," she said, "he had something he needed to check on first at work today. So, we can talk in the morning. You told me you're working tomorrow. What time?"

"Rocco wants me to go in a little early, by two so he can start showing me how to make the pies," Tom answered.

"Oh?" she asked.

"Yeah, he said he wants me to eventually work in the kitchen," Tom sensed some hesitation in her question, but did not say anything.

· · · ·

TOM WANTED TO SLEEP late that morning, like most young people his age do. His mother called him down at six so his father would not be late for work, "Gaetano, come down I'll make you breakfast," she said. Tom liked it when his Mamma made him breakfast, so he got right up. He remembered the conversation the night before and that his Papà would want to talk as well. His hair was messed up and all over the place. It looked like he had combed it with the pillow.

Tom's father's name was Filippo in Italy but just like Tom, they changed it when he came over and went through Ellis Island. They told him his name would be Philip or Phil as people ended up calling him.

"Good morning Papà," he said as he leaned over and gave his Mamma a kiss on the top of her head, "You too Mamma."

"I have to get to work soon so we'll have to get right to it," Papà said. He started right away as Fabiana got up to get Tom some breakfast. "Mamma said you talked last night?"

"Yeah, just as I got home," Tom answered, "Nonna isn't feeling too good these days she said."

"Not so much that," Papà continued, "she's probably fine for now."

"That's what Mamma said too," Tom added with a sigh of relief, "But something isn't right, or I'd still be sleeping." He looked over at his mother and smiled.

"You'd sleep all day if we let you," Mamma chimed in.

"Na, come on Mamma I always get to work on time," Tom quipped. His father suddenly seemed quite serious.

"We have little doubt in your commitment Gaetano," His father said. Philip had been calling him Tom around the house even though his mother always called him Gaetano. His Papà calling him Gaetano meant this was important. For everyday conversation, Tom was good. But when things got serious, his Papà called him Gaetano.

"You're the type of son most people wished they had," Papà continued, "you care about your family more than most your age. Especially, I hate to say it, here in America. In the old country family mattered more."

Tom was hoping this would not be another round of 'When we were in the old country' sessions. "What are you saying Papà?" he asked.

His Papà paused for a moment because he did not want to say what he needed to say. It was like going backwards. He sighed then said, "During the four years you were with your Nonna, we missed you and I swore I would never want you to be away from us ever."

Tom was sensing a bomb shell. "What are you saying Papà?" he repeated. It was all he could come up with.

"The tough thing here is I also love my Mamma just like you love yours and I can't go to take care of her," Papà said, "If I lose this job, I probably won't get another one. Things are tight because of the war in Europe."

"I'm glad Italy is not in that war," Tom added with relief.

"No, but with the unrest so close by, I worry for your Nonna more," he added, "your mother and I have discussed it, and we feel you should be the one to go and take care of her in her last days. We can only hope there will be many, but she is getting very old and I'm afraid rather frail." Phil was basing this on the tone in her recent letters along with some things Signor Rizzi said in his letters to Tom.

"Do we have the money for me to go?" Tom asked, "I know we try to save, but it must be expensive to go and then to come back, what if there is no money for me to come back?"

Phil paused for a moment. "I spoke with one of the dock managers yesterday," he said. "Every once and a while, there is a chance for someone to work their way for passage. I had asked him last week to let me know if anything came up and it did a couple of days ago. You would be a cook on a cargo ship. Not the only cook, more of a helper. They would show you what to do."

"More washing dishes?" Tom shook his head and grinned. His Papà knew he was not serious.

"I guess so. For what it cost to go to Europe these days, it will be the best paying dishwashing job you've ever had." his Papà said as he smiled and chuckled.

Tom knew it would be the right thing to do. He did not want to leave. But the thought of his Nonna growing old with no one to care for her was not something he wanted to bear for the rest of his life either. Signor Rizzi was available for many things. But it is not like having family right there. He also did not want to think about how long that might be. It could be for only a year or two. It scared him to think his grandmother might not be around for very long.

"So, when did you have in mind. Sometime this summer?" Tom asked. His Papà just sat there and looked at him. He could tell the next words were likely as hard for his Papà to say as they would be for him to hear.

"There is a boat leaving on the sixteenth and there is a position on it for you," Phil said. "It's not a liner like I said. It's a cargo ship going to Napoli. This is one of the ships we often see in port. I wouldn't feel comfortable with you on a ship that

I didn't have some idea of who was running it. I spoke with the captain yesterday and he is willing to let you go if you agree to work and not complain. He really means no complaining. Too many of the young people he takes on do nothing but."

"Is it at one of the docks where you work?" Tom asked.

"It is," Phil answered, "right now. But they need to unload and are not scheduled to reload until the twelfth. Figure a couple of days to load up and then they go."

"What do they do for the extra week, just sit there?" Tom was full of questions.

"Sometimes, if there are no other ships that need the dock," Phil explained, "If they do, they just anchor in the harbor and most of the crew has leave. The captain said he wants to meet you."

Tom felt a mixture of adventure and missing his home. At twenty-one every young man needs some adventure. This would be one to remember, especially the unknown. "Well, I guess that's it then," Tom said with the tone of acceptance his Papà had hoped for.

Phil knew his son and that he would do whatever was necessary when someone in the family needed him. His Mamma could not hold the tears back any longer. She grabbed him and gave him a hug like he had not felt from her in a long time.

"It's Okay Mamma," Tom reassured her, "it won't be forever. I'll be back." His Papà was getting up so he could leave for work.

"We knew we could count on you," Phil said as he looked at Fabiana, "I think we should write to her soon to let her know he is coming."

She looked at him sheepishly. "Wrote it last night," she said. "We just have to mail it." He just nodded his head not the least bit surprised then left through the back door.

Tom went back to his room to get dressed. "So much for meeting Margaret," he mumbled.

"What was that?" his Mamma asked thinking he was still talking to her.

"Nothing Mamma, nothing," he said as he left.

• • • •

TOM ARRIVED AT ROCCO'S a little before two o'clock and put on his apron but did not say anything to Rocco. He started to clean up the lunch dishes and put things away which did not need to be out. Rocco could tell something was on his mind but let it be. Once it looked like Tom was getting caught up Rocco noticed he went out back and sat down for a while without saying anything. It was not like him to be this quiet.

Rocco looked out wondering if maybe something had happened on his day off. He knew he was getting together with friends the day before. Maybe he had a falling out with one of them. He opened the door a crack and said, "You think you may want to try your hand at it?" referring to making pizza.

There was a bit of a pause but not enough so Tom would feel he was being rude. "Something I have to tell you," he said. Rocco was hoping it was not bad news. "Talked to my parents today."

"And?" Rocco questioned.

"Remember when we first met on the ship when I came over here?" Tom asked.

"Why," Rocco said, "are you going to work on a ship like I did?"

"Actually, sort of, not really, I mean...." Tom baulked back and forth. Rocco did not want to push because he could tell something was troubling him.

"I don't want you to think I'm not happy here," Tom finally answered. "It's my Nonna."

"The one you told me about when we met, back home?" Rocco asked, "Your father's Mamma?"

"She's the only grandparent I have left," Tom said, "My parents asked me to go back to care for her in her last days. It kinda scares me a bit. I want to be with her, but I'm not sure if I can really take care of her."

"Who looks in on her now?" Rocco asked,

"Signor Rizzi," Tom answered, "but we don't know how much these days. Maybe enough."

"Well," Rocco paused to be sure he would say the right thing, "he could probably help you with some things, don't you think? He's already there and didn't you say you worked for him once?"

"Yeah............" Tom hesitated, "he's very nice and close to the family for a long time. I'm sure he would be able to help."

Rocco knew this was not a subject where he should offer options. He felt a hole already thinking his favorite employee was going away. "So.......... any idea when?" Rocco asked.

Tom lifted his head. He had been looking down most of the time. "A couple of weeks," he replied.

"That's pretty soon," Rocco said trying to absorb the reality, "We're all gonna miss you around here. Don't know who I'll get to fill in. You won't be easy to replace."

That helped Tom feel Rocco was not upset with him. "I don't mean to cause you a problem," Tom continued, "its family, you know?"

"Sure do," Rocco said with a big chuckle, "Why do you think I stopped working on the ship? Now we have Francesca and her older brother Anthony. I couldn't think what it would have been like if I had stayed on the ship. Imagine if I had missed his first five years because I was away so much, and now a daughter too. Family has to come first."

Something about getting approval from Rocco helped him to know he was doing the right thing. "Now listen to me," Rocco said as he got a bit emotional, "When you come back, you remember, you always have a job here. No matter what. Even if I have to make up something for you to do. You come back. You have a job. Understand?"

Tom grinned and looked up at him, "Sure."

"So, you think you may want to try your hand at it?" Picking up where he had started. "You may need to know how to in order to support yourself in the old country. They do make pizza there you know........."

Chapter 9

• • • •

THE DOCKS IN ANY HARBOR can be an intimidating place unless everyone knows you. Jersey City was no exception. Most knew Philip Santorini. And his family was under the same umbrella of acceptance. Better known to his friends and coworkers as Phil, this tough and hardworking Italian immigrant had earned his place of respect over the past ten years. He was one of the faces which most knew and associated with the docks. When he asked for something, people would not hesitate to help him. So, when he needed to get his son to Italy to care for his aging mother, they worked together to make it happen.

The captain of the Hallwick was a seasoned seaman and had been navigating the Atlantic and Mediterranean for over twenty-five years. This trip was not to be as ordinary as others he had been on before. This was the first trans-Atlantic voyage his ship would make since the start of the war. Gus was Phil's foreman and had known Captain Stevens for a long time. The Hallwick had been making runs to Europe carrying lumber, coal, and textiles for the past fifteen years. Originally sailing out of Philadelphia harbor, most of her cargo was now coming out of New York.

The ship was completely unloaded by the third, but the dock was not booked for two more days. She would stay at the dock for the rest of that day then move out to harbor on the evening of the fifth. There they would wait until reloading on the twelfth. Most of the crew were given leave.

Phil arrived at the usual time on Monday morning. "What time did you tell your son to come by?" Gus asked.

"Just after lunch, around one," Phil answered, "Did you talk to the captain?"

"Yeah, I told him it would be sometime in the afternoon," Gus said, "he told me for us to just come aboard when Tom gets here." Gus had a few workers he would always go to in a pinch. Phil was one of them. "Does Tom know where to go?"

"Told him this morning," Phil answered.

"How's the Mrs. taking it?" Gus questioned.

"Eh. She'll be all right once he's on his way," Phil grumbled, "It's important. She knows that........... but....... she doesn't really like it."

"I don't think my wife would be able to handle that sort of thing. We talk about our oldest boy going off to college in New Brunswick next year and it gives her the hives," Gus said with a shiver.

Phil chuckled, "Yeah, that's what, thirty miles from here. He could walk home."

They settled into getting things done around the office. It was a bit light around the docks that day. "What do you have me on this morning?" Phil asked once he was on track.

"I'm gonna run you light," Gus answered, "Don't want to have you in the middle of something important and not be able to kick free when Tom comes. The Panaman is in. Two down from the Hallwick. We need to plan her load for tomorrow. Want you to check her out. That should only take the morning." Gus handed Phil the clipboard with Panaman's manifest.

"Panaman huh?" Phil sighed, "Everything in already for them?"

"Not till late this afternoon," Gus said, "train coming in from the cannery in Chicago was running late."

"Ah, the other windy city," Phil quipped.

"Got that right," Gus chuckled.

• • • •

THAT AFTERNOON WAS cold and typically breezy. Tom took the trolley from home and figured he would go to Rocco's straight from the docks. He knew where to go but was not completely sure he would not get lost. "Excuse me sir, I'm looking for the foreman's office?" he said as he stopped a man pushing a cart.

"Lookin' for a job kid? Not much available 'round here," the longshoreman barked.

"No I... I... I'm looking for my Papà, he works here," he replied. Tom was getting a bit shaky.

"What's your Dad's name?" the longshoreman said with only a slightly improved demeanor.

"Phil, Phil Santorini," Tom responded with pride.

"Oh, you're Phil's boy?" he said with a large grin coming over him, "Okay, here I'll show you where it is. Name's Jack what's yours."

"Ah.......... Tom sir," he answered with some relief.

Gus looked out the window and saw Tom coming. Phil was at the back of the office finishing the manifest for the Panaman. "Here comes your boy now Phil," Gus called back, "Looks like Jack's giving him an escort," he said with a grin, "You done back there?

"Just about," Phil said.

Tom came in and said hello to Gus. He had met him before and him well enough. The three of them all went up the docks towards the Hallwick. Inevitably Gus had to stop occasionally to deal with business matters. Tom was starting to shiver. It was a combination of the chilly wind and the nervous anticipation of meeting the captain. They got to the ship and Gus just walked right aboard as if he was the captain. Tom made sure he was the last in the line behind his Papà.

Captain Stevens was on the bridge working on the duty roster for the next week when they came aboard. He was not an exceptionally large man. Stood only five foot six inches and weighed in at only one hundred fifty-five pounds. But when he spoke, nobody dared cross him. "This your boy?" he said with a grunt. Phil gave him a nod.

Tom took off his cap and stood silently for a moment. He wanted to wait to be spoken to before saying anything. "Your father tell you the rules?" the captain stared at him.

"Yes sir, he said to do as I'm told without complaining," Tom answered hoping he was convincing.

"And what is it exactly you think I'll tell you to do?" Captain Stevens snapped back.

"Wash dishes, clean up the galley, and maybe help the cook if he lets me," Tom answered. He felt he was covering everything.

"What if I tell you to clean the toilets?" Captain Stevens said very quickly. He wanted to see his reaction.

"Someone has to clean 'em sir, may as well be the new kid," Tom quipped. He smiled as he said it thinking he was making the right impression.

"No complaining?" The captain continued, "Even if you're throwing up your insides from the rough seas huh? You still gonna clean the toilets?"

"Well sir, that's probably when they'll need cleaning the most," Tom said with a grin.

Captain Stevens could not keep a straight face after that one. "I guess he's right............What did you teach this boy?" he said looking at Phil and smiling, "Kid's got spunk. He'll work out just fine."

Phil was surprised and pleased he did not have to speak for his son. It does a man proud to see his son being able to carry himself that way. Gus just looked on and gave Phil a wink.

"We'll be out in the harbor starting tomorrow until the eleventh. He starts on the twelfth. Seven hundred hours, not a minute late. He'll stay aboard from there with a short leave before we set out," Captain Stevens said returning to his normal demeanor.

Phil replied, "Twelfth, seven hundred got it." He looked at Tom, "Got that?"

"Yes sir. Thank you, sir," Tom looked at Captain Stevens but did not know whether to shake his hand or not. Phil could tell he did not know quite what to do so he took his arm and led him out.

Now that they were off the bridge, Gus chimed in, "He seems tough, and he is. But there isn't a better skipper who comes through this harbor. You can count on him to do right by you." He put his hand on Tom's shoulder, "Just don't tick'm off."

"No sir," Tom chuckled understanding it was not something he wanted to do. "Papà, are you gonna be late tonight?"

Phil looked at Gus to double check, "Shouldn't be tonight, tomorrow I will be. We have a ship to load."

"Yeah, and they'll be in a hurry to make up for lost time waiting for the train from the cannery. Should have been here last night," Gus said as he slipped back into business mode. Phil grunted in agreement.

· · · ·

TOM FOUND HIS WAY BACK off the docks and headed for Rocco's. Some of the regulars had not seen Tom since Rocco told them he was leaving. He was not supposed to start until four. But since it did not take long with Captain Stevens, he decided to just go in early.

It was too cold to walk the entire way to Rocco's, so Tom hopped on the trolley. He did not have a lot of money on him, but he figured he would not need very much money for the next week. He really did not feel like walking in the cold that day. It made him wonder. 'Do I need to get a job when I get there? I don't even know how my Nonna pays for things. I don't think she has had any income since Nonno passed away. Is she poor? I don't remember.'

Tom was starting to realize when you are young, you take things for granted such as a meal on the table and clothes on your back. Not to mention a place to live. He became concerned for his grandmother even more. 'I'll get a job when I get there, I'll support her. Maybe she will even live longer if she knows someone is taking care of her. I wonder if Signor Rizzi would need someone to work............ What about the war? Does it mess things up for the people in the countries who are not fighting?'

The gravity of his voyage was starting to weigh on him. 'Worrying never solves things' his Mamma always taught him. It did not seem to stop him from worrying though.

The trolley came within two blocks of Rocco's. He knew the stop so well that he could fall asleep in the car and wake up just as it was pulling up to his street. Probably because the trolley would take a hard-right turn just before his stop. Today he was too preoccupied to doze off. His Nonna was on his mind.

"How did it go?" Rocco called out as he walked in.

"Short," Tom replied.

"Which, the interview or the Captain," Rocco asked.

Tom paused for a moment and then broke out into a full laugh, "Both."

Rocco laughed just as hard, "Just make sure you never get short with him."

"Me? Never, I'm mister nice guy remember?" Tom quipped back.

"Ok mister nice guy you got a lot to do," Rocco said as he tossed him an apron.

"Aye, aye skipper," Tom saluted Rocco as if he were a ship's captain and then laughed.

Later that evening, at about seven thirty, things were starting to wind down. Rocco's wife Sofia came in with the two kids. Tom also noticed some of the regulars were still hanging around even though they had been finished for a while. He also noticed some were coming in but did not order anything. Tom took it in stride until he heard a ruckus behind him, so he turned around. Rocco was coming out of the kitchen with a cake, and everyone started singing "For he's a jolly good fellow, for he's a jolly good................" Tom was both excited and embarrassed.

"What's this, a party?" Tom said wanting to show he was moved by the gesture.

"Only the best for the best," Sophia said as she gave him a hug and a kiss. Little Anthony hugged his leg too, then climbed up on the chair next to him to give him a bigger hug.

People took turns coming up to him and patting him on the back and wishing him the best of luck. Tom had never realized the regulars even took notice of him. He would just do his job from day to day and occasionally talk to some of the people. It was the way things would be expected in a restaurant setting.

Rocco handed him a small box which was neatly wrapped. "What...I.......... I'm.........I'm...." Tom stumbled.

"I'm trying to get the words out!" One of the regulars said from across the room which started everyone laughing.

"This is too much," Tom continued to stammer, "Why............... you .... it's just."

"Say it in Italian, you might get it out," one of the other regulars said, "you'd better start practicing. You'll be speaking a lot of it in a couple of weeks." Everyone was laughing.

"Open it," Sophia said.

"Okay," Tom said jumping at the chance, "Who wrapped this? There's four layers of paper here."

Tom's eyes lit up as he opened the small box. The place went silent while they watched Tom's face. He looked up and then around. "This......this...... this..."

"Is for you from all of us," Rocco said proudly.

"All of you?" Tom's voice quivered a bit.

"That's right," Rocco replied, "We figured one significant thing rather than a lot of smaller things. Make it easier to take with you also."

Sophia leaned inward, "we took up a collection," she said.

Tom reached into the small box and pulled out a simple but beautiful pocket watch and held it up in front of his face just staring at it. The whole place broke into applause and hooting then back to "For he's a jolly good fellow, for he's...................."

There were three pies in the oven and Rocco pulled them out, one Pepperoni, one Sausage and Onion and the other plain cheese. Tom thought they had been made for a customer when he saw Rocco putting them together just before Sophia came in. It turned out they were for his going away party. Tom spent the next half hour thanking everyone who was there and eating some pizza and cake.

He sat in one of the booths and little Anthony came over and climbed up on his lap. Anthony always ran up to Tom whenever he came to the restaurant. Rocco once told him, "That kid really likes you. He talks about you at home all the time. Tom this, Tom that. Little guy can't get enough of you."

"Think he knows?" Tom asked Sophia.

"No, not a chance, he's too little. He wouldn't understand," she replied.

The party wrapped up quickly since it was a weeknight, and everybody had to work the next day. Tom went in the back to finish up, but Rocco told him he could go home if he wanted.

"This is home too," Tom said with all seriousness.

Rocco and Sophia looked at each other and nodded without saying anything. Tom stayed and finished up. Not much else was said for the rest of the evening. Sophia left the room suddenly. Rocco figured she was crying. She came back a few minutes later.

"We all love you around here you know?" She said with a quiver and gave Tom a hug and another kiss, "You come back, hear?"

"I will, I promise," Tom said softly as she hugged him.

Tom caught the last trolley car for the night. He did not feel like sleeping on this ride either. He would not sleep very much most nights leading up to the twelfth.

Chapter 10

"Come on, get up," Phil said as he kept tapping Tom's foot. Tom jumped and sat up in bed. It was still dark, "What....... what.... what time is it? Uh. I can't believe it. What......?"

"No time for any of that. Get up!" Phil barked back.

"Okay............ Okay, I'm up.............. Let's see, packed, clothes over there, get dressed. I got it. I'm up," Tom mumbled as his head fell back on the pillow.

"Now!" His father snapped. Tom jumped to his feet and headed for the bathroom.

'Last time for a while I'll have such a nice bathroom' he thought to himself. Little did he realize, but this was indeed leaving home. He would be a man from here on. No more having Mamma pick up after him, No more meals without effort. He had not even thought about clean cloths. And Mamma knew it too. She had not slept for three days either.

Tom scurried to get dressed and grabbed a couple of things to pack. Then he went to the kitchen. "Gaetano," his Mamma called to him.

"Yes Mamma," he replied.

"Hurry and eat your breakfast it's ready and on the table. Your Papà is almost finished," she said like only a mother could.

"Not really hungry Mamma," he said knowing it was the wrong thing to say. Then he caught himself. "But I'll eat something."

She gave him a look like he was used to since he was young. Even back when they were all in Montoro Superiore. It said 'Do as I say. It's good for you. Or else.' Fabiana was not doing well with her son leaving home, "Hurry, you'll be late. Remember he said not to be late."

Tom looked to his father to see if he was anxious and showing whether they were late. Phil did not want to contradict Fabiana, so he did not say anything. But Tom could tell his father knew they still had some time left.

Tom had decided to pack light by advice from his Papà who knew a thing or two about traveling and told him he should only take what he could carry if he was running to catch a boat or a train. "Too much luggage will slow you down and cause you to miss one of them," his Papà taught him. Tom paid heed to this and had a medium sized duffle bag with his essentials and two changes of cloths.

"You can get what you need when you get settled in at Nonna's." his father told him.

For Fabiana, this was too short of a time for proper goodbyes. She knew he was going to be on the ship for three days before leaving harbor and she would see him once more. The plan was for dinner the night before he shipped out. Maybe there would be enough time then. Tom had worked at Rocco's the night before and then met some friends for a couple of hours before coming home. She did not feel there had been enough time to see him and prepare for him to leave.

Phil always took the trolley to work. He would have to transfer only once to get on the line which took him to the docks. From there it was a short walk to the office where he was to report each day. Gus had told him it would be all right if he were a bit late so he could see Tom to the ship.

As they were approaching the Hallwick, Tom started to think about the day his Nonna and Signor Rizzi brought him to the ship in Napoli. 'I wonder if people will be waving when we leave?' That just did not make any sense to him. His father would not be waving because he would either be working, or it might be during the night, and he would be home sleeping. His mother had never been to the docks. Neither Tom nor Phil really would want her there. Then he thought he may not even be topside when they left. There was to be a host of new thoughts for him as he ventured out on what could likely be the trip of a lifetime.

It was six forty-five when they reached the gangway. Phil and Tom walked up and saw what appeared to be a member of the crew just off to the left of the gangway. "You guys looking for someone?" he grunted.

Phil spoke up, "My son's first day. Looking for Captain Stevens."

"Not here. First day? He's part of the crew?" the crewman asked, "You that kid going to Italy?"

"That's me," Tom bounced back.

"Yeah, captain told me," he responded, "You'll need to see Hiram. He's in charge of the duty roster. Follow me."

Phil felt awkward because he knew he could not go with him. He also could not make a big deal about saying good-bye. So, he just patted Tom on the shoulder and said, "You all set then?"

"Sure Papà," Tom said with some hesitation but also with excitement.

"You have the money?" Phil asked him quietly. He had exchanged Tom's American currency for Italian. There was an office at the docks where they did currency exchanges for most countries. It was a service available to the crews of the ships which came into port so they would have American money with them if they needed to go into town. This worked out for them because they always preferred it when someone needed currency other than American. It saved them from having to go to the bank to exchange it. The fee for exchanging to Lira was almost nothing since they had a large supply of that currency.

"Yeah, got it on me," Tom said just as just as quietly. He spoke softly because he still did not know who he could trust.

"I'll check in before I leave tonight, see if you're free," Phil said at his normal volume. "Talk to you then." He was not sure if he should leave but it seemed like the best idea. He also did not want to embarrass Tom in front of a member of the crew. "Well, okay then, guess I'll be off."

"Thanks, Papà," Tom said trying to sound as mature as possible, "Thanks for walking with me." Tom did not want to be embarrassed either. Phil turned and left the way he had come.

"Tom is your name?" The crewman asked.

"Yeah, in America, my name is actually Gaetano when I'm in Italy. I suppose I should get used to going by that again," Tom said with almost some regret.

"Yeah well, Tom's easier for me, if you don't mind," The crewman said.

"No, that's what I'm used to anyway. I figure once I get to Italy, I'll just tell people that my name is Gaetano. But for now, Tom's fine. What's your name?" Tom asked.

"Frankie, I work in the boiler room," he said as if they had known each other for a long time. "Love it when we're in harbor, not much to do. Just a small boiler for hot water, showers, and cooking. You know?"

"I guess I'll learn," Tom said. He turned as they were walking towards the bridge and looked towards the dock in time to see his Papà walking away. It was both a sinking feeling and an encouraging feeling. At twenty-one, Tom needed to be out on his own. This was as good a way as he could imagine.

Hiram had been with the ship for three years. Before that he had been in the Navy for twenty years. He loved the sea and could not imagine himself doing anything else. "This is the Italian kid the captain told us about?" Frankie said as they came into the room where Hiram was working, "Tom is his name or is it Gitano?"

"Tom's fine," he replied as he reached out to shake Hiram's hand. Hiram gave him a quick shake and then grabbed the duty roster that was hanging on a nail.

"Galley hey? Not this morning though, captain says you should get settled in and see the entire ship, so you know who you're workin' with," Hiram said. He was all business as Tom knew he should be. "I'll take'm to Benny. He'll show him his quarters."

'Benny?' Tom thought. Could it be the same Benny he had met on the ship coming to America? Maybe so, how many Bennys are there? He did not meet one Benny while he was in Jersey City and maybe he had changed from passenger ships to cargo ships. He was very hopeful because he wanted to show him how well he could speak English now.

"This way," Hiram said as he pointed to the portal to their left.

"Thanks Frankie," Tom said as he gave him a quick wave as they left, "See ya around."

"Yeah, get the feel of the place," Frankie said, "See ya at dinner maybe." Frankie turned to go back where he had been.

Hiram started with the instructions right away, "Always watch where you're walking. You have to look both up and down. There are things to step over and things that are low. So, you're gonna trip and bang your head a lot until you get used to it."

Tom was thinking the captain would only have to worry about tripping, and he chuckled. Tom had grown to about five foot ten inches tall and knew he would have to keep an eye on the low bulkheads and pipes. They went down two levels and Hiram turned into a small room where Benny was supposed to be. Tom figured this would be when he would find out if it was the same Benny.

"Hey, got the new kid, you need to show him his bunk," Hiram said as he turned the corner before Tom could see, "Benny, you in there?"

"Yep," They heard a voice from the back of the room. Tom was disappointed because this was a much older and heavier man. He did not even look like the Benny he had known.

"I'll leave him with you," Hiram said as he left in a hurry.

"Captain told me about you. Workin' your way over to Italy? Something about your grandma being sick?" Benny said.

"Well not sick. Just getting old. My parents wanted me to go and take care of her during her last days," Tom replied. 'Hope it not days but years,' he thought to himself.

"We decided to have you bunk with one of the crew who's from your home country," Benny said, "His name is Augustino, he's from Rome. Street kid needed somewhere to go, something to do. So, the captain took him on when we were in Napoli last year. He's about your age, maybe a bit younger. Be a good match we figure." Benny was very pleasant. He was the nicest guy so far.

Tom wondered how well Augustino could speak English. He figured with a mostly American crew, he likely would speak it pretty well. They went down two more levels to the crew quarters and down the hallway. Benny stopped at a door and looked in.

"Doesn't look like he's here right now, probably on duty," he said, "Put your stuff over there and come with me. I'll show you around." Benny pointed to one of the bunks in the cabin.

The tour only took about an hour. The Hallwick was not a large ship and most of it was the cargo hold anyway. The most interesting part was the engine room. Tom had not seen a steam engine before and was amazed at the way heat from a fire could turn a propeller with just water boiling. Nothing was fired up though, so he had to imagine from the description the engineer gave him. He could not believe how much coal there was in the bins.

"Will they use all of it to get to Italy?" Tom asked the engineer.

"No, less than half," he replied, "We carry enough for a round trip these days. Coal costs too much in Europe compared to here. Especially since there's a war going on in some of those countries right now."

The engineer's name was also Tom, but Thomas was the name he was given at birth. He was raised in Philadelphia and his father worked in the shipyards when he was growing up. His father taught him about steam engines when he was fifteen. This Tom had been working on cargo ships for over twenty-seven years. These days however, he would only go out from April to September. The winter months were too rough for him at sea.

The last stop was the galley. Benny figured he would leave Tom there and then go back to what he was doing. Tom was surprised at how small the galley and the dining area were. There were only about thirty-two crew members to feed, and they would not eat all at once. They ate in shifts.

The galley chef was a Frenchman named Maurice from Marseille. He joined the crew about five years before. He had worked on several ships during his life. New York was the run he would get the most excited about. His favorite girl was in New York, and he always looked forward to seeing her. His English was not too good from what Benny had told him. Tom figured he could work it out with him.

The duty roster was posted in the dining cabin. "Make sure you read this every day, it changes all the time," Benny told him. "You don't want Hiram to chase you down if you're supposed to be on duty and not at your post. Stay on his good side and you'll be on Captain Steven's good side too."

"Good to know, thanks," Tom said with some trepidation. He remembered what Gus had said. 'Just don't tick'm off.' That must be what he was talking about.

"Stay here with Maurice for a bit, he'll show you what you'll be doing. I'll be back once the captain returns. He'll want to talk to you," Benny said as he turned to leave.

Tom stood there for a bit feeling very awkward because he noticed Maurice was just staring at him. "Italian Oui?" Tom knew what that meant.

"Oui," Tom said back trying to impress him.

Maurice continued to stare until it became uncomfortable. "I don't like Italians," he said, and continued to stare.

Tom did not quite know what to say but because this was not the captain he replied, "Sorry, nothing I can do about that. I guess I was born this way."

Maurice laughed. "Ah ha, good sense of humor, no?" he said as he smacked his shoulder. "Just joking about not liking Italians.................. Some of my best friends are Italians. Really, I mean it, really." He giggled while he rolled his eyes implying, he may not really mean it.

Tom figured he was still joking and decided to keep up the banter. "Well, they're not really your friends you know. They just feel sorry for you, so they pretend to be your friend. We Italians do that." He made certain he said it while laughing so Maurice would not take it the wrong way.

"Captain said you had spunk. I like you. You'll do good here, no? Hungry?" Maurice asked as he turned to walk towards the cupboard. "One of the luxuries of working the galley, you eat whenever you want. Just don't abuse it. The captain will take it out of your pay............... Oh, that's right, you don't get paid 'cause you're working off your fare. Je parie."

"So, I guess I'll eat a lot," Tom quipped.

"Guess you will," Maurice said, "Ever work in a galley before?"

"I work, oh, uh, worked at a restaurant here in Jersey City for the past three years. Rocco's, ever been there?" Tom paused to see if he had but got no reaction. "Mostly washing dishes and cleaning tables."

"So, you should be an old pro at this by now eh. C'est Bon, I won't have to keep an eye on you all the time?" Maurice said quickly as he nodded his head back and forth. Tom was quite sure he knew what C'est Bon meant.

"Maybe you could teach me some French while I'm working with you. You think?" Tom asked, hoping to build a friendship.

"Peut-être. If you work rapidement...... eh quickly and get done early, maybe I teach you French, eh?" Maurice liked the idea.

"Hey and maybe I can teach you some Italian too," Tom added.

"Italiano? Pourquoi devrais-je faire ça. Oh, oui Anglais, why would I want to do that? I don't like Italians," Maurice said with a face which was halfway between a pout and a smile. Tom smiled back knowing he was just joking.

Tom stayed with Maurice for about an hour looking over the place. He looked through the cabinets and under the counters. He looked at the dishwashing set up and wondered about the trash at sea. "What do they do with the trash? Do they just dump it overboard?" he asked Maurice.

"Mostly burn it in the boiler room with the coal," Maurice replied understanding why he would not know. He liked his curiosity about things.

Benny came in and gave Maurice a signal, "Takin' him to see the captain, are you done with him?"

"I'm just getting started with him," Maurice rolled his eyes and tilted his head back and to the right. "But you can have him for now. You start with me before noon saisir? You'll serve up lunch and clean after, okay?"

"Okay," Tom said almost with a salute.

This was right up Tom's alley and did not make him the least bit nervous. He was just glad he did not have to work in the boiler room shoveling coal all day or worse, all night. The galley was definitely a day job.

• • • •

CAPTAIN STEVENS HAD been at the dock master's office arranging the cargo load. They were to carry mostly food supplies such as wheat and oats. Some of it was to be livestock feed for dairy farms in Italy. The oats would be horse feed for the horses owned by the Italian government. There was also some canned ham and dried beef. It was sort of a jerky, but not exactly.

Some of the grain would be sold commercially, but the majority was for feed. The other cargo was flint. But that was not to be discussed by anyone. It was labeled Cornmeal and was in sealed containers covered with cornmeal to camouflage it. Only the captain knew. No one else on the crew knew. So, if the German's boarded them, the crew would appear to know nothing but that they were carrying food stocks.

"So, you met Maurice?" The captain asked.

"Yes sir, I start with him before noon," Tom said wanting to appear to be ready for working.

"Maurice is quite the character, isn't he?" Captain Stevens said.

"I like him," Tom added, "he's really funny."

"Yeah, but don't criticize his cooking, he's not the least bit funny when someone criticizes his cooking," Captain Stevens said with a smile, "Okay, you know where you bunk, you know where you work, and they showed you the head?" Tom did not know the term, so he looked puzzled. "The head, you know...............the toilet?"

Tom was embarrassed he did not know. 'Learn something new every day I guess,' he thought to himself as he nodded, he understood. "the one you said I may have to clean?" he added.

The captain grinned and nodded. They went over some basics until about ten o'clock then the captain dismissed him. He had enough time to go to his bunk to check it out a bit more. Maybe Augustino would be back by then. Now the only thing was to remember how to get there. The stairs were easy to find so he went down. Things did look familiar enough, but then again, the whole ship looked the same.

With only one or two wrong turns, Tom found the cabin with his bunk. No one was there so he just opened his bag and shuffled things about. There really was not much to take out and even less room to put it. So, he decided to work his way back to the galley and see if he could help Maurice prepare lunch.

Maurice had things under control when he got there but was glad to see his willingness to help. "Just watch for now," he told him, "you'll have plenty to do tonight after dinner. I am going to New York to see my Betty. 'She's waiting for me'," he started singing. "She loves me tu sais?"

• • • •

LUNCH WAS CONSIDERED an inconvenience to the crew when there was work that had to be done. They would always get anxious as the cargo was coming aboard. They would rather work straight through and be done with it. Dinner on the other hand was the time for relaxing and joking with each other. Some of the crew would have this evening off, but not the boiler room crew. They had to finish the system inspection procedures in order to fire up the boilers for a test run the next day. Tom was to stay aboard as part of his orientation and to be available if someone needed anything from the galley.

It was not that different working in the galley from working at Rocco's except it was much smaller. And at Rocco's there was the smell of pizza. The first wave came in for lunch. Maurice had put out some meat for sandwiches and a cold macaroni dish with a bit of oil and vinegar. Tom did not like it very much, but the men ate it without showing any preferences. He also put out some baked beans.

Frankie was in the first wave, so Tom said hello to him and told him he had been to the boiler room. "You wanna switch jobs?" Frankie said.

"Not a chance," Tom replied without hesitation.

The first wave was in and out quickly. That was one major difference from Rocco's. The people who came to Rocco's were just as interested in enjoying their time as their meal. This group just wanted to get fed and go back to work. The second wave came in and Benny was in that group. So was Augustino. Benny introduced them while Tom was dishing him the macaroni. "You guys will have a lot to talk about, both being from Italy," Benny said.

The thing Benny did not understand was the two of them came from completely different upbringings. Just because they were both Italian, it did not necessarily mean they had much in common. Tom was from a small town in the country and was close to his family. Augustino was a city kid and like most cities worldwide, there is an element of broken families which gravitate there. Augustino's father had died when he was two years old, and his mother moved to Rome to find work. So, he grew up on the streets getting into a lot of trouble.

The two of them exchanged a couple of words in Italian and agreed to spend time later getting acquainted. Augustino would be on board in the evening because he was under orders to not go into towns when they were in harbor. He could go out and about during the daytime if he was with other members of the crew but not alone, and definitely not at night.

This was a deal which he worked out with Captain Stevens when he brought him on board to work. It was to help him stay out of trouble. If he did well, eventually the captain would ease up a bit. Augustino knew it was for his own good and was more than willing to go along with the restrictions, most of the time.

The fourth wave was only about four men. That was partly because some were not on the ship but out doing things. Things like getting supplies in town for the crew and sending telegrams to various people they needed to notify in Italy regarding their schedule and cargo.

The dinner shift was different. Everyone was back on board and the meal was made up of soup and roasted chicken with mashed potatoes and canned corn. Maurice would try to cook what was traditional in the country they were in at the time and to serve roasted chicken with mashed potatoes sounded very American. All four waves were packed out and between each serving there would be a line outside in the corridor waiting for the next wave.

Tom realized each member of the crew was assigned a wave so there would not be any confusion. The crew stuck to it closely, but there would always be exceptions if someone were held up at their post during their wave. There would be times Maurice would be told someone could not make it to a meal. He would save something for them so they could come in anytime they were free.

Maurice told him the two of them would eat after everyone else was done and usually just after the fourth wave. They would sit down just the two of them and eat. Maurice made certain there was always something held back to make sure it was not all gone by the time they were going to eat. Then they would clean up. But not tonight, Tom had to clean up completely so Maurice could go see his Betty in the city.

Tom did not mind one bit. There had been many times Rocco had to count the cash do some paperwork, so Tom would do the entire cleanup. The only difference is he still did not know where everything was kept. Maurice knew this. So, he told him to just leave things on the table if he did not know where they belonged. It was not something they would do at sea because everything would need to be secured if they hit rough seas. Maurice would put things away in the morning.

He got done with everything at about eight thirty and realized he had not seen his Papà yet. He went topside and asked one of the crewmen who was smoking a cigarette if he had seen anyone asking for him and he described his father. As he was talking to him, he heard his Papà's voice call to him. He got excited and ran down the gangway to greet him.

"So how was it, your first day?" Phil asked.

"Great, long, what time is it?" Tom asked as he pulled out his pocket watch. "Wow, that late already."

"Looks like you're already settled in," Phil said.

"I guess," Tom replied, "I worked both the lunch and dinner. It's different than Rocco's, so small, just ten men eat at a time." Tom wanted to tell him everything, but Phil needed to get home and tell Fabiana Tom was doing well in his new position.

"Oh, one last thing Papà," Tom added, "they have me rooming with this guy from Rome. So, I'll get to practice my Italian on the way with someone other than you and Mamma. He seems like a nice guy. And the guy I work for, he's this Frenchman who's really funny." Tom caught himself going on and on. "But I know you have to go. Night after tomorrow they say I can have dinner with you and Mamma. I don't think I can make it home since we leave during the night so maybe I was thinking we could go to Rocco's. It's a lot closer. What do you think?"

"I think you're all wound up from a big day," Phil chuckled, "Hope you can sleep in a strange place. Ships can be very noisy even in harbor. I'll talk it over with Mamma and let you know tomorrow. I can check with Rocco too. He will like the idea, I'm sure."

"Okay, tell Mamma I miss her already," Tom said wishing he could spend more time with his Papà. Phil left so he could catch the last trolley, and Tom went to his cabin. He was asleep by nine fifteen. He did not even hear Augustino when he came in. Tom had to get up at six in the morning for galley duty. Augustino had told him there was an alarm clock in the cabin already set for five fifteen because that was the time he had to get up also. So, he pulled the lever out before he went to sleep.

Chapter 11

Sunday afternoon was relaxed and uneventful on the ship. The captain would not give demanding assignments on Sundays when they were in port. The engines had been tested the day before and all the cargo was on board. The plan was to set out at one o'clock the next morning because that was the window allotted for the Hallwick to have a clear channel out of port. The harbor master would try to schedule when ships would leave in order to minimize the risk of collision in harbor should the weather turn bad.

Tom had received permission from the captain to bring Augustino with him when he met his Mamma and Papà. They were under strict orders to not deviate from the plan of going straight to Rocco's for dinner and then right back to the ship. Captain Stevens would not have put that restriction on Tom. It was a condition of Augustino's probationary period.

Rocco had planned this to be a much quieter time than the going away party the week before. It would just be his wife Sophia, the two children and Tom's parents joining them for a peaceful time so they would not be distracted by anyone else. Rocco and Sophia had prepared a family style spread in the back room. They had soup, antipasto, lasagna, manicotti, and spaghetti with Rocco's special gravy which had meatballs and sausages on the side along with the best rolls in the region. This was to be a special night for the Santorinis. Their son was going back to the old country for a time, and nobody was certain how long that would be.

Tom and Augustino came in at about four o'clock. His parents were to show up at any moment. Augustino told Tom to call him Augie since most of the crew called him that. It was not really an Italian nick name he had grown up with, but it worked on board the Hallwick.

They came in the front and Tom walked to the back as if it were home. "Hey Rocco, want you to meet Augie?"

"Augie.......... Short for Augustino, right?" Rocco said as he reached out for a handshake. "What's your last name son?"

"Giovanelli sir, Augustino Giovanelli," he replied reaching back to shake Rocco's hand.

"Your Papà told me you had a friend from the old country on the ship," Rocco said as he turned to look at Tom, "Hope you boys are hungry. Sophia is at her best today. I'm even looking forward to this."

Phil and Fabiana came in around four thirty and went straight to the back room where they were all waiting. Rocco had told the rest of the staff to cover for him so he could spend the evening with the Santorinis. It did not take long for Augustino to feel at home. They spent most of the evening speaking in only Italian. Anthony sat on Tom's lap as usual.

"Did Tom tell you I used to work on a ship?" Rocco asked Augustino, "That's how we met." He looked at Tom and gave him a nod.

"Yes sir, he did," Augustino responded, "you were a cook, right? It was on a passenger ship?"

"That's right. But it was several years ago," Rocco said, "I did the job for about ten years. It paid well enough. That along with a little help from some of my family, I was able to save up to open this place. Not bad for a kid from Italy who started with almost nothing. Only in America. I do love it here. Any chance you'll end up in America Augustino?" Rocco did not want to pry into Augustino's personal life too much. He thought it was a good question to ask to get to know him.

"Maybe someday," he replied, "I do like it when I'm here. We came last October, and I went over to New York with two guys from the crew. The buildings were so tall, I couldn't believe it. Rome is beautiful but New York is amazing." Augustino was starting to loosen up a bit.

"Well, whenever you come into Jersey City, you come see us," Rocco continued, "I'll prepare something special for you." Rocco knew Tom would not be staying with the ship after reaching Napoli, but Augie would. He wanted him to feel welcome by himself if he were to return on the Hallwick.

Fabiana sat directly across from Tom and did not take her eyes off him all evening. She knew he was off on an adventure which would be good for him and help him to be a man. But mothers always hesitate when it comes to letting go. Especially if you have an only child. Having Gaetano filled her heart enough for four or five children. He was special to her, and she was proud of the young man he had become. She did not say much that evening. She just looked at him and remembered the years. Saying goodbye that night was one of the hardest things she had ever done.

• • • •

TOM AND AUGUSTINO WERE under orders to be back aboard by nine thirty so the captain could verify all of the crew was present and accounted for. They made it by only a few minutes, which did not bother the captain just so long as it was not a few minutes late.

A cargo ship casting off is quite different from a passenger ship. They did not need tugboats to line them up in harbor. The Hallwick was ready to set off and powered out of dock on her own steam. Tom was able to go topside to see everything as they cast off. It was just after one thirty on Monday morning April nineteenth, nineteen-fifteen, when they left the dock and headed to sea.

They passed the Statue of Liberty and could only see it by moonlight. The night was chilly, but not too cold. The wind was strong, and the current was rough. Tom could feel the ship in motion. It was not something he had remembered from his trip on the Saint Paul. That was a much larger ship, so the motion was not as obvious. He found it a bit unsettling.

It did not take him long to realize he was the only one who felt a bit uneasy. The rest of the crew saw it as calm waters and full speed ahead. Tom knew he had to be up for the breakfast shift, so he decided to go below and settle in. He barely slept a wink all night. Augie went right off to sleep and did not make a sound until the alarm went off at five fifteen.

· · · ·

AUGIE HAD TO GO BELOW and spend the next five hours shoveling coal into the boilers with only a short break for breakfast. Once at sea, the crew all knew their assignments and worked tirelessly knowing no one crewman could slack without creating a problem for the entire crew. Augie would work two five-hour shifts in the boiler room plus two hours of mopping and cleaning the toilets. Tom was glad he did not have that job. The captain had decided the crewmen who worked in the galley were best not to work cleaning the toilets. It was a good idea to keep them separated so the crew would not wonder if they washed up between duties.

Tom figured that out on the day he met Captain Stevens. The captain was pulling his leg when it came to cleaning toilets. But probably not about the rough seas. It was beginning to take its toll on Tom's stomach.

Tom got up with Augie and went straight to the galley. Maurice took one look at him and said "Mal de mer, you look awful. This isn't your first time at sea, is it?"

"No," Tom moaned, "I don't feel so good,"

"Tu n'as pas l'air bien. You must feel better. The others do not like to see the galley crew so pale. It upsets their stomach more than the sea," Maurice said knowing at that moment Tom could not care less how the others felt. He walked over to the cabinet and opened a jar, "Here chew on some of this, très bon."

"What is it?" Tom asked with considerable doubt.

"Ginger root," Maurice said as he broke off a tiny piece, "You chew some and then drink some of this seltzer water."

Tom hesitated at first but figured he had nothing to lose. "It's really spicy," he said as he took a small nibble. The seltzer water was a bit more difficult to swallow, especially first thing in the morning, so he only sipped on it at first.

"Try to keep moving, better to get your mind off of it. Bon pour vous eh?" Maurice continued encouraging him to try to focus on his job.

The first wave came through. Maurice was serving pancakes with syrup, breakfast sausages and coffee. It did not take too long for the first wave to be finished. Nobody on the crew wanted to hang around too much on the first full day out to sea. Tom realized by the third wave his seasickness was much better.

"Hey, the spicy stuff really works," Tom said praising Maurice for his remedy, "I feel much better. Don't even mind the motion as much. What did you say that was?"

"Ginger root," Maurice said, "we cook with it. Ever been to a soda fountain in New York, they use it in ginger ale."

"I've had ginger ale, but it wasn't this strong," Tom commented.

"Pleine puissance," he said, "that's why, they water it down for ginger ale." Maurice was glad his helper was not sick anymore. Augie came in on the fourth wave. He was concerned for Tom because he had seen him when he got up.

"You sure do look more like yourself," Augie said while chuckling, "I didn't think you were gonna make it."

"That man right over there," Tom said as he was pointing to Maurice, "he's the doctor. He made me feel better."

Tom did not know it at the time, but most of the crew would indeed go to Maurice whenever they did not feel well. He was not officially the ship's doctor but considering they did not have one, he was the next best thing. Maurice had a host of old-time remedies which always seemed to work.

The rest of the first day was rather calm. Tom went topside during breaks to look at the ocean. As evening came, clouds began to roll in. Frankie was also on break and was standing next to Tom, "Better get some of that ginger root from Maurice you were chewing on this morning. Looks like a storm ahead. Things may get a bit rough tonight."

They were passing Nova Scotia by nightfall and could see the lighthouse at Peggy's Cove in the distance. The Hallwick was headed into the open waters of the Atlantic. The forecast which Captain Stevens had received while in harbor did not call for it to be a very severe storm, but a storm none the less.

Augie was not working late so he stayed in the galley after the fourth dinner wave and offered to help Tom clean up. "No thanks," Tom said, "Maurice says the more I can stay focused on work, the less the seasickness will take hold."

He finished up and they stayed in the dining area with two other crewmen playing cards until it was time to go to bed. Tom was very tired from not sleeping well the night before and feeling sick in the morning. He decided he would strap into his bunk and sleep no matter how much the ship rocked. As he was going to sleep, he thought 'Too bad it was cloudy this evening. I was hoping to see the sunset on the water. Maybe tomorrow night.'

Tom fell into a deep sleep and began to dream about being on a hilltop looking down at a river below. He dreamt he was trying to hang onto a tree at the top of the hill because he felt as if he was going to roll down the hill if he did not hang on tight. Suddenly he could not hold on anymore and he felt himself tumbling down the hill and screaming for help. He was convinced he would end up in the river and drown.

At the bottom of the hill just before the riverbank was a large rock and he was aiming right for it. Just as he was about to hit the rock, he jolted awake and realized he was being tossed about in his bunk. The straps prevented him from falling out but not from going side to side within the bunk. He was bouncing quite severely. This put a scare into him. He looked over and saw Augie bouncing about as well but still sound asleep.

Logic does not play into it when you are frightened in a strange place with everything turning upside down around you. He tried to reason that if Augie were sleeping, things would be all right. It was not enough to get him to calm down though. 'Maybe if I get up and go where there are others awake' he thought to himself. 'No, they'll think I'm just scared' that would be worse than actually being scared in his mind.

After about fifteen minutes, he figured he could embrace the rhythm of the sea and turn it into music in his mind. As the ship went one way, he would see himself running to one side of the dance floor and then as it went the other way, he would go back to the other side. This seemed to work for a while, but the waves were too unpredictable to judge. Finally, he folded the mattress a bit and wedged himself in between it and the straps so he would not roll back and forth. He felt himself connected directly to the ship rather than being loose and free to roll around. He may have been rocking with the waves but not back and forth in his bunk.

Before he knew it, he was back to sleep and dreaming even more. By two o'clock in the morning the worst of the storm was over, and the ship went back to its normal motion. The next morning when Tom woke up, the motion of the ship was a bit worse than the morning before, but after the experience at night, this seemed calm to him. His seasickness was gone, and he hoped it would not return for the rest of the voyage.

Each day Tom reported to the galley and worked the three meals. Each evening, he would hang around with Augie and the crew playing cards and telling stories. One evening Augie told the men about the time when his mother threw him out of the place where they lived. It was because she thought he got into trouble with the police. They came looking for him because one of his friends on the street got caught breaking into a store. He implicated Augie as his accomplice instead of the person who had been the one to join him in the robbery.

His mother did not believe him when he came home since he had a history of getting into some trouble. But never anything like robbery. They had a terrible fight that night and both said things they wished they had not. His mother threw him out and he screamed at her saying he hoped he would never see her again. Words which haunted him ever since.

He spent several weeks living under bridges and around monuments until it became too chilly at night. He managed to jump on a freight train from Rome and ended up in Napoli dodging the authorities. He scrounged for food and a place to stay. Eventually he ended up at the docks and got to know people there who introduced him to Captain Stevens.

The one condition the captain had was that Augie had to be certain he was not wanted by the law. The captain would not harbor a fugitive. But he would help a kid to get his life on track. The crew could identify with him since many of them had been in trouble on occasion and understood how important it was to have some responsibility in order to get their life in order. They all contributed to guiding him and keeping the pressure on. It was best for him. Now that Augie was in a more stable environment, he was doing much better. His probation period would be over in three months, and he was almost ready.

• • • •

TOM CONTINUED TO GO topside each evening to see the sunset but every time it was overcast and sometimes raining. It had been over a week on board the Hallwick and this was beginning to feel very comfortable to him. They were three days out of Napoli. The rough seas had slowed down their progress some, but they were only going to be a day behind schedule by the time they pulled into harbor. The seas were indeed rough.

One evening Tom was standing next to Frankie on one of the upper decks and they were looking out at the high waves through a window. It was too rough to be out on deck. "Sure, would be nice if these waves weren't so high. Sometimes it seems like they're higher than the ship," Tom commented.

"Good thing," Frankie replied.

Tom was confused by what he said. "How could that be a good thing?" he asked, "Wouldn't it be better to have calm seas?"

"Not these days," Frankie added.

"I don't get it. What's different about these days?" Tom asked.

Frankie turned and looked at him and said very seriously, "U-boats."

"U-boats?" Tom asked, looking even more confused.

"Or as the Germans would say Unterseeboots," Frankie said without the slightest bit of humor, "You know submarines, torpedoes, boom we're all dead?"

Tom just stood there not sure what to make of it all. He had a look on his face which showed disbelief, fear, and confusion all at once. Frankie knew he should try to calm him down some after dropping that on him. After all, he was still young and had not seen war.

"You see," Frankie continued, "As long as the seas are rough, it is harder for the U-boats to see us. We can hide in the high waves and their periscopes can't get a fix on us. The rough seas make it harder for the torpedoes to reach their target." Tom continued to stare. This was not real to him. And it was not helping.

"But.......... wait a minute," Tom stammered, "We're not a military ship, why would they shoot at us?" Tom said trying to rationalize the situation.

"You think they care about things like that?" Frankie replied almost started to bark at him because he was scared too, "As far as they're concerned, we're carrying supplies to their enemies." Frankie was only trying to get Tom to see the reality.

"Italy is not in the war," Tom said as if Frankie could convince the Germans not to fire on them.

"Not yet," Frankie continued, "but give it time. This is Europe remember, wars are common and eventually everybody gets into it. Besides, they don't know what we're carrying. And they don't care." Frankie knew he was not going to calm him down. Rather it would be best to help him to grow up and face the world for what it was.

Tom stood there in a daze for some time not even realizing Frankie had left. He just kept staring out into the waves looking for anything that looked like a periscope or a torpedo in the water. His seasickness was returning.

Chapter 12

The last time Tom had seen the Rock of Gibraltar it was nighttime, and he could only make it out in the moonlight. This time they were passing it just after the fourth wave of lunch was finishing. Maurice told him he could go topside to see it and then come back to clean up. It looked as impressive as he had hoped it would be but this time, Tom could only think of one thing, U-boats.

The waves were much calmer than on the earlier portions of the voyage. Which at this point Tom realized was not necessarily a good thing. Especially now they were headed into the Straits of Gibraltar where it was relatively narrow and there was no place to hide from the U-boats if they were in the area. It took away the thrill of seeing the Rock even with it being a nice sunny day.

Tom also noticed the ship kept changing course. Every couple of minutes the rudder seemed to turn and never in a predicable manner. This started right after they passed a ship going in the other direction. The other ship sent a coded signal with their light, but Tom did not know what it meant.

He hurried back to the galley to clean up so Maurice would not be upset and finished in record time. Then he decided to go to the bridge and see if he could get some information. They were not really supposed to go to the bridge unless it was important. But he had been told he could come up once or twice to see the operation so long as he did not get in the way. He had gone on the first day but not again so he figured it would be all right.

The bridge was a very anxious place that day. He could see Captain Stevens looking at charts and reading messages. The captain was obviously upset. One of the crewmen who was about to take over the wheel was standing there. Tom decided to try him.

"Hey, Mike, what's going on?" Tom asked leaning over trying to speak as quietly as possible, "Everybody seems so upset."

"That ship we passed an hour ago," Mike replied, "they told the captain to be careful. They had reports of U-boat activity between here and Napoli. That's why we're taking evasive maneuvers. Can't be too careful."

Tom now understood fully what Frankie had been talking about. The Mediterranean was a bit calmer compared to the Atlantic. "The captain seems to know what he's doing though," Tom said trying to convince himself everything was under control.

"That's not the worst of it," Mike continued, "We just got a radio message with some really bad news."

Tom did not say anything, but his face had 'What???' written all over it.

"Italy joined the war," Mike continued with a whisper, "We're heading right into a war zone."

"There was no word of this when we left New York. Didn't we send telegrams back and forth? Wouldn't someone tell us?" Tom said in a near panic.

"Supposedly just happened yesterday. Something about them signing a treaty with England," Mike said.

"So, who's side are we, ah, they on?" Tom questioned.

"Well, I would assume ours," Mike replied, "It wasn't really clear which side they would join up with. After all, the war has been going on for a year and Italy managed to stay out of it up 'til now. My guess. They were probably approached by both sides at some point. You'd better get out of here. I don't think this is a good time."

Tom realized Mike was right and slid out. As he walked back to the galley, he started to worry about his Nonna. 'What if they come to take her home, what if there is fighting near our town?' The worrying escalated and Tom was not able to think clearly.

As they passed Corsica, they could see smoke rising up from near shore. The word was it was a ship on fire. This put everyone on edge. 'What if it was a torpedo? What if the U-boat that fired on it is looking at us right now through the periscope?' Tom thought but was afraid to let anybody know how scared he was. Truth was, they all were.

An hour or so later the ship took a sharp turn east into the direction of land. The captain told everyone to spread the word they had received a radio message from the Italian Navy to enter the small harbor at Civitavecchia on the west coast of Italy. There they could be protected from U-boats until the Navy could be certain of clear passage.

They could see several ships headed in the same direction which brought mixed feelings. On the one hand, there was safety in numbers. On the other hand, it was prime hunting for any U-boat captain who needed to get a couple of notches on his periscope.

A giant sigh of relief came over the men as they turned around the seawall and entered the harbor. This was an old harbor which was built originally by the Emperor Trajan in the beginning of the second century and was no stranger to wartime.

They stacked up the ships in the harbor less than one hundred feet from each other and then brought in barges to block the entrance. The harbor had been equipped with submarine nets, but they were not reliable, so the barges acted as another safety barrier. The barges would be left unmanned so if any torpedoes came through, they would be the first thing they would hit. They loaded them down with ballast to make certain they sat as low as possible in the water.

The crew could see the shore and all the buildings of the town as well as Michelangelo's Fort which was built right along the waterfront. They wondered if they would be able to go ashore, but it did not take long for them to find out they were to stay on their own ships. Word was sent to them, as with all other ships, anyone leaving their ship without permission of the Navy was subject to arrest or being shot on sight if they tried to run. That took away any idea of leaving the ship. They were all content to stay aboard.

Fortunately, they had stocked everything else they needed for the return trip for the same reason they had stocked enough coal. They had over a week's provision, and they might need every bit of it. Nonetheless, the captain immediately ordered rationing. There was no telling how long this would last or if they would get permission to get supplies from Civitavecchia. So near, yet so far as the saying goes.

The method of rationing had been predetermined on varying levels based whatever circumstances were upon the ship. For instance, if the ship was stranded at sea with no power, or ran aground in an uncharted area, the rule was one pint of water per day per crewman and one small meal based on the supplies on hand. The goal was to have a one-month survival plan.

The ship was equipped with some fishing gear as well so the crew could fish for food. The other plans were less limiting and sometimes left up to the captain to determine on a daily basis. There was high hope this would only last a few days. Then they would be underway to Napoli and unload their cargo. The rationing was mostly precautionary and prudent. After all, their cargo was mostly food supplies and at least one other item which no one was to know about.

Three days passed and the crew was anxious and frightened as well as being very bored. The captain decided to put everyman on repair duty in order to keep moral up. They only had to work four hours a day on repairs which included cleaning, caulking some windows on the bridge, minor engine repairs and painting. There was enough paint on board because they would do some painting each time they were in harbor. So, a standard quantity was readily on hand.

Maurice was not used to preparing only one meal per day, so he had time on his hands. "So, what do you think, maybe you can teach me some Italian, no?" he said to Tom after the meal was done, "We can go on the deck and relax." It was about two o'clock in the afternoon and the warm Mediterranean air was so pleasurable it almost took the stress out of the situation.

"Oh, so now you like Italians?" Tom quipped back.

"I wouldn't go that far," Maurice chuckled, "maybe if you can teach me some, I might be able to meet some nice Italian ladies peut-être oui?" Maurice had a smirk on his face which Tom had come to know and like.

Augie was there in the dining area since there was not any coal to shovel, and he had done his assignments in the morning. So, he jumped in, "Maybe you could teach him some words like............" Augie gave an extensive list of cuss words in Italian.

Maurice was on to him, "How do you know what I've been teaching you two isn't the same kind of thing in French?" He had been teaching both of them some French and they sort of wondered if maybe he had not slipped in a few embarrassing words.

"So, when I go into a restaurant in Paris and order dinner, the waitress might slap my face. Is that what you're trying to tell me?" Tom said as he threw a rolled up wet towel at him.

Maurice ducked just in time, and it hit some pots that were drying, making an awful racket as they fell over. They were all laughing when they noticed Captain Stevens was standing at the door to the dining area. Tom and Augie got a bit nervous, but Maurice did not skip a beat, "So what are you going to throw at me, dites-moi? Another towel?" he joked with the captain.

Captain Stevens was glad to see the men were getting a bit loose, but he had some business with Maurice. "Got a radio message from the Italian Navy," he said, "they told us starting today we can send a three-person party to shore to get supplies. Water is the priority for us, so you need to bring whatever containers you can fit on a lifeboat."

Maurice was responsible for supplies so that is why the captain came to him. "I know just the thing," Maurice chimed in, "I've been saving the wine jugs from dinner for the past week, and I already had quite a few before. Now I know why I've been saving them. We should be able to fill the lifeboat with them. Did they say how often we could go?"

"No, they didn't, they're not saying much of anything which tells me this may take a while. I was thinking you should take these two with you. They can help with the language if the locals don't speak French," the captain said as he looked towards Tom and Augie. "Besides, you may have to work a pump. So, you'll need some strong arms to be with you. We don't know what the set up is."

"Smart move, that's why you're the captain, sans doute. Ever row a boat before?" he asked as he looked at Tom.

"Not really," Tom replied, "But there's a first time for everything. Come on," he smacked Augie, "let's go, this is going to be fun."

Augie was not so sure. He was still a bit uncertain about being around the authorities. Even though there was no reason to be concerned. His memories of dodging the police in Rome and Napoli the year before were still fresh. "Ah sure, let's go," he said trying to be convincing. Maurice could tell he was uncomfortable.

"When do we go?" Maurice asked the captain.

"We have to be on standby and ready to go at a moment's notice," Captain Stevens answered, "they said they will send a boat by to let us know when it is our turn, and they will tell you were to go then. My guess is they will escort you. You'll need your papers. They'll check them to find out your citizenship. Make sure you don't deviate from their orders. They might shoot a hole in the lifeboat and then what would I tell the company." The captain smiled hoping to lighten up the situation a bit more.

"Okay, you heard the captain," Maurice said, "Tom, grab those bottles I had you store in the back, tout suite. It will take you a few trips. See if you can get some help from anybody who is standing around." Maurice was acting as if he was an officer in the military.

"You let me know if anybody doesn't help." the captain added. That was all they needed to hear. They each took four one-gallon jugs, two in each hand with their fingers looped in the jug handle and headed for the lifeboat deck.

At about four o'clock, the Navy boat came by with an officer and two seamen. They came on board the Hallwick to check the papers of the captain and the men going ashore for fresh water. Everything checked out fine, so they were on their way within twenty minutes. They were less than a hundred yards away from the dock they had been instructed to go to. Tom was chosen to row on the way in and Augie on the way back. Maurice would watch the cargo, to make sure it did not get away.

There was a wagon on the dock with a tank on the back and a waterspout. The crew from another ship was still getting their water so they waited for their turn. "If this wasn't such a pain, I could actually be enjoying this," Tom said to Augie, "This is a really nice place. I can just imagine what it's like without fifty ships all stacked up." Augie just nodded and kept looking around, still not comfortable. He could not wait to get back to the ship and away from all these uniforms.

It came their turn, and Augie started to fill one of the glass jugs with the water from the tank. There was a funnel there to help keep the water from spilling everywhere. Tom looked at the water as it was coming out and into the jug. He and Maurice looked at each other and said at the same time. "Boil it." This water looked like the water they had drawn in from the Hudson River for the steam engines.

Maurice looked at Tom and said, "Know any wineries nearby?"

"How about some apple orchards, apple juice is good," Tom chuckled back.

"You sure this isn't apple juice? It's the right color," Augie joined in, "Cider at that." It was a good thing they were speaking English. They figured the two guys working the tank wagon may not like their sense of humor. It was obvious they could not understand, so Tom and Augie started to engage in some small talk with them. They were not too friendly. Probably because they did not want to be there anymore than the crews of all of the ships which were stuck in the harbor.

"How did I end up rowing on the way back?" Augie complained, "This stuff is heavy. You sure we didn't overload ourselves? I don't remember being this low to the water."

"Hey, you know the captain's rules, no complaining," Tom snickered back.

"Captain's not here," Augie said with a mumble.

"I'll take over halfway if you want. But everyone is watching. You sure you want that?" by now Tom and Maurice were laughing hysterically.

"Yeah, you're funny, but your face beat you to it," Augie retorted.

"Oh," Maurice said as he started to act offended, "those are fighting words. You just wait until Mon Père comes. He'll teach you." This made them laugh even more.

By then they were coming up alongside the ship and the rest of the crew came down to get the jugs of water. "This what they gave you?" one of them said, "We could have lowered a bucket into the harbor for this,"

Another one said. "Maybe we can use it for bathing."

"You really want to wash with this?" Maurice chimed in. The initial enthusiasm left them quickly, but they still helped, partly because the captain was watching. It was obvious he was aware of the condition of the water as well. He told them they would only use it if they ran out of their supplies before they got to Napoli.

By the fifth day rumors were starting to fly around the harbor. Sailors from the other merchant ships were talking across from the deck of one ship to another. Some of the rumors were about their suspicions that they would all be taken prisoners and their ships confiscated. Or maybe the Germans were heading there with a large Navy, and they would be best to try to get ashore and run. Once the captain became aware of this, he called every crewman to the dining area. They managed to all squeeze in but there was no room to sit.

The captain knew it was time to address the issue. "Most of you men have been with this ship for some time. You know I would not steer you wrong. From this point forward, you are not to talk to sailors from other ships. It isn't good for morale and what they're saying is probably all made up anyway." The men knew this without the captain's comments but with the boredom setting in, even this crew was letting it get the best of them.

• • • •

THE MEN HAD NOT BEEN setting their alarm clocks in the morning since the workload was so light and the captain wanted them to enjoy the time to rest. Tom and Augie were woken up at dawn by a lot of movement and talking in the hallway. Tom got up to see what was going on. He saw Frankie heading towards him.

"What's all the commotion?" he asked Frankie.

"Tell Augie to get down to the engine room, we leave in two hours," Frankie replied.

"Napoli?" Tom asked.

"Must be, didn't say," Frankie replied, "just get ready to leave in two hours."

"Hey Augie," Tom turned to wake him, but he was already standing right behind him.

"Yeah, I heard. About time," Augie snapped.

Tom was not sure if the dining schedule had changed so he decided to run over to the galley to see if Maurice needed him. He threw on some clothes and got there in two minutes. Maurice was not there so he went looking for him. The captain was walking on the next level up and Tom could see him from the stairs. "Sir, did you need us to fix a breakfast for the men? Are we back on the regular schedule?" He suddenly realized maybe he should not be the one asking. "Sorry sir, I shouldn't be asking, I just got excited when I heard."

"That's all right," the captain said, "you had the crew in mind. Best if we just get underway, then see if there is time for a meal. We probably will have time for a late breakfast or early lunch once we're back out to sea." The captain was right. The men were probably too worked up to eat anyway.

"Yes sir, I'll tell Maurice," Tom replied sheepishly. He turned and went back down the stairs. Once he knew the captain was far enough not to see him, he ran the rest of the way to work off the nervousness from talking so openly to the captain.

The scene of the ships leaving was not too different from the day they arrived. It was obvious every ship's crew was as anxious to put this place behind them as was the crew of the Hallwick. The captain had the men spread the word the Italian Navy had radioed and said they would escort them to their destinations.

They were still several hours away from Napoli and with the evasive maneuvers they would be implementing, it would take even longer. The emotions ran high as they were leaving the harbor. As they came around the seawall into the open Mediterranean everyone's heart was racing and wondering if there may be a periscope nearby. Every spare man who was not assigned to ships operation was to watch the waters for periscopes and torpedoes. No one was really sure what to watch for, but it certainly beat staying below and wondering what every strange noise might be.

The captain was right. The men did not want to eat anything, but Maurice had food ready if anyone came by. Augie shoveled coal faster than he had ever done before hoping it would get them there faster. Tom joined the crew topside to watch for signs of trouble. Everyone prayed.

Chapter 13

> > >

It was getting to be evening in the interrogation room. Tom had been talking to the man with the cane for several hours. He had done all of the talking. To Tom's surprise, they had food brought into the room for them rather than have Tom return to his holding cell. They both ate together while Tom was talking. This meal was quite a bit better than the earlier. Likely because the man with the cane was eating as well.

"You know, I've been talking to you all day and you haven't told me your name," Tom asked as he was finishing his meal. This started the staring again. He could tell for some reason, this man did not want to divulge his name. The staring continued for a while longer so Tom decided to try again, "Maybe you could just tell me your last name."

After some more staring and hesitation he said, "All right, I am Signor Marcellino chief prosecutor for this region. That is all you need to know." Then he struggled again to get up and left the room.

Tom thought to himself 'was it something I said?' He was not sure what would happen next. There was no one else in the room but he knew they were likely watching and listening. "Excuse me, but could I go to the rest room please," he called out in an assuming voice. No one came right in, probably because they did not want him to know they were listening. A couple minutes later a tall woman came in to get the trays for the food. Tom repeated himself but in a softer voice.

"I'll ask," was all she said.

"Thank you," Tom replied figuring it would do no good. A few minutes later the two guards came in and escorted him to his holding cell. He knew where the clock was. So, he looked over as he walked by and saw it was after eight o'clock.

. . . .

JOE CAME BY TONY'S Pizzeria after he got out of court. Tony had gathered all the documents they could find. It was after lunch hour, so Joe was hungry and decided to eat at Tony's. They sat together and ate as they went over what they had found at the Santorini's house.

"Is all this stuff really going to matter?" Tony asked.

"Maybe not," Joe answered. It was not what Tony wanted to hear, and Joe could tell. "Maybe some," he added.

"You're sounding way too much like a lawyer now," Tony snipped, "so what's the point of it all?"

"One of the things you learn early on in law is to be prepared with all of the facts you can gather. Even if you're not sure if you're gonna need them," Joe said feeling like one of his law professors. "You may need something without realizing it until it's right on top of you. Then you're really glad you prepared. There's nothing worse than being caught without the answers when you need them."

"So, you gonna call them today?" Tony asked.

"By four, that seems to be the time they're free," Joe replied, "Oh by the way. I called my cousin who lives outside of Rome like you suggested. She said she would reach out to Maria and was more than willing to help."

"That's the best news so far," Tony smiled.

"Her name is Anna. She also told me her husband knew a lawyer who could give them a referral," Joe smiled back.

"I'm going to call Maria once you leave," Tony sighed.

"Call her now while I'm here, maybe she can give me some more information I can use when I call the consulate," Joe added.

Maria had returned by five o'clock and did not feel like having dinner. She had enough food left over to snack on from the night before. The radio was still set to the soft classical station, and she tried to settle in and wait for the phone to ring. It was after eight and she started to wonder if Tony was going to call when the phone rang.

"Person to person for Maria Santorini," the operator announced.

"This is Maria Santorini," she answered, "I'll take the call, thank you operator." Her heart started to pound. "Tony?" she asked.

"High Maria, you feel okay?" Tony answered, "Any word from Tom?" He figured there likely was not.

"Not yet, but I met a nice lady here today," Maria said as she was starting to calm down some.

"Is her name Anna?" Tony asked.

"Yes, it is," she replied, "I guess Anna's cousin Joe told you, right? Anyway, she's very nice."

"He said she might have a contact there?" Tony continued and was getting excited by now. "Someone her husband knows. A lawyer who could help on your end?"

"Yes. She did and I made an appointment to see him late tomorrow morning around eleven," Maria said, "It was the earliest he could see me. I hope my Italian is up to it. Supposedly, he doesn't speak a word of English. Anna said she would take me and help if I get tongue tied." Maria could tell Tony was wound up as she was speaking.

"Look, call me at the house collect once you get back to your hotel afterwards in the evening," he added, "I want to know what he says. You can even tell me in Italian. You'll have had enough practice by then." Tony chuckled with a nervous laugh.

"No Tony it will be the too early in the morning, you need your rest," she said trying to help him to calm down.

"What makes you think I'll be sleeping?" Tony quipped, "This is Tom we're talking about. He's like a second dad to me. I don't think I'll sleep until we get this thing straightened out. Before I go, Joe is going to call the consulate at four our time. Do you have anything to tell him that might help?"

"Oh, goodness I wouldn't know what to tell him," she pondered.

"Joe, what do you want from Maria? She doesn't know what you might need," Tony said looking across to Joe.

"Ask her if she knows the names of any of the people who took Tom and the exact address where he is being held or at least where he was arrested," Joe said.

"I heard him," Maria volunteered, "It all happened so fast, I didn't get anything, no names. I don't think they said their names. The man who was so angry seemed to be the office manager though. If that helps. The place......umm........ the place is where we went for the pension fund, you know the one in the ad? I don't know if they took him somewhere else."

"Yeah, I'm sorry I ever showed him that stupid ad," Tony sighed.

"Now Tony, don't punish yourself," she said sounding more like his mother than a friend. "It wasn't anybody's fault. This all has to be some sort of misunderstanding. None of it makes any sense. I don't even know what they meant by Tom impersonating a war hero. Tom never said anything about a war hero." She was starting to get upset again. "He was just drafted into the Army and then he came home. That's all he ever told me."

"Well, we'll figure out how to get this fixed," Tony said, "I promise you that. Look I'm gonna sign off. Don't forget to call me collect once you meet the lawyer and I'll let you know how

Joe made out calling the consulate, okay?" Tony did not want to end the call, but he could tell Maria would just get more upset if they kept talking about it.

"One last thing though Tony," Maria jumped in, "Anna offered for me to stay with them if this drags on. I told her I wanted to talk to Tom if I could and also get your feelings. Should I do that? The hotel is so expensive and staying here without Tom is not really fun like we had planned. What do you think?"

"That's very generous of her," Tony looked over at Joe again, "Joe, did Anna say anything about taking Maria to stay at her house."

"No," Joe's eyes lit up, "That would be great. Sounds like Anna all right. She's pretty amazing. I wish I got to spend more time with her."

"Well, my first impression is to stay put for a couple of days until we know something concrete. We can always have you move after," Tony suggested.

"That's sort of what I was thinking and what I would suspect Tom would say too," she replied, "Thanks so much for all you do. My goodness, look at the time. We have to go. Besides I'm sure your telephone bill will be more than your mortgage this month." Maria added. "You take care of yourself and get some rest. Tom can take care of himself and I'm doing okay too." She continued to care for him like a mother would. "So, you promise you will get some rest?"

"Yeah, you got it, I will," Tony surrendered. Tony hung up then turned to Joe. He just shrugged his shoulders and asked, "so, what's next?"

• • • •

IT WAS PROBABLY AFTER ten by now, so Tom decided to go to sleep. They would likely start the interrogation again in the morning. So, it made sense to get some rest. He was glad there was a toilet in his cell. That way if he needed to get up during the night, he would not have had to get someone to let him out of his holding cell and go to the restroom. However, he did regret not asking for an extra blanket, he had been chilly the night before.

• • • •

"YES, SIGNOR NARDINI please," Joe said to the receptionist when she answered the phone at the Italian Consulate. It seemed to take forever for him to come to the phone. Joe continued to review his notes the way lawyers do. The phone picked up again and it was still the receptionist. "Yes, Signor Nardini? I would like to speak to Signor Nardini please.................... Joe Carracci on the Santorini matter. I met with him briefly yesterday............Yes, Thank you." He was put back on hold again. After ten minutes the receptionist came back on the line.

"Signor Carracci?" she said.

"Yes, that's right, calling for Signor Nardini." He was starting to think there may be a problem.

"Signor, he says he will need to call you back in an hour," she continued, "Could you leave the phone number where you can be reached, please?" She did not seem to be concerned by the delay, even though it was obvious this was a very pressing matter.

Joe put his head in his right hand with the phone in his left and shook his head back and forth. "It is very important yes please could you have him call me as soon as he is free. I'll be in my office until I hear from him. My number is.........."

He hung up and wondered if he should call Tony or wait until after the return call. Over an hour later, the call had not come. Joe started to feel uncertain. Maybe this was not the right direction after all.

• • • •

MARIA DECIDED TO TAKE a late bath in the whirlpool tub. She figured it would help her to relax and go to sleep. The phone would not ring again until the morning when Anna would call to say she had arrived to take her to the lawyer. She decided to splurge and order some hot coco from room service. Once it arrived, she turned up the radio a bit so she could hear it in the bath and settled in for a little overdue pampering.

• • • •

JOE STAYED LATE AT his office to hopefully get a return call. It was almost six o'clock when the phone rang. "Signor Carracci please," the voice said. He recognized the receptionist from earlier.

"Yes, this is Signor Carracci," he responded with hope.

"Signor Nardini can speak with you now. Please hold the line," she said as the line clicked. There was at least a three-minute wait before anyone picked up the line.

"Signor Carracci?" It was finally Signor Nardini on the line.

"Yes Signor, were you able to find out anything helpful?" Joe asked without hesitation, figuring his time with Signor Nardini would be limited.

"It is a difficult situation Signor as you would imagine." Signor Nardini began. "When we spoke yesterday, I thought the name you gave me, ah, Signor Gaetano Santorini? I thought it was a very familiar name. When I called the prosecutor's office and then the pension office, it came to me. Have you never heard the name Gaetano Santorini Signor?" he asked.

"Not before yesterday, Signor, should I have?" Joe answered with some confusion.

"Well, that would be understandable. We do not teach our students about people like your general Patton for instance or any of your presidents. I learned of the heroism of Gaetano Santorini as a young child as did every child since the mid nineteen-twenties in Italy," Signor Nardini explained.

"That would explain the reaction I suppose if someone showed up calling themselves by that name," Joe said, "but Sir, you have to understand from our perspective he is just an innocent old man who was hoping to improve his retirement. If it had not been for the ad in the paper we discussed yesterday, he would have never even taken a trip to Italy because they quite frankly could not afford it. As it was, friends of theirs helped cover the cost for the trip." Joe was hoping these were opening statements and not closing arguments.

"I have been reviewing Signor Santorini's record here," Joe continued, "and I assure you they are all in order and his name is indeed Gaetano Santorini. So that leads me to believe he just simply has the same name as the man you were taught about in school as a boy. Surely the authorities would be willing to review his documents and then they would conclude this must be a very bazaar coincidence. Don't you think Signor?"

"Partly the difficulty here is the sincere admiration for our war heroes in this country we call home," Signor Nardini continued, "If someone were to try to swindle the government, it would be one thing. But to do so using the name of such a famous man. That is yet another. Imagine if someone claimed to be a famous person who had died like a celebrity who was killed in an airplane crash or maybe your James Dean who died in a car crash a few years ago. Imagine how upset people would be."

"I'm not sure I see the similarity," Joe said, "but I do certainly understand the admiration for heroes. We may not hold our war heroes in the same light, but we honor them in other ways on Veteran's Day and other holidays. We would not want anybody to belittle our heroes either. But Signor, there has to be some reason here. This man's name is what he says it is. Is there any way to contact the Gaetano Santorini who you are talking about and see if he can help to clear this up?" Joe asked, hoping he was not grasping for straws.

"That would be impossible sir," he replied, "I would not expect you to know this, but Gaetano Santorini survived almost all of the major battles of the Great War. But late in the war, regrettably he was found dead on the battlefield." Signor Nardini was obviously going to stay with his position.

Joe did not know how to respond to that. He thought for a second, which is all the time a lawyer has to think. Unlike other people, who can stop and think for a minute or two. "Well Signor, no one including Signor Santorini would want to upset anybody. How can we bring this forward to a resolution?"

"I'm sorry to say, it will simply have to play itself out in the system where he is," Signor Nardini said, "I must go now. I'm afraid I won't be able to assist you any longer." He was obviously putting an end to his involvement.

"I understand Signor. If I can resolve this, I will inform you as to the result. Thank you for your time." Joe hung up and began to sigh at the injustice. He was not sure if he wanted to call Tony but knew it was his duty. Tony was at the pizzeria, and it was a busy time. Joe decided to wait until after nine to talk to him, so he left the office and went home.

• • • •

THE PAMPERING WORKED wonders. Maria was able to sleep soundly all night. She got up and went down to one of the streetside cafés for some morning tea and a heavenly pastry which she had had her eyes on since they arrived. She had reached a peace about everything. Deep down, she felt the worst was over. Now if she could just hang on to that feeling for more than an hour at a time.

• • • •

THE DOOR OPENED IN Tom's holding cell and a new guard brought in the breakfast tray. "You will have exactly......" 'Oh not again.' Tom thought but still would not say anything which might cause him more trouble. After the usual recitation, the guard turned to leave.

"Thank you," Tom said keeping his polite demeanor. The guard did not acknowledge him and just locked the door. It was back to mess hall meals. He figured if he were going to have any decent food, he would need to be in the interrogation room with Signor Marcellino. He obviously had some influence when it came to the menu.

The door opened before the half hour was up and the two guards from the day before came in. "Signor, are you finished with your breakfast?" They asked.

"Yes, I don't really feel hungry. Can I take the rest of my coffee with me though?" Tom asked politely.

"No, Signor, there is coffee in the interrogation room," one of the guards said.

'Really?' Tom thought to himself as he got up to follow the two guards to the interrogation room.

< < <

Chapter 14

The harbor at Napoli had not changed a bit since Tom departed for America just six years earlier. The memory of that day was still vivid in his mind. He could almost see the crowd who had gathered on the dock to wave off those who were leaving for their new lives. He wondered what it would be like if his Nonna came to pick him up and maybe even Signor Rizzi. The chances were nonexistent.

Being they were on a cargo ship, they went to a different part of the harbor. They passed right by the docks where he had left from on the Saint Paul and continued to where the Hallwick could unload her cargo. Tom was a bit confused because the Navy had directly escorted their ship and seemed to not be as concerned about the others in the harbor at Civitavecchia. He had no way of knowing about the special cargo on board.

Augie had come topside as they were preparing to moor at the dock they had been assigned to. He was standing next to Tom as they were powering down the engines. "Too many uniforms," Augie said under his breath so only Tom could hear. There were many Army and Navy personnel on the dock and apparently waiting for the Hallwick. "Let's get out of here," Augie said as he pulled on Tom's arm, "Maybe we can stay out of sight."

Tom was not sure what he was concerned about but decided to take his advice if only to find out why his friend was so antsy. They decided to go to their cabin so Tom could gather his things. He knew he would have to look into getting a train to Montoro Superiore. On the way they stopped in the galley to see Maurice. He was complaining he had to throw away so much food because the men had not eaten anything since they left Civitavecchia with only a few exceptions.

"I'm going to gather my things in my cabin and then see if the captain can talk to me before he lets me go," Tom told Maurice.

"Do you know how you will get home?" Maurice asked him.

"I remember taking a train here from my hometown or I think it may have been the next town over. Doesn't matter, my Papà told me which streets to follow from the train station once I got there. It's not that far of a walk. I'm sure I'll find my way," Tom explained, "my Papà says to just ask the people there and they will show me if I get confused."

"You are doing a good thing, you taking care of your Mémé like this," Maurice said as he came over and gave him an embrace like only a good Frenchman could. "I miss you Je fais. You have been good here. You will do good wherever you go. You go take care of your Mémé now vous entendez oui?"

Tom almost cried but didn't, "You were nice to me, taught me some things and I'm glad you're my friend or, Je suis content que tu es mon ami.......... How was that?"

His French was not perfect, but Maurice got the point and started to tear up a bit. "Oui, Je suis content que tu es mon ami aussi. Je me souviendrai de toi," he replied in a soft voice.

Tom did not understand the last part but did not want to ask Maurice to say it in English. They shook hands and embraced again. Augie was anxious to find a corner to hide in, so he pulled Tom's arm. "Come on let's go." he said as he tried to lead Tom out of the galley.

They came to their cabin and Tom started to gather his belongings. Mike from the bridge crew came down and he looked like he had seen a ghost. "Hey, you guys, the captain is looking for you both," he said while Tom and Augie looked at him with disbelief.

"Why," Tom asked. It was obvious from Augie's actions, that he knew.

"You remember when you went to get the water jugs filled at the other place, the harbor we were stuck in?" Mike continued, "remember when they came to check your papers?"

"Yeah," Tom said still confused.

"We're Italians," Augie jumped in, "Don't you get it. We're Italian citizens. Don't you know what that means?"

Tom stood there dumbfounded. He looked back and forth at Mike and Augie trying to figure it out.

"There are two military officers with the captain on the bridge right now and they're looking for both of you," Mike said with a panic, "They figured out you were both Italians when you showed them your papers a couple of days ago. They know you're here and want the captain to bring you to them right away."

"What do they want?" Tom asked, still confused.

"Think Tom, think. There's a war on now. We're Italian, we're young men. Figure it out yet? The Army?" Augie said in a screaming whisper.

"You two had better follow me. They didn't look like they wanted to be kept waiting." Mike said surrendering to the facts, "Come on."

"Should we take our things?" Tom asked.

"No, just leave everything and come with me. Who knows, maybe it won't be what Augie says. All I know is you don't cross military people during a war," Mike said with resolve.

Augie stood there, almost unable to move his legs. "I have a very bad feeling about this," he said with a quiver in his voice.

"Yeah, but staying here isn't going to change that," Mike said.

They slowly made their way up to the bridge. Mike noticed there were even more uniforms there than before. 'All this for a couple of kids?' he thought to himself. He was not aware of the secret cargo they were carrying.

"Are these the two we were informed about?" one of the officers asked Captain Stevens.

"Yes Signor, just as you requested. Tom Santorini and Augustino Giovanelli," Captain Stevens said with much reservation. The officer looked them over for a bit.

"His papers say Gaetano Santorini," One of them said back, "Is that you?" he looked over at Tom. Tom knew he should not cause any problems.

"Yes sir, they called me Tom when I moved to America. I'm an American now," Tom said hoping to defuse the situation.

"You're not in America now. You are still a citizen of Italy and therefore bound by its laws," he snapped back exactly like you would expect from a military man.

Tom still did not want to make things worse. "Sir, I guess I don't know those laws since I went to school more in America. What does this mean?"

The officer stared at him as if to imply he should know and was just being difficult. "It means you are now a member of the Italian Army, both of you." His voice became loud and harsh.

"Ah, Signor," Captain Stevens interjected, "I realize Tom or Gitano here is just a passenger, but Augustino is a member of my crew. And I really do need him around here," he said then paused a moment, "Considering Signor the risk we have just taken for Italy." The officer knew precisely what he was talking about but no one else standing there did. Captain Stevens knew there was nothing he could do to save Tom at this point, but he would try to keep Augie. He knew the Army was not the place for Augie.

But he knew Tom at least well enough to know he could take care of himself.

The officer pondered the thought for a moment knowing Italy did indeed owe the captain some consideration for his efforts to conceal a shipment of flint for the war effort. He hesitated some but then said with a scowl, "We will need all of the soldiers possible to defeat our enemy. You can find an older man to shovel your coal."

The captain knew his effort was doomed. He looked at both of them and then at the officers. "May I have a moment with them before you take them Signor?" Captain Sevens asked as politely as possible. This was a request the officer could easily grant since Italy had only joined the war a week earlier and had a great deal of preparations to do before they could enter battle. A quick nod from the officer and the captain took them both by the arm and walked them to his quarters.

Tom was in a daze and Augie in a panic. Augie started to say something on the bridge. But the captain gave him the sign he had given to him several times before. This was a suitable time to shut up.

Once in his quarters, the captain sat them down. "Look boys, there isn't anything I can do from here. I'll try one last thing when we get back up to the bridge. I'll ask them if they can keep you both in the same outfit. That way at least you can look out for each other." Tom did not say much but Augie was in tears.

"I have a bad feeling about this," Augie repeated what he had said to Mike in their cabin.

"Tom, or I guess Gitano now, you're the oldest of the two, twenty-one, right?" the captain asked.

"Yes sir, twenty-one," Tom replied still not grasping the reality.

"Augie, you're only nineteen?" Captain Stevens said to Augie trying to calm him down, "So you stick close to Tom ah Gitano, or whatever it is, and he'll look out for you. Got it?"

They all resolved in their minds there was nothing they could do to change things, so they went back up to the bridge. Captain Stevens took the one officer aside who had been doing all the talking and spoke softly to him. "I know you can't let either of these boys go. So, I'm asking for one favor. Can you see to it they stay in the same outfit and serve together? I would see it as a personal favor to me, and I will be forever in your debt." He nodded and said nothing else.

The officer pondered for a moment and then a moment more. He looked at the two young men and then back at the captain. "You have done a service for our nation. I will see to it."

"Thank you, Signor," The captain concluded knowing there was not anything left to say.

Tom wanted to be perceived as cooperative, so he said, "I guess we'll be going with you Signor. Shall we go and gather our possessions from our cabin now?" thinking he was making a good impression.

"No. You will have no need for your possessions in the Army," the officer ordered. "What you are wearing is what you will take with you, nothing else. You will receive uniforms, and we will take anything you are carrying with you to use for the war effort." Tom knew he meant the personal things they carried such as all their money.

Augie was trembling but Tom was keeping his cool. "Yes Signor, I understand. When do we leave?" Tom continued.

"Immediately," he said.

"Yes Signor," Tom said just short of saluting but did not because he was not certain how to and did not want to appear foolish. Augie just stood there as the officer looked at him. Tom gave him a facial signal.

"Oh, Yes Signor," Augie finally said.

"I'll keep your possessions on the ship boys," Captain Stevens said, "Augie, once the war is over, you find us, and I'll return your things and even give you a job if you need one. Tom, I'll give your things to your father when I see him in New York later this month."

Tom suddenly realized his parents had no idea what was happening. And what about his Nonna, how would he tell her what was happening? "Could you tell my parents where I will be?" Tom asked the captain. He did not want to say what he was thinking, 'tell them what has happened to me.' He pondered for a moment and then asked, "And could you get word to my Nonna I won't be coming?" This broke the captain's heart because he knew how important it was to the Santorini family to have someone looking after her in her last days.

"I'm sure I can tell your folks," The captain said and then he looked over at the officer, "Can I arrange to get word...."

"No Signor, no one communicates the whereabouts of our soldiers," the officer snapped again.

"If we don't say anything other than he is not coming?" Captain Stevens was grasping at straws.

"Only if you deliver the message in person. Letters and telegrams get intercepted," he said with an obvious 'Don't ask me again' tone.

"I understand Signor, we can't be too careful during war," he said while looking at Tom and saying with his eyes, 'I tried' knowing he would not be able to help. They would be leaving earlier than scheduled with no load to bring to New York. The shipments which were to be loaded for New York were confiscated for the war effort. They would load down with some gravel for ballast. Tom now knew he was looking at a big man. They just gave each other a nod.

Many of the crew were standing around on the deck when they escorted Tom and Augie out. "Signor, may we be allowed to say good-bye to our shipmates?" Tom asked, "Just for a moment. I promise."

The officer looked at him and because he was not resisting, he said "For just a moment. Stay where I can see you. When I say come, you come."

"Thank you, Signor, you're most kind," Tom said and dipped his head.

The crew members walked over, hesitant at first and gave them a hug and wished them well. One by one they gave their farewells while cautiously watching the officers and soldiers with rifles to make certain they were not stepping out of line. Maurice could only watch from afar. This was the worst thing he could imagine. "Mon Dieu, pourquoi" he kept saying over and over with tears in his eyes.

Tom reached into his pocket and took out his money and slipped it to Frankie. "Give this to the captain and ask him to get it to my Papà. I don't want these thieves to get it," he whispered to him.

"You got it. Keep your head down, I want to see you back here once this war is over," Frankie said sadly.

There was a truck which had pulled up several minutes before they came down from the bridge. It was an open troop carrier that could be converted with a canvas cover for the rainy season. They were entering the dry season, so it was pulled open with the canvas tucked up near the front of the truck. The crew watched as they were led down the gangway and put in the back. There were at least fifteen other young men on the truck already.

It was obvious their ship was not the only one which had been checked for young Italian men who were ready candidates for the Army. Many of them were trying to leave the country on ships which were outbound. They were the easiest to catch. It was all the young men who were already on ships who forced them to search the crew manifests and passenger lists. Gaetano and Augie were easy pickings for them.

This was a brand-new model truck that the Italian government had commissioned Fiat to build for the war effort before Italy entered the war. They had been short of Army vehicles in nineteen-fourteen. It was understood by all that one of the reasons for Italy holding out for a year once the war started was because they were so ill prepared.

As Gaetano climbed aboard the truck, he took a seat at the back. Then he remembered his pocket watch Rocco and his friends gave him at the going away party. He regretted he had not given it to Frankie with his money. Once they closed the back flap of the truck, he looked to make certain no one could see him. As the truck took off, he carefully took it out of his pocket and hid it in his shoe. The others were all watching in the direction the truck was driving, so they did not see him, not even Augie. He felt they may see him and insist it be turned over for the war effort. It would have to stay hidden if it could.

The truck drove for four hours into the country until darkness set in. It was nine o'clock when they arrived at what was to be their home for several weeks. It was a newly constructed Army camp that would be used for their combat training. There, these young men would be turned into fighting soldiers. They would be trained in hand-to-hand combat, weapons use, explosives, and something new to warfare.......... the radio.

Chapter 15

During the long drive from Napoli, most of the men on the truck tried to get to know one another. They exchanged their stories about how they had all been 'recruited' into the Army in the same way, at gunpoint. Gaetano and Augie felt fortunate they had not been taken by force but by inescapable authority. It had been comforting to them to know how hard the captain had tried to fix things.

They made no stops during the four hours while they were on route. Most of the men were thirsty and hungry from the journey. Like Gaetano and Augustino, most were taken from ships arriving or leaving Napoli.

Three of the men had been scheduled to leave on passenger ships to America just like Gaetano had six years earlier. These men were treated more harshly because the officers accused them of trying to desert their duty as Italian citizens by leaving their country during wartime. There was no consideration taken that their travel plans had originated long before the Italy joined the war.

One man named Anthony was with his wife and two children. They were ready to depart for New York like so many other families had been doing for over a decade when the soldiers came. He had figured they would not take him into the Army because he was twenty-seven and had a family. The Army officers took him away from his crying children and pushed him to the ground. He lay there on the dock while they walked around him mocking and kicking him. It was mostly for show in order to ridicule him in front of everyone. It was sending a message to anybody who knew someone that was thinking of fleeing the country. They called him a coward and traitor in front of his wife who was trying to shield her children from seeing this humiliation of their Papà. They then insisted she board the ship and leave the country without him. He did not know what would come of them since he was carrying all of the money they would need to get settled in America.

Gaetano's first thought was to offer to have his Papà help her in New York. But he was just now realizing he had no way to contact him. So much had changed in such a brief period of time. What was going to happen next was all he could think about.

After arriving at the camp, they had all hoped for something to eat and drink. The dust of the trip had dried all their throats to the point where they could barely speak.

"All out," the sergeant ordered, "and absolutely no talking, no questions, no exceptions."

Augustino was about to say something, and Gaetano could tell. He gave him a jab and shook his head 'NO!!!' It went against Augustino's nature, but he remembered what Captain Stevens had said about listening to Gaetano and held back.

They were lined up and shown how to stand at attention. Most men complied but two were complaining about being hungry and thirsty. Gaetano was glad he was smart enough not to have been one of those two. The sergeant walked over to one of them and another sergeant walked over to the other.

They were both severely beaten and left on the ground while the rest of the men were given instructions. Occasionally the sergeant would walk by them a give them a kick. One of the men realized he had messed up and forced himself to his feet. "I wish to apologize for my disobedience," he said loud enough to be heard by everyone. The sergeant walked up to him and stared him in the face. "I have learned my lesson and will never disobey again."

The sergeant put his face right in his, "the next time, you will die." he screamed.

This prompted the other man to struggle to his feet and offer the same apology. The sergeant walked up to him and struck him down again. "That man meant what he said, and I know you do not. You're just trying to copy him," he screamed even louder.

"Please Signor, let me prove myself, I will never disobey you or anyone again. Please I swear it on my mother's grave," he continued to beg. This irritated the sergeant even more. The sergeant knocked him back to the ground and began to kick him until he did not move. The men were not certain what happened to him afterward, but they never saw him again.

They were ordered to march, best they could, until they reached a small building. They stood at attention outside while they were called in by name, three at a time. The men would go in and fifteen minutes later come out dressed in a uniform and ordered to stand at attention again. Gaetano went in before Augustino. He walked in and was ordered to empty his pockets of all his possessions. He was concerned about his pocket watch. 'What if they see it' he thought. He did not want to lose it and certainly did not want them to have it. Moreover, he did not want to get caught disobeying a direct order.

There were three soldiers who had been in the Army for some time processing the recruits. They reviewed his papers and kept looking up at him and then down at his papers. This reminded him of going through Ellis Island, but the end result would not be the same. He would not be seeing his parents when he was through. They looked at the two items he had in his pocket, a small clipper and knife combination and a picture of his Mamma in a small leather pocket folder.

"Do you have any money?" One of them asked.

"No Signor," he responded.

"Everyone has some money, where are you hiding it?" one of the other soldiers said.

Gaetano did not want to appear to be lying, "We were escorted off the ship we were on this morning, and I asked the officer if I should gather my things that were in my cabin. He said I would only take what I had on me. My money was in my cabin, so I never got it."

This seemed plausible to the three soldiers, and it was getting late. They too wanted to call it a night. "Very well," one soldier said, "you wouldn't need it here anyway." Gaetano just nodded his head.

One man came up to him and measured him for his uniform then reached down to the third pile from the left and took a bundle. It had a pair of uniform pants, one shirt, a jacket, three pairs of socks and a pair of boots. He handed it to Gaetano and pointed to some chairs in the corner. Without saying a word, Gaetano walked over and began to undress. 'How am I gonna pull this off' he thought while thinking about the watch. He needed to appear to change quickly so as to not draw attention to himself.

Gaetano put on his uniform which did not really fit him. It was a bit tight. The watch was in the shoe he had been wearing, and he was concerned it would be lost forever. As he went to pick up his clothes to place them in the bin they had shown him, an officer came in to see what was taking one of the other three so long. With the distraction, Gaetano was able to tilt his shoe over and catch the watch. He then pretended to drop his shoes and bent over to pick them up. The officer gave him a dirty look but did not say anything. As Gaetano stood, he slipped the watch into his boot.

This process took them past one o'clock in the morning. They were then ordered to march to a makeshift barracks. There they were each given an assigned cot which was to be theirs. They still had been given nothing to eat or drink.

The next morning, they were stirred at dawn after just three hours of sleep. The lessons of the previous day made certain none of them would complain. They were told to fall in at attention and shown how they were to line up. Everyman jumped to it without hesitation.

The sergeant walked up to one of the men who had been on their truck and stared him in the face. "Are you hungry?" he asked him.

The soldier did not want to appear complaining so he responded. "No Signor!" this brought about a severe slap to the face.

"We will not tolerate liars here," he yelled at the top of his voice and then walked up to Gaetano and repeated the question.

"Yes Signor, I am," Gaetano responded loudly.

"And what are you going to do about it?" the sergeant asked hoping to get the wrong answer.

"I will eat when I am told to Signor," he said without a hint of expression on his face.

The sergeant simply shook his head up and down with approval, "then you shall all eat." He proceeded to order the men to march to a mess tent nearby. They were all incredibly happy Gaetano gave the right answer. It was clear any wrong word would have resulted in all of them remaining hungry for the rest of the morning.

Just as Captain Stevens had asked, Gaetano and Augustino were placed in the same unit. All the men who had come in with them the night before from the docks of Napoli were placed in the same unit. It appeared as though the officer who approved Captain Steven's request knew all along that Gaetano and Augustino would be in the same outfit. Either way, it was fine with them.

The rest of the day was no surprise to anyone. They spent the morning doing calisthenics and running. The weather was cooperating. It was a beautiful spring day in central Italy. It had rained two days before, so the dust was not flying. The air was fresh and clear. The men were allowed to drink as much water as they could. There was a well pump next to the mess tent and even though their arms were like jelly from all of the pushups, pull-ups, and anything else ups they could throw at them, each of them were more than glad to work the water pump. It meant getting a drink of the most delicious well water Italy had to offer.

They were all glad to not have any display of authority when it came to lunch as meager as it was. Any nutrition was welcome. None of these men were used to this type of workout. Many of them had been farmers and were used to working hard in the fields. But this was nothing like what they were used to. It was difficult for Gaetano since he exerted most of his energies bussing tables and washing dishes at Rocco's. 'Oh, to taste one of Rocco's pizzas right now,' he thought to himself and then realized that type of thinking would only cause him trouble.

It was a bit easier for Augustino. All the tons of coal he had been shoveling aboard the Hallwick were paying off. Of course, not all the exercises were what he was used to, but it definitely helped with his endurance. It was his attitude that worried Gaetano who was watching him closely to make sure he did not spout off about anything.

By late afternoon, the men were marched to a large tent and sat down on the dirt floor of the tent. There, they were lectured on the merits of a well-trained soldier and the importance of obeying orders. A lesson which had already been illustrated quite well. This took them until it was time to march back to the mess tent for what would be the only warm meal of the day. No one was quite sure what it was. But by that time of day and with the entire workout they had done, their meals disappeared before they could even tell if they were edible.

They were allowed to rest for the evening. More than half of them went straight to their cots and went right to sleep. Gaetano and Augustino spent a little time talking over the events of the day.

"So now what?" Augustino asked.

"We do as we're told and hope this war doesn't drag on like most do," Gaetano replied.

"You mean like the hundred years war that we learned about in school?" Augustino said. Gaetano just chuckled and shook his head.

The next morning came fast. They were all hurting from the day before. It did not matter as with most Armies. They still had to fall into formation. By now they knew what that was. The morning began with exercises before breakfast and most men had not realized a trip to the latrine was best done before roll call. A mistake none would make again.

The breakfast at the mess tent was the same as the day before. It consisted of black coffee and bread with a spread of lard on it, supposedly for flavor. Knowing what the previous day was like, no man hesitated eating what was given to him. They all were remembering the breakfasts their Mammas would make for them. Gaetano had already made the decision to avoid thinking about that.

After they had breakfast, the sergeant ordered them to do a five-mile run. The area in which the camp was located was in a valley. The dirt roads leading out of the camp were mostly winding uphill. Gaetano looked at the hill side and could see a truck coming down towards the camp. It was kicking up a significant dust cloud behind it. The sergeant was too far away to hear him, so he said to Augustino. "Looks like we'll be breathing that all the way up the hill," because it seemed to linger behind the truck. Dusty roads were common in most of Italy and when trucks, wagons and even horses would pass, the dust cloud could be seen for some distance.

"Well," Augustino said, "think of the good side."

"What's that?" Gaetano said sarcastically.

"We run downhill all the way back to camp," Augustino snickered back. Then they both looked up the hill again and then back at each other, "If we make it up the hill in the first place."

Making it up the hill was not optional. Several of the men collapsed and several more wished they had not eaten the lard on the bread as they threw up their breakfasts. Gaetano and Augustino made it up the hill with only about half of the men completing the run. They thought they would be able to rest once they got up to the top but because some of the men had not yet completed the run. Instead, they were made to exercise until all the men made it to the top. This was to send a clear message that every man needed to stay together while running without some falling behind.

Once all the men made it to the top, the sergeant had them stand at attention and began to lecture them. "So, you men wonder why we made you exercise after running up the hill. You think we were harsh, and you were being punished." No one would say it but that is exactly what they were thinking.

"Now you must think. Look at the men who made it to the top first," he said then waited a moment before continuing, "They did not quit. They got to where they were supposed to go without giving up." He gave another long pause. "If you were in a battle, you men who fell behind would come to the top to find these men all dead. Why? Because you were not there to fight with them." It took a moment to sink in for some of the men. "And then, your enemy will kill you because you allowed yourselves to be divided which made you all weak.

You need to stay together to maintain your strength as a fighting force. Your country needs every soldier ready to fight when the enemy is before you. You will not be able to catch up. You must keep up so you will be there when they need you. Or all will die." Sometimes too many words will defeat the message. The sergeant stopped right there and ordered the men to run back down to the camp.

That afternoon, after they had another basic lunch, they marched to a field. There they were each given a rifle and bayonet. For two hours they were taught how to load and clean their weapons. Mounting the bayonet proved to be more of a challenge for some than others. Most were able to snap it into place without too much trouble. Three men managed to slice open their hand by not holding it right. One of them needed to go to the infirmary to get his hand stitched up. The other two just needed to wrap it until the bleeding stopped.

At the end of the afternoon training, each man was required to show the sergeant his weapon was unloaded. All the men were instructed to watch the entire process. The soldier who had received the stitches came up to the sergeant with his rifle. "Have you checked your weapon?" the sergeant asked as he had with each and every one.

"Yes Signor, I have," The soldier replied.

"You are certain your weapon is not loaded?" he asked again, unlike the others.

"Yes Signor," he said trying to show confidence.

The sergeant took the rifle from him and told him to stand at attention, which he did without questioning. He then walked up behind the soldier and pointed the rifle at his head. "Still certain your rifle is not loaded?" he asked again.

Then the soldier made the smartest move of his life. "Well Signor, considering I cut myself today putting on my bayonet, I think I may have made a mistake. Could you check it for me............ just to make certain?"

The sergeant snickered and looked up and down the ranks waving the rifle about. Some of the men figured he knew something they did not. It was a bit discomforting. Then suddenly the sergeant pointed it down at the soldier's feet and pulled the trigger. Even though the men had been hearing gunfire all afternoon, this startled all of them. The sergeant was standing behind the soldier when he pulled the trigger, so the soldier did not know where the rifle was aimed.

The men dared not laugh though they wanted to. The soldier, whose gun it was wet himself and his pants were soaked down to the knees. There were a few who could not hold back a chuckle though.

After only a moment the sergeant ordered the men to silence which they made certain they did. "Losing a man to a bullet from the enemy's gun is a tragedy. Losing a man to a bullet from one of your own rifles is a crime. Men die from this incompetence. You will know your weapon and use it properly or men will die who should not."

Gaetano was coming to an understanding as to why the sergeant was the way he was. This sergeant was about thirty years old and had obviously had war experience. He had been one of the soldiers who fought in the war against the Ottoman Empire and the Turks in nineteen-eleven and nineteen-twelve. It was obvious he had seen many of his fellow soldiers die and was more interested in saving the lives of his men than intimidating them. Gaetano would treat his orders with more respect going forward.

The men were once again allowed to rest for the evening. They were shown the tent where there was a shower set up. The water was cold but was a welcome refreshing. The soldier whose rifle was not unloaded went in with his pants on at first and came out holding them after giving them a rinsing off. He did not want to start the next day with day old urine on them. This led to even more laughter, but he knew he had it coming so he played it up by taking a bow as he came out.

The next afternoon the men spent most of the time between lunch and dinner in survival training. They would be given a canteen and two-day rations. Most men also carried a shovel. All would carry their rifles and two grenades. Each man would be responsible for his own rations. One of the men told the rest his older brother had fought in the previous war in nineteen-eleven. "My brother said it was common to take rations off of the dead soldiers so you would have an extra supply."

"Isn't that considered stealing from the dead?" another asked.

"When you consider most soldiers have to make their two days of rations last sometimes a week when they're pinned down, you can understand why men do," he responded. That brought an eerie silence to the conversation. The thought of being in that position was not something they wanted to spend too much time thinking about.

One of the things they were instructed on was hygiene. The men were taught to keep their feet dry. That is why they were given a couple of spare pairs of socks to help. All the men were trained in basic first aid techniques. Some men were given specialty training for things that would be necessary when the troops were in the battlefield for extended periods. Some were taught how to cook. Some, radio communications and for Gaetano, he was taught .... how to cut hair.

They had now been in training for two weeks. The men were getting used to the pattern beginning with exercise before breakfast and a run up the hill before lunch. Then training in hand-to-hand combat in the early afternoon. But on this day, there was no lunch. No one dared question why. They marched to the field where they would practice their weapons and hand to hand combat. Something was different this day. They were told to leave their rifles unloaded.

There was a truck parked along the road with crates inside. The men were ordered to unload the crates but not open them. As they were finishing, the sergeant told them all to sit around in a circle. "This war has been going on for a year now," the sergeant began, "Our nation has stayed out of it so far. We now have no choice but to engage our enemies." The men could tell this might take some time. "Our allies to the north have been fighting the same enemy you will soon fight. And they have fought in ways we have never seen before. You must be prepared for all types of warfare." With that he looked down and opened the nearest crate. He reached in and pulled out something no one had ever seen before. "You may never have to use this and with the grace of the Lord above let that be true." He placed it over his face and a cold chill went down the backs of all of the men because they figured out what this was............. a gas mask.

Chapter 16

It was late May. Gaetano and Augustino along with their outfit had been in training for nearly four weeks. There was no way for them to know when they would see battle. The sergeant told the men about the brave soldiers who had been conducting attacks before the official declaration of war. They fought against the Austro-Hungary Army under the command of Armando Diaz. Their efforts were intended to bring an advantage to the Italian forces once they officially declared war. The plan was called 'The First Jump.' The sense of pride in which the sergeant spoke of these soldiers was intended to give the men a passion to join the fight. For the most part, he was succeeding.

The men would usually have combat training or equipment training in the afternoons. It was the best time to engage them and have them remember what they had learned. To have them exercise in the afternoon under the extreme heat would not work as well. The first thing in the morning was best for that. Usually though, on Saturday afternoons, they would have some type of entertainment for the men. They would either play a sport, or a local musician would play for them.

This Saturday they were told to go after lunch and change into their dress uniforms. Which essentially meant their clean uniform. Not the ones they would exercise and work in. It was mid-afternoon when they all went to the mess tent. They saw four stations set up for taking their pictures. There was an Italian flag set up behind where they would stand, and a green curtain hung from a set of pipes.

These photographers were very professional. They appeared to have the latest cameras and equipment. Each was given an assigned time to report to the mess tent so they could stand in line for their pictures. Gaetano and Augustino ended up going at the same hour.

They were scheduled for four o'clock, so they just sat around trying to find a shady spot in the camp. By four thirty there were only three ahead of them. They had been in line for about twenty minutes. The men before them were playing it up to try to look as handsome as possible. Some looked very awkward and stiff while most just stood there and either smiled or looked serious. It was left up to each man which way he preferred.

"You think they're going to put my picture in the paper?" Augustino asked.

"You'd better hope not," Gaetano responded.

Augustino thought for a minute and was obviously quite confused. "Why not?" he asked.

Gaetano looked back over his right shoulder and answered, "Because if they do, that means you're dead. They use these pictures for the obituaries." Suddenly the fun was taken out of it for Augustino and for the rest of the men who heard him.

The next morning on Sunday, May twenty-third, the men arose at the regular time and began their exercises. Everything seemed normal as normal can be when training for war. As they were marching to the mess hall they were not dismissed as usual but told to stand at attention. Unlike other mornings, the men could smell a rather pleasant aroma coming from the mess tent. Usually, breakfast was a cold meal or bread and all they could smell was coffee.

There was a large group of soldiers and officers standing nearby. A captain was standing with them, who the sergeant said served directly under the command of the Chief of Staff Luigi Cadorna. They were all told he was there to address the men.

Captain Marcello was a slim man about five feet seven inches tall. There was a slight limp in his right leg when he walked.

He had fought under, at the time, General Cadorna since nineteen-ten when he had been appointed to command the Genoa Army corps. Captain Marcello had seen battle numerous times during the previous conflict with the same enemy they were now about to engage.

It was a breezy day, and it made it difficult to hear for all of the men. Gaetano was close enough to hear most of what the captain said. "You men have been working hard this past month to make your country proud. Soon you will have the opportunity to truly make them proud. It was made official on this day that we as a nation have declared war on our old adversary to the north. We will be assembling the largest force of fighting men our nation has seen in many generations. We must fight our old adversary on this new day. They will not prevail." Captain Marcello was pacing back and forth before the men. When he had his back to Gaetano, it became difficult for him to hear exactly what he was saying but based on what he could hear, it was obvious they would soon be moving out. The rest of what he was saying was likely predictable.

The sergeant dismissed them to the mess hall with instructions to gather in front of their barracks once done in an hour. They went into the mess tent and saw what it was they had been smelling while in line up. The men were quite excited to see their breakfast was steaming hot scrambled eggs with sausage along with hot oatmeal. The bread they had become used to was actually toasted. This day they had also brought in fresh cream for those men who enjoyed some in their coffee.

Augustino made his way over to be next to Gaetano. "Last meal?" he said with some degree of sarcasm.

"Come on Augie, just enjoy it. It may be the last warm food we see for a while." Gaetano said back with a minor rebuke.

The men who filled the mess tent were treating this morning as a celebration even though the idea of going to battle is usually not something you rejoice about. That is usually seen when returning from battle. However, this was probably the only nice thing that happened to any of them for at least a month. Life is best when you can enjoy things as they come.

After breakfast was over, the men were allowed to make their own way back to the barracks. There, they were to gather all of the things they had been assigned to carry. A canteen filled with water for the trip, rations, weapons, and whatever specialty items they were told to keep in their pack. Gaetano of course packed his hair cutting tools. The sergeant told them to fall in at exactly nine o'clock.

There were twenty-five trucks just like the one they had been brought in on. The Fiat 18BL had 5.655 c.c. four-cylinder engine which developed 38 h.p. at 1.300 r.p.m. It had four speeds and reverse. This was the pride of the Italian Army for troop movement and supplies in nineteen-fifteen. It was designed to hold twelve men, six per side in the back. This day it would squeeze in eighteen men.

The camp had held four hundred men plus training personnel and support staff. Medical personnel, cooks, and weapons experts were permanently stationed. They would prepare the rifles and specialty items for the soldiers. The training personnel would stay behind to train the next group of recruits.

Some new army people showed up that morning. They were the field sergeants and officers who would be leading this new group of soldiers. These were the combat experienced leaders they would be assigned to. They would be part of the division headed by Captain Marcello.

No one would say how long the trip would be and no one dared ask. Questions like that might be considered complaining. One of the men knew enough about the current conflicts up north to figure they were headed somewhere in the northeast region of the country. That would take them towards the Austro-Hungary border where it was no secret the enemy Army had an entire year to dig in and get ready for this offensive. The outcome was dubious. All that was certain was they were headed for battle and the more they prepared their minds for it, the better off they would be.

The sergeant ordered the men to load onto the trucks at nine thirty in the morning. The trucks sat in the morning sun for nearly two hours before they left the camp. This time the men would ride up the winding road which led from the camp wishing they still were running because that would mean they would run back to camp for a meal and possibly showers. There was no telling what was next this day.

Some of the men chose to sit on the floor of the truck because they were so crowded. They could put four men sitting on the floor which meant only seven were on each side. Depending on the size of the men on each truck, things could get rather personal. The roads were bumpy and often men seated towards the back would have to hold on so as to not fall out.

Then there was the dust. The first truck seemed to kick up enough dust by itself but there were twenty-five trucks in the convoy. It was a good thing they were not trying to sneak up on the enemy. The dust cloud from all those trucks lingered and the men in the rear of the convoy had to breathe it in. Most men fashioned a dust mask with a handkerchief, but it still got into their eyes. It was always welcomed when a cross wind would push the dust away from the road. The area was very dry, and the heat and dryness of summertime was coming upon them. The dust would be a challenge for them to deal with for some time.

They knew they were supposed to use their canteens for water that day, but some were confused about whether they were allowed to eat from their rations. No one had told them if they would stop along the way. In Gaetano's truck, one of the men knocked on the back of the cab and asked. He was told to wait and not eat their rations because they were reserved for the battlefield. Not everyone in the convoy thought to ask.

The trip took them through some of the most beautiful countryside they had ever seen. As they would pass through villages, some people would stand along the roadside and cheer. The men enjoyed this part of the trip especially when the ones cheering were pretty young ladies.

In the late afternoon, the trucks came to another training camp. There, they were allowed to get off the trucks. But were instructed to remember which truck they had been on so the officers could keep track of who was on each truck. They could not take a chance someone would find a way to jump off or stay behind in the camp.

The trucks pulled up to the mess tent and there was a meal waiting for them. "Did they bring the same cooks from the other camp?" Augustino said to Gaetano, "This is the same food we've been eating for a month."

"Army standard. Shut up and eat," Gaetano snapped back. "Sorry............ long trip and my skinny behind is killing me," he said when he noticed Augustino's face grew long.

Augustino looked up at him and grinned, "mine too."

After they ate, they went back to the trucks, but it was getting late. The original plan was to make it there by lunch. They had hoped to get much farther that day. However, with some delays at the camp in the morning and the size of the convoy being larger than they had planned, they were delayed. Then there were even more delays on the road. It was decided to keep the men at this camp for the night. The men knew they could not cheer, but they felt like it. "All right, somebody show me my cot," one man said. But there was not going to be any cots that night.

They were instructed to find a place close to the truck they had been on and roll out their sleeping blanket to settle in for the night. It became obvious the days of having a cot were mostly over. At least the weather held up and the night air was crisp and breezy. It was better than riding all night on the truck. They likely would have if they had fresh drivers to take over. Most of the reason for staying at this camp was to give them a rest.

The next day rather than the convoy being delayed with breakfast, they were given packages with food for the day's trip. The only time they would stop would be for refueling the trucks. There the men would be allowed to get out and stretch and take care of other more personal business. They had added two trucks to the convoy at the second camp loaded with barrels of gasoline. Gas depots would not be available for fueling the trucks on route.

As they headed north the terrain became more mountainous. The goal was to reach Bologna by nightfall. As they were working their way up a mountain pass, word came that the road ahead was blocked by a landslide.

"It looks like we're gonna be doing some roadwork," one of the men on Gaetano's truck said.

"Maybe so, but something doesn't seem right," Gaetano replied. He was standing up at the front of the truck and looking ahead. His was the fifth truck in the convoy.

"What's happening up there?" Augustino said having just worked his way to the front where Gaetano was peering.

"I don't see anyone gathering shovels. I see them getting their rifles," he said stretching his neck to see, "Someone is coming towards us, and he doesn't look happy."

One of the sergeants from the lead truck was coming down the line of trucks and as he stopped at each truck, the men got out and headed off the road and took cover in the brush and rocks.

"Something's up," Gaetano said to the men in his truck. The sergeant got to the cab of their truck and Gaetano could hear him.

"Not taking any chances. We don't like the looks of it," he told the sergeant in the passenger seat, "Have your men take cover off the road and be prepared for anything."

"You think anything could happen this far south," their sergeant asked.

"We'll find out soon enough," the first sergeant answered.

Sergeant Patrizi was assigned to their truck. He was riding up front and jumped out. He climbed up on the runner board and ordered, "Everyone out, snap to it, this is not training anymore."

The men were not the least bit organized in their attempts to evacuate the truck. The first two men hopped off without any trouble, but the third man who was seated on the driver's side jumped out without looking where he was going and landed wrong on his right leg twisting his ankle. He let out a scream like he had been shot, which made everyone around him nervous thinking they may be under attack.

The next two men to jump out grabbed him and dragged him off the road. "Shut up, you want to get us all killed," one of the men said, "you cry like a baby. Oh, Mamma I hurt my footie. What are you?"

"That's enough," Sergeant Patrizi said as he flagged the medic to look at it. He leaned right into the face of the man who fell, "You do that in a real battle, and you could get everyone killed. You don't jump without looking, understand?"

This put the soldier on track, "Yes Signor, it won't happen again."

"What would he do if he really got hurt like getting shot or something?" Augustino said to Gaetano under his breath.

"Let's hope he never finds out," Gaetano replied just as softly.

"All right. Keep a close look out around the ridge for anything that moves. You do nothing but tell me. I'll decide what to do. No one fires a shot unless I say to. Got it?" Sergeant Patrizi commanded. He could not take a chance his men would shoot the first innocent farmer who came by to see what all the commotion was about.

They took cover wherever they could find it and began to look around. The truck was less than fifty feet away. About ten minutes went by and then they saw eight men walk up from the back of the convoy. The sergeant of the squad walked up to Sergeant Patrizi, "We're going to set up a perimeter along the ridge. If it's all clear, your men are to go to the front and rotate one-hour shifts clearing the road with the men from the other trucks."

"Any idea if there's trouble," Sergeant Patrizi asked.

"Probably not. But the captain said he's not taking any chances. Something happened like this last week, and it was an ambush," the other sergeant said.

"I heard about that. But that was much further north, up by Treviso. Does the captain think they could have made it this far south?" Sergeant Patrizi asked.

"He lost some good men that day. He's not taking chances. Give it twenty minutes or so and then head up to start the rotation. It looks like we will camp here tonight," he said then turned and continued walking with the other men from his squad to the next group of men.

"What is it?" Gaetano asked Sergeant Patrizi, "What was that about an ambush?" he continued trying to sound supportive and engaged.

"It's because of our attacks over the last few weeks," Sergeant Patrizi replied, "The enemy had sent some snipers into the woods near Treviso. The road was blocked by a tree and when the men got out to cut it out of the way, the snipers picked off ten men and wounded eighteen others. I guess the landslide looked suspicious enough to warrant the precaution." Gaetano was surprised he was so open about it. But then Sergeant Patrizi was not an officer, but a fighting man like them. He just had a higher rank.

Once the perimeter was set, the men calmed down and went to work clearing the road. The engines of the trucks were all shut down and they took until nightfall to clear the road enough to pass. Some of the boulders were too large to move so they made a temporary bend in the road for the trucks to pass. There was a sharp drop off on the right side of the road which made it difficult to manage.

It became necessary to fill in some of the hillside to make for a roadway. They used a winch connected to two trucks to pull a couple of boulders off the road and down the side. Then they needed to establish some gravel for a roadway. They tried a couple of trucks just to make certain they could pass before nightfall. Once confident the road had been restored, it was confirmed they would camp there for the night.

Word passed truck by truck as to the plan. They told the men to eat the food they had in their day packages but to save some for the next day since they were so far behind schedule. Some of the men realized they had not planned correctly and had already eaten everything. Others had actually listened during survival training. As night came over the mountain, the men once again pulled out their sleeping blankets and tried best they could to get a comfortable spot in which to settle in for the night.

Gaetano told Augustino to set up with him next to the truck. "I don't like those clouds," he said.

Everyone found what seemed to be a soft spot along the side of the road where they could push down the brush to pad the ground. Gaetano set up right next to the truck on the roadway which brought some ridicule from the men who thought they would have a more comfortable night's sleep in the brush.

During the night, the weather turned, and it began to rain. Not a hard rain, just a pleasant spring rain. Gaetano tapped Augustino and they slid in under the truck to get out of it. Some men had the same idea, but they could not fit all eighteen men underneath so some of them had to sleep in the rain.

"Captain Stevens was right," Augustino said.

"How's that?" Gaetano asked.

"He said you would look after me. Don't know what I'd do," Augustino replied. Gaetano just looked up at the bottom of the truck and wished they were both still on the Hallwick battling rough seas.

Chapter 17

While on perimeter watch the next morning, some of the men could see a stream on the other side of the ridge. It was only about a hundred yards away from the road. The captain ordered the men to go fill their canteens and told them to wash up downstream of the men filling the canteens. They were given only thirty minutes before the trucks were going to move out. Most men ran to the stream so as to have time to wash up some and get the dust from the day before out of their eyes.

Gaetano made a point of getting to know the men's names in his truck. Not all of them were familiar to him. They had not loaded the trucks with the same men they bunked with at the camp. A couple, but not all.

Nevio was from Napoli and worked on the docks. He was recruited because he offered to help the officers check the ships for Italian citizens. They ended up recruiting him after he was finished. Anthony was the family man who was ridiculed at the docks when attempting to board a ship for New York.

Luigi lived in Napoli as well but did not work at the docks. He was making deliveries there when he was recruited. Rinaldo, like Augustino, worked on a ship shoveling coal. His ship was a passenger liner. The captain of his ship thought he may have been able to talk the Italian Army officers out of taking him because he had some political connections. But it was to no avail. Rinaldo was a large man, very strong and not someone any captain would want to lose from his crew.

Gregorio was the quiet one. He was a man of small stature and kept to himself most of the time. Gregorio was a cook on the same ship as Rinaldo. Sad to say the captain did not try to keep him from the officers. There were three men they wanted to recruit from his ship. Rinaldo and Gregorio were not really certain of the third man's name. They did not know him very well on their ship and thought his name might be Macario. He was one of the two men who complained on the first day. The one who was never seen again.

Two of the men were named Lorenzo. The two could not be more different. They were not recruited from the docks but were workers in Napoli. All of the employers throughout Italy were instructed to provide a list of eligible recruits to the Army. The other men called them 'The Lorenzos' as though they were a pair of acrobats who did a high wire act in the circus. It was the source of quite a bit of ribbing which they did not seem to mind too much. Not that it would have stopped it.

Valentino was the prankster of the group. If someone had a trick pulled on them, they would assume it was Valentino even if it were not. He worked in the market in Napoli when he was recruited. Tomaso was from Rome. He had applied to be a police officer and was waiting for his application to be approved when the Army came in and recruited any man who was not essential to the operations of the Roman police. His name came up and they took him.

Paulo was a bit older. He was thirty but had some problems with the police in Rome, so they offered him an opportunity to redeem his record by joining the Army. They were happy to see him leave Rome. Angelo regretted not entering the priesthood. If he had, he would not be in the Army. He told the men he had decided to hold off for one year and then enter the seminary. He was afraid now the Army would get him to heaven even faster. Angelo also worked on the docks in Napoli.

Pierre was originally from France. His father had to leave Marseille over a gambling debt in quite a hurry five years earlier. Pierre's father worked on the docks in Marseille some years earlier, so it was a logical option to go to Napoli to look for work on the docks there. Once his son was old enough to work, he got him a job also. Pierre's father was too old for the Army, so they only took Pierre. They considered him an Italian citizen because he and his father had lived there for five years.

Dino and Enrico were brothers. Dino was the older. They both worked on a cargo ship which sailed mostly out of Napoli. They would make regular runs to North Africa and Palestine. Dino was the steam engineer and Enrico worked on the bridge. Their father had worked on the same ship until his passing three years earlier. The captain of the ship had promised him his two sons would always have a job on his ship as long as he was captain. He did not count on them being recruited into the Army.

Armando was the ladies' man. He was from Napoli and was a waiter at one of the finer restaurants. He bragged about meeting a different girl every week. Armando was much more impressed with himself than the others were. When Armando would brag, some of the others would think about their sisters and hope Armando would never find out where they lived.

The youngest was Mario. He was only eighteen and did not know when to be quiet. If someone spoke out of turn, it would be Mario. Some of the men attributed it to his youth but others did not let him off the hook that easily. He was also the one who was most likely to start a fight. Mario worked on the dock loading cargo ships.

• • • •

THE LAST TRUCK PULLED around the spot where the landslide had taken place by six thirty in the morning. It was the beginning of another long day with sore bottoms and dusty eyes. Bologna was within sight by late morning. There was a training camp on the far side of the town. The convoy went right through the center. It would have been just as easy to bypass, but the cheers of the people on the streets were an important morale booster for the troops as well as a show of support to the people.

Once arriving at the camp, the men were amazed at how much larger this camp was. This was an established Army camp which had been there for several decades. Rather than tents, there were buildings made of stone. The mess hall was large and airy. That was where they let them off and told them they would have only a half hour to eat their lunch.

"Why couldn't we train at a place like this?" Augustino said.

"Yeah, did you see those showers we passed?" Gaetano added, "they were inside a brick building. I'll bet you they have hot water too."

"Hey, wonder if they got girls here. You know, nurses?" Armando said, "there were signs for an infirmary. Find an infirmary, find nurses. I can see it now.......... Oh, Mamma, I don't feel good. Please take my temperature." All the men laughed partly at the humor and partly at the predictability of Armando.

"It hurts right here," one of the Lorenzos said, "kiss it and make it feel better, just like Mamma used to."

"Oh nurse, could you please tuck me in, just like my Mamma used to?" Paulo added. By now they were all laughing loud enough for everyone to hear.

• • • •

AFTER THEY FINISHED lunch, none of them wanted to get back on the trucks and the sergeants knew it. Sergeant Patrizi was waiting at their truck as the men came out of the mess hall. "Everyone hit the latrine and then fall in," he said, "We're going for a run to loosen all of you up for the rest of the trip." This actually seemed appealing to the men. Anything to avoid getting back on the hard seats at this point.

Sergeant Patrizi had them line up for marching formation. Rather than start running right away after eating, he had them march for a bit and then break into a trot. The road they were on took them by the infirmary and some of the men saw the nurses they hoped were there. As much as they were tempted to call out to them, they did not want to get on the wrong side of the sergeant. Seeing all the nurses was the thrill of the day. It did not really matter if they were good looking either. They were women.

The run was relatively short compared to the training exercises. But the intent was different. All the men returned to their respective trucks. There was travel time to make up, and the day was rapidly disappearing.

There was a water pump nearby and the men were told to fill their canteens again while the other trucks were loading up. Some drank what was in their canteens to make room for more water even though they may not have a latrine break until the trucks needed gasoline. "Stand here," Sergeant Patrizi said. He looked up and down the line of trucks to see the loading progress. "You men are at ease but stay right by the truck," he added, "When I say load up, you have thirty seconds, or would you like to load in right now?" The men all appreciated the wait. It also showed the sergeant was looking out for them.

It was nearly two o'clock when they were ordered onto the truck and headed out immediately unlike the first morning when they left their training camp. North of Bologna was not as hilly as it had been south of the town. This meant they would be able to make up for some lost time. The roads were straight and level.

The trucks could up their speed a bit which also resulted in more dust. But the day was breezy enough so most of the dust was being blown to the side of the convoy. Again, it was a good thing they did not have to conceal their approach. The enemy would have seen this dust cloud from miles away.

Captain Marcello had originally planned for the convoy to be past Padova by the previous night. This would set him back an entire day. A day that would be necessary for digging in. It also would have given him enough time for some orientation of the terrain for the troops. To delay the offensive was not an option and he would have to make up for lost time once they arrived.

The convoy made it past Padova by six o'clock. They stopped for about thirty minutes so they could join two other convoys which had munitions and supplies. One convoy was coming out of the port at Marghera. The harbor had been sewn up to prevent attacks from U-boats for several weeks. Ships that made it in had come from England mostly. More ships had been scheduled in, but some had not made it past the effort to blockade most of the Mediterranean by the German U-boats and battle ships. They were either sunk or diverted to other ports which were closer to their location when Italy joined the war. It was at the discretion of the ship's captain as to which.

The other was from the west in Verona where the Italian Army had established some secret munitions depots years before. This convoy had to come directly east to Padova because the mountain passes which led directly to the front were not secure. That and they were likely not passable for another month yet due to the spring thaw.

The three convoys collectively were made up of over one hundred trucks. Their goal now was to reach the walled city of Cittadella before they camped for the night. There would be no stopping for a meal. The men were now under battlefield conditions.

The convoy that came out of Verona carried most of the supplies for troop support which included food, medical supplies and even a mobile hospital which would set up three miles south of the front line. The thought of a mobile hospital made many of the men feel somber.

Driving at night on dusty roads can be as dangerous as driving in inclement or foggy weather. The visibility is limited to the tail gate of the truck in front of you. If the wind is not in your favor, you could easily lose them in the cloud. The troop convoy was first followed by the supplies and then the munitions. This way if the convoy came under attack the first line of defense would be the armed personnel. They would protect the supplies and munitions. Fortunately for all that evening, the road was clear. They all understood this would not last.

Late evening at about nine o'clock, the convoy pulled into the field where their camp would be for the night. The soldiers were instructed to use their rations. They would be resupplied in the morning before they headed up to Asiago for preparations of the assault. The men on Gaetano's truck were very quiet as they unloaded. The same rules applied as the night before. They were to camp close to their assigned truck for easier deployment the next morning.

Sergeant Patrizi seemed very solemn that evening. A soldier with experience knows when a battle is looming. No one knew exactly when the offensive would begin or how it would take place. The only people who knew for certain were Chief of Staff Cadorna, General Frugoni head of the second Army and the Duke of Aosta with the third Army. They were not about to share that information with the troops or even their captains.

• • • •

GAETANO AND AUGUSTINO along with the rest of the troops settled in for the night expecting the next day would bring them to the front lines. The eighteen men plus the driver and Sergeant Patrizi set up a fire. It was acceptable at their location, and they all knew this would not be acceptable once on the front lines. They opened up their rations and tried to figure out if they were worth eating.

"So, what is this stuff? Canned meat?" Anthony asked, "My Mamma would turn in her grave, rest her soul."

"You smell this? What is it?" Luigi added.

"My brother Alfonso ate worse than this when he was in the Army a few years ago," Nevio said, "this stuff is actually an improvement from what he told me."

"So, what do you think is going to happen?" Augustino asked.

"There's going to be a lot of people getting killed, what do you think?" Mario snipped.

"Hey, don't talk like that," Rinaldo complained, "how would you know, you trained with us. You were recruited at the dock just like all of us at gunpoint. You don't know any more than the rest of us. I don't wanna hear that kinda stuff." They knew not to mess around with Rinaldo from the days at training camp. He was the toughest of them all.

"Sorry Rinaldo," Mario said sheepishly, "didn't mean to get you riled. Just meant things are gonna get ugly for all of us. Can't deny that, can ya?" Mario tried to calm things down.

"Funny thing is," Gaetano added, "we all get to find out real soon."

Sergeant Patrizi was just watching and listening to this to get a sense of what the men were thinking. "Remember," he finally said, "We all fight together, there will be no disagreements on the battlefield, or we all die. Got it?"

No one said anymore about the fighting. The conversation went back to the rations. "So, what is this stuff?" Anthony repeated himself.

• • • •

THE TEMPERATURE WAS a bit colder than the night before. They were getting closer to the Alps at that point, and it had an effect on the temperatures, especially at night. Everyone had the same idea as Gaetano and Augustino from two nights before and it was a rush to get a place to sleep close to the truck so they could slide under if it started to rain. Gaetano thought first when they got off the truck and staked out a place for him. He made sure there was a place for Augustino as well without making it obvious. He figured it would be best if the other men did not think of Augustino as needing to be looked after.

As morning broke, they were told they would be held in the area for a couple of days while they waited for some other supplies to arrive. Those supplies were artillery batteries and the shells they would use to bombard the enemy positions.

By noon time however, the officers had decided to continue with the original plan to move the troops to Asiago. They would get direct field training sooner and also dig in there just in case they needed to fall back from the initial attack point.

The officers knew that even though the Austro-Hungary Army was entrenched and ready for a defensive war, there was always the possibility they would take the offensive. So, the trucks were loaded up and they went on their way.

The trip did not take long, just two hours. They wasted no time starting to dig in. The first trench was to be five feet deep, and the dirt was to be piled up on the side which faced the enemy positions making it almost seven feet of protection. Augustino and Rinaldo had the easiest time of it due to their work experience shoveling coal on their ships.

"I could do this all day," Augustino said to Gaetano and Valentino who were working next to him. "Coal is filthy. You breathe that black dust all day inside of a tin can. Give me the fresh air any day."

"Know what you mean," Rinaldo added, "But at least on the ship, no one is trying to shoot you."

"Guess you never met my boss," Augustino quipped back.

Gaetano laughed, "hey Frankie wasn't all that bad."

"Not Frankie, Brian the night boss," Augustino added, "I don't think you ever got to know him. He usually slept during the day and wouldn't have been at dinner very often."

"Short ugly guy, looked like he lost a lot of fights?" Gaetano asked.

"That's him," Augustino replied.

"You're right. I never got to know him," Gaetano concluded, "We always kept some food out for him though."

Every man other than the officers contributed to the digging, even the truck drivers. They would not be using the trenches right away, but they had to make up for a lost day and Captain Marcello ordered all of them to dig. As evening came, they noticed that even some of the medics had joined the digging.

"I feel like we should sing a song or something patriotic," Valentino commented.

"What did you have in mind?" Pierre questioned.

"I don't know, Marcia Reale or something," Valentino added.

"That's the national anthem and it doesn't have any words. What's wrong with you?" Mario jumped in.

"You never heard the words?" Valentino asked, "There're a couple of versions that people have written. 'Long live the king, Long live the king' you know they teach it in school."

"I wouldn't know," Pierre said.

"Well of course not. It's not the French national anthem. How does that one go?" Valentino paused.

"Don't think these guys want to hear some Frenchie singing something that isn't Italian right about now," Pierre sighed.

"Yeah, you're probably right about that. I guess I'll just shut up and dig," Valentino resigned himself.

"Good," Augustino said under his breath to Gaetano.

Gaetano chuckled and said, "Don't let him hear you say that."

"Eh, I'm not afraid of him," Augustino added.

"Not the point," Gaetano said, "You'll have plenty of fighting to do soon enough."

It got too dark for the men to dig anymore so they were ordered to eat and prepare for sleeping. The trucks would be leaving in the morning, which would mean fewer diggers the next day. Most of the men were exhausted but, Augustino and Rinaldo were just getting started. Two five-hour shifts shoveling coal each day made digging dirt for three and a half hours seem like a trip to the park.

The troops ate a bit and then settled into the best spots they could find to sleep the night away. Some men had planned ahead by piling soft dirt then flattening it to make the ground more comfortable for at least one night. The ground the night before had been packed down and was quite hard. This was more comfortable considering. It was a technique they figured they could repeat as long as they had shovels, which they knew would be for quite some time.

In the morning, the men were woken up to the sound of the truck engines starting and driving off. "Well, I guess we're here to stay," Augustino said.

"Let's hope so," Gaetano replied.

"Yeah, I guess that's a good point," Augustino realized what he meant. It would certainly beat the alternative.

Chapter 18

It took six days to dig the trenches near Asiago. The troops were not just digging but also training. The training involved such things as rock climbing and the proper way to operate a hoist. The retaking of the northern territory would be right in the midst of the Alps. One of the reasons for not delaying the offensive was the Italian Army would have to do most of the fighting in the summer months due to the extremes in weather at the elevations they would be fighting.

The enemy had been entrenched for almost a full year and knew the landscape. Fortunately, Captain Marcello had two officers who had lived in this area while growing up and had gone hunting with their fathers often. Lieutenant Fabrini's father would take him up to a cabin they owned at the six-thousand-foot level during the summer. That was close to the area they would have to retake. It was understood Lieutenant Fabrini was not to be on the front lines. The captain made certain of his safety for the sake of the rest of the men. It would not be in their best interests if something were to happen to him.

• • • •

ON THE MORNING OF JUNE fifth, Sergeant Patrizi organized a squad of soldiers to venture out on a reconnaissance mission. He took five men. Paulo, Armando, Nevio, the younger Lorenzo and Gaetano. They left at dawn. The mission was to scope out which mountain passes were occupied, and which may be safe for troop movement. They would be out for four days. Three other squads also went out in other directions with pretty much the same instructions.

Sergeant Patrizi was a skilled mountaineer. That is why he was given this assignment. Paulo had done some mountain climbing several years before and was comfortable working the gear. The only mountains Gaetano ever saw were the bluffs overlooking Hoboken. The hills around his hometown did not count. This would be a different mountain experience for him.

All of the men were informed as to the route and knew the map. They had studied it for two days prior to leaving. It was important for them to all know where they were going and how to get back in the event Sergeant Patrizi or any others would be killed. The danger was not only that they may encounter the enemy, but the terrain itself was potentially deadly. The goal was to reach Rovereto and circle to the south towards Lake Garda.

They took their rifles and the normal amount of ammunition that was allotted to every soldier. Each man carried two grenades and a full travel pack. It was not the intent for them to engage the enemy, but they had to be prepared to defend themselves. They had to make every effort to avoid a conflict in order to report back to Captain Marcello. He needed to know the enemy troop strength in the region.

The mountain ranges south of Trentino were among the most beautiful in the southern boundaries of the Alps. The area around Asiago was three to four thousand feet above sea level. Even though, this area was only considered the foothills.

The squad headed straight north. The first day, they saw no signs of enemy troops. The men were ordered not to talk or make any unnecessary noise on the trail. At any moment, they could come around a ridge and be face to face with the enemy. They did not want to give them advanced warning they were coming. Silence was the rule.

At midday on the second day, it began to rain. Rain is always welcome when trying to be inconspicuous. The sound of the rain on the ground covers many noises a man can produce. Stepping on fallen branches and the occasional rocks rolling down the hill because someone was not watching can draw attention very quickly.

It turned out to be true because a couple of hours after it started to rain, they came upon a group of about fifty enemy soldiers. They seemed to be staying put waiting out the rain showers. There were a couple of trucks which had supplies and munitions. Sergeant Patrizi gave the men a sign to back out and circle around them in order to avoid detection. The enemy was over two hundred yards away when the squad first saw them.

"What do you think they were up to?" Gaetano asked.

"There must be an outpost nearby. It looks like they're restocking it. No telling exactly where it is and we're not sticking around long enough to find out," The sergeant answered, "We'll just report there is an outpost is in this region. They likely move them on a regular basis anyway."

"Won't the captain need that information?" Gaetano continued.

"Not that detail," Sergeant Patrizi replied, "Just they were in the area should be enough. We can't risk detection."

The map showed an alternate ravine just to the west, so they went towards that direction. It was easy to avoid the enemy since they probably were not expecting any Italian troops in the area for several more days. Their intelligence had informed them the formations of Italian troops were still close to Verona. They had spies watching to see when they would move out. Those troops had been placed there for the sole purpose of keeping the enemy's attention off the movements to the east.

Rovereto had considerable evidence of enemy troop buildup. Sergeant Patrizi ordered the men to pick up the pace a bit in order to report back to Asiago. They made it to Lake Garda by noon on the third day and realized they were behind schedule by a day. The route back would take them south of where they had been and over less hilly country. At times they would go double time to catch up. If they were too late, the captain might suspect that something happened to them. Their original schedule called for them to return by night fall on the fourth day or very soon after.

The sun was setting behind them as they approached Valdagno. They saw an old farmer in his field. He had been struggling with a broken wagon wheel for most of the afternoon. Sergeant Patrizi did not want to commit the entire squad at first just in case he was sympathetic to the enemy. Paulo and the sergeant went alone to size up the situation while Armando, Gaetano, Lorenzo, and Nevio stayed behind on the other side of the hill.

"Ciao Signor," Paulo called out from the edge of his field.

"Buonasera," the farmer answered, "Soldiers? That either means I'm safer or in for a lot of trouble."

"Safer for now Signor, we can't account for what the enemy will do once we start sending them back where they came from," Sergeant Patrizi added.

"And not a moment too soon, Sergeant I believe? I recognize the uniform. My son is in the Army. He too is a Sergeant," the farmer said with pride.

"Looks like you have a problem, Signor. Can we help?" Paulo asked.

"You men are an answer to prayer," the farmer sighed, "this wagon is just too heavy to repair the wheel on my own. I don't think even the two of you will be enough."

"No need to worry," Paulo replied and then waved the sign that said the situation was safe. The others came over the hill quickly.

The farmer gave the sign of the cross and said, "Thank you Lord, you always come through for your humble servant."

As they approached, it was obvious they would need to help the old farmer. They wanted to make sure he would be able to get home before sunset. He had everything they needed to pry the wagon up and properly set the axle. With a couple of whacks of the hammer, the wheel was set. They helped him hitch up the work horses and he was all set to go home.

"You men, you're welcome to stay at my home tonight," The farmer said with a big smile, "I'll even give you dinner. My wife has plenty. She always cooks for an Army. Wait, you are the Army," the farmer started to chuckle at his own joke.

"That's very gracious Signor, but there are too many of us. We could not impose," Sergeant Patrizi responded.

"I do not take no for an answer," the farmer jumped, "I could not have done this alone. My son............. he is also off to war. He would have helped if he were here. It will make my wife feel like she is feeding our son's friends. I insist." He was not going to let them go easily. "I'll open some of my favorite wine for tonight. Then you can sleep in the barn. There is still enough hay so you can be comfortable."

"Vino?" Armando perked up.

"My favorite, we celebrate my son Giuseppe and his fellow soldiers," he concluded figuring he had won them over.

The five men looked to the sergeant for a reaction. He hesitated for a moment. "Well, for your son. That would be a good reason," Sergeant Patrizi said hesitantly. Then he looked at the men. "One small glass of wine each." They all nodded with acceptance at the restriction.

The farmhouse and barn were less than half a mile away. They moved as fast as the horses could pull the wagon. "How is our schedule?" Gaetano asked the sergeant.

"We would have only gained five miles tonight. Hope you feel up to some running tomorrow," he said to all of the men.

"Yes Signor," Lorenzo piped in, "All the way back to......."

"That will be all," Sergeant Patrizi jumped in. Lorenzo suddenly realized he was not supposed to divulge the whereabouts of the troops just in case the enemy would ever question this farmer. Even though he was loyal, they could not risk that information be out.

"What is your name Signor?" Gaetano asked.

"Giuseppe, my son is named after me just as I am named after my father Giuseppe," he said with pride.

"That's a good name," Paulo said, "My father's name is Giuseppe. I'm Paulo, this is Armando, that one over is Lorenzo, the funny looking one is Nevio."

"Hey, watch that," Nevio said with a laugh.

"Up ahead are Gaetano, and the Sergeant you know already," Paulo said.

"You boys came along at a good time. Thank you all again," the farmer said as they came into the barnyard. His wife came out to see why soldiers were with him. Many things went through her mind at first. 'Are they here about Giuseppe? Is there trouble coming?' She thought to herself. Once she saw that her husband was jovial with them, she realized everything was all right.

"Alessa, these men will be joining us tonight," he called to her, "they came as an answer to prayer. I would have never fixed that wheel alone and Alfonso is in town this week." Referring to the farmer who lived up the road. They would often team up when something was too hard for just one man to do.

"Do you men know our Giuseppe?" she asked thinking it might be possible.

"No Signora, we are not from this area," Sergeant Patrizi said without saying any more about where they were from or how long they had been in the area. His experience showed and the men were learning by watching him.

They sat around the table, which was not large enough for so many, but it could manage to seat eight. Gaetano offered to help. "Signora, I used to work in a restaurant in America. So, I know my way around a dining table. Let me help you, there are too many of us to sit back and watch you."

"America?" she replied, "If you were in America, why did you come back? Did you come to join the Army?"

"No Signora, it's a long story. I came to care for my Nonna. I hope she's all right," he sighed.

"You came all the way from America to take care of your Nonna? You're a good boy. We need more good boys like you," she said taking on a motherly tone, "Where are you from young man?"

"South near Napoli, a small town called Montoro Superiore in the province of Avellino. Have you ever been in that area Signora?" Gaetano asked.

"No, I'm afraid not. The farthest I have ever gone is Bologna. My sister moved there with her husband. He is a builder, a mason worker. There was much more work there for him............well, at the time," she answered, "We have gone three times. And one time we met them at Venezia. We spent some time enjoying the sea. Someday maybe we can go back. Very expensive, very expensive."

Gaetano chuckled.

The evening rolled on with pleasant conversations and great food and wine. Signora Alessa had prepared some linguini with dried tomatoes and peppers in a garlic olive oil. She had baked bread that would have been enough for two days use for her and her husband. So, they had enough to go around. She told her husband she would just bake again tomorrow. Giuseppe opened a jug of his favorite rose' and it was as if there was no war on the horizon. But they all knew better.

Gaetano left to go to the outhouse. "Take your rifle," Sergeant Patrizi said quietly so their host would not hear. Gaetano discreetly took it with him understanding by now the sergeant knew what he was talking about. Coming back, he stopped by the window and some light was shining out. He reached into his boot and took out his watch. Nine thirty-five, he knew they would be heading for the barn once he went inside. He slipped the watch back into his boot.

"The rest of you take liberty like the private and meet at the barn," Sergeant Patrizi said, "We have taken up enough of our host's time. Thank you, Signor and Signora, your hospitality was most gracious. We probably will be gone at first light, so please accept our thanks and blessings to your household."

They exchanged farewells and the men left to go into the barn. Giuseppe was right. There was enough hay for the men to get comfortable. "All right, listen," Sergeant Patrizi said, "Guard duty, one-hour shifts. It's not like sleeping in a ravine behind some boulders. As much as I trust them, we can't risk that someone will come. We leave two hours before dawn." The men respected him for his tenacity. Lorenzo took the first watch.

• • • •

BY THE TIME THE SUN rose in their faces, they were several miles from the farm. The route was clear, and they took advantage of the open fields to run some of the way. It was not a rapid pace but faster than walking. Sergeant Patrizi did not want to over work the men just in case they did confront the enemy. It was not likely there would be any enemy troops in the area they were in. They did not let their guard down, but they felt more comfortable than when they were heading for Rovereto.

They ran for twenty minutes and walked for twenty. Once every two hours they rested for ten minutes and drank water. At one point they came across a wild strawberry patch. "Can we take our rest here?" Nevio asked the sergeant. He loved strawberries and the wild ones were his favorite.

"Ten minutes, we're not on a picnic here," the sergeant replied.

Nevio was able to pick almost enough strawberries to fill his helmet in the ten minutes they had. The others only picked about half of that, which was plenty for them. Nevio could have eaten twice as much. Lorenzo did not pick any. He said they gave him the hives.

There was a stream in view of the strawberry patch, so the men filled their canteens and washed off their faces. They were ready for the rest of the journey. The next part was walking so Nevio kept moaning in ecstasy every time he put a strawberry into his mouth. After a while it got on everyone's nerves.

Armando was walking behind him, and he had quite a few of his strawberries left so every time Nevio moaned, Armando threw a strawberry at him and tried to hit him in the back of the head. The first few missed or hit his jacket so Nevio could not tell. Lorenzo and Gaetano were walking with Armando and chuckled every time he threw one and it hit his back. They soon joined in until Nevio caught on.

"How could you waste such a perfect berry?" he said as he bent down to pick up the ones they threw, "Oh they didn't mean it," he said to the fallen strawberries as he popped them into his mouth.

It was past two o'clock when they decided to run some more. Nevio had eaten all his strawberries, and the others had eaten some but thrown the rest at Nevio. It was time to get serious and get back to camp. "We should be able to get back by sunset," Sergeant Patrizi said, "That sign is for Thiene, so we are about fifteen miles out."

They made good time and returned to the camp by five thirty. While they were gone, the Army had set up a mess tent with hot food. They arrived just in time to get dinner and wash up. Several of the men they knew saw them and could not wait to get a report as to what they saw. It was agreed during the walk they would keep the farmer and the pleasant evening before to themselves.

• • • •

SERGEANT PATRIZI WENT immediately to Captain Marcello's tent to report. He gave him all the information regarding where they had seen troop movements and fortifications. The concentration was around Roverto and north. There was some activity between there and Lake Garda, but not enough to have concern. Lieutenant Fabrini was there. They reviewed the maps together, so the captain had a better idea of what was to be expected once they launched the offensive.

The sergeant did, however, tell the captain about the evening before and the cautions they took. The captain was all right with his decision to befriend the locals. It would have been unwise for Sergeant Patrizi to not tell the captain. The other men not knowing about it was one thing. But keeping information from a commanding officer would have been wrong.

The planning was nearly complete. The troops were ready for battle and the officers knew too much idle time would not be good for the men. They were conditioned and ready. It was now just a matter of giving the orders and it would all start. But no one could know how long it would last.

Chapter 19

The next day, a high-level officer's meeting was well underway in Captain Marcello's command tent. All the lieutenants were present, and it was made clear none of what was discussed would be repeated outside of the tent.

"We will have the advantage," Captain Marcello announced to his staff, "Two hundred thousand men at our disposal to their one hundred thousand, who could ask for better?"

"What will we have for heavy guns?" Lieutenant Fabrini asked.

"To start off, two hundred guns, more on the way," the captain answered, "the first strike will be to bombard across the Isonzo. That will break them down."

"How long until we move in with the troops?" The lieutenant added.

"We give them a full week of bombardments, then the frontal assault. They won't know what hit them," he said with pride.

"Do we have a date?" another asked.

The captain was not certain if he wanted to tell them a date just yet until he had the right feeling about it. Then he figured he needed to get their reaction to see if it helped him to finalize his decision. "The twenty-third," the captain said, "each of you prepare your men. We move out in two days." The reaction was all positive. They were all on board. After two and a half hours of each lieutenant being briefed on his deployment, the meeting was broken up.

• • • •

IT WAS MID-MORNING, about nine o'clock. Men had been lined up for two hours to get their hair cut. Gaetano was getting sore hands from all the scissor work. The older Lorenzo was up next. "I don't know if I can trust you with those scissors," he joked.

"If you like, I can use my bayonet," Gaetano joked back, "It's sharper. I can cut even more than hair with it."

"That's what I'm afraid of," he pounced back, "hey someone find me a real barber. This man is not fit to serve."

"So, what's the word?" Gaetano asked.

"About what?" Lorenzo said.

"The big hush hush meeting in the captain's tent. When do we go?" he asked again.

"Oh, that meeting. They decided to cancel the war. We're all going home tomorrow." Lorenzo quipped.

"Now I am really getting my bayonet," Gaetano said and bent over to reach under the table behind him.

"Someone, please help me. There's a mad man with a knife," Lorenzo called out. All the men around were laughing at the show.

"Hey, remember, I can either make you look great or make you look very silly. Just one slip of the scissors and half bald," Gaetano said then looked at the men watching. He pointed back and forth to either side of Lorenzo's head with his scissors, "Let's see, bald on the right or bald on the left."

"Bald on the left," one man called out.

"No, the right," another said, "how 'bout both?

"Both? That wouldn't look silly," Lorenzo quipped, "how can you be bald on both? You would be just bald."

"You'd have a stripe of long hair running right down the middle," Gaetano answered.

"Then I was right," he chuckled, "I would look silly."

"All right raise your hands, all that want bald on the right," Gaetano said, "Hmmm...............Not bad, now all that want bald on the left......... .... Left it is."

"Doesn't anybody care about how Lorenzo will look for the ladies?" Lorenzo pleaded with a fake crying voice.

The crowd all shouted, "No!"

"What women? You haven't seen a woman since we ate at the camp near Bologna," Gaetano said, "besides you'll need more than a good haircut to get a woman to look at you, you ugly......"

"Nobody loves me," Lorenzo interrupted.

Augustino walked up during the show, "Hey both of you. The sergeant wants you both back in ten minutes for a briefing. I think we're packing it up soon."

Most of the men standing in line were glad not to have to sit through a haircut. Gaetano was still an apprentice barber, and his teacher was missing in action. Based on some of the haircuts that morning, these men were thankful for the interruption.

"How long did he say it would take? I have heads to cut," Gaetano said holding up his scissors in a threatening manner. The men scurried away pretending to be in real danger. "Hey, get back here, I'm not through with you yet." Gaetano said with a lot of chuckling. Lorenzo and Augustino joined the laughter.

"It looks like I'm out of trouble as well," Lorenzo said.

"Oh, I'll get you once we're through with the sergeant," Gaetano said, "I'm sure he wants you clean cut."

• • • •

THEY WENT BACK TO THEIR tent to meet up with the rest of the men and waited for the sergeant to come in. He was delayed for half an hour then he came in with the lieutenant. All the men jumped to their feet and stood at attention. "At ease men," Sergeant Patrizi said. They relaxed a bit but remained standing at near attention.

"You have all heard some things about moving out. Well, it's true," the lieutenant said, "Day after tomorrow we head for the Isonzo and watch the artillery pummel them until there is nothing left. Then we move in a cleanup." He stood and looked at the men for just a moment.

"Dismissed," the sergeant said and left the tent with the lieutenant.

The men stood for a moment and then started to look at each other, "That's it?" Armando said, "No big talk about serving your country and being proud? I'm disappointed." With that he walked out. The rest of the men followed slowly. Gaetano and Augustino stopped once they left the tent.

"You ready for all this?" Augustino said.

Gaetano just looked at him but did not say anything. His eyes did the talking.

• • • •

THE NEXT DAY BROUGHT a different type of training. All of the men were instructed on how to assist an artillery division. With the level of bombardments that would be implemented there would be a need for extra manpower to supply the guns. They would be going round the clock and hopefully opening a door the infantry could simply walk through without much resistance.

They received instructions on the proper handling of the different shells and which types of cannons would fire them. In order to maintain a continuous barrage of gunfire, they would need every available man to feed the gunners. Just like for some digging was a different exercise, this would tax them beyond their abilities.

At one point the men were competing to see how fast they could carry the forty-pound shells which were placed for them to practice with. Rinaldo won by a long shot. Everyone figured he would, and Rinaldo was hoping maybe they would transfer him to the artillery division. He dropped a few hints around so he might get someone to suggest it. That could keep him off the battlefield. At the end of the day, Sergeant Patrizi called him over and told him how impressed they were, and they had requested he be transferred permanently. It worked.

All the men were happy for him. If they were to lose one of their own, this was a good way to do it rather than some of the alternative ways. Rinaldo packed his things and was transferred immediately. There was not any time for a real farewell, so he just gave everyone a handshake and left.

The next morning came fast. All the men were exhausted from training with the cannon shells. It was time to load up on the trucks which had returned during the night and head to the front lines. The trip only took two hours by back roads that had not been intended for use by trucks. Horse drawn carriages were about all these roads could handle so the trucks had to take it slowly. Gaetano thought 'This time, they're definitely going to see the dust cloud.'

The Isonzo River was the barrier between the Italian Army and the Austro-Hungarian Army. As the trucks approached the area, it became very evident to the men this was going to be an uphill battle, an actual uphill battle. The river was at the base of the foothills which led to the Alps. The enemy Army was deeply entrenched and ready for anything they were going to throw at them.

On the morning of June twenty-third, they arrived at the Isonzo River. The cannons had been set up the week before. Trenches deep enough to hide several large cannons were dug over the previous month and the munitions for the first barrage were in place. As they were making the final approach in the truck, the first rounds went off. Even at the distance they were, the sound was earth shattering.

Augustino and Gaetano looked at each other but did not say a word. The rest of the men on the truck just looked back and forth at each other. This was the most intense sound they had ever heard. There had been some cannon fire at the training camp, but those had been mostly battlefield cannons which could be moved on the back of an average truck. These guns were much larger.

Sergeant Patrizi seemed to take on a new personality. He had seen war before and was better prepared than the other men. As prepared as anyone could be for the presumed carnage which was before them. The last mile was deafening. Mario looked the most frightened. Paulo appeared to be getting angry. That was how he dealt with it. Most just looked at each other and said nothing. If they had spoken, no one would hear anyway.

The barrage seemed to be nonstop. There might be an occasional lapse in gunfire. But just as nerves would begin to calm down, another barrage would begin. The men in Gaetano's truck were brought to a trench that held two large cannons. They went to work immediately transporting shells to the gunners. There was a significant supply of shells already in place, but that would not last long.

As the battle raged on for several hours, they rotated men so the first wave would be relieved. They were sent to the mess tent for a meal. It was hard to swallow. Each time one would try, another cannon went off and made them jump. There was no getting used to it. The shifts were long, and the breaks were few.

Everyone figured the shell that just went off, might take out the enemy soldier who would likely be the one who would kill you once you mounted the offensive. Carrying the shells became a bit easier with that in mind.

Nightfall came and most did not notice. How could one sleep with all of this? But they did. That level of fatigue eventually catches up with you. Gaetano and Augustino along with all the men under Sergeant Patrizi retired at midnight to get some rest for another day's constant barrage. Gaetano did not cover himself with his sleep blanket. He used it to cover his ears. It did not help very much.

Each man could only get about three or four hours of sleep. Once awoken by the cannon fire, there was no going back. Gaetano lay in the tent for two more hours unable to sleep but would doze off occasionally for brief moments.

The next day was a repeat of the first. The second night they slept for five hours. By the end of the week, they could sleep through the night as if there was nothing going on. The last two days saw a reduction in cannon fire. Partly due to supplies drying up and partly to fatigue. It was more likely though everything in range had already been hit. Or so they hoped.

On the morning of the twenty-ninth of June nineteen-fifteen, the frontal assault began. There would still be some artillery fire, but only when it was needed to support the ground effort. The men crossed over the Isonzo River and began to rush up the hillsides. The shock that came over the men was quick and to the point. It was as if there had been no artillery at all. The Austro-Hungarian Army was still in place and firing at will.

The first wave was nearly completely eliminated. The second, almost the same as they found places to take cover. The real fighting had begun. The Italians were in an unbelievably bad location for taking the hill. They had the river to their back and everything in front of them was straight uphill or worse. They had to cross the river under fire and hope to make it to the other side. The enemy was well secured, and everyone knew it. The battle should have been a success based on the numbers of men on the side of the Italian Army. It should have been enough to defeat this enemy. But the terrain was not allowing them to gain any ground.

The battle raged on for an entire week both day and night with little gain and much loss. By July seventh, Chief of Staff Cadorna ordered a cease fire and had the Armies fall back to more secure locations to regroup. Reports began to come in. They only managed to gain slightly in some regions. They took the heights near Plazzo and Mount Colowrat. There were also some slight gains made around Mount Krn. Nearly fifteen thousand men were lost in this battle for the Italian Army.

Sergeant Patrizi called for all his men to meet at one part of the camp. Many were missing. Mario had been killed along with the older Lorenzo, Gregorio, Angelo, Dino, Enrico, and Luigi. They first had thought Pierre and Anthony were killed as well, but they came a bit later because they had been separated from the others for three days and were fighting with another squad. They were told where the rest of Sergeant Patrizi's men were regrouping and found them later.

A pep talk would have been a waste of time and Sergeant Patrizi knew it. He tried to encourage the men based on their survival and the overwhelming odds, "You all held your own out there. I'm proud of each and every one of you." It was not the answer to their dilemma, but they were glad he was making an effort to acknowledge their struggles.

"So, what's next?" Gaetano asked him.

"We should be getting orders within the hour. That's how things usually work, sometimes longer," he answered.

"What good did all of those cannons do?" young Lorenzo asked, "It was as if none of them hit the targets. How can that happen?"

"It's the trenches," Paulo said, "and the hills, did you see how high those hills are? Can't call them hills. They're mountains, real mountains. How high up are we?"

"Over six thousand feet," Sergeant Patrizi said, "and the enemy is even higher. Once we take the foothills, we have some real mountain climbing to do. If you think the air is thin now, just wait until you reach ten thousand feet. I used to go that high with my Papà when I was a boy. Keep in mind. The enemy has had a year to get used to it."

"Well, that's encouraging," Augustino said, "I heard there are airplanes fighting this war. Why can't they just fly over them and drop a bunch of grenades? Wouldn't that work?"

"Not a bad idea," Gaetano added, "You know how to fly one of those things? I sure don't. Not sure I want to either. Where do you hide when they start shooting at you?"

"Well at least you can see the enemy," Augustino said with some resignation, "all I could see was a puff of smoke and a lot of dust flying. That's probably what saved my life this week. They couldn't see me through the dust clouds."

There was a relative peace at the camp. Men did not have any energy for the type of horseplay they had grown used to in training. They ate what they had and drank as much water as they could find. They tried to rest anywhere there was nothing moving. The sun was strong, and the air was dry. Gaetano remembered days like this when he was young and worked at the vineyard for Signor Rizzi. He wished he were there now so he could pop open a bottle of wine for himself. When he was younger, they would only allow him to have a bit of table wine with his dinner. And then only as much as they said he could.

But to have one of those bottles now would be heavenly. He imagined himself finishing the whole thing.

The fighting had been going on for two weeks but in some ways, it felt like only a couple of days. It went by quickly. Most of these men had never seen a battlefield. The sight of their fallen comrades was more than some could endure. But endure they must. There were no alternatives.

The next day some men started to talk about desertion. That did not go over well. They learned quickly not to say anything about that because other soldiers might report them. They would need every man to pull his weight. True they had not succeeded in their efforts to push back the enemy, but that was no excuse for cowardice.

It seemed to be forever that they did not receive their orders. Four days passed and things were almost falling into a routine again just like three weeks earlier. Gaetano went back to giving men haircuts and Augustino pulled a lot of kitchen duty.

"I'd rather do what you're doing," Gaetano told Augustino, "I'm use to restaurant work at Rocco's and like on the Hallwick."

"Yeah, but on the Hallwick, Maurice would let you eat whenever you wanted. If I get caught eating anything, it's off to the cell for the rest of the day without anything to eat until morning," Augustino complained, "It happened to a guy named Franco. He couldn't believe it. Neither could the rest of us.

A new reality had set in for them. Live going forward would be vastly different.

Chapter 20

The heat of the summer sun was both a pleasure and a burden. The men still had to do exercises to keep in fighting shape. They worked on techniques of hand-to-hand combat because they had begun to see what they were up against. Near enough to the enemy trenches, they would be soon on top of the soldiers from the Austro-Hungarian Army. The artillery would help but not accomplish the task at hand. At some point they would have to face their enemy head on.

"You think they're going to start up again in this heat?" Augustino asked.

"Same for the enemy, they're burning up too," Gaetano answered.

"I'd just as soon get to it anyway," Augustino said, "This hanging around pretending to be a soldier is getting to me."

"Yeah.............know what you mean," Gaetano added, "you on kitchen detail today?"

"Seems like every ......," he started to reply, "hey, what's that? You hear that rumble?" Augustino stood up and climbed onto the truck next to them to look. "Will you look at that?"

"Look at what?" Gaetano stood up and stretched his neck.

A convoy of cannons and munitions trucks was working its way into the camp. "These are the big ones," Augustino said, "maybe they can shoot high enough to take out some of the enemy before we have to face them again."

"I don't have much confidence in the cannons with those trenches so well dug in," Gaetano grumbled. The convoy did not go close to where they were but moved east. It was still a loud noise.

That evening the men broke loose a bit and started a game of football. Paulo was the goal tender for their tent and Gaetano played as a striker. The game only lasted a half hour. One of the men mentioned the good times playing football at the training camp in the evenings and Sunday afternoon. Once they started to talk about the men who used to play with them and that did not make it off the battlefield the week before, the fun was gone. Everyone just went back to their tents.

On the morning of July seventeenth, Sergeant Patrizi called his men to order. They were to head further west to take a slightly different approach. The attempt would be to flank the enemy if they could and penetrate what seemed to be a weak spot in their line. By noon they were loaded up onto the trucks, and on their way. They went towards Roverto where they had conducted the reconnaissance mission the month before. The truck passed right by the farmer's house where they spent one night on the mission. No one was visible to them as they passed. It was just as well. The farmer and his wife had likely headed south to be safe once they heard the artillery.

The morning of the eighteenth saw immediate action. The cannons were firing, and the men were getting ready for an assault. This time there would be no bombardments for a week leading up to the attack. The cannons rang out for three hours and the order was given. The artillery was primarily used to break apart the barbed wire barricades so the men could penetrate and rush the trenches. There, they would engage the enemy directly for the first time.

The terrain was just a bit more level allowing for the type of attack the Italians were more used to. This was intended to surprise them since the first battle had such a long bombardment first. The hope was the enemy would take the cover needed to protect themselves from the bombardment and not be aware the Italian troops were coming.

It was as if Sergeant Patrizi had a special sense for battle. He knew when to order the attack without anyone telling him that the artillery was about to cease. This man was a natural soldier and the men under him felt secure knowing he was in charge. They started for the river as the artillery was still going off. The men were not sure if it would stop before they arrived. The shells were exploding all around the riverbanks on both sides. Normally, the men would be in fear of being hit by their own side, but they had grown to trust Sergeant Patrizi. They just knew by the time they got to the edge of the Isonzo, the shelling would stop. And it did.

The river was shallow at that point, so the crossing was not difficult. The cannon fire must have been doing the intended distractions because they did not draw any fire while crossing. The hills at this location were more gradual and they seem to make some headway.

Two hundred yards past the river, they came to the first enemy position. The Italian soldiers were practically right on them by the time they first realized they were on the move. Most of Sergeant Patrizi's men jumped into the enemy trenches at about the same time and began to engage in hand-to-hand combat. They were not able to use grenades with the exception of when they first approached the trench.

If they had continued to use them, their own men would be at risk of being killed by their own grenades. Rifles and bayonets were the weapons of the hour. The fighting began with the sound of exploding shells just beyond their position which was intended to prevent reinforcements from reaching the first line of trenches. Gaetano and Sergeant Patrizi ran side by side over the hump where a shell had opened up the barbed wire just enough for two men to enter.

They had the benefit of surprise on their side this time. The Austro-Hungarian soldiers were hunkered down to weather the shelling. The first eight enemy soldiers were killed without much effort. Two of them did not even have their rifles ready. Paulo and Pierre were right behind them. Sergeant Patrizi signaled for them to turn to the left and rush up the trench. There was only room for one man at a time. Gaetano took the lead with Sergeant Patrizi right behind him. He stayed to the left so the sergeant would be able to fire to his right.

For the first twenty yards they caught the enemy off guard. They seemed to be falling quickly. Gaetano turned a corner in the trench, and they came to an opening. There they found thirty enemy soldiers. Bullets flew but seemed to miss their intended targets. The Italian soldiers were moving so quickly the enemy soldiers seemed almost confused by their tactics. The opening led to what seemed to be a command tent and mess. The men scattered some and began more hand-to-hand combat. The bayonets were in full use.

Sergeant Patrizi tapped Gaetano on the shoulder and signaled him to follow. They began to run towards what was the next trench to the left. Sergeant Patrizi mis stepped and tripped on a dead soldier. He landed his right knee on the ground and began to regain his stance when an enemy soldier jumped into the trench from above. He was not fully stabilized when the soldier was upon him. Gaetano fired but missed.

The enemy soldier hit Sergeant Patrizi with his gun butt and the sergeant fell to the side. As he tried to regain his footing, the enemy soldier pointed his rifle at him and pierced the side of his neck with his bayonet and then fired. The bullet entered right behind his left ear and Sergeant Patrizi fell instantly. Gaetano screamed, "No!!!" and proceeded to hit the enemy soldier in the head with his rifle butt. He hit him repeatedly until he did not have a head anymore.

The other men had secured the trench area where they were and saw Gaetano pounding his rifle into what remained of the soldier's head. Blood was flying everywhere, and Gaetano was screaming over and over again, "no, not him, not him." Augustino, Paulo, and Pierre came up to him and stood there. They just let him get it all out.

There was no time for pondering. More enemy soldiers were on the way, and they had to move up the line. They jumped out of the trench on the enemy side to get a sense of what was before them. Without the sergeant to guide them, they felt lost. Paulo noticed a truck with supplies on it. It was munitions and they decided to try to destroy it. Gaetano threw two grenades at it and the gas tank exploded instantly. 'That was easier than I thought it would be' he thought to himself. They proceeded to approach some tents and fired before they entered. Some were occupied but most were not.

The rest of that day and all of the next were mostly constant hand to hand combat and moving forward towards the enemy positions. Near the end of the second day, it seemed the enemy reinforcements were becoming overpowering. The decision was made to pull back to the river. They had done some damage but were unable to hold the position. The enemy knew exactly how to take back what they had lost.

Casualties were even higher than the first battle. But the only one that mattered to the men in Gaetano's squad was the sergeant who would not come back. He was their backbone and their strength. They would have to find another way to get by now.

• • • •

ONCE BACK ON THE OTHER side of the Isonzo, most of the men collapsed wherever they could find a location that was out of the way of moving trucks. They ate whatever rations they had on them and fell asleep sitting up and leaning back on trees or rocks. Some of them had fought through the night and all the previous day.

At dawn, the remaining men from Sergeant Patrizi's squad were sitting together. A lieutenant came up to them. "Where is your sergeant?" he barked.

"Out there," Paulo answered pointing across the river.

The lieutenant looked over to where he was pointing and understood their sergeant was killed across the river. "You're all with me now. Stand up and come this way," he ordered. They knew his type by now and did not hesitate to follow his orders. All of them snapped to it, grabbed what they had with them and followed the lieutenant.

There was a group of about eighty men waiting when they arrived with the lieutenant. Out of the twenty-five men who started with Sergeant Patrizi, there were only seven left. They sat where the other men were and barely said a word to them. The lieutenant went to a nearby tent and entered. After only a few minutes he emerged with a determined look on his face.

As he approached, one of the other eighty men said, "I know what that look means."

"What?" Augustino asked.

"He just volunteered us for something. I've seen it before," he replied.

The lieutenant could barely contain himself. It was as if he had the mission of the century before him. He looked determined and excited at the same time. There was a truck nearby, so he walked over to it and pulled down the tailgate. The map he was holding unfolded easily. He began to run his finger along what appeared to be the Isonzo River.

"Right there!" he said pointing and tapping the map hard with his index finger, "That's where we go."

Gaetano was close enough to see. It was about three miles to the west. There was what appeared to be a gorge or a deep ravine which led into the hills from the river.

"Our reconnaissance of this area shows there is little activity in this ravine. That is where we will go and flank the enemy," the lieutenant said.

Gaetano took a closer look at it and thought he recognized it. This was the pass where they had begun to go into on their reconnaissance mission. They had seen about fifty enemy soldiers and some trucks. This had not been unoccupied just a month before. He hoped the enemy had relocated since he was there last. He hoped the lieutenant's information was correct.

The order was given, and they moved out right away. They kept south of the river to avoid detection. There was a squad of soldiers resting by the roadside while they passed. "Any activity up that way," one of the eighty asked.

"You must be kidding. There all over this area," one of the soldiers resting said.

"That's just great," Augustino grumbled.

By noon, they reached the place where they could cross the river. It seemed narrow but deep. This would be the place for them to cross. The deep nature of this location made it a less likely place to cross so it would be less guarded. It would work to their advantage. One man swam across with a rope tied to him. He secured the rope to a boulder on his side. The rope was then secured to a tree on the south side. This was because not all of the men could swim. The rope would guide them across.

They formed loops from their belts and hooked them around the rope. They could slide across that way without sinking or being swept away. There were almost ninety men in the group. They managed to cross quickly. Some swam since the currents were not strong there. The key was to keep your rifle dry. Not all men did. Some of the men knew how to slide their rifle along the rope so it would not touch the water. As they reached the other side the lieutenant ordered the men to inspect their rifles. They checked to see if they were dry and if not, they needed to clean and dry them quickly so they could move on.

Gaetano and Augustino were able to keep their rifles dry, but Paulo slipped, and his rifle went underwater. "All that training is paying off," he said as he rapidly disassembled his rifle. "I didn't understand why we had to do this in less than five minutes. Guess I know now." Paulo said. He was one of the first to succeed in meeting the timeline during their training.

"This is the ravine we scoped out," Gaetano whispered to Augustino.

"What did you find?" Augustino asked.

"About fifty soldiers and trucks that looked ready to restock an outpost," he replied.

"Outpost?" Augustino asked, "what kind of outpost?"

"Don't know. We didn't get close enough," Gaetano said wishing they had.

"Think you should tell the lieutenant?" Augustino said showing his concern.

"Not sure if he wants to hear something like that. Let's see what we come up with." Gaetano said as he shrugged his shoulders.

"I think you should tell him. I'll go with you," Augustino added.

Gaetano hesitated for a moment, "Guess you're right, let's go." They walked over to where the lieutenant was standing. "Signor?"

"What do you want?" he snapped at them.

"Signor, I came to tell you something," Gaetano said beginning to think this was a bad idea.

"Well? I don't have all day. Out with it," he barked again.

"Signor, my sergeant took a squad of us to this area for reconnaissance about a month ago and we entered this ravine," he said confidently.

"And?" the lieutenant sneered.

"Well Signor, we came across about fifty enemy soldiers and some trucks the sergeant said looked as if they were restocking an outpost of some kind," Gaetano continued.

"Did you pursue the enemy and destroy the outpost?" he sneered even more.

"No Signor, the sergeant said we were under orders not to engage but report back to the captain," Gaetano added knowing this was not going well.

"Your sergeant was a coward. When you get that close to the enemy you engage them," he said with a tone of disdain.

"Ah Yes Signor. Just thought I would report. Thank you, Signor," Gaetano said hoping he could turn around and leave.

"Well maybe you'll get a chance to make up for his failed decision," he sneered again.

"Yes Signor," Gaetano said and turned to leave hoping he would not say anything more. Fortunately, someone else came over to talk to the lieutenant so Gaetano and Augustino slipped away. They were infuriated by his comments. The coward he talked about was their respected Sergeant Patrizi.

Ten minutes later they were given the order to move out. Paulo had finished cleaning his rifle and was ready. Two other soldiers nearby were not quite ready and did not seem to be able to put their rifles back together. Paulo helped them both and reassembled the first one in less than one minute. The other just needed adjustments, so he did that once they started walking.

Because of that, Paulo, and the rest of the remnant from Sergeant Patrizi's outfit were near the back of the line. The ravine was wide at first just as Gaetano remembered it. He thought maybe they could go by way of the alternate route they had used the previous month. But it was obvious the lieutenant was not open to suggestions.

Two miles into the ravine, it began to narrow. They were past the point where Gaetano was familiar with so it was now a guessing game as to when they might find the enemy. It was extremely hot and dry. It had not rained in over two weeks. The ground was hard and dusty. Gaetano was glad he had filled his canteen at the river. So was Augustino who had finished half of his.

The lieutenant's plan was to have four soldiers take the point and the rest come up about fifty yards behind. This would give the lieutenant some warning if the enemy were nearby without exposing all the men at once. It was almost three o'clock when the unthinkable happened. The four soldiers who were walking ahead walked right into a trap. They walked up through a relatively narrow part of the ravine and then into what appeared to be a small clearing.

Once they were all in the clearing, a large machine gun began to fire on their position. Because they were all in the clearing, none of them made it to cover. It took less than ten seconds for them to all fall. The rest of the men dove into the brush and looked for any protection they could find. They were not in any immediate danger since they were not yet in range and the enemy in the machine gun nest had not seen them. The lieutenant's plan had worked, sort of. But cost the lives of four men.

Chapter 21

There was no hiding the fact there were more soldiers behind the four. The lieutenant ordered twenty men to take up a position where they could see the machine gun nest but not be in any direct danger. The report came back. It was a pillbox built into the hillside with a small opening in the front. Giving little option for attack. This was obviously a very secure setup for the enemy and both sides knew it.

Everyone else moved forward to be a bit closer. Each man took a turn to look above the hillside and see the layout. There was no place to hide once you entered the clearing where the dead soldiers were. There appeared to be somewhere to take cover about twenty-five yards to the left, past the clearing. But getting there seemed impossible. Four men had fallen within ten seconds of being fired upon.

The lieutenant wasted no time ordering two men to try to make it to the point of cover. The order given was for the twenty men who were posted in view of the machine gun nest, to fire on it while they made their way to the first point of cover. Gaetano and Augustino watched as the two ventured out. They could see the men, but neither of them was in the sights of the enemy.

The signal was given to provide cover fire, and the two men ran out into the clearing. The rifles of the Italian soldiers were not powerful enough to make any impact on the enemy machine gun. Some of the bullets reached the area but most fell short. The machine gun was nearly over hundred yards away, But the sound it made seemed almost as loud as some of the cannons they had become used to. The difference was, they could see the instant results of the machine gun. The cannons did their damage too far away to see.

The two soldiers did not make it more than ten yards when they were cut down. Immediately, the lieutenant grabbed two more men and ordered them to run out into the clearing. They must have thought the enemy might need to reload because they did not hesitate. They ran out and did not make it any farther than the previous two.

Then the lieutenant ordered one man at a time to go out. Five men ran out to their immediate deaths. Then there was a short lull in the action. The men were hoping the lieutenant was contemplating a change of strategy. He began to walk up and down the line of men who were laying low for cover.

The lieutenant grabbed Augustino and pulled him up. "You next," he screamed.

Augustino leaned away from him, and his street attitude took over, "Signor, this isn't working," he cried, "we should go around them. They'll kill us all."

The lieutenant shoved him toward the opening to the clearing and said, "Coward, you will obey orders."

Augustino continued to resist, "But Signor, there must be a better way."

The lieutenant pulled out his pistol and screamed at him, "follow orders coward."

Augustino began to plead with him, "but Signor."

The lieutenant pushed him forward and put the pistol to the back of his head and screamed for all to hear including the enemy, "Move!"

Augustino just froze.

The sound of the lieutenant's pistol going off was much louder than any cannon fire they had ever heard. It seemed like slow motion to Gaetano as he saw his friend fall forward and his blood shoot out of the front of his head. All the men stopped and stared at the lieutenant. No one dared to say anything.

The lieutenant panned back and forth, "Are there any more cowards?" the lieutenant screamed, "Are there anymore?" Still, no one dared to speak. He grabbed another man and pushed him forward. The man nearly tripped on Augustino's lifeless body as he just looked down at him with total fear.

The soldier reached the opening in the rocks where the clearing was and hesitated for a moment. He turned and began to ask the lieutenant, "Can't we......"

The lieutenant screamed and pointed his pistol at the soldier, "Cowards, you are all cowards."

The soldier ran out in fear that the lieutenant's aim at close range was probably better than the enemy's from over fifty yards away. He ran in a zig zag pattern hoping to avoid the machine gun. The bullets hit the dirt in front of him, and he dodged them for some time. Gaetano noticed the bullets hitting the dirt were kicking up a great deal of dust. It began to form a bit of a cloud.

For a brief time, the soldier was able to avoid the bullets because the dust was getting thick. But to no avail. About five yards short of the first point of cover he fell. He was not killed but he could not run because both of his legs had been shot. He cried out for help, 'Shut up,' Gaetano thought to himself. The machine gun opened fire again and finished him.

'How many more are going to have to die?' Gaetano thought to himself as he looked at Augustino lying on the ground. He thought for a moment and looked around at the area around the clearing. Then he thought to himself. 'Dust.......... dust, I've been choking on it for three months. Lots of dust.'

Gaetano ran up to the lieutenant and called to him, "Signor!" The lieutenant turned to him with his pistol in hand and Gaetano was not sure if he was getting ready to use it on him. "Signor. I have a plan," he said not giving the lieutenant a chance to speak.

"Each man has two grenades with him, right?" Gaetano said almost out of breath continuing the verbal takeover. The lieutenant nodded, not certain what to make of this private coming at him. "Give me more grenades. As many as I can carry," he said starting to grab all of the men around him to take their grenades. The lieutenant stood there and did not say anything. He had never seen this type of behavior before, and it was taking him by surprise.

"Signor. Order the men with rifles to fire at the ground just beyond the clearing, as much as they can, please Signor just order it," he said frantically as he continued to grab grenades from anyone nearby. By now, he had over sixteen grenades hanging from his straps and belt.

Gaetano rushed up to the opening just before the clearing and gave the signal he was ready. The lieutenant hesitated but then told the soldiers to do what Gaetano had asked. It all was happening so fast the lieutenant did not have time to think about it. The men started to fire at the ground just beyond the clearing and with that Gaetano pulled the pin out of one of the grenades and threw it as far as he could trying to miss any of the men who had fallen just in case any were still alive.

The grenade exploded and kicked up a dust cloud. Gaetano ran out towards it at the same time pulling the pin on another grenade. He ran fifty feet and threw the other grenade towards the right side of the ravine. He had run into the dust cloud which the first grenade created and was between the first and second. The machine gun fire was nonstop but ineffective. Gaetano did the same zig zag approach as the previous soldier but with the dust cloud to hide in, he managed to avoid getting shot.

The other Italian soldiers could not see him because the dust cloud from the first grenade was still lingering. Gaetano threw a third grenade to his left but ran to the right. The machine gun fired into the dust cloud which the third grenade caused. While the machine gunners were watching the left side to see when he would appear Gaetano ran up the right side of the ravine.

They had not seen him and continued to fire into the area where the third grenade went off. Gaetano dove into a spot behind a short brush about twenty-five feet up the side of the hill and stopped. There were some boulders as well which had rolled down the hillside.

The machine gun fired some more, and the Italian riflemen continued for a bit. No one knew where Gaetano was, including the lieutenant. "He must have been killed," he said to his assistant, "But he had the right idea."

The firing stopped on both sides. Gaetano was safe for the moment but knew he could not stay there. The lieutenant ordered the rifles to fire again and two men ran out throwing grenades as Gaetano had. They were not as careful to avoid the fallen men. One landed in the midst of them, making certain of their demise. While they were being fired upon, Gaetano made a run for it to see if he could get up higher on the side of the ravine. He dared to look up long enough to see that from where he was, the machine gunner likely could not see him. He began to crawl towards their position.

The next two men were in the clearing trying to get to the point of cover. One made it, but the other fell to machine gun fire. Gaetano crawled more and faster. It was mostly rock where he was, and he was not stirring up any dust. The man who had reached cover was pinned down. He was thankful for not only having cover, but also for being far enough away from the lieutenant. More men tried to make it to his position, but none made it. The count was up to nineteen dead, including Augustino.

The lieutenant had finally decided to rethink his strategy. He did not send out any men for a few minutes which was a mixed blessing for Gaetano. The man who made it to the point of cover was looking back to see if anyone was coming. It was a few minutes before Gaetano realized things were on hold. He thought for a moment and then decided to try something. He was hiding behind a small rock formation on the side of the ravine.

There were several rocks around him and some dry clay which had rolled down from uphill. He remembered as a boy, he and his friends would play soldier. They would throw what they called dirt bombs at each other. They were dried clumps of clay which were laying around where they played. When they hit the rocks, they would create a puff of what looked like smoke, thus the name smoke bomb. He was hoping he was far enough away from the machine gun nest so they would not see where it came from. He grabbed a handful of small clumps of clay and threw a couple down into the base of the ravine.

They fell just behind some rocks and created the puff he had remembered. The machine gunner figured someone was running in that area and began to fire. With that, Gaetano pulled the pin on another grenade and threw it forward of where the dirt bombs had landed giving the impression the supposed soldier who had created the puff of dust was throwing the grenade. This resulted in everyone firing their weapons. The lieutenant thought it was the man taking cover at the other side of the clearing who started this and ordered the men with rifles to cease fire until he could calculate another plan.

While the guns were firing, Gaetano managed to gain another fifteen feet slightly uphill and much closer to the machine gun nest. He could make out the shape of the pillbox now and realized the closer he got, the harder it was for them to see him. But he still needed a distraction. He was not sure if the dirt bomb trick would work again but he had to try since there was not much activity behind him. Once again, he grabbed as many clumps of dried clay as he could pick up with one hand and threw them.

They hit some rocks but did not make much of a puff this time. He worried maybe they were on to him, but nothing. Gaetano peeked up for just a moment to see the pillbox. The enemy soldiers inside were visible to him. It was now or never. He decided to try his trick one more time with just a single large clump of clay. It flew through the air, and he prayed they did not see where it came from. If they saw him now, it was all over.

He could not run back, and it was only him out there. So, he would be no match for the machine gun or even a group of soldiers with their rifles. There was only one solution. The large clump of clay hit the side of a boulder. This time the machine gun opened fire on where the puff came up at the base of the ravine.

While they were firing, Gaetano decided to throw one more grenade down into the ravine. It must have been the enemy never considered someone could be where Gaetano was because they did not see the grenade come down from the right side of the ravine. It exploded and created the largest dust cloud thus far.

The obvious thing to Gaetano was the enemy soldiers in the pillbox were getting nervous about where this grenade had come from. They were firing at anything and everything in the area of the last grenade. The lieutenant could see the grenade go off and knew it could not be the soldier who was taking cover at the end of the clearing. He ordered the men with rifles to shoot at the ground beyond the clearing to create a distraction.

With that opportunity, Gaetano made a dash further uphill and towards the pillbox. He was twenty yards, fifteen yards, ten........ Then he saw one of the soldiers in the pillbox look his way. He ducked in behind a boulder to his right. This had to be it. They had to have seen him. The rifles kept firing from behind him, and the machine gun was roaring at full capacity. It seemed there were no bullets hitting anywhere near him. It was possible he had maintained his effort to remain unnoticed. 'Do I look?' he thought. 'No choice now.'

He popped his head around the boulder, but the enemy soldier was not looking at him because he had moved slightly back into the pillbox. Gaetano could not see any of them directly, but he could hear them now. They were speaking in German in an obvious panic. Gaetano figured they were talking about where this mystery soldier must be. Not only was the machine gun firing but also the three other soldiers in the pillbox were firing their rifles into the area where the last grenade had gone off.

Gaetano knew it was now or never. He paused for just a moment to think about his Mamma and Papà back home. If he did not make this happen, they would never see him again. Then he thought of his Nonna and wondered if word had made it to her, he was not coming. And then he thought of Augustino. Augustino was just a scared kid. Life had not dealt him a good hand, and he certainly deserved better than what he got. This was going to be for Augustino.

His rifle was still strapped to his back. He had not taken it off since he ran out. There were nine grenades left. Gaetano grabbed two off his strap and pulled the pin out of the one in his right hand holding the other in his left. 'One more look.................. Clear,' he thought.

Gaetano ran around the right side of the boulder and made a dash for the last ten yards to the base of the pillbox. The sound of the machine gun firing nonstop covered any noise he made. The opening of the pillbox was about twelve inches high and four feet wide. It was eight feet off the ground. He stood less than six feet tall with a reach of about twenty more inches. The grenade would have to go in first shot. If he missed the grenade would likely kill him instead.

With a slight hop up, he threw the grenade, and it went right in. He heard a shout from the enemy soldiers inside and then an explosion. At the same time, he pulled the pin from the second grenade and threw it in the same way. It too went right in and exploded.

Then there was silence.

The firing had stopped from inside the pillbox and also from the Italian soldiers. Gaetano ran around to the other side of the pillbox. As he stepped around, he drew his rifle to his front and got ready for whatever was before him. A dazed enemy soldier was coming around trying to make sense of what had happened.

They came face to face and Gaetano plunged his bayonet into his stomach and fired one shot. The man went down. Gaetano continued to run to the other side of the pillbox. Two other soldiers were there and obviously not expected to see an Italian soldier that close. He fired at both, striking them. One was killed right away from the shot to his chest and the other was shot in the arm. Gaetano rushed him as he was reaching for his pistol, and Gaetano plunged his bayonet into him just below his left ribcage.

It was over. There were no more enemy soldiers in the area that Gaetano could tell. These men must have just been all there were at this outpost. It must have been placed there to prevent anyone from getting into the next region. Gaetano went back around to the front of the pillbox where he knew the others could see him and waved back and forth with his helmet. One of the men with rifles saw him and called out to the lieutenant.

The lieutenant ordered twenty men to rush to where Gaetano was and help him in verifying all of the enemy soldiers were subdued. Gaetano leaned up against the front of the pillbox and slid down to a seated position. He watched as the other men came running up the ravine and up the hill to meet him. The one who was the most relieved was the soldier who had made it past the clearing and had been pinned down. He stood up and began to jump up and down. Then he ran to where Gaetano was to thank him.

Within five minutes most of the other men had made it up to where he was. They verified all the enemy soldiers were dead and there were no others in the area. The lieutenant ordered a perimeter be set up to protect the men as they examined Gaetano's handy work.

Gaetano got up to meet the men and they all gave him a pat on the back and a hung. He was in a daze and did not really want any of it. He walked back down the hill and along the ravine to the clearing. As he passed some of the soldiers who he had taken grenades from, he handed them one or two back and said, "thanks for the grenades." And that was it.

He walked by the dead soldiers in the clearing looking down at them as he passed hoping maybe at least one would still be alive. There were none. Then he walked around the rocks to the hiding place on the other side of the opening where he had been. Fifty feet back was Augustino. He paused for quite some time and then walked over to him. Augustino was lying on his stomach with his head turned to the left. Gaetano knelt next to him and touched his back. Then he turned and sat next to him.

He grabbed Augustino's shoulder and pulled him over holding him on his lap. He did not care that Augustino's blood was getting all over his uniform. It mixed in with the blood of the soldier who had killed Sergeant Patrizi. Gaetano began to cry.

Men were walking past him but, saying nothing. Half an hour went by. Eventually Gaetano stopped crying and just sat there with Augustino on his lap. He heard someone walking towards him but did not acknowledge him. It was the lieutenant standing in front of him. Gaetano eventually looked up at him but did not say a word.

The lieutenant stared at him for a moment and then said, "He got what he deserved."

Gaetano paused, thinking of all of all the things he could say but said nothing.

"He was a coward," the lieutenant spewed.

Gaetano looked up at him. The evening sun was in his eyes, and the lieutenant was partially blocking it. He thought further for a moment and then said, "he was my friend."

> > >

Chapter 22

Tom was just returning from the restroom with one of the guards. He saw the clock on the wall which said eleven forty-five. His breakfast was not particularly good that morning, so he kept drinking coffee they set up in the room. This was his third trip to the restroom. The previous one was at nine thirty. By now he was getting hungry and hoped since Signor Marcellino was in the interrogation room, maybe lunch would be coming, and it might be palatable.

They escorted him back to his seat still facing the mirror. Signor Marcellino had left while he was in the restroom. Tom was glad no one was present. At least that he could see. Likely there were still observers behind the mirror. He needed a moment to compose himself. Many of these memories had been buried for most of his life and the thought of reliving some of them was troubling. But he realized he was actually all right. The years had brought a resolution about it all. Still though....

The door to the interrogation room opened and a tall lady brought in a tray. She set it down on the table and left. Shortly after, she returned with two bottles of sparkling water and set them down as well. Tom was not sure if he should thank her since she had not told him whether or not any of it was for him. For all he knew, he would be escorted back to his holding cell and given the required thirty minutes to consume his rations. He hoped not.

Ten or twelve minutes passed, and the door opened again. Signor Marcellino entered looking more worn out than Tom. Tom had been doing all the talking and could not understand why he looked so tired. Then again, Signor Marcellino was not a very talkative person. Maybe Tom was better off that way.

"You spoke of your being recruited reluctantly," Signor Marcellino said which surprised Tom, "Would you have enlisted if things had been different?"

"I often wondered that," Tom answered, "I'm not sure. You can't see a decision like that after you've seen what was to be. Knowing what it was like................ probably not."

"What if you had stayed in America, would you have joined the Army there," he asked.

"I would have been drafted if I had stayed in America," Tom answered, "Most of the guys I knew when I lived there during the early teens were. I had a good friend, Steven. His girlfriend tried to set me up with her friend just before I left for Italy, but I didn't have time meet her. Can't remember her name now, how 'bout that." Tom paused for a moment and chuckled. Then his face grew long, "Steven was killed in France. We didn't know for certain, but the story was he was gassed."

"What was the lieutenant's name?" he asked Tom.

Tom was not certain why he was asking. He put a very stern look on his face and said, "I will never speak his name. It would bring shame to his family."

Signor Marcellino just stared as usual. He had done more talking in the last two minutes than he had done all morning. "They brought lunch. Help yourself," he said pulling the cover off the tray. Tom looked at the tray but realized he was not really hungry anymore. Signor Marcellino reached over and took some bread and began to make a sandwich. This did not seem like a typical lunch in Italy, it looked as though they had intentionally prepared something more American for Tom. He decided to try and eat something anyway figuring he may not get a chance to later. It may be a long afternoon.

• • • •

ANNA HAD COME TO THE hotel early, to take Maria to breakfast. But when she arrived Maria told her she had already gone to the café on the street. "I'll join you even though I've had my breakfast. I could get another cup of tea," she said.

They went down to the same café and took a table on the sidewalk. "Did you rest last night Maria?" Anna asked.

"I hate to admit it but, yes, I did. They have a whirlpool tub in the room, and I decided to pamper myself. Something told me that's what Tom would tell me to do, so I did," Maria said with a smile.

"That's terrific, I was worried about you. I can't imagine what you must be going through," Anna said as she patted her on the left hand.

"Last night I had a peace about it all. I just know that everything will work itself out," Maria sighed.

"But still, we have to take care of business," Anna replied because she was not feeling the same peace as Maria. "I got a call from the lawyer's office this morning before I left the house. He will be ready to meet us just after eleven. There may be some last-minute distractions they told me. But not to worry. We'll get to spend the time needed. His secretary said he will work through his lunch to meet with us if he has to."

Maria did not want to get shaken up about it. She knew if she were going to get through this, she would have to keep a positive attitude. So, she just nodded her head in agreement.

Anna had her car with her, so she drove Maria to the law office. They went right by the government building where Tom had been taken into custody and was being held. Maria had a sinking feeling as they passed the building. She tapped Anna and pointed to the building. "That's it, that's where they took Tom," she said. Anna just glanced over at it. She was familiar with the area but had never taken notice of that particular building before. Maria turned her head after they had passed the building and could not help looking until it was no longer in sight. 'Hold on Tom,' she said under her breath.

Traffic was rather heavy after passing the government building. What could have taken ten minutes on a day when the traffic was light, took over thirty minutes. Anna was familiar with driving in Rome, so she made certain they allowed plenty of time to reach the lawyer's office. It took them four times around the block to find a parking spot on the street. It was a side street just eight blocks from the office. "They say if you can get a parking spot within ten blocks of where you're going in Rome, you must have connections," Anna said jokingly.

Maria started to get nervous as they walked up the stairs to the office. Anna could tell and put her arm around her to give her support. The office was at the end of a long corridor on the third floor. There were double doors and the windows on the doors were opaque. The name of the law firm was stenciled on the glass. It read Carlo Rossetti Procuratore.

The office looked quite impressive. That is part of what makes a lawyer effective. The image that is presented in the office when you first arrive. It gives the impression this lawyer gets results. In contrast, when you go to see a lawyer, whose office is a two-room rental over a tailor shop with no name on the door and no receptionist, you know you have a problem.

Anna did all the talking with the receptionist. Maria understood every word even though the dialect was different, and they spoke rather fast. Maria and Tom always spoke Italian in the home, even with their children and friends. But this setting was different. For Anna and the receptionist, this was their first language. All the expressions they used were a bit unfamiliar. Maria was able to follow along though.

They waited in the lobby for thirty minutes because they were about ten minutes early and the suspected delays which Anna had been warned about had indeed taken place. It was about eleven twenty when they were shown into Signor Rossetti's office. Anna introduced herself and dropped the name of the lawyer who had recommended Signor Rossetti. He was all smiles when she turned to Maria. "Questa è Maria Santorini da America," she said to him in Italian.

Signor Rossetti smiled and greeted her in Italian as well. Maria assured him she could speak Italian fluently, but it was now her second language and if he could please excuse any errors she might make with her American dialect. This resulted in some laughs and smiles which helped Maria to relax a bit. Anna began to tell him what had happened to Tom two days before. "Quale hai detto che era il suo nome?" he asked still speaking Italian.

"Signor Gaetano Santorini," Anna responded.

Signor Rossetti suddenly leaned back in his chair and looked very confused. "Gaetano Santorini? Il famoso Gaetano Santorini sappiamo tutti?"

Maria looked even more confused. She understood that. 'Famous?' she thought to herself. "Signor, I think this person they say Tom is impersonating is a different man with the same name," she said in English and then Anna translated.

"Well, if that is true, then we should have no problem convincing them," he said and Anna again translated, "I will have my office make an appointment for tomorrow morning about this time."

Maria's face dropped. She had hoped he would be able to go today. Tom had been there for almost two whole days, and she was running short on patience. "Is there anything that can be done today?" she asked him. Even without translating he knew what she was asking.

"No Signora, my schedule if full today. I will have my office call this afternoon though," he said sadly knowing it was not what she wanted to hear.

Anna hurried things along because she understood every law firm bills by the hour. Maria knew that also but was motivated a bit differently. They left the office by twelve o'clock.

• • • •

ANNA KNEW THE REST of the day would be troublesome for Maria. No news in this case was not good news. She could see the look on Maria's face of despair. "I know what you need," Anna said as they exited the building, "You need to shop."

Maria did not really feel like shopping but figured it might take her mind off things for a while. "I had wanted to go shopping while I was in Rome, but I didn't want to drag Tom with me," she said, "I had planned to go one afternoon if he wanted to nap. Things sure have changed, haven't they?"

"That they have," Anna said, "That they have. Let's get a quick lunch and then we hit the stores. I know just the place for the best prices."

The shops Anna took her to were priced way out of her pocketbook. These were similar to some of the New York stores she had always wished she could shop in. 'Maybe someday' she would think to herself whenever she was tempted to go into one of them while she and Tom were on the other side of the river walking down Fifth Avenue.

"This looks like it wants to be on your head," Anna said holding up an expensive looking hat, "It looks just right for you. What do you think? Try it."

Maria did not want to spoil it. Two girls shopping can be a lot of fun. She had gone shopping with friends before and tried on hats which she could not afford. It was always good for a morale boost.

"No, I don't think so," Anna commented, "look in the mirror, what do think?" Maria was in agreement this one was not for her. "How about this hat?"

They spent about forty-five minutes looking at most of the ones on display. None of them suited her. It was not a problem though. It was the shopping, not the buying that mattered. Anna was keeping a close eye on Maria, hoping she was being distracted long enough to get her mind off of things. Most of the high-end stores were close together and they went into at least ten of them. Some were boutiques and some were larger stores much like the department stores Maria was used to in New York.

It was getting close to five o'clock and Maria realized she was quite tired. "We should head back to the hotel," Maria said.

"I was thinking, why don't you come to my house and join us for dinner tonight," Anna said hoping she would accept.

"Thank you so much but I was hoping to hear from Tony tonight to see what your cousin Joe was able to find out through the consulate," Maria said regretfully.

"I could call Joe from my house. We could find out then," she added.

"I would rather talk to Tony if you don't mind. Thank you though," Maria said as she touched her hand, "he might worry if he tries to call the hotel and I'm not there."

"That's fine," Anna said, "You need your rest too. Any further thoughts on coming to stay with us?"

"Tony and I spoke yesterday, and he thinks it's a good idea," Maria said, "hopefully I can talk with Tom tomorrow and get his feelings on it. If so, maybe Saturday? Would that be all right? You're probably right the hotel bill will get out of hand fast." She did not volunteer that Tony had offered to pay for the hotel. But she also did not want to take advantage of the favor either.

Anna drove her back to the hotel, but it took a long time. It was the end of the business day and traffic was the heaviest Maria had seen since coming to Rome. Anna purposely took a different route so as not to go past the government building again. She said it would save some time and have less traffic that way. It was not really true, but it was probably best. Maria had been distracted enough to get it off her mind for a while. Driving past the building would likely undo all of that.

"Would you like me to stay with you for dinner?" Anna asked.

"Thank you but I would like to be alone this evening," Maria replied, "I'll get something light at the café where I ate breakfast. I like it there, probably eat inside though. It'll be quieter. Tony will call by eight, I think. I should be back to my room by then."

"All right then," Anna agreed, "I'll drop you off in front. Are you sure you don't need me to go in with you to make sure you're settled?"

"Oh no, I'll be fine. This place is getting familiar now," Maria smiled.

"Hey, maybe you can pamper yourself again tonight. Use it while you can," Anna chuckled.

"That I will, I assure you. Thank you again so much for everything today. I wouldn't have been able to do any of it on my own," Maria said solemnly.

"I'll call you tomorrow early afternoon to see how you're doing, all right? Maybe we'll have heard something by then," Anna said as Maria was closing the car door.

The window was open, and Maria leaned in. "Have a good night, and thank you again," she said and watched as Anna drove away. Maria went up to her room briefly before going to dinner.

As she said, her dinner was light. She ordered a small side of pasta with olive oil and a house salad. That with a bit of bread and Maria was set for the evening. It was after seven thirty when she headed back to her room. As she walked past the front desk the clerk called her over. "There is a message for you, person to person call from New York. The operator asked for us to call back when you arrive so she can connect you with a Signor DiDonato. Shall I call right away, or would you like to get settled in before I call?"

"Just give me five minutes to get into my room and then I can take the call. I can get settled afterwards," she said and thanked him.

A few minutes passed once she was back in the room. Then the phone rang. "Person to person for Maria Santorini please," the operator said.

"Yes operator, I can take the call, thank you," she answered, "Tony? What did Joe say? Did he get any help from the consulate?"

"Well Maria," Tony said with a sigh. "The news wasn't good........."

< < <

Chapter 23

S till under the command of the lieutenant, Gaetano, and the remnant from Sergeant Patrizi's squad had been patrolling the valleys and ravines for three days. Along with the rest of the outfit which had at one point been eighty men strong, they were constantly reminded of the risk of attack from another machine gun nest. Occasionally they would encounter enemy resistance but nothing substantial. So, the lieutenant decided to head back to the base camp where they had set out from.

From what they saw on the map, they had been mostly circling around with the intent of flanking the enemy once a battle had started. The plan was to be positioned to attack from a direction where the enemy would not expect. The sounds of gunfire were at a significant distance. It became obvious this mission was not accomplishing what it was supposed to.

The men were frustrated and disappointed. To have been able to surprise the enemy in that way would have been a boost for the campaign. With the loss of men at the ravine, the ability to effectively surprise the enemy was lost as well. The remaining number of soldiers would not be able to have the impact that ninety would have had. The enemy machine gun nest had done its job. Even if Gaetano did manage to take them out.

The men left from Sergeant Patrizi's squad were Gaetano, Paulo, Pierre, the younger Lorenzo, Nevio, Anthony, Tomaso, Armando, and Valentino. They stuck together like a fraternity during the mission. Paulo tried to keep an eye on Gaetano to see how he was holding up. He had been the one to go through the worst of it thus far. They returned to the base camp midday, Saturday the twenty-fourth.

The lieutenant went straight to the captain's tent to report not much had transpired, with the exception of the overtaking of the machine gun nest and how it happened. While he was there, Paulo brought the remnant together for a talk. "We have to get away from this madman," he said to the others, "he's gonna get us all killed if we ever see the enemy again."

"How can we?" Nevio asked, "he said we were with him now."

"You're not talking about desertion, are you?" Armando chimed in, "I'm not doing that."

"No, nothing like that," Paulo said, "anybody says anything we just say we thought he only needed us for the mission, and we went off to find the rest of our outfit once we got back."

"That could work," Tomaso jumped in, "I like that idea. Anything to get us away from that lunatic, what do you think Gaetano?"

Gaetano had not been doing too much talking the previous couple of days. The others were concerned but completely understood what it must have felt like to do what he did. "Whatever it takes, just get me away from him," he muttered.

As they were talking Nevio noticed a soldier walking about twenty yards away. He was a large, formidable man. "Rinaldo!" he called out.

"Rinaldo? Where?" Lorenzo said, looking around.

Rinaldo turned to see who was calling his name. Once he saw his old mates he ran over to where they were. "Hey, what are you guys doing here?" he yelled, "I haven't seen you guys for over a month. Where's the sergeant?" he could tell by the sudden silence that the news would not be good. "When?" he asked.

"Last week when we went over the wire and into the enemy trench," Pierre said, "he was one tough guy."

He looked at Gaetano and asked, "What about Augustino?" knowing they were good friends.

"Hey, how's your sister Rinaldo?" Valentino interrupted, "still as pretty as ever?" He walked over to him and put his arm around him. "You gotta let me go out with her sometime. I'll be good, I promise." Rinaldo caught on right away. He dropped it quickly and figured he would find out later.

"You still in artillery?" Anthony asked.

"No, they didn't need me anymore so I'm with a new outfit," Rinaldo answered. "we're right over there behind those trucks. They say we move out today to head further east for a big push down river."

"There's our outfit boys," Paulo exclaimed.

"What do you mean?" Rinaldo looked confused, "Aren't you in an outfit?"

"Not anymore," he laughed, "let's get out of here before that lunatic comes back."

"I'm with you," Pierre snapped.

"We all are," Nevio added.

They followed Rinaldo to his outfit, and he introduced them to his sergeant. "These guys were with Sergeant Patrizi like I was before getting transferred. They're lose now since he was killed. Can we take 'em?"

The sergeant looked them up and down and thought for a bit, "We could use all the help we can get. You're not assigned?"

"No sergeant," Paulo said, "we had a short mission for about four days, but nothing official."

"All right then, fall in. We leave right away," he looked over at Gaetano and noticed the blood all over his uniform, "Looks like you've seen some action."

Gaetano did not say anything. He looked down at his uniform and noticed it was not tight on him anymore. Just three months prior, he had a tough time with the buttons. Now it was a bit loose and starting to tear in places. The return trip across the river did not wash away all of the blood either.

As the men walked away, Tomaso kept turning around to make sure no one was aware they were leaving. "What if they come looking for us?" he said to Paulo.

"Just remember what I said and play stupid. Oh, I'm sorry I didn't know. I thought you guys were done with us. I didn't know," Paulo said with a silly voice to make himself sound stupid. Tomaso and Nevio laughed.

"Hey Rinaldo," Valentino asked, "What did you say the sergeant's name was?"

"I probably didn't tell you guys his name, did I?" Rinaldo said somewhat apologetically, "It's Sergeant Grillo. I don't know his first name."

"Grillo eh?" Tomaso said, "How well do you know him?"

"Not very well. Not as well as we knew Sergeant Patrizi," Rinaldo answered.

All this time Gaetano had not been saying anything. He looked up at them and they were all surprised to see him chiming in. "Best if you don't get to know him. Easier that way," he said. The comment made the conversation change its tone quickly. The others realized there were still tough times ahead and no one knew who would make it out alive............. if any of them.

They stayed together and got on the same truck with eight other soldiers. Gaetano went back to being quiet. It took until they were over the first hill for Tomaso to stop looking back to see if anyone noticed them leaving. The drive was not long. It was over two hours through some of the roughest roads in the region. Unlike the first long drive from the training camp, the men were glad to have a seat and a ride. It was sure better than walking the entire way.

Fortunately, they arrived at the next location just in time to eat at a mess tent. The men who were on the mission with the lieutenant had been on rations for days and the smell of boiled potatoes was like heaven to them. They were let off and told they could go right to dinner but needed to meet by the trucks immediately after they had something to eat. They were given just a half hour.

The potatoes were good, but they could not really tell what was in the gravy they poured on them. It had chunks of some type of meat, but they could not tell what it was and knew better than to ask.

"Stop looking up the road," Paulo said to Tomaso, "No one is looking for us. We're too far away and I doubt anybody cares what that lunatic would say anyhow."

"Guess you're right," Tomaso conceded.

After they ate, they went back to the trucks to meet Sergeant Grillo and the rest of their new outfit. Rinaldo was more connected with his new mates and did not really stay with the original group. They all understood he had been with these guys for a while now and had a new allegiance. It was really all right with them. They were just thankful they came upon him when they did so they could get away.

That night, the men were sent to a large tent to sleep. There were a couple rows of cots there and they managed to each get one. Gaetano took the one at the end farthest away from the opening and laid right down. He was asleep within seconds. It was only seven thirty.

At five o'clock in the morning they awoke to the sound of artillery fire nearby. This was the most rest they had enjoyed in over a week, and they could feel it when they got up. Most of them had become so used to sleeping on the ground, a cot seemed uncomfortable. But it was nice to be able to sleep in a place where you did not have to worry about waking up to an enemy soldier possibly pointing his bayonet at you.

There were crates in a truck just outside the tent with fresh rations. It was time to move out and they would not have time to go to the mess tent for a warm breakfast. With a fresh set of eyes, they could see the front line was just sixty yards to the north. Fortunately, the artillery fire was from their side, but they knew what that meant. Before long, they would cross over to the other side of the trenches and make a run towards the enemy. Just like the week before when Sergeant Patrizi was killed.

All the men in Sergeant Grillo's outfit were first to get to the trenches. The artillery continued for over an hour once they got there. So, the sergeant had told them to take in some rations. "No telling how long we'll be out there. If we're successful, we'll be eating in their camp tonight," he said to a small group nearby. The men started to show their fear and were getting nervous. Most began to pray and some shake. Gaetano did not show any emotion.

The artillery stopped at nine o'clock. Within moments the order was given, and they prepared to climb the trench. The bullets were already flying over their heads before they even began. By now the enemy knew once the artillery stopped, the soldiers were on their way. Several men did not make it up onto the field between their trench and the enemy's. The enemy bullets took them out as they raised their heads above the trench.

Gaetano sat for a moment looking back away from the enemy. He then let out a scream. He lunged upward with his back still toward the enemy and rolled onto the ground above the trench where he had been. The others followed but could not understand how he jumped up like that. As they managed to get on top of the hump of dirt, they noticed Gaetano had already crawled twenty yards and was starting to get up.

Even with the gunfire, they could hear Gaetano screaming. None of them could keep up and many got pinned down in craters which had been made by exploding cannon shells in previous days. For the next fifteen minutes they made gradual headway to the enemy position. Nevio saw Gaetano throw a grenade into the trench before them. Then jump in.

The grenade had killed several enemy soldiers and made an opening which enabled others to follow. Gaetano jumped in and grabbed the grenades off the first two dead enemy soldiers he came across. He pulled the pins on them and tossed them. He threw one to his left and one to his right. The enemy did not think grenades would come at them from that direction, so they were not prepared. Gaetano ran towards his right through the trench.

Whenever he saw a dead soldier with grenades, he took them and would throw them up the trench. Then he would follow and shoot his rifle in the general direction in which the trench was dug. All the while looking up to his right to be certain no enemy soldiers would jump in on him the way it happened to Sergeant Patrizi.

As the other Italian soldiers reached the trench, they found all the enemy soldiers either blown up by a grenade or shot at close range. Some of the Italian soldiers needed to fire beyond the trenches to fight back the reinforcements who were heading their way. The battle raged on for seven hours. This one was theirs.

When it was over, Sergeant Grillo walked up and down the trench looking at the carnage. So much of it had been done by this screaming soldier named Gaetano, and everyone knew it. He came up to where Gaetano was sitting in one of the trenches. He was back to being quiet. Sergeant Grillo looked up one side of the trench, then the other, then back at Gaetano. "Well done," he said to him with almost a whisper.

Gaetano just looked at him and remained silent. "You'd better head back to camp and get something to eat," the sergeant said. Gaetano got up and climbed over the edge of the trench. The sergeant watched him. He put his rifle over his shoulder and began to walk back. About halfway back he noticed Gaetano stopped and jumped into a ditch. He came out with a wounded soldier on his back and carried him back to camp. The sergeant turned and continued to assess the results of the day's battle.

About two hours later, Sergeant Grillo went back to their camp figuring by morning they would move the camp up to the next line of battle. He went by the field hospital and noticed Gaetano was still there with the man that he had carried. It was young Lorenzo. His right leg was being amputated. "Will he make it?" Sergeant Grillo asked Gaetano.

"Yeah, he'll make it," Gaetano answered, "The bullet shattered his thigh bone, there was no saving it. Doc says too much artery damage."

"He get hit anywhere else?" the sergeant asked.

"No, but it's his ticket out of here," Gaetano said as he stepped away. Lorenzo was unconscious from the morphine. The others managed to survive the day and assumed they would be able to use the cots in the tent again. As they went in, they noticed Gaetano was already asleep in the last cot.

• • • •

THE NEXT DAY THEY ALL took part in moving the camp. Extra trucks were brought in to help, but the roads moving forward were not passable. They reverted back to the old standby their Army had used for centuries, donkeys and wagons. The donkeys pulled some of the smaller field cannons. Paulo was helping to guide some of the donkeys that were pulling the cannons. He thought for a moment and then drifted over to Nevio and asked, "how are we gonna get these cannons up into those mountains once we get there? The donkeys won't be able to pull them."

Nevio stopped in his tracks and looked up to the north. The Alps were easily another five thousand feet above where they were. "Got me, didn't somebody say something about airplanes?"

• • • •

IT WAS NEARING THE end of July, and they seemed to be making some progress in their area. Word spread fast though that most of the efforts were fruitless. The tactic of using full frontal assaults was not working. This should have been expected since the war was now over a year old in other parts of Europe. All the commanders who used the frontal attacks were met with the same limited result. The trenches were a solid defense along with barbed wire which stretched as far as the eye could see in places.

The effort continued for another week until Chief of Staff Cadorna ordered a cease fire. It was August third when the fighting stopped. Most of the Italian Army had accomplished little and, in some areas, had lost territory. A new strategy would have to be embraced, and better techniques would have to be utilized. They would have to take the higher ground. The planning for the new strategy would take months and bring them closer to their most dreaded enemy.............................. winter.

Chapter 24

The commanders were aware there would be a lull in the action. They allowed the men to rotate furloughs. Trucks would leave every Friday and return the following Sunday with the previous group of men who had been on furlough the week before. The location for furlough was the camp just outside of Bologna where they had stopped on the way to the front. The trip would take just over a day.

This facility had the needed room for several hundred men at a time. From there the men were allowed to go into town for whatever fun and sometimes trouble they could find. The Patrizi men as they had come to be called managed to get furlough together.

Their time to go was on August twenty-seventh. The trucks left at noon just after lunch. The men had played a game of football in the morning, so they were adequately tired for the truck ride. Valentino rolled his jacket up and tried to lay down with his head at the end of the truck. The other men did not care for him taking up so much room, so they made a point of accidently kicking him just as he started to doze off. He eventually got the message and sat up with the rest of them. Fortunately, the truck was not carrying eighteen men this time. Only twelve men were in the back of the truck. Two were in the front with the driver. They agreed to take turns sitting in front. There were three men who could drive the trick. A couple of times one of them would relieve the driver.

Gaetano got the first shift to sit in front. He put his jacket up against the window and fell asleep. He had not been sleeping well for the last three weeks since the fighting stopped. While the fighting was going on, he behaved almost the same way as the first day when Lorenzo got shot. They all knew there was no stopping Gaetano when the order was given. It was not clear to the men if he wanted to be killed, or if it was just how he processed being angry about what had happened to Augustino. Maybe he felt the harder he fought the sooner it would be over, and he could go home.

They had been told Lorenzo might be in the infirmary at the camp they were headed for. If so, they agreed they were going to find out where he was, and all go to surprise him at the same time.

As evening came, the trucks drove into a tent camp which was just off the road. There was not much to it but three tents with cots, a mess tent, and a mechanics tent for servicing the trucks which were on route to the front. It was also a fuel depot for the trucks to fill up. This was a new concept for the veterans who had been in the Army for some time. They had been trained strictly on horseback and these noisy trucks which kicked up dust and kept breaking down seemed like more trouble than they were worth. But to the young soldiers, they were happy they were able to ride.

The dinner was a typical Army issue with a lot of boiled potatoes and little else they could identify. Still, it was good to be away from the front and have a place to sleep out of range of the enemy cannons and snipers. In the morning, they were able to get a warm breakfast, hit the latrine and jump back on the trucks for the trip to the camp.

The weather was still quite warm. But the evenings were getting shorter and chillier. No one wanted to say it out loud in fear it might not be so. But they all hoped that when they got to the camp, they would be able to take showers or baths with hot water.

The trucks pulled in just before five o'clock in the afternoon. They would have been there an hour earlier but one of the trucks got a flat tire and it needed to be changed. The policy was the convoy always stayed together. Never leave anybody behind. Further away from the front it was not as critical, but it was a standard. It broke down just outside of an apple orchard. The men were ordered to stay away because they did not want to upset the owner of the orchard.

"The Army is there to protect its citizens, not to steal their harvest," Sergeant Grillo told them as they were waiting.

"What about just taking some of the ones that fell already?" Tomaso asked, "My Papà had a small orchard when I was growing up and he never cared if someone took what was on the ground."

"They all look so ripe and ready to eat," Valentino pleaded.

"Only if the owner comes by and says we can," the sergeant continued, "the last thing I want is for the owner to come around and I have to explain to him why I let my men trample his orchard. Got it?" They all shrugged their shoulders and grunted a reluctant agreement. They were like young children when told he cannot have any candy in the bowl on the table right in front of him.

• • • •

THE FIRST NIGHT AT the camp the men would be confined to barracks to help them get settled in. Also, they did not want the men to go into town on a Saturday night. That was the most likely time for them to get into trouble.

"So, do they have showers?" Tomaso asked Sergeant Grillo, "I can't wait to wash off those trenches."

"Yeah, there's a shower building at the end of this row of barracks. Go in groups of ten so things don't get too crowded in there. There should be plenty of hot water from what they told me," he said to the men. He was quite familiar with this camp. It was where he had trained five years earlier.

There was hot water indeed, for the first twenty men. The third group had a disappointing experience. After that, they decided to wait an hour between groups to let the boiler catch up. Gaetano was in the first group to get his shower. He had plenty of hot water and soap, real soap.

As the evening wore on, Gaetano looked around for a place where he could wash his uniform. He found some soap which could be used for washing clothes while he was drying off near the shower. He stuffed some into a small bag he found and put it in his uniform jacket as he left not certain if he would be able to use it. He looked around and found there was a basin outside. He did not waste any time getting to it. There was no hot water but did not matter.

The last thing he wanted to do was to go into town with his filthy blood-stained uniform. Most of the men had some rips and stains on their uniforms but Gaetano's uniform was so beat up that he looked as if he had been fighting a great deal longer than the rest. And in many ways, he had been.

He washed and scrubbed his clothes three times. Some of the other men followed his lead. The barracks smelled of the damp uniforms hanging around drying. It was still warm enough at night for them to leave some windows open. That helped to dry the clothes. By morning they were mostly dry. There was just some dampness in the seams. They did not care. It felt good to have something clean on.

· · · ·

NEVIO ASKED AROUND and found out Lorenzo was there at the infirmary in one of the long-term wards. Everyone agreed to visit him in the afternoon. It was a pleasure for them to eat breakfast knowing they really did not have anything to do. They were allowed to sit outside of the mess hall and relax on the grass. If they wanted to go back in during the morning and have another cup of coffee, that was all right too. This was like a real vacation for some of them.

Several of the men fell asleep while lying out in the sun. They had been in the sun plenty during the past months but never just to relax. Gaetano asked around and was able to get some stationery. The Army base could mail a letter to America for him if he had the right address. That was no problem. Gaetano could do nothing but remember home and wished he had never left.

He sat under a tree and started to write a letter to his parents. He had not reached out to them since being taken into the Army at the docks. Captain Stevens would have likely told his Papà by now what had happened to him. Then he thought. 'What if the Hallwick was sunk by a torpedo and never made it back to New York?' He could not allow himself to assume such things.

'Just write the letter,' he thought, 'how long would it take to get there?' he wondered. During peace time the letters his Nonna would send took over a month to get to them. With the war on, who knew if it would even get there? Maybe the ship carrying the mail would be torpedoed. 'Just right the letter' he thought again.

What would he say? '*Dear Mamma and Papà having a great time.*' That would not work. '*How are things at home?*' was silly. 'Just right the letter' he repeated to himself, 'just right the letter.'

Dear Mamma and Papà,

By now you must have heard what has happened. Captain Stevens should have told Papà I was recruited into the Army here. I am all right, but I miss you both. Please pray this war ends soon so I can come home.

I could not get word to Nonna that I would not be coming. Please make sure she is all right. I will go to her first when I get out of the Army to make sure she is all right. I fear she will not be.

Papà, please tell Captain Stevens Augie will not be coming back. He did not make it. That is all I am allowed to say about him. They asked us not to talk about the war or what we are doing other than that we are close to the mountains in the north. We always wanted to go to the mountains and see the snow on the tops in the summer. For that, it is beautiful.

I will try to write again if I can. There are limits to mailing letters. But I will try. I love you both and miss you. Please pray for me and the men I serve with.

Truly yours always

Gaetano (Tom)

He sealed the envelope and took it to the office where they mailed the letters. The others wanted to see Lorenzo at the infirmary right after lunch and Gaetano did not want to miss that. He hurried back to the mess hall and found the rest of the Patrizi men already eating at one of the tables.

"Hurry up and get something to eat Gaetano, we want to surprise Lorenzo," Pierre said.

"I'm not really hungry," Gaetano replied, "Maybe I'll just grab a roll and something to drink." He made it back to the table in no time and sat for five minutes with the men eating his roll. They all left the mess hall at about one o'clock and headed off to the infirmary. The rule for visitors was they could not stay too long. It was supposed to be a place to recover, not socialize.

Lorenzo was happy to see them. "I thought you guys might come by here at some point," he said with the biggest smile he had given in a long time. "Other guys were getting visits by their squads on furlough. I figured if was just a matter of time 'til you made it."

"Hey, are they taking good care of you here?" Valentino asked, "meet any pretty nurses?"

"Actually, there is one named Francesca," he said, "she's really nice. I think she likes me."

"Francesca? She has a sister?" Valentino continued, "I'm always looking for......"

"You're always looking.... that's right," Pierre jumped in, "give it a rest."

They all had a tough time avoiding looking down at his missing leg. But they all did. And Lorenzo noticed. "Hey that's all right. I've gotten used to it a bit," he said, "at least I have one good leg. Some of these guys really got messed up. You don't want to know. I see some of them and I'm very thankful I only lost one leg." The tone got a bit more serious.

"We've seen them, before they leave the battlefield," Anthony said, "never know if they make it this far. I suppose if they do, they have a chance."

"Not really," Lorenzo said, "They take quite a few out of here with sheets over their heads. Then there are those guys who will not ever be able to be in public again. Their faces are so badly messed up or burned they................" Tears started to roll down his face.

They hoped they had left the war up at the front but realized these men had their own wars which would not be over when the shooting stopped. Some of these men would carry the wounds and the scars forever.

"We were told not to stay long," Nevio said, "Looks like you could use some rest."

"Sure," Lorenzo said, "They told me the rules too." They all shook his hand and patted him on the shoulder as they got ready to leave.

"Be well," Paulo said.

"Gaetano," Lorenzo said, "could you stay for a second?" They all looked at each other and realized why.

"We'll be outside," Paulo said as he gave Gaetano a tap on the arm.

Lorenzo paused for a moment. He was trying to hold back the tears. "I didn't get a chance to thank you for pulling me off the battlefield. I would have bled to death the doctor said." Gaetano hung his head and looked at him with his eyes raised in humility.

"I couldn't just leave you there," he replied, "you're my friend."

"I know what it means to have you as a friend Gaetano. You're one in a million," Lorenzo continued and sounded like he had rehearsed this. "Some of the other guys here were there that day. They all remember that one guy nobody could stop. Most of us might not be here if it were not for you. And don't think it went unnoticed. I heard two officers talking about you. But they didn't know your name. So, I told them. That was Gaetano Santorini, my friend." Now it was Gaetano's turn to hold back the tears. He could not say anything, so he just nodded his head and gave Lorenzo a hug.

The other Patrizi men were hanging around outside sitting on some benches near the entrance. Gaetano came out and it was obvious that it had been an emotional time for him, so they did not say anything to him other than "All set?" Then they started to talk about going to Bologna for the evening. The trucks were leaving just after dinner and if they missed them, they would be out of luck until tomorrow.

• • • •

THE MEN WERE ONLY ALLOWED to stay in town until twelve midnight and then they had to be at the trucks. Any man not on the trucks on time would be left behind, considered A.W.O.L. and spend the rest of his furlough in the brig. The evening before, they had all been given money to spend. It was considered combat pay. Gaetano was surprised because he did not realize soldiers got paid. The Army did not give the men a regular pay. They would give them some when they were on leave and then the rest once discharged. Some men were having money sent home to support their families, but most men were not married.

There was enough money so they could do some drinking, and get into some trouble if they chose. Most were glad to have something happen that was not life threatening. The Patrizi men stayed together and went to several places to see all the town had to offer. At ten o'clock Pierre said he was hungry and wanted to know if anybody else was. They went to a café to sober up a bit and get some decent food to fill them up. Some of the other men who were leaving told them what was good to order.

It was getting close to midnight, and they were not far away from where the trucks would be to pick them up. They made it with a few minutes to spare. None of them wanted to lose their furlough to the brig. On the way back Gaetano was thinking about what Lorenzo said to him after the others left. He was glad this friend would make it unlike his other friend who was never coming back.

• • • •

THE REST OF THE WEEK had the men relaxing during the day, playing some football in the afternoon, and returning to town in the evening. On the last day, however, they spent the entire day in Bologna so they could see more of the town in daylight. Most men still had enough money left to buy lunch and dinner at the places of their choosing.

Gaetano spent some time in the Piazza Santo Stefano and went to the Fountain of Neptune. Later they all met at the San Petronio Basilica so they could go to dinner together. They found a restaurant with a sign out front that said it welcomed soldiers. It said there was a discount for men in uniform. Gaetano looked down at his uniform and thought 'Even a beat-up uniform like this one?'

Being it was their last night in town before going back to the front. They were all told they had until two o'clock in the morning to get back to the trucks. Thursday evenings in Bologna were active a bit later than earlier in the week. But it was not like Saturday nights when men from the base nearby would often go in looking for fights. The local merchants knew the difference between the men stationed there and the men coming in for furloughs. The men on furloughs were better behaved most of the time.

The next morning, they were scheduled to head out at nine o'clock. The plan was to make it to the same small camp they had stayed in on the way down. They spent Friday night there and left before dawn. Everything was on schedule, and they arrived by noon on Saturday at the front. Nothing had changed and it did not take long for them to feel like they had never left. The fighting still had not resumed.

Chapter 25

Rumors can spread like wildfire in the trenches. Men were talking about the first two major offensives. Many had heard things about the strategies which were tried and failed. The large numbers of men rushing the very secure trenches of the enemy who were well situated on higher ground was becoming obviously very foolish. Yet the same method seemed to be the plan for the next offensive as well.

The other problem was trying to accomplish too much with too few men. For the first two battles they had tried to take on too wide of a battle line. With the enemy being so well entrenched, this strategy was proving fatal.

Chief of Staff Cadorna was beginning to realize he had not utilized enough artillery. The places where they had seen some slight success was due to the fortunate and usually accidental artillery strikes which opened up access for the men to go in. Having learned from those incidents, he was now going to enhance the artillery significantly. They had added roughly twelve hundred more artillery pieces and began to place them. But still they were being spread too thin to truly be effective.

One of the problems was the enemy positions high atop the mountains allowed them to observe the Italian Army's every move and prepare a proper defense against it. The men in the Italian trenches were rapidly becoming disheartened. What would the next battle be like? Would they have a new plan which would work and not cost so many lives?

Then there was the waiting. Waiting for something to happen. Day after day just more waiting. At least by this point Gaetano was getting better at giving men their haircuts. It was something to do which was a bit more than the other men. This helped him and those he would banter with while giving them haircuts to break the boredom.

Word came in early October they were going to move out. This time they were to head east. Even though they planned to attack on multiple fronts, they were going to attempt to focus on Gorizia. Again, Captain Marcello made his promotional appearances to the troops. He would meet with several each day and deliver the same rally speech he had given at the training camp about mounting the largest fighting force in a generation. However, many of those fighting forces had already fallen during the first two battles.

During the late morning of October twelfth, the men began to load onto the trucks. The weather was no longer working to their advantage because the rains had started and there was new snow on the mountain tops above the eleven-thousand-foot level. The Patrizi men were still a unit and serving under Sergeant Grillo. They managed to get on the same truck again.

The men were issued warmer jackets than what they had been given at training camp. Some of them smelled very musty because not all of them were stored in a dry place during the warm months. A couple of the men preferred being chilly over smelling the mildew. It would be nice to have another furlough so they could wash them in the basins with water and soap. There would be none of those where they were going now.

The troops gathered near Valerisce just west of the Isonzo on the other side of the river from Gorizia. This would be the staging ground somewhat away from the view of the enemy. No one was certain when the fighting would start, but in some ways the men would prefer to get on with it. It was not getting any warmer.

On the morning of the eighteenth, the artillery began its more concentrated assault. Sergeant Grillo was to stage his troops and prepare for an attack on the bridgeheads at Tolmino and Plezzo. If successful, they may be able to move forward enough to possibly take the town of Gorizia itself. There was some time to wait during the initial artillery barrage.

Paulo had been promoted to corporal just after returning from furlough. Partly because he was a bit older than most of the other men and he had shown leadership in the previous two battles.

"You think it's gonna be different this time?" Paulo asked Sergeant Grillo.

"Well, based on what I'm seeing, it doesn't really look any different," he replied. "We're still spread too thin. We should be tighter, more focused. We need to win something significant and then we can spread out." Sergeant Grillo had seen a few campaigns and some of them were done right. This approach had obviously not been working thus far.

"At least we have a lot more artillery," Paulo replied.

"They have to hit something worth hitting though," The sergeant said pessimistically, "just making craters for us when we retreat is not enough. They need to open things up."

By mid-afternoon, the order was given to move out. There was a bit of a trek to get to where the fighting would begin. The artillery had done some good for the advance. The hope was to reach the Isonzo. The barrage focused on the shores by where they needed to cross. As they moved ahead, they saw the effective work of the cannons firsthand. The heavy bombardment had opened up what they needed. The real fighting was imminent. They still had not reached the Isonzo.

The first confrontation started around five o'clock and continued well after dark. There were some advances and some push back. The elevation in this area was not too high, so the men were not short of breath as in the previous battles. Gaetano and Paulo stayed close together during most of the fighting. Paulo wanted to see if Gaetano was doing better now there had been a break in the fighting.

He was fighting along with the men this time and not running out on his own, at first. But as the night wore on, he would take on more and risk exposing himself in order to advance. He was inspiring the men around him by the way he would not settle for minor advances. The Austro-Hungarian Army was definitely outnumbered. But their commander Field Marshall Boroević was wise and positioned his troops well to maximize their defenses.

There was a pause in the fighting after one o'clock in the morning, but it did not last long. At the first sign of daylight the fighting began again and the Patrizi men were all on the move. The entire morning was made up of a constant but slow advance. The artillery was being moved up as the battle line advanced. There was a slight risk. If the Austro-Hungarian soldiers went on the offensive and took back enough ground, they could lose the artillery to them. It would be too difficult to move them back quickly if the counterattack were swift.

Two weeks went by with constant fighting and little gain. There was some retreating, but not enough to bring down morale. The areas to the north saw little or no gain. But the Gorizia region saw significant advances. This was a good indication that a focused offensive would work better than attacking an area which was too wide.

With the minimal success to the north, Chief of Staff Cadorna called a cease fire on November third. There was no official notice given but it seemed the success in the region of Gorizia gave Cadorna the notion he should expand on the focused approach. He redeployed the troops from the north down to the Gorizia region but still intended to maintain a fighting front all the way south to the Adriatic Sea. The troops were still spread too far apart to be effective as they could have been. ·

Just one week later, on November tenth, the fighting resumed. Sergeant Grillo's men, including all the Patrizi men hit hard along the enemy trenches. Gorizia was in sight, but the enemy troops held their ground.

On the evening of November fourteenth Sergeant Grillo's men found themselves pinned down in a trench just twenty yards west of the enemy. Casualties were extremely high that day. Twenty-five of Sergeant Grillo's men were not accounted for and feared dead on the battlefield. Armando, Anthony, and Nevio were also missing. Gaetano thought he had seen Nevio dive into a shell crater.

"Paulo, hey Paulo," Gaetano called to him. Paulo was about thirty feet away, "Did you see Anthony or Armando?"

Paulo worked his way over to him, "Armando's gone Gaetano. I saw him get hit this morning. I haven't seen Anthony."

"Doesn't look like we're going anywhere soon," Gaetano added, "they've got us pinned really good this time."

Valentino and Tomaso crawled over to them, "You guys see Nevio or Armando?" Tomaso asked.

"We were just saying," Paulo answered, "Armando is gone, Anthony.......... don't know."

"What about Nevio?" Valentino asked.

"Gaetano said he thinks he's pinned down in a shell crater," Paulo said, "but with all the shelling, who knows." Gaetano nodded in agreement.

Darkness settled in quickly. By six o'clock they could not see anything on the battlefield. The shooting continued even though it was impossible to see what they were shooting at. It dwindled over several hours. No one was certain exactly when, but at some point, the fighting stopped. They could only guess at the time.

Gaetano reached into his boot and pulled out the pocket watch he had managed to keep hidden all this time. He opened it but could not see the time. It was cloudy in the late afternoon, and it became very cold. Usually, Gaetano would be able to make out the time by the moonlight. He dared not take out the watch during the day when someone might see him with it. The best he could figure was it was somewhere between eleven and midnight.

Most of the men had eaten some of their rations and were trying to rest. With the silence of the guns, the moans and screams of the wounded began to ring out. They had heard cries for help before but never like this. What was the most difficult to hear, was the men pleading, "Kill me, someone please kill me." Men were crying out for their Mamma's and screaming in agony.

Gaetano was exhausted and was trying to fall asleep but there was no rest while those men were suffering. Occasionally the enemy would fire in the direction of the screams to try and hit one of the men in agony. It seemed to be a game for them. Two hours went by. The moans and screams were only getting worse. Paulo was on one side of Gaetano and Valentino on the other. They could not sleep either.

"Somebody please, do something," Tomaso said, "put them out of their misery. Anyone would understand."

"They'll be dead by morning," Paulo said sadly.

That was the last straw for Gaetano. He leaped up and rolled onto the battlefield before either Paulo or Valentino could stop him leaving his rifle behind. They peered over the mound to see where Gaetano had gone. "Gaetano!" Paulo said with a whisper scream, "What are you doing?" but no answer.

Gaetano ran to the first sound he heard. He found a soldier moaning and leaning against the stump of a tree that had been blown away by artillery. He grabbed him and flung him over his shoulder and began to run back. The enemy soldiers heard something and began to fire into the darkness at whatever they thought they might see moving. Gaetano reached the side of the Italian trench and slid the wounded soldier over the mound. "Get a medic," he said in a whisper then he turned around and went back out onto the field.

The next man he came across was one who was screaming the loudest for someone to kill him. "Please kill me," he screamed as Gaetano reached him.

"Shut up stunad, you wanna get us both killed," Gaetano said to him in a firm whisper. "You may want to die, but I want to go home someday, so shut up."

With all the commotion, the enemy was firing at any sounds they heard. Gaetano realized he would not be able to run with this one, so he hit the ground and began to drag him. He took hold of the back of his jacket collar and pulled with all he had. This caused the wounded soldier to scream even louder. But it was a technique that worked. Gaetano knew this would be a useful method of getting men off the field. They reached the mound, and Gaetano lowered him in like he had the first. "Get a medic and a mussel for his mouth," he said.

"Get down here," Gaetano heard someone say, "You're gonna get yourself killed out there." It was Sergeant Grillo.

Gaetano leaned into the trench with his head lowered just a bit, "You know I can't do that. I can't stand the screams." With that, he turned and crawled out again looking for more wounded.

The sergeant just shook his head after Gaetano left. Looking at Paulo he said softly, "No, I guess he can't."

The shooting continued but no one was able to see where Gaetano was, not even his own men. He decided to stay put behind the stump where he had found the first soldier. The screams and moaning continued and the enemy would shoot whenever they thought they might hit something. Word spread fast on the Italian side. They did not shoot back in fear they might hit Gaetano.

At first, he noticed a couple of drops of rain, then a light rain, then a full rain. Within fifteen minutes a cold heavy rain had begun. The good thing about a heavy rain is it can cover up a lot of noise. Gaetano was on the move again. He could hear the screams and moans, but they did not fill the night air in the same way which had become so unnerving when he was in the trench.

He reached another soldier who was lying in the open field afraid to move. This one was not screaming because he was afraid to get shot. Gaetano did not take the time to see how he was injured. He just grabbed his collar like he had the previous soldier and began to drag him. 'This guy is big' he thought to himself as he struggled to pull him. They approached the mound, and two men reached up to grab the wounded soldier.

Another reached out and grabbed Gaetano. "What are you doing?" Gaetano rebelled, "let go of me." It was a lieutenant he had never seen before.

"Get down here you fool," the lieutenant said.

Gaetano pulled away and broke his grip from his arm. The lieutenant grabbed him again. "I told you to get down here," he said.

Without thinking about what he was doing, Gaetano punched the lieutenant in the face and broke free. He turned and went back out onto the battlefield. The lieutenant got up and looked out where Gaetano had been and then at the men around him. It was very obvious the men around him did not agree with what he had done and had deserved the punch in the face.

Gaetano reached another soldier and could tell he was alive but was not saying anything. He grabbed him by the collar and began to drag him like the others. 'I'm glad this one is smaller' he thought as he was able to move him much easier. This time Gaetano went in a different direction to avoid the lieutenant who he had punched. They reached the edge of the trench and Gaetano began to lower him in. That is when he realized why this man was much easier to drag. He had been hit by artillery and had no legs. Gaetano had been pulling only the top half of a man. But he was still alive, maybe not for long, but still alive.

At about two in the morning, he climbed into a shell crater to get a soldier he heard moaning. It was Nevio. He had taken a bullet to the abdomen and had lost a lot of blood. "Is that you Nevio?" Gaetano asked.

Nevio had lost so much blood he could not respond. But Gaetano could tell he knew it was his friend who had come to get him. There had not been any shooting for a while, so Gaetano decided to risk it. He stood up and put Nevio on his back and made a run for it. They almost got to the trench when the firing started. Nevio had let out a grunt as they dropped down into another crater and it got the enemies' attention. It was still too dark for them to see what they were shooting at so both of them made it to safety.

During the next four hours, almost until the first light of dawn, Gaetano continued to pull men off the battlefield and into the care of the medics. As dawn came, Gaetano was lowering the seventeenth soldier into the trench. He was right where his friends were at this time. Paulo reached out and took his arm.

"You've done enough. It's over," Paulo said, "come down now. It's getting light, they won't keep missing now." Gaetano looked at him with a look of rejection towards his warning. "Please, come down, you've done enough. Please."

Gaetano paused a moment more and then looked out on the field. They could see the enemy now and the light of the sun beginning to show behind them from the east. He looked back at Paulo and then back at the field. There was an obvious conflict in his eyes. "There's more out there," Gaetano said.

"There will always be more out there," Paulo said softly, "But you've done enough, more than enough." Gaetano still looked reluctant to stop. "If you get killed, then you won't be around to save others on another day. Don't be foolish, you've done more than enough."

With that, Gaetano rolled into the trench. It was almost as if a switch had gone off and he suddenly began to shiver. All the time he was out on the field, he was getting wet from the rain and muddy from the dirt that was no longer dusty as it had been in the summer months. Sergeant Grillo came up to where he was and saw him shivering. "Get some blankets," he ordered, "you all right soldier?" he asked Gaetano.

Gaetano could not answer him with all the shivering. It was not just the cold. It was also the fear which finally settled in. He had not allowed it to take over during the night. Hot coffee was what he needed but there was not any to be found. Sergeant Grillo started to rub Gaetano's shoulders to help him warm up. As he was trying to help him, the lieutenant who Gaetano had punched came by.

"Sergeant, arrest that soldier for assaulting an officer," he said barking out the order. Sergeant Grillo just looked at him and continued to rub Gaetano's shoulders. "I said place that man under arrest."

Sergeant Grillo got up and walked up to the lieutenant, "Could I have a word lieutenant?" he said as he took him by the arm to a place where no one could hear what they were saying. The grip he had on him convinced the lieutenant to follow. "That man just pulled over a dozen men from certain death and all you can think about is getting even?"

"We can't have privates thinking they can go around hitting officers now can we Sergeant," the lieutenant said sarcastically.

"No Signor, we can't," Sergeant Grillo said, "Just leave him to me. I'll make sure he understands that."

"But he struck me in front of my men. We can't have that," he continued.

"Some of those men he pulled in were their friends. Do you think placing him under arrest is going to go over well with them?" Sergeant Grillo pointed out. "I'll take care of him. I'll put him on kitchen duty for a while. I'll say he snapped or something and he's getting punished for hitting an officer. That will cover two things. It will also give him a break from the battlefield and look like he's being reprimanded for hitting you. Will that work for you lieutenant?" The look on the sergeant's face was near rage. The lieutenant's selfishness was overwhelming, and Sergeant Grillo had no time for it.

The lieutenant did not want to give it up, "I say he should be court-martialed, that's what he needs."

"I don't know about you, but I wish I had fifty men like him. I've seen him fight. I don't want to lose him," Sergeant Grillo scowled having now lost his patience with him.

"Well, then I'm going to put it in my report and let the captain decide," the lieutenant said with a sneer.

"Do what you have to do, but I'm going to see to it that he's taken care of," the sergeant said sternly. With that the lieutenant stormed off.

Sergeant Grillo walked back to the men. Paulo came up to meet him as he got close, "So, what did you say?"

"Good thing he left," Sergeant Grillo replied, "or I would have punched him myself."

"Just got word, Nevio didn't make it," Paulo told him.

Sergeant Grillo was hoping for something good to hear. He shook his head, "Don't tell Gaetano just yet. I'll break it to him when I think he's ready."

The sun was up now. It was starting to warm some but, the brisk morning air of November was still sharp. This day would not be a day of rest for anyone. By ten o'clock the shooting had resumed, and the battle raged on until dark.

Chapter 26

The fighting continued for just over two weeks. Since the previous battles had stopped at about the two-week mark it, was expected maybe things would stop for a while. But due to the coming winter months, Chief Cadorna planned to finish the year with at least some success.

The remaining Patrizi men were still a tight unit. They had not lost anyone else since Nevio on the fourteenth. Anthony showed up two days later. He had been separated and diverted north with another squad. It took him a couple of days to make his way back. The only ones left at this point from the original group were Paulo, Tomaso, Pierre, Gaetano, Anthony, and Valentino. Rinaldo was around but was no longer considered one of the Patrizi men since he had transferred out early on. And then there was young Lorenzo whom they were all glad had survived and was likely home by now.

With several slow points in the fighting the men had many hours of waiting in the trenches. They would try to rest when they could but much of the time was spent simply looking up and down the trench and talking to one another about nothing. No one wanted to look over the mounds of dirt because the enemy was just as bored and would occasionally take some target practice at any soldier who did not keep his head down.

"What day is it anyway?" Valentino asked.

"Thursday," Paulo answered.

"The date?" Gaetano asked.

"Ah.........the twenty-fifth, I think," he paused, "November twenty-fifth............. yeah."

"Last Thursday of November...Thanksgiving Day!" Gaetano said.

"What?" Tomaso said with a chuckle.

"Thanksgiving Day," Gaetano answered, "It's an American holiday. I guess you guys wouldn't know about Thanksgiving Day, would you?" They all looked confused. Something about their history when some folks first went there in a small boat and almost all died. They taught us in school."

"I'm not liking this story," Valentino moaned, "They almost all died? Why celebrate that?"

"The ones that survived. They celebrated. You know?" Gaetano laughed, "Every year they fix a huge meal, and all the relatives come over. They all eat turkey and then fall asleep."

"Why fall asleep? When my family gets together, we all want to see each other," Tomaso said.

"Got me! They just do, that's all," Gaetano said with a puzzling look on his face, "It's a tradition there."

"Huge meal?" Paulo said, "I could eat a huge meal right now. I see a huge plate in front of me and my Mamma serving it up to everybody. Awe, why did you have to remind me?"

"Stop, you're breaking my heart," Valentino cried.

"My friend Steven invited me over last year to his house," Gaetano continued, "my parents didn't really celebrate it too much since we don't have family there yet. I never ate so much. His mother made this enormous turkey with bread inside of it called stuffing and potatoes that were mashed all covered in gravy."

"Gravy on potatoes?" Paulo asked.

"What they call gravy," Gaetano answered, "is different than the gravy my Mamma makes. It doesn't have any tomato in it."

"No tomato in the gravy? How could you eat that?" Paulo joked.

"It was good," Gaetano laughed again, "hey, you think we can talk them into giving us some turkey today to celebrate that we've all survived?" They suddenly got serious again. Survived, it was an ominous concept.

. . . .

DINNER THAT NIGHT WAS a bit disappointing after the discussions of feasts and family. But at least they did not have to eat rations that day. Because there had not been heavy fighting where they were, a mess tent was set up. The potatoes were not mashed and did not have what Gaetano had described as gravy on them. But there was something on them. Some may call it gravy, chunky gravy. There were plenty of other descriptions for it which were not as pleasant.

They also managed to get some sleep that night. But the reprieve did not last for long. The next morning saw an upswing in the fighting. The Austro-Hungarian Army had the same idea to keep or take back as much territory as possible before the winter set in. Most of the fighting had been the Italians trying to take territory they claimed belonged to Italy and the Austro-Hungarians trying to keep what they had claimed for themselves.

This time though the enemy was on the offensive. Any gains made by the Italians had been a demoralizing blow to the Austro-Hungarians and they had a score to settle. The battles continued for several more days. The Italian soldiers became scattered in places. Gaetano got separated from the rest of his men in the late morning of November thirtieth. He had been holding a position with two soldiers from another squad which just happened to be next to him after three hours of fighting that morning. The fighting had lasted through the night, and everybody was a bit disoriented. An assault by the enemy had cut right between them and the rest of the Italians.

Gaetano knew they were cut off. He looked over at the other two soldiers who were with him in the shelled-out ditch and could tell they were both very scared. "I'm Gaetano, who are you guys?" he asked the other two.

"I'm Luigi," one said with a quiver in his voice.

"Vinnie," the other said sounding just as frightened. They were both young. Likely not even nineteen years old.

"We gotta make a run for it," Gaetano said.

"You're crazy," Vinnie responded, "They're everywhere. We're trapped."

"I think we should surrender," Luigi added.

"Now who's crazy?" Gaetano snapped back, "we should head north and circle around. We're already behind their lines. We should be able to get through if we go around and don't go straight back."

"We'll never make it," Luigi cried.

"You do what you want, I'm going for it," Gaetano said with an obvious lack of willingness to compromise.

The other two stayed in the ditch and watched as Gaetano crawled out heading north. He crawled for about eighty yards and pulled into a line of brush. There was some shooting close by so Gaetano turned to see what was happening. Through the brush he could see six enemy soldiers had overtaken Luigi and Vinnie. Luigi put his hands up to surrender but an enemy soldier ran his bayonet into his chest and fired. Vinnie tried to run but was shot in the back by three enemy rifles. Gaetano realized he was on his own.

He also knew he would be in constant danger of being discovered. There were no Italians anywhere to be seen. He hid wherever he could, stayed low and figured he would try to move once it got dark. Even in the dark, he crawled were ever he went and listened. Listened for anything that would be a sign of where the enemy might be.

Two days later, the fighting stopped but he was still behind the enemy lines. He moved slowly over several days, hiding the best he could. His rations had run out.

One night he managed to find a barn near a farmhouse. It appeared no one was living in it. The owners had obviously fled the fighting in fear. The barn had no animals inside. They likely had been taken by the owner when he fled, or the enemy soldiers had taken them for food.

The fortunate part was there was no sign of the enemy there either. Gaetano decided to stay in the barn, well camouflaged behind some hay for a couple of days to get rested up. Early in the morning of the second day, before sunrise so as not to be seen, he went into the house to see if maybe some food had been left behind. There was nothing in sight.

He remembered his Nonna had a hidden root cellar and began to look around for signs of an entrance. He started to pull away some carpets to see if there might be a hatch. He began with the kitchen. The most obvious place would have been under the table but there was nothing there. There was a carpet just inside the back door which led to the woodshed. He pulled it back and there it was. He removed the carpet and went down a short staircase. It was only about five steps. The area was shallow, about four and a half feet high, so he had to stay low.

The enemy soldiers must not have seen this place because Gaetano found some roots, potatoes, and several jars of canned goods from the farm including some canned apples and peaches. He had his Thanksgiving feast a few days late. No turkey though.

After he ate three jars of fruit, he decided to look around upstairs. There was a supply closet which had been ransacked. He found a winter coat hanging behind the door. It surprised him the coat had been left behind. 'They must have been here during the summertime' he thought to himself 'or of course they would have taken the coat.' The coat had deep pockets both inside and out. He looked around a bit more and he found a sling they likely used for picking vegetables.

That night Gaetano slept in the root cellar under the kitchen so if the enemy returned, they would not find him. He had figured out a way to pull the carpet back over the trap door with some string to hide himself even better. It was the first night in weeks he slept soundly.

The next morning, he stuffed as much food as he could from the cellar into the pockets of the coat and more in the sling. There was not anything worth eating left behind. It was December eighth, and the winter was coming fast. He had not seen any enemy soldiers for a few days, so he decided to venture out during the day and lay low. If he heard anything or saw anything, he could hide in the trees. This way, he could cover more ground in daylight.

With that in mind he set out from the farmhouse with his rifle which had just a few rounds left and one grenade. 'This will be enough food to cover me until I get back to my outfit,' he thought, 'going north should get me free of the enemy.'

During the day he would take out his pocket watch from his boot to see the time. After a while he just kept it in his pocket. The plan was to go north for a day more and then head west. Maybe he could find a hole in the enemy line and make it through. There was no sign of fighting, and he did not hear any gunfire or cannons. This was a good sign, but no guarantee. The coat was very warm, and he almost forgot he was a soldier fighting in a war.

The area became more mountainous as he continued north for an extra day. After a while Gaetano noticed what appeared to be a ravine to his left. He decided to go through it to see if he could get back to his outfit that way. Several hours later, he came upon what appeared to be a small outpost which did not look occupied. But he was not taking chances. He looked a little closer and saw it was similar to the pill box outpost which he had come across earlier that year. This was not something he wanted to relive. Maybe there was nobody manning it or maybe there was. He did not have enough grenades to take them on.

He backed out the same way he had come in and circled around to miss it completely. 'Maybe I could have slept there for a night,' he thought, but the thought of someone stumbling in on him while he slept was enough to end that idea. Hiding behind some rocks or trees would be much better even though it was getting very cold at night.

As he walked, he noticed a road and followed it for a while. Down the road, about two miles, there was an overturned truck on the side of the road. It was an Italian Army truck which had been attacked at some point. Maybe during the summer by the looks of it. Gaetano took out his pocket watch and saw it was getting past six o'clock.

Walking during the day had seemed safer than before and nighttime walking in this hilly terrain was just as dangerous as coming across the enemy. He decided to sleep behind some brush close by. During the night, the weather turned and began to rain, a very icy rain. Gaetano remembered the truck which was not far away and decided to make his way there. The driver's window had been broken out, but the other side was intact.

Gaetano crawled in through the driver's window and lay down on the overturned roof of the cab with the seat above him. He thought the seat might not be fastened too well so he pulled on it. The seat was only fastened in with spring snaps and it came right out as well as some dust, debris and several packages of bullets that must have been pushed in there by some soldier figuring he'd get them later. They were the standard issue for his rifle.

He could not see them but knew what they were since every soldier had to learn to load his rifle in the dark. The seat would be slightly padded compared to the cold metal of the roof, so he repositioned himself and managed to get the seat below him. It was not ideal. However, it was better than sleeping in the rain.

With the seat now below him, he would not be able to get out of the driver's window because the seat blocked it. Since the seat was light enough, Gaetano figured he would just move it out of the way in the morning to get out of the truck. He could barely see out of the other side as well. It raised him up and hid him pretty well. This helped him to relax and fall asleep. It was nice to be out of the rain. He just hoped he would not snore and be noticed if someone came by.

• • • •

THE NEXT MORNING, GAETANO was awoken by the sound of voices. It was the most frightening sound because they were speaking German. He stayed perfectly still. 'Do I get my rifle ready?' he thought, 'No, that might make noise and there's no way to know if they have any friends with them up the road.' Gaetano decided to wait it out hoping they would be on their way soon.

It appeared they were taking a break from their journey, and it was only the two of them. Still, he had no reason to start a fight. 'What about a grenade?' he thought again. That would just let everyone for a mile around know there was an Italian soldier nearby. The sound their grenades made was different from the enemy grenades, So it would be obvious whose side he was on. 'Just wait it out!' he thought to himself, 'Just wait it out!'

Twenty minutes went by. Gaetano could smell the cigarettes they were smoking. He wished he had stayed out in the rain behind some rocks on the hillside. Even if he had to stay still and out of sight, he would not have been right next to them.

A moment later there was a startling sound just above his head. It was the sound of running water hitting the passenger window. 'Awe.................. why couldn't he pee on a rock or something?' Gaetano thought to himself trying not to think about the fact an enemy soldier was peeing right at his head. 'Thank goodness the window on the passenger side isn't broken out.' he thought. But that did not stop the smell.

He waited a couple of minutes and then the sound again. 'Why would you pee right where someone else just peed?" he thought with disgust, 'go pee someplace else!'

This was a good sign though. Maybe it meant they would be on their way before long. Gaetano's biggest fear was they might be waiting for someone to meet them there. Then he may have a larger group to contend with. He had gone undetected thus far, so he decided to wait it out some more. It finally paid off after another hour had passed. Gaetano listened carefully as they left so he would know which direction they headed. This day was beginning to improve. The two enemy soldiers went in the direction which he had come from the day before.

He waited another twenty minutes and gradually moved the seat out of the way. There was no way to do it quietly, so he hoped no one was around. He poked his head out of the driver's side window where he had crawled in. It seemed clear so he grabbed the bullets he found and crawled away from the truck to some brush that was up the hill a bit. From there he was able to size up the situation and determine if it was safe to continue.

This region was unfamiliar to Gaetano. He had taken part in the reconnaissance mission which was much closer to Asiago and had access to the maps. But he did not have time to study any maps of the Gorizia area. He just counted on using the sun for a compass and to try his best with that.

• • • •

WALKING AS MUCH AS he was over rugged terrain, Gaetano had time to think about this past year. A year before at this time he was home in Jersey City with his Mamma and Papà. Each day he would get up and go to work at Rocco's and on his days off meet up with his friends. 'I wonder what Steven is up to right now,' he thought. Gaetano had not really contemplated whether the Americans might become part of the war since he had not seen any American soldiers fighting where he was. These thoughts helped to pass the time, but they were also taking their toll on his attitude.

'Maybe I won't go back,' he thought to himself. At first, he was not willing to admit he was really thinking that way. It was mostly to blow off some steam for the rough year he had had. But after several days of wandering and obviously having become lost, he started thinking more about honestly considering it. 'They'll think I was killed or taken prisoner. That makes sense. Besides, I've done my part already.' This was the beginning of an exercise to convince himself it was all right to run away.

'I'll make my way to Spain or go north to.......... what's up there...Denmark or something. Then I'll get a boat to New York. Once I get there, they'll know I'm an American now and not a new immigrant because I can have them look up Rocco and he can tell them I used to work for him.' He was starting to reason it all out in his mind.

It was obvious he was far from the battle zone by now and there was no indication fighting had taken place where he was walking. Gaetano had gone much farther west than he originally had planned, maybe unintentionally, or maybe......

Occasionally he would come across a farm or a house on the hillside. It was wise to avoid them. This area was not very heavily populated and most of the time he was able to remain inconspicuous.

After a couple of more days, he began to think maybe he could start to trust some people by telling them he was on a furlough and was told he could go to his ailing mother. That way he may be able to get some food. The jars and roots which he had taken with him from the farmhouse were running out and he had maybe one day's supply left.

He could always hunt. He did have his rifle with plenty of bullets and knew how to use it. But sneaking up on an animal to hunt was a different thing. Would he hunt for a rabbit or something larger? Since he was not a hunter, he really had no idea. As he would walk through the wilderness areas at the foothills of the Alps, he would watch for any motion that might be a possible target for dinner.

There was no lack of water though. The streams were running with plenty of water because the wet season had come and the storms from up in the mountains were supplying the streams well. 'Maybe I can fish.' he thought. His Nonno had taught him when he was staying with them before joining his parents in America. "No hook," he said out loud.

It had been many days now and he was still heading west. One afternoon in mid-December, best he could figure it was around the nineteenth or twentieth, he heard something coming up from behind him on the road he was on. Ordinarily he would find a place to hide in order to avoid detection. This time he thought this might be a good chance for him to try out his furlough theory. It was a man on a horse drawn carriage. As the man came closer, Gaetano put on his best smile and waved to him. The man did not seem too impressed with his gesture of friendliness but stopped, nonetheless.

"Ciao Signor," he said with his plastered smile, "might I be able to ride in your cart for a while? I am headed home on furlough to see my Mamma. She's not well, she sent a letter to me, so they let me go see her while there is a stop to the fighting."

The man looked at him without saying anything at first. He just stared at him. Gaetano was not sure if the man was just going to leave or even if he was going to speak.

"If you really wanted me to think you weren't running away from the war, you should have left your rifle behind," he said very matter of fact. Gaetano could not cover up his surprise at being so easily found out. "Soldiers don't take their guns home on furlough young man."

Gaetano stood with a chill running all the way down his back. 'What now?' he thought. He contemplated turning and running into the woods, but his feet would not move. 'Why didn't I hide?'

Gaetano stared at the man for what seemed to be an eternity. "Get on. You can sit up here with me," The man said with little emotion.

His feet were still stuck in place as he tried to figure out what was happening. The man almost started to leave but tried one more time, "Do you want a ride, or will you continue walking wherever it is you're going?"

Gaetano shook off the fear and confusion and climbed on board. They rode for a while and then Gaetano could not keep his curiosity to himself any longer. "You're not angry with me?" he asked him humbly, almost hoping he was a bit angry.

"Each man has to make up his own mind when it comes to war," the man said quietly, "not everyone makes the same decisions you know." There was a long pause.

Neither of them said anything for some time. They rode in silence, but Gaetano did not mind. Then unexpectedly the man said, "We got the letter in late August." he had not turned to say it. He just looked forward at the horse and became very stern.

Gaetano was afraid to ask, but this man seemed kind. "What letter Signor?" he asked hoping he had not already figured it out. The man kept silent. Gaetano paused for a moment and figured he was already committed. "Was it your son Signor?" The man stayed very quiet. Gaetano could feel this man's agony and could not help but wonder if maybe he had fought alongside his son. He decided to leave it alone and turned to look forward also.

After some time, they began to talk again but this time it was about simple things. "What is your name Signor?" Gaetano finally asked.

"My name is Arturo, and what is yours, young man?" he replied sounding like a teacher Gaetano once had.

"It's Gaetano Signor, Gaetano San...." he started to say.

"Just your first name if you don't mind," Arturo abruptly interrupted, "that way if someone asks about you, I can tell them I only knew your first name." he obviously wanted to avoid trouble.

"I guess I understand," Gaetano said sadly. This was not making him like the decision, which he actually had not completely made yet. It also was a bit embarrassing. "Maybe I should walk before we get to where other people might see you with me."

Arturo paused a bit and then nodded his head, "I'll let you know when we are getting close." They did not talk much after that. Around forty-five minutes later they crossed a small bridge and started uphill. Gaetano could see up the hill far enough to know there was a small village coming up and figured this was the end of the line.

Arturo stopped the carriage and stepped down from the carriage. He walked to the back and opened a pouch. There was a considerable load of supplies. It seemed he was stocking up for the winter. Out of it he pulled a loaf of bread and then he opened another sack and pulled out some potatoes. Gaetano got down and walked to the back where he was.

"Here," Arturo said, "this should hold you for a couple of days." He handed them to him. Gaetano was moved by his generosity.

"Are you sure Signor," Gaetano said humbly, "You will need this during the winter."

"I'll have enough," Arturo said calmly, "I always plan for extra in case someone comes to visit. Besides, we have one less to feed this year."

Gaetano's eyes filled up with tears and he choked up, "May I ask Signor, what was your son's name?"

Arturo hesitated and almost did not answer, "Nevio............my son's name was Nevio."

Gaetano had another chill down his back thinking this could be his friend's father. 'But no,' he thought to himself 'Nevio was not killed during the summer. He just died recently.' But it just as well could have been his father. He could feel the loss of this man's son and wished he had known him.

"Thank you, Signor, you have been too kind to me, and I don't deserve it," Gaetano said with a sinking feeling. He did not like the new him and was growing to dislike it more with each passing hour.

"Go over that ridge and follow the tree line for about four hours," Arturo said pointing to their right, "you'll come across a train track. They have to slow down for the turn ahead so you can jump on. Don't try to get on the passenger train, just the freight train."

Gaetano wondered why he was trying to help him get away. Maybe deep down inside this man was wishing he had told his son to do the same months before. "It's getting late Signor. Do you know anyplace that would be good to spend the night?" It was mid-afternoon and it got dark early in December. He only had about two and a half hours of daylight left.

"Maybe," Arturo said with a pause to think, "you'll have to decide once you get there." He put his hand on his shoulder and pointed again. "When you get to the tree line, go for a couple of miles and you will see a horse path leading up the hill into the forest. Go up for less than a mile. There is a hunting shack there. You should be able to stay if no one is using it. It's usually only used during the summer. Being winter now, most people will be home."

"You know this place, Signor? Is it yours?" Gaetano asked.

"No one really owns it. Everyone takes turns using it when they are out hunting," Arturo said, "If no one is there, you can build a fire to keep warm. Do you have flint?

"No Signor," Gaetano answered.

"There's probably some there," he added, "most people leave a bit behind rather than take it home with them. It's just in case someone forgets theirs. We all help each other out around here."

"I'm not much of a hunter Signor," Gaetano said apologetically, "maybe I should leave my rifle with you." He was paying heed to the earlier advice and trying to return something for the man's generosity.

"Believe me Gaetano, the last thing my wife wants around is an Army rifle," he said shaking his head, "maybe if you're lucking you can shoot something for dinner." Arturo patted Gaetano on the back.

"Like I said Signor, I'm not a hunter," Gaetano repeated.

"You'll have to learn some time," he said, "you had better get along now. I have to be home for dinner."

Gaetano nodded his head, "Thank you again Signor." He took the items Arturo gave him and headed towards the tree line.

Chapter 27

Gaetano always had a good sense of direction. It also helped that Arturo had given him detailed instructions. The tree line was easy to find but the horse path left a bit to interpretation. It was essentially a break in the trees with a narrow path used by people as well as horses. He could have easily missed it.

Nonetheless, the hunting cabin was right where Arturo said it would be. He approached it cautiously even though there was no real reason too. Maybe he had been fighting the enemy long enough to know to fear any unknown place. As expected, there was no one using the cabin, so Gaetano moved right in. At first, he did not know exactly how to light a fire. Arturo had told him about some flint, but Gaetano had never started a fire with flint before.

After some contemplation, he figured out he needed to use a piece of flint and his Army knife. He scraped his knife across the flint and made a spark. Once he saw the first spark, he understood.

It was late December, there were plenty of dried leaves to start up the fire. 'These hunters are very thorough.' he thought to himself. There was some firewood under a covered area just next to the hunting cabin. The process was a bit frustrating at first. The leaves were not creating enough heat to start the wood on fire. The logs were too large. He needed some twigs.

Fortunately, there was a bit of daylight left. Gaetano went around in the woods and picked up some branches that were on the ground. He was able to break off some of the smallest branches and stuff them into the stove. That did the trick. With a good flame, he was able to gradually add larger twigs and then small branches. He remembered when he was younger and working for Signor Rizzi that he had shown him how to set the flue on the chimney pipe to get the best flame. He tried a couple of different settings and before long the cabin was warming up nicely.

'I should stay here for a while. This will be the first night since summertime I'll be able to sleep without freezing,' he thought to himself. But at the same time, he knew he would need to move on the next day.

Once warmed up, Gaetano opened the sack with the potatoes. The hunters had put a water pump from a well right in the cabin. It was over a small basin with a drain that went outside. He worked on it for a while, and it started to pump out water. It was very cold but was the best water he had tasted for some time.

There was a small pot sitting on top of the stove, so he put some water in it, cut up a potato and left it in the water to boil for a while. He looked at the loaf of bread that Arturo had given him and figured he had been fortunate thus far. With the food at the farmhouse, the bullets in the truck and the kindness of Arturo, he felt very thankful.

While the potato was cooking, he decided to look around the cabin a bit. There were a couple of cots along the wall as well as a table and three chairs. The light from the stove was dancing around the room as darkness settled in and Gaetano was beginning to enjoy the experience. Above the stove just to the left, he noticed a shelf with some spices in jars. There was a piece of garlic there, so he cut it up and added it to the potato in the pot. He also found some salt. This was shaping up to be a nice evening.

The potato was cooked in about fifteen minutes. It took a while for the water to boil but once it did, it became a hardy boil. While searching, he found some utensils. He had his Army kit with him, but he decided to use one of the forks and a knife from the cabin. It made him feel a bit less like he was at war.

He could have eaten a lot more, but he knew food would become harder to find until he managed to find his way back home to Jersey City. He had some money with him that he saved from furlough but wanted to save every bit of it to pay for passage to New York if he could find a way. He hoped he could make it to a port somewhere which was not under siege from the U-boats. That, he knew, would be difficult. So, buying food was out of the question.

The evening wore on and he found himself having a lot of fun stirring up the fire. There was no chance of running out of wood and it appeared even if he used more than he should, the next hunters to use the cabin would still have all they needed. It looked like there was a full year's supply outside. He brought in enough for the night and bolted the door behind him. There was no chance of any enemy soldiers coming by, but he kept his rifle loaded and ready anyway.

As he laid down on one of the cots, he took out his pocket watch and stared at it for quite a while. This was his link to home. As long as he had it, he still could think of home. Without it, he felt he would be lost and not remember everyone who cared about him. It was after ten o'clock. With the warmth of the stove and quiet of the cabin, he drifted off to sleep.

• • • •

DURING THE NIGHT, HE needed to get up to tend the fire and take a short trip outside. All the fresh well water he drank during the evening had done its bidding. It was frigid outside, so he made it quick. He took notice of the silence of the area at night. There was a peace about it that was inescapable. If he had not been so tired, he might have stayed up to enjoy the tranquility. However, he went right back to sleep and slept straight through until after nine o'clock in the morning.

There was a bit of canned fruit left in a jar from the farmhouse, so he planned to eat that for breakfast. He looked over at the shelf above the stove and noticed there was some coffee in a can. He had never made coffee by himself before but figured it was an opportune time to try. 'Why not,' he thought. There was what appeared to be a percolator in a cabinet. He had never used one but recognized it from when his Mamma made coffee. He knew he had to crush the beans some to save time. Whole beans would take a too long, and he was not sure how long. With a bit of water and crushing up some beans, he placed it on the stove.

It was the worst cup of coffee he had ever had. He used far too much coffee and not enough water. It was very bitter and strong. But it was coffee. After he ate, he felt like he could run all the way to the train tracks carrying two of his friends from his unit.

It was close to noon when he finally ventured out. The sun was out, and it was a bit warmer than the day before. As he went back down the horse path to find the tree line, he turned back to look at the cabin. He had doused the flames in the stove the best he could but figured it would be safe to let it die out on its own if it flared up again. It looked to be a very solid stove, and he was certain the hunters would leave a fire in it when they went out to find some game.

This morning, Gaetano had a bounce to his walk, not just from the coffee but from the rest and the peaceful evening which he had enjoyed so much. He was sure to remember it for a long time. The tracks would be less than two or three hours away now since he had walked the tree line for a bit to reach the horse path.

He did not see anyone while he walked. It was not the season for workers to be in the fields so everyone would be home.

Just as Arturo had said, Gaetano found the tracks. He followed them for about twenty minutes and found the curve which he had been told about. Arturo told him to jump the train from the outer part of the bend in the track so he would not be seen by either the engineer or the conductor in the caboose. "They don't treat riders very nicely when they catch them," Arturo told him, "You could end up in jail or worse."

Gaetano put his ear to the track to see if he could hear anything. He was not sure if that even worked but his friend Steven from New Jersey had told him that once when they were walking along some tracks heading to Hoboken. 'What if there isn't a train today?' he thought. With the war on, there was the possibility most businesses were reducing their activity which might limit the amount of freight trains.

The thought of starting a fire was on his mind to keep warm. There had been plenty of flint left behind at the cabin, so he took the two smallest pieces just in case he needed to start another fire someplace. Since he did not know the train schedule, he decided to hold off.

As evening approached, he started to get disappointed. Maybe there will not be any trains today. What about tomorrow and the next day? How could he be certain these tracks were even used anymore? He thought of something his friend Steven had told him while they used to walk on the tracks in Hoboken. "Don't walk on the shiny tracks when there is a train passing. If there is a second train, you won't hear it."

"Why not?" Tom would say.

"If the tracks are shiny, then trains are using them regularly. If they are rusty, then they are likely not used very often, if ever," Steven told him.

'I wish Steven were here now...' he thought, 'well actually I would rather be there.'

Darkness was soon upon him. So, he had to figure out where he might sleep. He decided to lie down alongside the track so if a train came, he would be close. After some more thought, he realized he needed to be more hidden so the train engineer would not see him on the side of the track. That would be too obvious he was about to jump on the train.

This region was hilly farmland, and the terrain was rocky. Farmers in the area would make rock walls and sometimes just piles of rocks along the edges of their fields while plowing. There was a pile of rocks like that within sight of the tracks and considering how quiet it got at night, a train coming down the tracks would certainly wake him from a sleep. So, he worked his way over to the rock pile and tried to figure out a place where he could get comfortable.

It was too late in the year to make a bed out of fallen leaves, so he made the best of it on the ground. After all, he had slept many nights inside of the trenches between battles. At least he did not have to look forward to a battle in the morning.

Even though he had slept past nine o'clock in the morning that day, he was still tired. Partly from the cold and partly from all of the long walking he had been doing over the many days since running from the enemy in the ditch. 'Maybe I should go back to the cabin,' he thought, 'I could be there in two hours. I know the way even in the dark. There's enough moonlight.' He realized that type of thinking would never get him home. Plus, there was no certainty trains did not run at night. If he missed one, it could be days before another came through.

He slept, but not soundly. Every little noise woke him up because he thought maybe a train might be coming. Morning came and there was still no train. There was a bit of bread left in his pouch, so he ate some. He had passed a stream just before finding the tracks, so he headed there to fill his canteen with water. It was worth taking a chance to get the water since he knew he could hear the train coming from far away. There was only a little water left in his canteen.

As it turned out, the train did not come while he went for water. It was past noon, and the train still had not come. He was starting to wonder if he should keep walking along the tracks to keep on the move. What Arturo told him about the train slowing for the curve made him decide to stay put. If he missed the train because he was not in a place to get on, then it would mean walking all the way. All the way............ what did that mean exactly?

By late afternoon, he decided to start a fire close to the rock pile. He took some rocks off the pile and made a little fireplace to contain the fire. There was plenty of dry grass near the rock pile and loose wood just inside the tree line. He figured it would cover him for the night should the train not come. This time, the fire started much easier. He now knew how to use the flint and start it with the right fuel.

That night, he barely slept a wink. All he could think about was whether he was doing the right thing. Should he go back to his squad? Should he find a town where he could go to see the magistrate? He could easily say he had been wandering while getting more lost every day. They may not believe him, but it might not matter all that much just so long as he was there and willing to fight. 'Fight?' he thought, 'not my fight.' Leaning towards going home was winning out at that moment.

In anticipation of possibly needing to run to the train quickly, he built up a pile of dirt near the fire. The dirt in the field was loose from all the plowing each year so it was easy to loosen up with his knife. He also remembered when he had first dug the trenches in Asiago how the men would use freshly dug up dirt to sleep on because it was a bit softer. This ground was not too bad. Just before dawn, he managed to fall asleep for a while.

Morning came and there was still no train. The day was quite chilly compared to the previous two. He decided to keep the fire going. Waiting is not so bad when you know at some point the waiting will be over. Gaetano was starting to wonder.

'If no train comes today, I'll start walking tomorrow,' he decided. There would not be enough food to stay put for much longer. After a while you just have to face the facts. There may not be a train for days or even weeks.

Several trips past the tree line to get more firewood kept him busy enough to not get upset at the wait. Again, he reminded himself it was better than being in a trench. Nightfall came again and this time he had even more wood to cover the needs for the fire. He let it get larger than the night before to warm him up. It did and he was able to sleep longer, but not as well as in the cabin two nights before.

As dawn was approaching, he decided to prepare to leave once it got light. His timing could not have been better. Just as he had completely doused the fire with dirt and rubbed out the coals, he heard the sound of a whistle in the distance. Then he had a frightening thought. 'What if the train is going in the wrong direction?' He listened for a bit longer and then realized the train was coming from the south and headed north just as he needed it to.

This was his chance. He had scoped out a place to hide along the track so the engineer would not see him as he passed by. Once the locomotive had passed the curve and no one could see him, he would run up to the train and hop on. But what if all of the cars were closed or full of something? How would he get on and where would he ride? How long would he ride? He was not even sure where it would take him. 'Doesn't matter,' he thought, 'anywhere is better than this war zone. What if it's a passenger train?'

The train seemed to take forever to reach where he was. The first sign of the whistle had come over a half hour before and still no train. Maybe it made a stop further up the tracks. But he kept hearing the whistle. If it had stopped, they would not blow the whistle so often. Eventually he could see the plume of smoke the locomotive was putting out. His chance was right upon him.

The train reached close to where he was waiting, and he was able to see quite a bit of it from where he was. It was a long freight train with over thirty cars. Many of them were empty and the doors were open to air them out for the next shipment of livestock.

Just as Arturo had suggested, the train slowed down to accommodate the curve. The engineer was not looking towards Gaetano's side of the train as he passed. Gaetano made a run for it and headed for the eighth car which had its door wide open. He had feared other people would have had the same idea and he may have to compete for the space in the car. This was the first time he had never done this and wondered how many people did.

He realized he had nothing to fear about anyone giving him trouble. He was, after all, carrying a rifle and was now a trained soldier. The thought of fighting someone though was the last thing he wanted. But, if necessary, he would have the advantage.

He ran alongside the track just like he had planned over the previous two days and grabbed hold of the side of the opening. With a quick lunge upwards, he jumped on. Once on the train, he realized he had the car to himself. 'Should I close the door to keep warmer?' he wondered. If he did, maybe the conductor might see it then figure someone had boarded the train and come looking. It was best to leave it open and sit in the front most corner to minimize the wind.

There were four bales of hay in the car. Few, but enough to set up a comfortable seat. The hay would also help to keep him warm. The coat he found at the farmhouse was now his most treasured possession. It was large enough to cover him and his Army gear including his sleeping blanket which he had with him even in the last battle he was in. They had trained them to fight with most of their gear because they would likely not return to where they had been the night before. So, if they did not carry everything, they would soon have nothing. He took it out and wrapped himself up best he could and waited for what was next. Whatever was next was likely to be determined by the circumstances. He would have no control of it. It would not be by a decision he would make for himself but likely made for him.

The train did not stop all day. Gaetano slept part of the time and looked out the door part of the time. He also did a lot of thinking.

The scenery was breathtaking. The tracks took them through the foothills of the Alps and then gradually through the valleys. Looking out the door, he noticed they were running right alongside a vertical wall of rock. He went right up to the door to see how close it felt. Suddenly he was frightened by darkness. The train had entered a tunnel. The first of many in the area. He was initially nervous but soon grew to enjoy it.

At the third tunnel he had an idea to try to hold his breath once they entered and see if he could hold it until they reached the other side. The next one was easy, as many were. But there were some that were too long for him to hold his breath the whole time. This made him feel like a young boy again. He was actually playing. Maybe he was free.

The train started to slow down. Gaetano wondered if he would need to get off. As the train came to a stop. He put the four bales of hay in a row close to the front wall but left enough room to lay behind them for cover just in case the conductor decided to look in the cars for riders who did not belong. The stop was a supply station for the engine to take on water and some coal to burn.

Gaetano stayed very still and quiet. At one point he thought he heard someone walking up the tracks. Maybe it was the conductor going up to talk to the engineer or gather some supplies. 'Wouldn't it be nice if I could just get off and go into a restaurant to get dinner?' he thought. It was almost dark now and he realized he had been on the train for over ten hours. How far had they gone? Wherever they were, it was much colder and there was more than two feet of snow everywhere. He did not dare look out in fear he might be discovered.

The layover took more than an hour. He had found a comfortable position to lie in and found himself falling asleep. He realized he was sleeping when the train lunged forward to continue its journey. By now, it was completely dark. There were some lanterns along the side of the tracks where the water tower was. They lit up the inside of the car as the open door passed by. He knew he could get up and look out the door again, but he was quite comfortable where he was. Besides, it was probably too dark to see anything anyway, so he drifted back off to sleep.

Because he fell asleep so early, he woke up in the middle of the night. He was freezing. The temperature had dropped even more than it was at the water tower. 'Maybe I should go up to the engineer and ask him if I could shovel coal to pay my way on the trip.' He started joking to himself as he took a sip of water from his canteen. 'At least then I'd be close to the fire.' The water in the canteen was partly frozen.

As the day went on, he got even colder. The four bales of hay provided some insulation but not that much. He broke up one of the bales and started to stuff hay into his coat and up his sleeves. 'Maybe running away in the winter and straight up into the Alps wasn't such a good idea,' he thought. He could not remember ever being this cold.

By early afternoon, the train began to slow down again. Gaetano decided to take a look out the door and see where they might be. They were passing through a town and there seemed to be a lot of activity. He kept out of sight best he could so as not to be detected. This was probably a good place to get off and try to find some place to warm up. The constant wind from the motion of the train made it even colder. Maybe he could find a barn someplace where he could hide. Then he could try another train on another day.

As the train came to a stop, he heard a commotion. He peeked out to see what had happened. Four cars back, a rider was discovered and was trying to run. There was a local constable there and they chased him down and hit him repeatedly. 'What now?' he thought to himself. Then he had an idea. He shook all the hay out of his coat that could be seen and jumped out of the train. But he did not run. He just stood by the side of the train looking into the car which he had been in.

As he kept looking back and forth in the car, he heard a voice call out to him in German. "Wer sind Sie. Was machst du?" It was the conductor who had returned to the train after letting the constable take care of the other rider and cart him off.

Gaetano looked at him as if to greet him warmly. "No sprechen," he responded. The conductor looked at him confused as to what to do next. "Italienisch sprechen?" Gaetano asked him.

He shook his head to affirm he could speak Italian. Gaetano pointed to the empty freight car and said in Italian, "Do you think I could get a ride on your train? I'm going to see my Mamma, she's not well."

"No, no one rides free, buy a ticket at the station like everyone else," he replied back in Italian. Then he noticed Gaetano had a rifle with him. He looked down and saw his Army boots and realized he was a soldier. "They let you go see your Mamma?" the conductor asked a bit more cordially but still not friendly.

"Yes, but I have to be back in two months once the weather clears a bit," he said hoping he was being more convincing than he had been with Arturo.

"Well, I would, but they are harsh with free riders these days with the war on. You must pay to ride and only on passenger trains." The conductor was warming up a bit more, but he still would not let Gaetano on the train. It did not matter though since Gaetano was getting off the train.

"Thank you anyway," he said as he patted the conductor on the shoulder, "Do you know when the passenger train will come?"

"Two days, maybe," the conductor replied, "maybe not. The weather is not looking too promising and maybe the trains will not come for another month. It all depends on the weather. You just can't tell this time of year."

Gaetano started to wonder if he might be stranded. What would he do if he could not get to a port back to New York? He was not sure what to do next. "Thank you, I guess I'll just have to get lucky," he said and then began to walk away.

"You have a place to stay?" the conductor asked.

He wanted to maintain the ruse that he had not been on the train but looking to board the train. "Yes, I'll go back to where

I was staying before your train came," Gaetano said then waved and continued walking as if it was the natural thing to do. 'What now?' he thought.

There was what appeared to be the main road out of town just ahead so he decided to go that way to see what he might find rather than try to stay in the town. Maybe he could camp in the woods and build a fire like two nights before by the rock pile. But with all this snow everywhere, where would he find wood to burn.

The road led him up the side of a mountain and along a ridge. It would narrow at times but was passable. The weather had not been too harsh thus far in the area even though there was some snow. There were sled tracks on the road and evidence that horses had been pulling them. Gaetano had to watch where he walked. He went for two hours looking for a place where he might be able to stay for a while and get warm.

Several miles up the road it opened into a valley. The view was spectacular. The road followed the east side of the valley for some time. It was now getting late, and the sun had gone behind the mountains on the west side of the valley. He looked toward the side of the hill. There was a large house and about fifty yards to the right of the house was a large barn. This might be a place to hide and get warm. Nightfall was soon on him, and he figured he only had half an hour of daylight left.

The sled tracks from the road led right up to the house. Gaetano decided to circle around and come at the barn from behind so as not to leave any tracks in the snow which the owner of the house could see. He had to hurry because it would be dark soon. The hilly terrain made it more difficult. But it was a clear shot without any obstacles to the rear of the barn.

As he entered the barn, he heard chickens making some noise. He hoped they were not reacting to his presence. There were also two horses, and they too made some noise. It was important to keep as still as possible to get the animals to settle down. Gaetano was very hungry, and the sound of chickens made him think of eggs. He had not had real eggs since they had furlough at the Army base near Bologna. Looking around, he noticed a couple of eggs sitting in a small cubby near the back door which he came in. They were warm as if they had just been laid. The thought came to him to try to eat them raw. That was not very appealing since he had never tried it. And what if there was a chick inside. He would feel awful cracking the egg open.

It was enough just to have some place warm to sleep for the night. As he looked around for a place to settle in, he passed right by the front door. At that very moment, his worst fear happened. The front door of the barn which led to the house opened and there stood a rather large man. He was an older man, well into his sixties but very formidable, nonetheless. Gaetano just stared at him not knowing if he should run or just melt.

"Und was machst du?" The man said in a very calm voice which surprised Gaetano. He had expected an angrier greeting and not such a peaceful one.

"No sprechen," he said nervously. The man looked at his uniform pants and boots and the rifle Gaetano almost forgot he was still carrying.

Then he looked at Gaetano some more and saw the fear on his face. Realizing this trespasser did not speak German, he tried another language. "E cosa stai facendo?" he repeated the same question in Italian.

Gaetano's face lit up. "Just trying to find a place to stay out of the cold," he said to him back in Italian.

"By any chance to you speak English?" the man asked him in English, "My Italian isn't very good anymore."

Gaetano's face lit up even more. "Yes, I speak English. Very well, I used to live in America," he said wanting to immediately tell him the whole story of the past year. He paused a moment and then asked him, "Are you going to throw me out?"

"Throw you out?.......Hmmm," he said with a half-smile, "No.............no, I'm not going to throw you out. I couldn't. After all, it's Christmas Eve. I seem to remember a story. Something about someone needing a place to stay on Christmas Eve and only finding a barn."

Gaetano looked surprised and confused. This man had no reason to be so nice to a stranger who had invaded his barn. "So, it will be all right if I sleep here tonight?" he said almost pleading, "I promise I'll leave in the morning."

The man looked at him for a moment. "No............... you can't stay here," he replied. Gaetano looked even more confused as he said, "I have a guest room in the house. You can stay there. Besides, you look very hungry. And very, very cold." The older man smiled and chuckled.

Gaetano stood there dumbfounded. 'How could this man have me stay in his home? He doesn't even know me,' he thought.

Knowing what this young man before him was thinking since it was written all over his face, he smiled and said, "Like I said, it's Christmas Eve."

Chapter 28

Günter Hass was a retired train engineer. He had retired two years earlier and chose Gifbourg Switzerland in which to settle. His familiarity with the town grew because he would pass through the town on layovers and often stay for periods when the trains were not running. It had grown over the years due to its location on the converging train tracks. Four different lines met there so naturally the need for train services was great. Three different companies had set up shop in Gifbourg to meet the requirements of the trains passing through.

Restaurants had sprung up to serve the people on passenger trains. Most conductors would schedule a couple of hours in Gifbourg. It would give enough time for the travelers to have a meal and maybe purchase some items of interest from the region. Men who were well experienced in engine repairs came here for what proved to be steady work. There were two veterinarians in town who would help in evaluating and possibly treating livestock being transported to faraway places. They would make certain the livestock endured the train ride and seeing to it they arrived in a healthy state.

On the far side of town was a train yard which some carriers used to store their extra cars based on the need of the season. One company had tried to relocate their operations for constructing train cars to Gifbourg twenty years earlier. It never got off the ground due to stiff competition just one hundred kilometers away. That along with poor management caused them to fold within two years.

Günter had many friends there having been in the train business his entire life. He started as a boy shoveling coal. He was a strong and rugged man who knew his way around most of Europe and parts of Asia. If there was danger in front of him, he knew exactly how to deal with it. On more than one occasion he was confronted by robbers who threatened him while he was engineering his train. He would manage to keep his head, which resulted in him keeping his head. Finding a scared kid in a soldier's uniform in his barn on Christmas Eve did not pose what he would consider to be a true threat.

Gaetano stood at the doorway of the kitchen and looked in amazement at the sheer size of this house. The first floor was lit by several gas lights mounted on the wall. It was large but did not look overdone like he would imagine a palace or mansion to be.

He stood with his coat on and his rifle on his back, not realizing he had not taken them off yet. Günter returned to the kitchen holding some clean clothes. The sight of this young soldier standing there with his mouth opened just gazing about made him chuckle.

"You can take your coat off if you like. You'll find it is plenty warm in here," Günter said as he walked over to where Gaetano was standing, "Here.......... some clean clothes for you. They don't fit me anymore." He looked at Gaetano completely understanding why he was just staring. "Please, if you could. Leave your boots over there by the door in the mud room. My cleaning lady doesn't come until Thursday, and I would rather not spread mud everywhere."

Gaetano looked down at his boots and his coat. He snapped out of it as if he had just woken up. "Oh, yes, of course, umm where did you say?" he asked.

"Right there," Günter said with a chuckle then pointed to the area by the back door.

"What time does your cleaning lady come on Thursday?" Gaetano asked, not sure how to make conversation.

Günter let out a big laugh. "Little secret, don't tell anybody," he said leaning over to Gaetano a bit, "I'm the cleaning lady."

Gaetano stood confused for a moment and then realized what he meant and started to laugh.

"So, you tell me," Günter asked, "which would you prefer to do first, eat dinner, take a bath, or even better, take a shower?"

"A bath?" Gaetano said with amazement, "You mean I could take a bath...With hot water.... you have hot water?"

"You don't realize who you're talking to young man," Günter's chuckle increased with every statement that Gaetano made, "I spent my whole life as a train engineer. I know how to work a boiler, I assure you."

"This is the most...............I mean...............it's just............." Gaetano began to stammer.

"Over there," Günter pointed again to the mud room by the back door. Gaetano shook the cobwebs out of his head and walked over to the mud room.

"Umm, what should I do with this?" he said as he started to take off his rifle.

"I suppose it's loaded?" Günter asked.

"Well.........yes, it is. Part of the training I guess," Gaetano said apologetically, "I'll unload it. That'll be much safer for inside the house............... right?"

"That's how I store my guns too," Günter said. But this time without a chuckle. He had a profound respect for the power of a gun.

Gaetano took off his rifle and had it unloaded within seconds. That too was part of his training, to be able to load and unload quickly. Then he leaned his rifle against the wall in the corner by the door. "Is this a good place for it?" he turned and looked at Günter.

"That'll be fine for now," Günter replied, "You can hang up your coat right there on those pegs."

As Gaetano hung it up, Günter asked him, "That doesn't look like a uniform coat."

Gaetano paused and looked at it hanging there. Then he said, "It's.......... well............. it's a long story." Günter just nodded.

"So, have you decided?" Günter asked.

"Decided?" Gaetano said curiously and wondering if Günter figured out, he was running away.

"Eat or bathe?" Günter said.

"Oh, ah, that depends. Depends on what you were going to do I guess," Gaetano said wanting to be polite.

"Well, I've been eating later and later these days, so you will have time to bathe if you want," Günter offered, "that way you might enjoy your dinner more with clean clothes and warmed up a bit. Come on, I'll show you where everything is."

"Oh, I guess I should have told you my name," he said realizing he had not introduced himself, "My name is Gaetano Signor."

"Günter, my name is Günter," his host replied.

Gaetano could not believe this was happening. He followed behind Günter towards a grand staircase in the center of the house. The house was spacious and open with only a few walls on the first floor. There were several columns around to hold up the next story. From the base of the staircase, you could almost see the entire floor. As they walked up, Gaetano kept turning from side to side and looking all around at the size and scope of the first floor.

The second floor was more what one would expect with a hallway down the middle of the house and rooms off to the sides. Günter walked him all the way down to the end of the hallway and entered a room to his right. Gaetano followed him in and looked with even more amazement at this bathroom. He had never seen anything so majestic before. There was a bathtub to his left and two sinks right across from it. Behind the bathtub was a wall with a door. Behind the door was an area that measured four feet by four feet. It was the most beautiful shower he had ever seen.

Across from the shower was another door. Günter opened it and there was the toilet in its own little room. "The only thing I ask," Günter said, "is that you leave it the way you found it."

"Yes, of course, my Mamma taught me well to respect other people's homes," Gaetano said without hesitating, "I promise."

"Fair enough then," Günter said with a smile, "Towels are in the cabinet behind those doors. Hang them up right there when you're done, and I'll leave your clean clothes over here by the door. Your room is the one directly across the hall with the blue quilt on the bed. Dinner in an hour?"

"Oh, yes, thank you," Gaetano replied, "Umm........." Gaetano did not know how to ask.

"What's for dinner?" Günter asked for him. Gaetano just nodded in embarrassment. "Have you ever had sauerbraten?"

"Ah............I don't.........." Gaetano stammered.

Günter just laughed, "You let me know if you like it."

"I'm sure I will," Gaetano said trying to be reassuring.

With that Günter left and headed downstairs. Gaetano looked around in utter disbelief that he had gone from sleeping in a train car and on the ground to this. A beautiful home with running hot and cold water. He turned the water on in the bathtub and waited about ten seconds before feeling some extremely hot water come out. It was actually too hot for him to touch. Turning the cold-water side on, he was able to set the temperature just the way he wanted it.

He took off his uniform and set it on the floor near the shower door. Then he climbed into the tub while there was only a little water in it. As the tub filled up, he made adjustments to the temperature of the water to get the best feel. At first, he thought the water was discolored coming out of the faucet. It had been clear when he got in. He soon realized the water was discolored by his not having taken a shower in weeks. The dirt was just rolling off him.

He put his head under the water. Then came up with water dripping down his face. This was heaven. He began to soap up his head and then rinsed it off. His head just did not feel clean, so he did it again. By now the tub was full so he stopped the water from running. The bar of soap was hard and abrasive. He had never used this type of soap before. It was rough on his skin, but it sure did the job of cleaning off the dirt. So much was caked on from the battles and the traveling.

The water became so dirty, he decided to drain the water out and start with fresh water. 'What if I use up all his hot water?' he wondered, 'Well, we'll see.' The second filling was just as hot as the first. "There's no shortage of hot water in Günter's house," he said softly to himself. This time he lounged back and soaked for a while.

He did not want to lose track of time and delay his host's dinner. So, he got out after twenty minutes of soaking and dried himself off. The clothes Günter had left him did fit, sort of. They were a bit baggy in places and a bit long. But they were clean, and they were not blood stained. He looked at his uniform and wondered if he would ever wear it again.

The room across the hall was lit by a single candle. Gaetano took his uniform and carried it into the bedroom in order to leave the bathroom the way he had found it. He set the uniform down on the floor by the window not knowing what he should do with it. He did not want to put it on the clean furniture. On the bed was a robe and on the floor was a pair of slippers which had been left there obviously for his use. He slipped them on and put on the robe then went downstairs.

• • • •

THE AROMA OF VINEGAR was strong by the time he reached the top of the stairs. He was familiar with the smell of vinegar in antipasto but that was usually served cold. This was cooking on the stove, and the aroma filled the air and almost took his breath away. Günter had set the table and was preparing to serve up the dinner.

"Excuse me young man, but did you see a very dirty soldier up there before you came down?" Günter said with a chuckle, "He needs to come down for dinner. You don't look a thing like him."

Gaetano smiled and laughed, "Yes, I did Signor. I believe he was rinsed down the drain, never to be heard from again."

"Pity, he was such a nice young man," Günter laughed some more then pointed to the far side of the table, "Come sit over here. You can feel the warmth of the stove that way."

Gaetano knew so far, everything Günter said led to something good. So, he went right over. He sat down and could feel the warmth right away. "You were right of course. It is nice and warm over here. What did you call it sour something?" he asked.

"Sauerbraten," Günter said, "with red cabbage and Chnöpfli."

"Can......canup.... what is it?" Gaetano said feeling lost.

"Chnöpfli," Günter repeated, "fancy name for noodles here in Switzerland."

"It looks like popcorn in America, but softer," Gaetano added.

Günter chuckled some more, "Popcorn, I've never heard of that. Is it like regular corn? I've heard of corn."

"Yeah, it is corn," Gaetano said trying to figure out how to explain it, "they take dried corn. I guess it's dried somehow. And they put it on the stove with some oil. When the corn gets to a certain heat, it pops and makes a fluffy looking thing like this. Oh, you have to shake the pot too. You've never seen popcorn?"

"No, can't say that I have," he replied, "you let me know if my Chnöpfli tastes like your popcorn."

"Oh, I doubt it," Gaetano said with a smile, "I'm sure that you're....... how did you say it?

"Chnöpfli," Günter repeated again.

"Right, that canuplee. I can't wait to try it," he said hoping not to sound patronizing.

Günter placed everything on the table and sat down. Gaetano waited a moment. His Mamma had trained him to allow the host to make the first move and direct the meal. It was rude to reach without knowing what the right protocol was. Günter folded his hands and began saying grace. Gaetano saw him and folded his as well. He was glad he had not reached for some food.

"Dear Lord, we thank you for this meal we are about to eat. We thank you tonight we celebrate your birth. Please guide us in our ways in the days to come and help young Gaetano find his way with your guidance. Amen," Günter looked up and smiled.

Gaetano paused yet again. This time because he was so moved by this kind man named Günter. "Amen," he said after, "So, Sour brotten and canuplee."

Günter could not hold in his laughter, "Yes."

• • • •

THE DINNER CONVERSATION was easy and light. Günter was not interested in prying into how this young Italian man came to be at his home on Christmas Eve. "Tell me about America," Günter asked, "I've always wanted to visit there, but it takes so long to get there and back. I hear they have a rather good train system there."

"That's what my Papà says," Gaetano responded, "he works on the docks in Jersey City. It's right across the river from New York. There are so many train tracks in Jersey City it isn't even funny. They bring things from all over the country to Jersey City to ship overseas. My friend Steven and I used to go play on the tracks all the time when I was younger."

"Oh, kids play on the tracks there as well huh?" Günter interjected, "A lot of kids get killed that way you know."

"Actually, I do," Gaetano said shaking his head, "There was a kid in my school who was hit by a train just past the tunnel leaving Hoboken in the marsh land. He was standing on the tracks watching a train go by and didn't hear the other one blowing his horn. I can't remember his name.... Ted, I think."

"You can imagine what the engineer felt like knowing he couldn't stop the train on time," Günter said.

"Yeah, we never stopped to think about that when we were young," Gaetano added.

"From where I sit," Günter said, "you're still young."

"I guess you're right about that," Gaetano said then nodded, "you were also right about this sour brotten. It's really good."

"Glad you like it," Günter smiled.

As Gaetano finished his plate, he looked around the table for possibly more to eat. The sauerbraten was quite different, but he ate it all without any questioning if he even liked it. Günter had originally planned to eat alone and normally would prepare extra and keep some left over in the icebox. But he never prepared too much extra because the icebox did not keep it for more than a day or so.

If he had known he was going to have a visitor, he would have likely sautéed more. It usually takes two or three days to properly sauté sauerbraten to get it right. He did have enough time to increase his Chnöpfli and cabbage though, so it was adequate for the meal. There was nothing leftover. Gaetano easily realized this as he noticed they had eaten everything Günter had prepared. He did not want it to be obvious he was still hungry though.

It was not hard for Günter to see this young soldier was able to eat more. "Well," Günter said teasing a bit, "I suppose you wouldn't be interested in a special treat a bit later on, would you?"

Gaetano felt like a ten-year-old kid who was just offered a pile of candy. "A treat?" he replied trying not to give himself away, "What kind of treat?"

"Something I discovered while I was doing a weekly run to Denmark," he said, "I'll have to bake them after I clean up."

Gaetano saw his chance, "Oh, I'll clean up. I used to work in a restaurant in America. I cleaned up the entire kitchen by myself and did the dishes all the time. I actually don't mind doing them. Especially when it's cold outside. It warms me up and I sleep better."

"I seriously doubt you'll need help sleeping tonight," Günter said with a slight snicker, "You were looking forward to sleeping in a barn, remember?"

"I'm trying not to," Gaetano said rolling his eyes.

"I'll take you up on your offer," Günter said with a smile. Behind the smile was a self-assurance he had made a wise choice to help this young man. "I'll get started on the æbleskivers."

"The what?" Gaetano asked dumbfounded by yet another thing to eat he had never heard of or could pronounce.

"Æbleskivers," Günter said, "you'll see."

Gaetano jumped right to it and started to clear the table just like he had done so many times at Rocco's and on the Hallwick. He stacked the dishes and carried a big pile of them to the sink. This made Günter a bit nervous because these were his good dishes, not the everyday ones. He took them out specially for the Christmas Eve dinner. Gaetano noticed the look on his face and wondered what might be wrong.

"Am I doing it right? he asked Günter.

Günter did not want to be ungrateful for his help. "Well, these aren't my everyday dishes," he said, "You can take your time to wash them. I'm sure in the restaurant you had to work fast, but not here. You can take all the time you need."

Gaetano felt badly he had not thought of that himself. "Oh, umm, what should I do?" he asked humbly.

"Just stack the dishes with ones the same size. That way they won't fall over," Günter replied trying to be instructive rather than critical.

Gaetano looked over at the dishes and saw what he meant. They were stacked rather precariously. Then he started to wonder if Rocco worried about the way he stacked dishes too. He had knocked over quite a few poorly stacked dishes while working there but had learned to stack them better on the Hallwick because of the rough seas.

"You're right, I shouldn't rush," Gaetano said as he walked over to the sink and began to restack them properly.

Günter stood and observed. 'This is a young man who is willing to be taught something.........that's good,' he thought to himself.

Gaetano made certain he took his time to finish the dishes. He had visions of sweeping up Günter's good dishes from the floor and going out to sleep in the barn after all. That was good motivation to be careful. Over his shoulder, he could see Günter working on the treat he had promised. "Are those able.... aver...skivvies things something you make all the time?" he asked.

"More than I should," Günter responded, "these things will put the weight on fast. I save them for special occasions."

Günter had finished mixing the ingredients and reached under the counter to pull out the pan. Gaetano had never seen an æbleskiver pan before. It was cast iron with small pockets on the bottom to separate the æbleskivers.

"That's different," Gaetano said, "It looks like a frying pan that someone used for target practice."

Günter laughed again, "It does. You would have to be a fairly good shot to get the divots so even though. I used to know a man who could do it."

"I thought you said you would bake them," Gaetano questioned, "That pan has a handle just like a regular fry pan."

"You bake them on top of the stove," Günter said knowing he was just confusing the young man even further, "Sort of like pancakes."

"I guess I'll have to wait and see," Gaetano said as he finished the last dish, "Where do you want me to put these?"

"Just leave them stacked where you have them, I'll put them away later," Günter said, "It's almost treat time."

The rest of the evening was restful. Gaetano had not had an evening like this for a long time. Home was always a pleasure, but this was almost like a vacation for him. The æbleskivers were indeed a real treat. It was just as Günter had said. He had made a full pan just for the two of them. It held seven and Günter only had two. He said it was so he would not put on weight. The truth was he was happy to see Gaetano enjoy them so much.

Things quieted down by nine o'clock. Gaetano had found what could easily become anyone's favorite chair to sit in. Günter took out the book he had been working on and within minutes Gaetano fell asleep. Two hours later Günter tapped him on the foot.

"You'd better head upstairs," he said, "you'll sleep much better in the bed."

Gaetano barely opened his eyes and grumbled some pleasantries. He made his way to his feet and took a not so straight path to the stairs. "Goodnight," he said as he reached the bottom of the stairs, "and thank you again for dinner and every......." he was already drifting back to sleep.

Günter went down to the basement to stoke the fire for the night and set the steam pressure for the system. He knew just how to set things so they would have heat without needing to get up during the night to add fuel. Everything was in perfect balance. Just the way Günter liked things to be. It had taken him most of his life to figure out how. As he went upstairs, he put out the gas lights which were all around the first floor and looked out the front window. It was snowing heavily. He sighed and went upstairs to bed.

Chapter 29

Gaetano opened his eyes and wondered for a brief moment where he was. The reality of the previous day seemed intangible. Yet here he was waking up in a warm house, in a warm bed, covered by a quilt that could have been made by Günter's mother when he was a child. The sun was shining in through the window. It looked as if it had been up for some time. He reached over to the side of the bed and grabbed his pocket watch. "Eleven thirty?" he said out loud.

A quick calculation led him to realize he had been asleep for fourteen hours. He got up and went to the window. 'I thought I saw it snowing when I went to bed,' he thought, 'that's a lot of snow.' There had been about a foot or so of snow on the ground when he walked from the train station to Günter's barn. This seemed like so much more. The road was invisible. Even if you knew where it was, it would not do any good to try to follow it.

'It must have snowed three feet last night. How am I going to make my way in this?' He thought some more. His door was open, and he could see the bathroom was empty, so he went across the hall and closed the door. The mirror in the bathroom was the largest he had seen. He noticed it the night before but had not thought about how big it was. After a few minutes he realized he was just staring at himself.

The back door to the house closed and it snapped him out of it. He finished up and went downstairs. Günter had been out in the barn gathering eggs from the ten chickens that he owned. "Good morning Günter," he said with a smile.

"So, you are still alive," Günter joked, "I was beginning to wonder. You must be starving."

Gaetano had not really thought about it because he was still in disbelief of being where he was. "Now that you mention it...." he said.

"There's still coffee if you want some," Günter offered, "I had two cups earlier. I wasn't sure when you would get up. So, I decided to wait for breakfast." He went over to the sink and put the basket of eggs down. "I also have some jars of apple cider. There's an apple grove on the south side of my property. I make my own."

"Apple cider!" Gaetano exclaimed, "I love apple cider. Rocco always kept some at the restaurant even though he didn't sell it. We all loved it.......................during the fall that is."

"Well according to the fine people of Gifbourg, I'm the only one who makes it here," he added, "seems the only thing they do here that is similar is a fermented beverage."

"Must be strong," Gaetano said almost asking rather than observing.

"The hard stuff really isn't my cup of tea," Gunter said, "or should I say cup of cider. But I like mine much better."

The night before Gaetano thought things could not get any better. But now a homemade breakfast with real apple cider. This was more than he could have imagined. "What can I do to help?" he said energetically.

"Well, how would you like your eggs cooked?" Günter asked.

"However, you make them......and whatever is easiest for you," he replied.

"All right then, scrambled it is," Günter said as he clapped his hands together, "You can get the white bowl from the cupboard over there and break six eggs into it. Do you like it with milk? Please say no."

Gaetano chuckled, "My Papà doesn't like milk in his eggs either. But my Mamma always makes them that way. I prefer no milk as well."

"Good to hear," Günter said with a smile, "I'll go downstairs to the root cellar and get a jar of apple cider."

Gaetano went to the cupboard and pulled out the bowl. He cracked open six eggs and noticed two of them had double yokes. "These eggs are huge!" he said to Günter when he came back upstairs, "Two of them had double yokes. Does that happen all the time?"

"Sure does," he quipped, "I have big chickens I guess."

"You mentioned milk," Gaetano asked, "I didn't see a cow in your barn."

"I have a neighbor with ten cows," he replied, "I trade with him. Some eggs or cider for the little bit of milk I need, which isn't much."

"How long have you been here?" Gaetano asked. He was starting to show his curiosity. Günter did not mind one bit.

He put the cider on the table and walked over to the stove to set up to scramble the eggs. Gaetano finished beating them with the fork he had taken out of the drawer. He handed the bowl to Günter. "I finished the house just over two years ago. Just in time for my retirement."

"You said you were a train engineer?" Gaetano continued, "When did you start that?"

"Well," Günter replied, "You can't just walk into that kind of work. You have to work your way up. It took me until I was almost thirty to land the engineer position. For years I did the demanding work, shoveling coal, hitching cars, throwing switches, and tossing logs in the early days.

"My father worked in the train yards outside of Zurich. He got me my first job. His job was to set up the trains with their engines and get them ready for their journey. Back then, he did everything from engine maintenance to stocking the cupboards in the caboose. The closest he ever got to being an engineer was moving the engines around the yard. Some engineers aren't really very good at that. But then he never had to learn how to judge speed and weather conditions."

"How did you learn to speak English so well?" Gaetano asked.

"Huh," Günter grunted, "Like most real motivators in life. It was a girl."

"Yeah?" Gaetano smiled, "What was her name?"

"Not sure I remember," Günter said while looking up as if the answer was on the ceiling. "Bess, I think. She was from England. I was about thirty-two at the time. Fell hard for that one."

"Must not have been all that hard," Gaetano quipped, "you can't remember her name."

"Wait until you're my age young man," Günter grinned, "you'll be lucky to remember what day it is. Never mind the name of an old flame." They both laughed. "We met in Zurich. Her father was in banking and would come twice a year from London to do business. You know how it is, if I wanted the girl, I had to go to England to be with her."

"How long were you together?" Gaetano asked,

"Just four months. I stayed in England for four years though," he went on. "Eventually I moved back. There was too much rain."

"Well, your English is very good," Gaetano added, "It took me almost two years before I was comfortable speaking it once I moved to America. How many languages can you speak?"

"Seven," he said quickly, "Eight if you count Arabic."

"Seven?" Gaetano said sounding amazed, "And some Arabic? Why Arabic?"

"In my late forties into my early fifties I landed a job on a line that took me out past Turkey," Günter said with some pride, "we would run from Paris to Istanbul weekly. I had to learn some Arabic as well as Turkish in order to get by in the train yards at the end of the run. There would be layovers as well. So, I had to learn the languages."

"Which others? Besides English, obviously German and I thought you spoke some Italian yesterday," Gaetano continued to ask.

"For some reason, I never got very good at Italian," Günter said, "probably because I only worked on a line that went through Italy for a couple of years. The others on the train spoke Italian so I never really needed to. Besides those you mentioned, let's see, Danish, French, and Swedish."

"Swedish?" Gaetano questioned, "Let me guess, a girl?"

Günter laughed, "How did you know? Actually no, Swedish and Danish are similar. Like Spanish, French, and Italian are similar. Some of the people I worked with would teach me and I would teach them other languages. Surprised I never learned Spanish though. Guess I only learned the languages I came in direct contact with on a regular basis. I didn't do any runs to Spain and none of the others I worked with spoke much Spanish. At least not that I ever knew.

"So why settle here?" Gaetano asked, wanting to know all he could.

"Not far from where I grew up, I suppose," he continued, "besides, this area is so beautiful year-round. Just look outside. Have you ever seen that much snow before?"

"I was going to ask you," Gaetano seemed a bit nervous to mention it, "how am I going to find my way, I can't even see the road."

Günter put his hand on his shoulder, "It looks like you're stuck here for a while. That's if you don't mind listening to an old man's stories."

"No," Gaetano said reassuringly, "I like talking to you. You kind of remind me a bit of Signor Rizzi I used to work for in my hometown in Italy before I moved to America."

Günter nodded his head in humble approval. "This snow makes things impassable. The trains won't be running for a few days and then on a very limited basis............ if at all."

Gaetano had not contemplated being stranded. The thought came with mixed feelings. Part of him wanted to leave and find his way home to America. Part wanted to stay and enjoy this beautiful home. And part was tugging at him to return and finish his job in the Army. It appeared that decision was being made for him, at least for the time being.

"I don't want to be a burden on you," he said with a serious tone, "you've been very generous to me. I really don't deserve it."

"Generous has nothing to do with it. Remember, it is Christmas, or have you forgotten," Günter said trying to reassure him.

"Christmas? That's right, I had forgotten completely. I didn't even think about it when I woke up this morning," Gaetano said a bit embarrassed he had forgotten Christmas, "So Merry Christmas then."

"And to you," Günter replied.

Gaetano continued, "I remember my first Christmas when I had just moved to America. I got up before everybody. We didn't have much, but it was still nice exchanging presents. I wish I had something to give you. You've been too kind to me already."

"Someone to spend Christmas with," Günter said, "That's all I wanted. I prayed about that just last week and look, here you are. I got what I asked for. Eggs are ready. Let's eat." They sat down and Gaetano folded his hands waiting for Günter to say grace. He did and they began to eat.

"Were you ever married?" Gaetano asked and then wished he had not. It was a very personal question.

Günter paused for a moment and looked to the ceiling for the answer again. "Yes............. for a brief time," he replied.

Gaetano was embarrassed he had asked. So, he did not follow up. But Günter continued anyway. "It was shortly after returning from England. We met in Zurich. I figured a girl from my home country would be better than someone I would meet in my travels."

Gaetano did not want to pry but Günter seemed willing to discuss it. "What happened?" he asked hesitantly.

"Well, I was in my late thirties nearly forty. We had been married for three years," He began to speak softly, "I figured I would never have children. I was almost forty like I said. And she was thirty-three. One day she told me I was going to be a father."

"That must have been exciting!" Gaetano jumped in.

"Yes," Günter added, "I even thought about taking a job in the train yard like my father did so I could be home once the baby came. But there wasn't anything available." He paused for a couple of moments. It seemed like an hour. Gaetano did not want to push on this subject.

"I was in Paris and planned to be home the next week when the doctors said she was due," Günter continued, "they had given me some time off knowing we were about to have a baby.................. Something happened, she was early. We had someone checking in on her with her parents standing close by........................ She died giving childbirth. Neither one made it. It came on so suddenly............. Her mother never forgave me for not being there.......... But her father understood."

Gaetano wanted to say something like 'I'm sorry' but he just sat there stunned. After a bit he asked, "Did you ever think of getting married again?"

Günter gave a half smile and a chuckle, "A lady like that only comes along once in a man's life. There was never anyone who even came close."

"She must have been very special," Gaetano said trying to be consoling, "that was terrible. You must be sad."

"Not anymore," Günter said with a smile and glassy eyes, "they're in a much better place. Someday, I'll be there too."

Gaetano sat trying to figure out what to say next, but he was lost. His heart went out to Günter and wondered if he might be able to deal with things as well someday.

"That was then this is now," Günter said with a change in tone, "So I saved all of my money in order to build a house to live in when I retired and here it is. You like it?"

"Very much!" Gaetano said glad Günter was cheerful again and changing the subject.

"Tomorrow, I'll show you around," he said having moved past the memories. "Have you ever fed horses?"

"No, they're really big," he said, "they must eat a lot."

"Not as much as you might think," Günter replied, "I try not to over feed the animals. They aren't like us humans. We eat too much and keep eating."

"I want to learn," Gaetano jumped at the chance to help again, "I'll do whatever you need me to do around here. I like to work."

"I'll take you up on that too," Günter said, "but not today. Today is Christmas and I just want to enjoy the peace and the company. Do you play cribbage?"

"I don't know what that is, a game of some sort," Gaetano asked.

"I'll teach you," Günter said with a smile.

. . . .

THE DAY WAS FILLED with joy and rest as these two unlikely roommates talked and played cards. By mid-afternoon, Günter broke away to start the dinner. He had picked up a goose the morning before in town. The sled tracks he had left on the way to and from town were what Gaetano ended up seeing when looking for a place to hold up. "Come with me," Günter said to Gaetano. He led him downstairs and showed him the root cellar. "This is where I keep things that need to stay cool but not on ice." He grabbed two potatoes and two carrots and handed them to Gaetano, "You have the honors of peeling them."

"My pleasure," Gaetano responded, "Like I said, anything you need me to do."

Gaetano looked over and could see the boiler set up Günter had made. It looked very elaborate to him. But he figured it was simple to Günter. He remembered Günter said he would show him around tomorrow, so he did not ask to go see it right then.

They went upstairs and Günter started to prepare the goose. Gaetano peeled the potatoes and carrots and cut them up into two pots. "This reminds me," he said to Günter. "It was just last week. A man gave me a ride in his carriage and then told me about the train tracks which led me here. He also told me about this cabin he used sometime for hunting and told me I could stay there that night."

"Did you?" Günter asked.

"Just the one night," Gaetano said.

"What made you think of it?" he continued.

"The potatoes," Gaetano chuckled, "he had given me some food to take, and I had a couple of potatoes. I cooked them with some crushed garlic in the water."

"Garlic? Was that any good?" Günter questioned.

"I guess," he shook his head, "it could have been better. I put some salt in too."

"Ah, I always add salt to my potatoes," Günter said, "let's put some water in these to keep them fresh until the goose cooks enough."

Once the goose was in the oven, they went back to playing cards. Three hours went by quickly and it was time to eat the Christmas goose. A tradition not all cultures embrace, but it was a standard for Günter growing up. So, Gaetano was introduced to it.

The evening was like the previous one with Gaetano sitting in his new favorite chair and Günter reading his latest book. And just like the night before, by nine o'clock Gaetano had fallen asleep.

Chapter 30

Sunday morning December twenty-sixth saw even more snow. It was coming down hard when Gaetano woke up. This morning it was closer to eight o'clock. He woke up to the sound of the steam pipes clanging. Günter had not stoked the fire as well the night before, so things had cooled down some. As he fired the boiler up again, the pipes began to expand.

Gaetano put his pants on and ran downstairs because he wanted to see Günter working on the boiler. Günter was surprised to see him up that early. "So, you get enough rest?" he asked.

"Yes, I'm fine," Gaetano replied.

"Didn't wake you up, did I?" Günter sounded a bit concerned, "I didn't want this to cool down too much."

"Not a problem," he replied, "Besides, I can't sleep my life away, as much as I would like sometimes. And I wanted to help you today. You said something about feeding the horses?"

"They're probably hungry by now," Günter sighed, "There's enough hay to hold them over until I can give them some grain. There'll be some eggs out there too."

"I was thinking," Gaetano hesitated, "they must need to be cleaned up after, the stalls and everything."

"Hmm," Günter grunted, "smart kid."

"Not that smart," Gaetano laughed, "I think I just volunteered to shovel horse poop."

"That you did," Günter laughed nodding his head.

"So, what is all this," Gaetano asked as he was looking at the gauges and valves.

"My little invention?" Günter smirked,

"Yeah?" Gaetano replied and kept looking around. He knew not to touch anything. "This is some contraption. How does it work?"

"Well, I'm glad you asked," Günter answered. He was in his glory. "I modeled it after the steam engines on the trains where I used to work." Gaetano did not have to keep asking questions, his eyes were doing all the asking.

"You have two ways to heat a house with steam," he continued, "the most common method is to have a shut off valve that opens and closes with a thermostat you put in the living area. The thing I don't like about that is the clanging pipes like you heard this morning. What I do is a bit different. I set the pressure levels to keep some level of steam going through the pipes at all times."

"Is that better?" Gaetano asked.

"I think so, but most people wouldn't want this system," Günter said enjoying the chance to explain it, "You have to keep a close eye on the fuel supply, the pressure, and the water levels. Most people would not want the extra effort. The other thing is the heater design in the living area. You probably didn't notice any of those large cast iron heaters around, right?

"Uh, I hadn't really looked," Gaetano stammered.

"Most people use them because they work well with steam and hot water," Günter continued, "Did you see any heaters?" Gaetano shook his head. "You didn't. That's because I put the pipes in the floors. Back and forth between the joists, see?" Günter pointed to some that they could see where they were standing. "Then I added some grates in key locations for the heat to rise."

"The same on the second floor?" Gaetano asked, sounding even more interested.

"Pretty much," Günter replied, "but we don't need as many because the heat from the first floor rises. Plus, all the rooms on the second level have grates that I can open or close based on which rooms I want to heat. The floors on the first level radiate an even heat constantly and the pipes never..............well I mean rarely get cool, so therefore, no clanging pipes, except when I forget or get lazy like last night."

"A lot to be proud of," Gaetano smiled.

"Well, I prefer saying happy with, I've seen what pride can do," Günter said trying not to be contrary.

Gaetano looked around for a couple of moments and then changed the subject. "They say that when you live in the country, you do all the chores before breakfast."

"You're catching on fast," Günter said, "There's a lot to do. Let's head out to the barn. Oh, you'll need the coat you wore when you arrived."

They headed upstairs and bundled up. There was a lot of snow between them and the barn. Günter had made a path the morning before, but it was already covered by the new snow. The two men trudged through creating something of a path for them to follow back when they were done. The snow was coming down like a blizzard. Fortunately, there was a fence line which ran straight from the house to the barn. The snow was coming down so hard, someone could easily take a wrong turn and end up going away from the house. All they needed to do was to follow the fence. Which at this point, was only sticking out of the snow by about a foot and a half.

The path to the barn was packed down some but it was still difficult to get through. The large doors opened out, so they were impossible to open with the snow piled up. There was a smaller door to the right of them which opened inward. That was the target. It took them quite a while to reach it. Gaetano understood how someone could get lost going just fifty yards.

Günter showed Gaetano where everything was so he could start cleaning up the stalls and laying down some new hay. He showed him how to mix up the grains for the horses and where to put it for them so they would not knock it down. While Gaetano was doing that, Günter went to the usual places to find the eggs. If there did not seem to be the regular amount, he would hunt around for any new creative places the hens may have chosen to lay eggs since the day before. He always counted on each chicken laying one egg per day. It was rare if he was not able to find them all. They could be very clever and reach places which were difficult for Günter to get to.

Such was the case this day. He was four eggs short. Two he found easily but the other two were not so easy to find. Sometimes if he took out the chicken feed, they would come running and then he would see where they came from and look for the eggs in that direction. Once Gaetano was finished, he helped join in the search. They each found one of the two missing eggs.

The horses were fed, and the stalls cleaned up. Gaetano broke up the ice on the water troughs. Günter had the builders drill a well from inside the barn. This gave him the ability to pump from inside on days like this and it was less prone to freeze up. The pump was right next to the trough, so Gaetano pumped up some more water.

The chickens were fed, and the eggs gathered. Günter did not own a rooster. So, he never had to worry if any of the eggs were fertilized. One of his neighbors would bring by a couple of roosters twice a year to help Günter keep his supply of hens up. Any males, he would give to the neighbor.

In nicer weather, there would be far more chores to do, but with another blizzard on them, they decided to go back to the house. "Guess I won't be making it to church today." Günter said as they were about to open the door of the barn to leave. Günter figured this blizzard would carry over until nightfall. He was normally able to hitch the horses and make it to church even if there was snow. But, in a blizzard like this. These conditions were such that only the people who lived in town near the church made it to service.

"Do you have a shovel I can use to cut a path to the house?" Gaetano asked.

Günter looked at him sheepishly. "It's at the house," he said, "Besides, it's just going to keep coming down. We can tackle cutting a path when it stops. If not, I do have a pair of snowshoes."

Gaetano had heard of snowshoes and had even seen pictures of them. But he had never seen a pair up close, let alone wear them. Just in the hour they were in the barn, it snowed another three inches. The return trip was even more difficult, but they made it.

As they got back in, Gaetano looked down in the mud room and noticed his pack. He had put it down first thing when he came in the door two days before. "How do you wash clothes?" he asked Günter, "is there a basin somewhere? I should wash my uniform and blanket. I can wash things for you also."

"You don't have to wash my things," Günter said not wanting to put everything on Gaetano.

"No, I want to help around here. I don't mind," He insisted.

"Downstairs behind the boiler," Günter replied, "I have a sink set up there."

Gaetano opened his pack and looked in at his regular items. His canteen, mess kit and his hair cutting tools. "Oh," he exclaimed, "I can give you a haircut."

This surprised Günter. It was not something he would expect to hear, "Haircut?" he asked surprised.

"They trained each of us to do things in the Army," he replied, "different things so not everybody did the same thing. Me? They taught me to cut hair. I still have my tools. Well, scissors, comb, and a brush.......... see."

"Maybe I'll take you up on it next week sometime," Günter said almost trying to change the subject. Some men just do not like getting haircuts from someone they are used to.

'Next week?' Gaetano thought to himself. The realization was getting more obvious he would likely be stranded for some time. The thought was quite reassuring. This would give him time to get things settled in his mind.

Gaetano set himself to get washing his uniform and blanket. He wondered if the coat needed to be washed too but did not know if he could. He had remembered his Mamma once taught him winter coats do not get washed like regular clothes. He went upstairs and grabbed his uniform and tried not to let it get him dirty. Günter met him in the cellar and pulled out the wash basin for him.

"Soap is up on the shelf right there in front," Günter said.

"Thanks," Gaetano said looking around, "Did you want me to wash anything for you?"

"No thank you," Günter responded, "I do mine on Wednesdays and I usually don't break my routine. You can hang things up by the boiler." Günter had set up a couple of ropes for hanging clothes to dry during the winter since they could not hang up outside. "They'll dry fast there and be very warm when you wear them which come to think of it, probably doesn't matter since you're likely not to use them anytime soon."

Gaetano just nodded because it was not a subject which he was ready to discuss with his host. He was not sure he even wanted to discuss it with himself. There was much too much turmoil in his heart about what was the right thing to do. Günter had a sense it was still too sensitive a subject to bring up, so he just patted Gaetano on the back and started upstairs to have a cup of coffee and prepare breakfast.

"Do you want me to bring you some coffee?" Günter asked him as he reached the bottom of the stairs.

Gaetano had almost forgotten about breakfast and looked down at his wash thinking maybe he should have waited until after breakfast to start, "No thank you. This won't take long and then I'll be up. Or maybe I should let them soak for a while and finish after breakfast."

Günter nodded his head and went upstairs. Gaetano was motivated to get it set up and start soaking quickly. So, he went right to it. He opened the faucets and got the hot water right away. Once he had enough water he put in a bit of soap. He did not want to put too much and figured he could add some after breakfast if he needed to in order to get things clean.

Gaetano walked upstairs and went over to the stove to get some coffee. "Where does your running water come from?" he asked Günter.

"Here, I'll show you," Günter said as he got up from the kitchen table and walked over to the window which faced the back of the house. Gaetano walked over and looked out as well.

"See back there," Günter said pointing to a break in the trees, "You can see the hill go up steep right there."

"Yeah, I see it," Gaetano said leaning toward the window.

"Follow that path up the hill about two hundred yards. It gets steep just beyond the bend," Günter said, "you can't see that far. It goes almost straight up at one point. I buried a pipe through that area. I had them cut the trees, pull the stumps, and dig down almost four feet."

"Them?" Gaetano asked.

"Five men who were out of work one summer about four years ago. Just before I put in the foundation below us," Günter said remembering back, "They had to use some machinery for parts of it, but some places were just too steep for machines."

"So, where does it all lead to?" Gaetano asked very curiously.

"Well, there's a spring on the side of the mountain," he continued.

"A well?" Gaetano said with a smirk.

"A spring," Günter said confused by the question.

"You said 'Well, there's a spring...'" he giggled.

"Oh, I get it.... well.... hmmm....... funny," Günter said very patronizingly, "where did you learn to joke like that?"

"My friend Steven and I went to a Vaudeville show in New York," he answered.

"Vaudeville? Oh yes, I heard about that," Günter said, still a bit confused by the style of humor. "It's a type of American theater thing, isn't it? We don't have that kind of theater here. Not I've ever seen."

"It originally started in Europe," Gaetano added, "Poland, I think. Sorry, I couldn't help myself," Gaetano said giggling some more.

"Well," he continued and then realized he said it again. Gaetano giggled again. "The spring is up there a ways," Günter pointed out the window and shook his head.

"It seems to have a lot of pressure," Gaetano continued to question, "Can a spring be that strong?"

"Good question," Günter said, "At the top of the line I set up a tank to catch the water. It works like a water tower. The weight of the water pushes down on the line and creates the pressure."

"What kind of tank?" Gaetano was starting to sound like a four-year-old asking too many questions.

"I made it out of stone and mortar," he replied, "It's twenty feet in diameter and eight feet deep."

"Is it full all the time?" he continued relentlessly.

"This time of year, probably," Günter speculated, "Definitely during the spring."

"Doesn't it get dirty with things falling into it?" Gaetano was asking more interesting questions.

"Ah," Günter said, "No, I built a lid for it. It's supported in the middle by a stone pillar I put in and made something of a roof with a door so I can get in to do maintenance if I need to."

"So, nothing can get in the water then," Gaetano said starting to get the idea.

"Pretty much," Günter replied, "Most of the time."

"Why? What do you mean 'most of the time'?" Gaetano asked. He figured there was a story he wanted to hear.

"Last spring......." Günter hesitated wondering if he should tell this story. "Last spring I had been away for a few days and in the morning the day after I got back, I came down to make some coffee and I let the water run for a bit. I always do when I've been away, flushes out the pipes." He looked at Gaetano. still not certain if he wanted to tell him this. He had such a curious look on his face, he could not hesitate, so he continued. "I was running the water and all of a sudden, it was an instant change, the water smelled very badly."

"What kind of bad?" Gaetano asked with his eyes getting wider at each answer.

"You don't want to know," Günter said with a terrible look on his face, "It was one of the worst smells I've ever smelled."

Gaetano hesitated a bit and then asked, "So what did you do?"

"I got dressed and went up the hill," Günter added.

"And?" he prodded.

"I got to the tank and opened up the door," Günter said with a look of disgust on his face, "There was a dead animal of some sort in there. I think it was a raccoon, but it was too hard to tell."

"Why was it too hard to tell?" Gaetano asked and then realized why without Günter having to say, "Oh, you're kidding. It had been there for a few days and............. Oh, that's disgusting."

"You're right," Günter said with a shuttering tone in his voice coupled with a laugh.

"So, what did you do?" Gaetano asked, not really wanting to know the details.

"Fished it out," Günter said shaking his shoulders as if he had a chill, "Then I put some large rocks on the door. It probably pried the door open and got inside." The memory was still fresh in his mind. "Then I came down and opened every faucet in the house to drain out the tank."

"How long did that take?" Gaetano was shivering from the thought as well.

"I ran it for over a week," Günter said, "Just to be sure. The smell went away after two days, but I didn't want to take any chances. I went into town and bought some chemicals the merchant said would disinfect the water. I went back up the hill the day after to put it in. But I ran it all week anyway."

"What did you do in the meantime?" he asked.

"Went out to the barn and used the pump you were using this morning," Günter said proudly, "I knew I would need it for a backup. So that's the main reason I had them drill the well in the barn.... Well?" They looked at each other and laughed. "Sometimes during the summer, I have to use the pump because the tank loses pressure. I like to let it build up and not get too empty."

• • • •

GAETANO HELPED WITH breakfast the same as he had done the day before and they sat, ate, and drank coffee for a couple of hours watching the snow fall. Remembering his soaking laundry, Gaetano took a fresh cup of coffee and went downstairs to finish up. It did not take him long since he was not interested in getting his uniform all that clean. His blanket was not something he really needed either. After all, he had a bed with a quilt and flannel sheets to keep him warm. Sleeping outside was not something he could see himself doing anytime soon.

He could not help but wonder how his friends in the Army were doing with the weather. Did they have to sleep outside or were there tents? Maybe some of them were even sent to camps where there were barracks with heat. It was not something he needed to think about. That kind of thinking only made him glad he was not there to find out.

The snow stopped at around three in the afternoon. It had slowed down some shortly after noon, but Günter suggested waiting until the snow completely stopped before going out to clear the path to the barn. After a couple more hours, it was time to get started and they were ready to go. Günter had two snow shovels in case one broke.

Günter gave Gaetano an old pair of gloves he had laying around and they ventured out. There were only a couple of hours of daylight left so Gaetano wanted to work fast. They were about halfway finished when it was getting dark. Gaetano started to pick up the pace.

"Don't kill yourself," Günter told him, "we can always finish tomorrow or...." he turned and went to the house. A second later he came out with a lantern, "We can light this up," he said as he struck a match and lit the lantern. Günter hung it up on the back porch. That little lantern lit up the entire back yard between the house and the barn. The fresh snow reflected the light, and it was beautiful to look at. There was a gentle amber glow that evenly filled the yard.

Gaetano noticed Günter was getting tired. "Why don't you go in the house, I can finish," he told him.

"I'm all right," he replied, "but I do think I'm going to slow down some."

"How about if you go clear off the porch," Gaetano offered, "It's not heavy there. You can take it easier. Take your time." Günter nodded his head in agreement and headed over to the house to slowly clear off the porch.

By seven o'clock they were done. Gaetano was tired but glad he had had a chance to put in some hard work. He knew it would help him sleep that night. They both walked into the mud room and shook off the snow from their clothes. Günter was very tired and just wanted to sit for a while.

"Are you hungry?" Gaetano asked.

Günter nodded his head, "a bit."

"I noticed you have some rolls left," he continued as he walked over to the cupboard, "I can make us a couple of goose sandwiches." There was quite a bit leftover in the icebox.

"Sounds good," Günter said leaning his head back into his chair.

"Why don't you close your eyes for a few minutes while I fix these up?" he said with a smile glad he could help some more. Günter grunted and closed his eyes. He was asleep within seconds.

Gaetano made the sandwiches and looked over at Günter. He saw he was sound asleep and did not want to disturb him. He put a pot lid over the sandwiches and went to his favorite chair and sat for a while himself. The house was toasty warm, and he almost fell asleep himself. He dozed a bit but did not fall completely asleep.

About an hour later, Günter opened his eyes, "Oh my," he exclaimed, "how long was I out?"

Gaetano looked at his pocket watch. "About an hour," he replied.

Günter looked around not completely awake, "Did you eat?"

"No, I wanted to wait for you," he replied and pointed to the table with the sandwiches under the lid. "We can eat whenever you want, the sandwiches are made."

They got up and walked to the table. The sandwiches were still fresh because they had been covered. Gaetano poured some water for them, and they sat down. Günter said grace and they began to eat.

"You sure can put in a hard day's work," Gaetano said referring to the shoveling.

"Well, you have to remember what I did my whole life," Günter said, "a whole lot of shoveling at all hours of the day and night."

After they ate, they sat in the living room and played cribbage until almost midnight. They talked about a number of things in each of their lives. Günter told him about the four years he spent in England and Gaetano told Günter the story of when he confronted the purse snatcher in Napoli when his Nonna was bringing him to the ship to go to America. He began to wonder how his Nonna was doing and whether he would ever see her again.

The two unlikely roommates decided to call it a night and went off to bed but not before going downstairs to stoke the fire for the night. Gaetano wanted to watch how, so he would be able to help. He felt an overwhelming desire to repay this man's kindness. The only way he knew was to offer to help him do things around the house.

Chapter 31

The following mornings Gaetano got up early and went out to the barn first thing to care for the horses. Günter would come out around the time he was getting done so he could gather the eggs. Thursday morning Günter's neighbor Karl came by to drop off some milk and get some eggs. Gaetano could hear them talking but they spoke to each other in German, so he did not understand much of their conversation.

"Who's the boy?" Karl said noticing Gaetano working in the barn.

"That would be Gaetano," Günter said wondering what Karl was making of it. Gaetano heard his name and realized they were talking about him. He just kept working and pretended he did not hear them.

"Where did he come from? I know he's not family," Karl questioned. Karl had a tendency to be curious and not let things go unanswered.

"Oh, he just wandered in. Found him in the barn on Christmas Eve," Günter said.

"Just took him in? Just like that?" Karl asked with a slight bit of condescension.

"He's just a young man trying to find his way. That's all," Günter said with a slight sigh, "We all have to find our way, right?" Günter knew Karl's story and how he had struggled when he was young and still getting established.

"Guess you're right," he conceded, "how long is he staying for?"

"You ask a lot of questions Karl," Günter said a bit sternly.

"Just concerned for my friends, that's all," he said trying to soften his prying, "I'm sure you know what you're doing. Thanks for the eggs. Will you be needing more milk now there are two?"

"I'll let you know. Thanks Karl," Günter said hoping he was about to leave. Ordinarily their exchanges were more pleasant. They were good friends, but Karl had a way of sticking his nose into everyone's business. He left and Günter shook his head glad he did not have to deal with him anymore that day.

After he was out of sight Günter walked over to Gaetano and pointed to the sled in the barn, "I'm going to hitch them up and go into town. Do you want to come?"

"I sure do," Gaetano answered. He was getting a bit of cabin fever and wanted to get out.

"I have some errands to do now that the snow is packed down some," Günter continued, "you mentioned you like to work."

Gaetano looked at him curiously, "Yeah?"

"Well, I had an idea," he said looking at Gaetano to see his reaction, "There's a barber in town...."

Gaetano thought he was going to say he preferred getting his haircut from his own barber, which was likely true, "If you'd rather go to him, I understand. I was just offering."

Günter put his hand on his shoulder, "I was going to ask you if you wanted me to talk to him about having you cut hair at his shop if he has the need for an extra barber."

Gaetano looked surprised and was a bit embarrassed at what he had said, "Oh................ sure............. that sounds good." He thought about it a second more and then realized it was a great idea. "That way I can pitch in to help with the food, I'm eating you out of everything."

Günter just smiled, "If it were a problem, I wouldn't have let you stay. I have enough food. I'm not worried about it. I just thought you would like to have some activity out of the house. Just until you figure out what you want to do. Since the trains are not running very often. That plus, you will need to make money all your life and the more things you know how to do, the better off you'll be. It'll keep you in practice."

Gaetano thought a moment and nodded his head, "That's a good idea. How well do you know him? Will he listen to you?"

"I've known him his whole life," Günter added, "I knew his father, another railroad man."

"I know it's not the right thing to ask," Gaetano said hesitantly, "But how much does a barber make?"

"If it's your shop," Günter responded, "the entire charge for the haircut or shave." Gaetano looked at him hoping for the best. "And if you're working there, I'm pretty sure you get about half plus whatever tips you can get."

Gaetano's face lit up. He had some understanding of what a haircut cost but not in this area. It was the motivation he needed to speed up his chores. They went inside the house and ate a fast breakfast which consisted of some coffee and muffins Günter had made the night before. Once done, they headed right back to the barn to hitch up the horses. A task which was mostly Günter's effort. It was yet another thing Gaetano was able to watch and learn. He tried to help some though. Günter wanted him to get a bit of hands-on experience. This was a chance for the horses to learn to trust him as well. He had been with them for a few days now and they were no longer afraid of him. This was a good next step.

"Should I bring my tools?" he asked Günter.

"Not today," Günter answered, "Not sure if he needs anyone yet." Günter was pleased to see his enthusiasm.

The ride into town was shorter than he would have thought. It had taken him almost three hours to walk on the day he got off the train. With the horses and the sled, the trip went much quicker. They were somewhat limited as to where they could go with the sled. The snowpack was not as thick in town, so they left the carriage in the place that Günter was familiar with. It was close enough for them to carry back the things Günter needed.

Before the shopping errands though, there was the trip to the barber shop. As they approached, Gaetano struggled to see if he could make out anybody inside. He was curious to see how busy he might be the week between Christmas and New Year.

Günter went in first with Gaetano close behind. There were four barber's chairs but only one barber......and five men waiting for haircuts. This was starting to look good for Gaetano. The barber waved to Günter obviously acknowledging he knew him well. He did not give Gaetano a second look though figuring he was another customer.

"Eber, haben Sie kurz Zeit?" Günter said to him in German but Gaetano sort of
understood.

He was at a point where he could break away. The haircut was finished, and he just needed to clean up the customer. Günter took him to the side near the front door so others would not hear the conversation. Eber looked over at Gaetano a couple of times as they talked. He started to nod his head in what seemed to be agreement then looked over at Gaetano again.

Günter signaled him to come over. He spoke to him in English. "Gaetano, this is Eberhard Rheingold, he owns this shop," Gaetano reached out to shake his hand, "I told him you don't speak any German even though you may know a few words. He does, however, speak enough Italian to get by. So, you can speak to him in Italian."

Gaetano looked straight at Eber. "Signor, it is a pleasure to meet you," he said to him in Italian.

"Günter tells me you have enough experience to do some barbering," Eber said, "and you need to find work."

"Yes Signor," he replied, "I would like to have a chance to prove myself to you." Günter had told him not to mention he was taught to cut hair in the Italian Army. That would bring up too many questions Günter knew Gaetano was not ready to answer. Not just yet. With Günter's referral, all of those types of questions would not be necessary. He would simply have to cut hair well enough to please Eber's customers.

"I can use you two days a week," Eber said getting right to business, "Friday and Saturday, all day, or until people stop coming in."

"Friday and Saturday, that's good, very good," Gaetano said nodding his head up and down in approval. "Thank you, Signor. I will work hard."

"I believe you will," he added, "especially if this man brought you in." he pointed to Günter.

"This week is the new year, so we are closed on Saturday," Eber continued, "be here at eight o'clock tomorrow morning. It has been busy lately, so I could use the help."

"I should bring my tools, right?" Gaetano asked him, trying to sound very professional.

"You have your own tools?" he questioned, "that's very good. Yes, bring your own tools."

Gaetano was tempted to ask him how much he could make but Günter had told him not to discuss pay right away. He told him Eber was an honest man and would do right by him. Gaetano realized he was busy with a shop full of customers who figured they were going to leave right away. But Günter sent Gaetano back to where he was standing before and said something else to Eber. Eber nodded his head and shook Günter's hand.

As they left, Gaetano could not wait to thank Günter. "He is a very nice man," Gaetano said, "I appreciate you doing that for me. What did you talk about after?"

"Eight o'clock in the morning was a bit early for me two days in a row," Günter said which made Gaetano wonder if there might be a problem. "He has a room upstairs from the barber shop which is not used right now. I asked him if you could stay there on Friday nights and I could come get you on Saturday afternoon."

"What did he say?" he asked.

"He was fine with that," Günter answered, "you just have to feed the stove to keep warm. You will have to eat at the restaurant on Friday night as well."

"I can do that." Gaetano replied. He felt like he did when he was living with his grandfather. He would take him places to teach him how to grow up.

• • • •

THEY HAD SEVERAL OTHER errands to run including a stop at the grocery store for some fresh meats Günter wanted to pick up. He told Gaetano he would put them in a chest in the barn. It was exposed to the cold enough to keep it frozen until they needed it. The chest was secure enough to keep animals out.

Before they stopped for the meat, Günter said he was hungry, so they went to the hotel and had lunch. It seemed everybody knew Günter on a first name basis. He had a lot of friends, and everyone obviously liked him.

The hotel restaurant was known around town for its special soups. On the menu this day was a lentil soup which the owner had developed over the years. Günter knew the schedule of which soups they served each day and part of his plan for coming into town this day was to get a bowl of Herman's lentil soup.

They sat in the back of the restaurant near to the fireplace. Gaetano had developed a chill from being out. The soup hit the spot for both of them, and they continued to talk about it all the way home.

Gaetano told him he wanted to learn how to make things like soup. "I was hoping Rocco would let me start doing some of the cooking at his restaurant," he said as they were leaving town, "I didn't mind cleaning up and doing dishes, but I sure wanted to try my hand at making the gravy."

"Gravy?" Günter asked, "I plan to make some gravy for the beef I just brought tonight. You can put some on the potatoes also if you like."

Gaetano began to giggle a bit without trying to make fun of him, "Our gravy is a bit different than that," he added.

"How is it different?" Günter said looking very confused.

"We serve the gravy on our spaghetti and penne," Gaetano replied.

Günter had a very puzzled look on his face trying to understand why gravy on spaghetti would be a good thing. "Well, I guess it takes all kinds," he said trying not to show he was still confused. However, it was obvious to Gaetano.

"Some people call it sauce, like spaghetti sauce," Gaetano said trying not to giggle.

"Oh," Günter said then he paused for a moment trying to figure out if he was still confused or if he really understood what gravy was to Gaetano. "That's different. I think I know what that is. Things are called by different names, depending on where you're from."

They arrived back at Günter's house before dark and Gaetano put the horses in their stalls. He gave them some fresh oats and spent a little time with them because now they were more friendly with him. Günter went straight in and started dinner.

Gaetano came in and helped with the usual things like peeling the potatoes and the carrots. It was like clockwork by now. They kept working and talking about things in their lives and mostly good memories. Günter was getting a better idea of what America was like and Gaetano was getting a feel for the life of a railroad man.

The evening was short since they had to get up early in order for Gaetano to get to the barber shop by eight in the morning. He put his haircutting tools by the door so he would not forget them in the morning. Günter went straight to bed and after a nice hot shower, Gaetano went to bed also.

• • • •

GÜNTER HAD A WIND-UP alarm clock which he left in Gaetano's room. It went off at five thirty in the morning and it was still dark out. Having been in the Army for most of that year, Gaetano knew when it is time to get up, you get up. They rushed down some coffee and hitched up the horses. If there had been a place for Gaetano to leave the horses during the day, he could have gone by himself. But Günter decided it would be best to bring him in and then come home after to catch up on some rest.

Gaetano's first day on the job came with some mixed feelings. He was glad to get a chance to make some money and cut some hair, but many of the customers were reluctant to try a new barber. Especially someone who was not from their town. Italians were plentiful in Gifbourg but not everybody could speak Italian. Some of the customers could speak it well and Eber tried to use that as a reason for them to try Gaetano. There were periods during the day when there might be two or three people waiting for a haircut but decided to wait for Eber. Gaetano just sat in his chair and read the paper.

The customers would ask him where he was from. He told them about the town where he was born, but few knew the area. He would also talk about America. The most engaging conversations that day were the men's curiosity about New York. Some of Gaetano's stories were a bit embellished though. He told them of the times he would go across the river with his Papà to Little Italy in lower Manhattan around Canal Street. It surprised them that the different European nationalities stayed so close to each of their own communities rather than mixing more. They figured it had been the reason for moving to America.

Günter came at about four thirty to see if they were finished for the day. There were only two customers left in the shop, and both wanted to use Eber. When they saw Günter coming, Eber called Gaetano into the back room and gave him his pay for the day. It was slightly more than he had expected. Eber gave him almost everything he had taken in because he felt bad about some people not wanting to use him right away.

"They will get to know you and start to use you," Eber said to him, "eventually you will get half of what you take in and all of your tips."

Gaetano was more than pleased. "I understand why they feel that way," he said, "I would probably do the same thing."

"I'll see you next Friday morning then," Eber added, "unless you come into town during the week." That was not likely. Günter usually planned to do his errands on either Friday or Saturday based on what he needed to get done. That way he was only making one extra trip into town to pick up Gaetano each week.

Günter spoke briefly with Eber and thanked him again for letting Gaetano work at his shop. They left and went straight home for what Günter promised would be a special dinner to celebrate the New Year. It was December thirty-first, and Gaetano was more than glad to put nineteen-fifteen behind him.

That evening they played some cribbage and talked more about their histories. Never anything too deep or troubling. Just telling each other about things which had happened and people they had known. Gaetano took out his pocket watch and set it down next to the cribbage board so they could see the clock reach twelve midnight. About eleven forty, Günter got up and went to the cabinet. He took out two shot glasses and opened a bottle of Schnapps and set one down next to Gaetano. "For the New Year," he said.

Gaetano looked a bit surprised. Günter had not had a single drink all the time he had been there and had wondered if he was a teetotaler. The look on his face was obvious so Günter explained, "I only have a small amount on special occasions like New Year's Eve." Gaetano nodded his head and took a sniff of the shot glass. He could tell it would be strong. He had dinner wine enough times, but never anything like this. When on furlough, he only drank beer.

They gazed at the watch closely as the last five minutes counted down. The cribbage game went on hold for a few minutes while they anticipated the new year. At the stroke of midnight, they toasted the hopes and dreams of the year to come, "May it bring much happiness and wisdom," Günter said, and they each took their shot of Schnapps.

For Gaetano it was a pleasure to have a toast with his new friend, and he was happy he was where he was. He also did not think he would be drinking more Schnapps any time soon.

Chapter 32

The New Year brought something of a routine for Gaetano. He would help Günter in the barn and around the house during the early part of the week and cut hair on Friday and Saturday at Eber's. There were several snowstorms during January and early February, but none of them interfered with Gaetano making it to work at the barber shop. The last two weeks of January were so busy Eber had Gaetano come in on Thursday also. The customers were getting used to him and he had more work to do.

One of Günter's horses took ill for a couple of days in early February, so Günter summoned one of the veterinarians in town through his neighbor Karl the morning he came to get some eggs. He was headed into town that day, so he agreed to get the message to the vet. It was a slow time of year for them due to the limited or almost nonexistent train service. It turned out to be nothing serious. But it did mean Gaetano had to walk into town that Thursday. He arrived by nine o'clock and Eber was concerned about why he was a bit late. Once he heard Günter had a problem with one of his horses and Gaetano still walked all the way to make it to work, he was not only relieved but grew to respect Gaetano even more than he had already.

The only downside to Gaetano working at the barber shop was the room he would stay in was not a clean place. One Saturday he got up early and tried to clean a bit, but he needed to get downstairs by eight o'clock and did not have much time to get things done. Each week he would try to do a little bit more. But it still was not anything like staying at Günter's. Günter's house was like a palace to him. He appreciated every moment he was there.

Eber would keep a pot of coffee going on the stove on Saturdays as a complimentary gesture to his customers. Saturdays were a popular day at the shop, and it usually brought in a larger crowd. He knew better than to have free coffee all week long. The men would just come for coffee and hang around but not get a haircut. He had tried that early on when he first started in business and learned the hard way.

Winters were long in the Swiss Alps even though they were far enough south for the season to change early. They were at a high elevation, so it stayed cold longer in the Gifbourg area. Gaetano became quite familiar with clearing a path to the barn and riding on a horse drawn sleigh.

As March approached the conversations between Gaetano and Günter became more in depth. Some evenings would go late into the night as Gaetano would talk about how he had come to Italy to care for his aging grandmother and was reluctantly recruited into the Army.

The twenty-seventh was the last Sunday in February. Günter and Gaetano went into town for church like they had become used to doing. That particular Sunday was a bit different. The sermon was about forgiveness and how we needed to be willing to forgive those who have hurt us, no matter how badly.

That afternoon Günter noticed Gaetano was very agitated. He was not unfriendly or short with him, but he was just on edge. Something was bothering him. They had a chicken dinner that night and after cleaning up they sat down for one of their lengthy conversations.

"You've seemed troubled all-day Gaetano," Günter said as the opening to the conversation, "Is there something on your mind?"

"Not sure," he replied, "I keep thinking about something that I hadn't been for some time. Not since the fall it seems."

Günter looked at him with a look which said, 'You can tell me. It's Okay.' It took a couple of minutes because Gaetano just could not get it out. "You don't have to tell me," Günter said, "if you don't feel right talking about it." He knew the young man who had come to stay with him had many things he needed to sort through. But it would have to be at the right time. Gaetano wanted to take him up on the offer to drop it, but it had been eating at him all day. He thought about it some more and then decided to tell him some of what was bothering him.

"I had this sergeant," Gaetano said "he was a very brave man. We all respected him because he knew how to be a soldier. And he taught us well." Gaetano took a deep breath and continued. "One day they started by bombarding the enemy positions pretty heavily. We ran out to catch them off guard because we assumed they would expect the bombing to continue for some time. It was a good plan. Two of us got there ahead of the others and jumped into the enemy's trench."

Günter sat and listened and made a point to not interject. He knew this would be a one-sided conversation for a while. They had brewed some coffee, and he took a sip of his as it was not yet cool enough to drink.

"We fought hard that day..................... His name was Sergeant Patrizi. Funny though, I can't really remember his face, just his uniform. It wasn't that long ago either," Gaetano said shaking his head. "He and I ran to the left after taking down some of the first enemy soldiers we encountered. Then he tripped over a dead soldier, lost his balance and just then another enemy soldier jumped down on him. He couldn't regain his balance and went down. If only he hadn't tripped."

"What happened?" Günter asked.

"The enemy soldier. He got him with his bayonet," Gaetano paused, "And then he shot him to make sure he killed him."

"What did you do?" Günter asked but did not want to pressure him. He knew there was something Gaetano needed to talk about.

"I went crazy. They told me after," he said then paused again. "they told me that I just kept hitting him and hitting him until he didn't have a head left. I hit him with my rifle butt over and over. The memory seems more like a dream than reality."

"That's what's been on your mind all day?" Günter asked, thinking maybe he was getting to the bottom of what was bothering him.

Gaetano's eyes glazed over. He hung his head and did not say anything for a minute or so. "No," he said, "that's a part of war. You lose people you fight with all the time. It was his time to die that day."

"But that had something to do with what has been troubling you today?" Günter asked, trying to help him say the things he obviously really wanted to say. He knew him well enough by now to pry some.

"It's what it led to," Gaetano said, "after the battle was over, the rest of the men who reported to Sergeant Patrizi met back at the base camp and got scooped up by this lunatic lieutenant. He took us on a mission to circle around the enemy positions and take them by surprise." Gaetano noticed his coffee was there and took a sip to see if it was cool enough to drink. Günter also reached over for his and held on to it because it was just the right temperature now.

"Did it work?" Günter asked.

"Not really," Gaetano continued, "ultimately, we never got to where we were going. It all started to go wrong right away." Günter kept an interested ear, and Gaetano knew he was listening very intently. "Late afternoon on the first day out, we came across a machine gun nest, a pillbox they called it."

"I know what those are," Günter said, "we often would see them on hillsides along the tracks. All overgrown and abandoned from some earlier conflict. What happened?"

Gaetano looked like he wanted to quit before he got any deeper into it, but he continued anyway, "We found them the hard way. The lunatic lieutenant had four men walk ahead to supposedly scout. But I think they were just bait, and he knew it full well." Gaetano shook his head in disbelief. "They knew how to set the trap all right. And the four dumb clucks walked right into it. We had been walking in a ravine with fairly good cover but when these guys walked into a clearing, they were waiting for them. There was no place for them to run. Five to ten seconds. That's all it took." Günter's look asked the question without him having to speak. "Oh, we all ran for cover when the shots rang out. We weren't the ones they were shooting at. At least not right then."

"So, did you circle around?" Günter asked.

A look of disgust came over Gaetano's face, "If only we had............ This crazy.... lunatic............ I can't say it. I was in church today." Günter gave a safe chuckle. Not a chuckle that would say it was funny, rather he understood completely. "This............... lieutenant started ordering men to rush the machine gun nest two at a time at first. Did that twice and all four were killed immediately. Then he started sending them out one at a time and went through four or five more before he stopped."

"It doesn't sound like he knew what he was doing," Günter added knowing this was tough for Gaetano to talk about. "Then what?"

Gaetano looked even more disgusted now. "Remember the friend of mine I told you about on the Hallwick?"

"The kid from Rome?" Günter questioned.

"Yeah, Augie," Gaetano said, "The guys on the ship used to call him Augie. I usually called him Augustino. I think it made him feel more grown up. He liked that." There was another long pause and some more facial expressions as he continued. "This............ I still can't say it....... lieutenant started walking up and down the line of soldiers who were all trying to stay invisible. I was wondering what he was doing. It didn't make any sense for him to keep walking back and forth like that."

Gaetano paused for quite some time. "He grabbed Augustino, pulled him up, and started screaming at him 'you next'..................... Augie was scared, I mean really scared. We had just watched eight or nine men get cut down on top of the four who got it walking ahead of us and there was no sense to any of it." A change came over Gaetano, his voice deepened. He was no longer scared to tell it. He was angry.

"What happened?" Günter asked, afraid of the answer.

"Augie started to argue with him," Gaetano said in a very stern voice now, "He tried to reason with him. At one point he dropped to the ground, I think. The lieutenant pulled him up and started screaming at him calling him a coward. Augie just kept pleading with him................ Then he shot him."

Günter was not sure he heard right, "Who?"

"That........I can't say it..... he just shot Augie. He shot him right in the back of the head," Gaetano started to shutter as he was telling it. "He just shot him. One of our own, he just shot him." Gaetano hung his head down and stared at the floor.

The tears were obvious to Günter. He now realized why Gaetano had been edgy all day. "The sermon today, right?" Günter asked.

Gaetano looked up at him lifting his head only halfway and looking up with his eyes the rest. He shook his head acknowledging Günter was right on the money. "How can you forgive someone who does something like that? He never said he was wrong. He never said he was sorry."

Günter knew he needed to choose his words carefully. This was a tough thing for a person to struggle with. He paused and gave Gaetano some time to settle down.

"There are different ways to forgive Gaetano," Günter finally said softly.

This confused Gaetano as he looked straight at him now with his head all the way up looking curiously but wanting to hear what he meant by this. "The preacher said we need to forgive no matter what right?" Gaetano said.

Günter nodded his head to agree but needed to qualify things a bit. "Think of it like this," he said, "if you have a friend or neighbor and they do something to hurt you. There is no doubt about what they did, and everyone knows it. At some point they realize what they've done, and they regret it. Then they come to you and say they're sorry for hurting you. You forgive them, right?"

"That's the easy part," Gaetano said agreeing, "they're your friend you should forgive them. Or you won't have any friends after a while." He added a chuckle.

"True," Günter nodded, "and like the preacher said about Peter asking how many times you were to do this. Seven? He said, thinking he was so noble."

"Seventy times seven, I know," Gaetano responded, "But that's when they keep coming back to ask you to forgive them. What about when they never acknowledge they hurt you or anyone for that matter?"

"That's the other kind of forgiveness I was talking about," Günter said making Gaetano a bit confused, "What would you like to do to that lieutenant right now if he was standing in this room?" he asked, posing a question for which he already anticipated the answer to.

Gaetano was stern enough to blurt it out, "do what he did to Augie," he said.

"What does that do to you every time you remember your friend and what happened to him?" Günter said leaning forward in his chair, "it hurts, doesn't it?" Gaetano nodded his head. "How would you like to not have it hurt anymore?" Günter asked.

Gaetano looked for a moment and tried to figure out how on his own. But obviously could not. "I don't see how," he replied, "how do you forgive someone who would just hurt again and again and never apologize or admit what he did?"

"Look at it like this," Günter said sitting back a bit in his chair, "Forgiveness is surrendering the right to get even. Do you feel getting even would make you feel better?" Gaetano nodded his head to say yes. "It wouldn't," Günter added, "then you would be him. You see that's why we're told to love our enemies. Because, when you hate your enemy.............. you become them. And how can you hold someone in un-forgiveness when you have done exactly the same thing yourself. Surrender it and let it go so it no longer hurts you."

"But what comes of the person who hurt you, or in this case hurt your friend?" Gaetano asked sincerely.

"Doesn't matter," Günter said, "you're free, and that's all you should care about."

"He probably got himself killed anyway," Gaetano said with a snicker.

"No," Günter said with a sigh, "that type usually gets everyone around them killed."

Gaetano nodded in agreement. He did not tell Günter he then volunteered to go out, after yet another soldier lost his life trying, and took out the machine gun nest single handed. That would have been a distraction from the hurt. This was about Augie and not him.

Günter knew they had probably had enough heavy discussion for one evening and offered to go a get a muffin for Gaetano. He brought over the coffee pot and added some to Gaetano's cup. Then he sat down and reached over to the side table and opened the drawer to pull out the cribbage board and the deck of cards.

They spent the rest of the evening playing cards and talking about lighter things. Gaetano had some thinking to do and periodically would stare off while they were playing. Günter just waited patiently figuring he would eventually come back to the game. And if he did not, so what? This was a big hurdle for Gaetano to get over, and Günter knew it may take some time. With the evening coffee, the game went on late into the night. No matter though because it was starting to snow again. And they knew there would be some work to do in the morning once they got up and had to clear snow.

By two o'clock in the morning they decided to call it quits. Gaetano was no longer agitated so when he went upstairs to go to bed. He fell asleep and was starting to come to terms with the thing he had been struggling with for months.

He dreamt about coming back to Italy on the Hallwick that night. Augie was in the dream, and they were on the deck of the ship during one of the storms they had encountered. The waves were crashing over the top of the deck. Augie was trying to hang on, but a wave caught him and took him. Gaetano called out to him and tried to reach out to catch him as he washed by. He caught a piece of his shirt but could not hang on. He went overboard with the next crashing wave and Gaetano could not see him anymore. He just kept calling his name. Then he was screaming his name as if Augie could hear him with the crashing waves all around. Gaetano sat up quickly and woke up realizing he was calling out Augustino's name in his sleep.

He sat in his bed for a second and caught his breath. He was shaking all over. "You all right?" he heard Günter's voice from the doorway. His silhouette was visible, but Gaetano could not really see him.

"Yeah, I guess," Gaetano said shaking the nerves off, "was I actually calling out?"

"For a while," Günter replied.

"Sorry, I didn't mean to wake you up," Gaetano said falling back onto his pillow.

"Not a problem," Günter said, "I'll fall right back to sleep. What about you though?"

"I guess I will," he said getting up to make a trip to the bathroom, "If I don't start dreaming again."

Günter stepped aside to let him go across to the bathroom. "See you at breakfast," he said. Gaetano grunted and closed the bathroom door. Günter turned and went back to bed.

Chapter 33

March of nineteen-sixteen was upon them now. It was the first of the month and a rather lovely day. The weather was showing the first signs of warming up. Snow was starting to melt, and the horses were livelier in their stalls. It was Wednesday morning and Gaetano was still doing his chores in the barn when Günter came in to gather the eggs. Karl would be coming by soon and he wanted to have the fresh eggs picked up for him when he came.

"Tomorrow, I'm going into town," Günter said. This was a bit out of the ordinary since he had planned his schedule of in town errands to coincide with Gaetano's work schedule.

"Anything going on?" Gaetano asked.

"With the weather starting to get better, they get things geared up at the train yard and often want me to be there to help out some," Günter replied.

"Trains starting to run again?" Gaetano asked with a sound of uncertainty in his voice.

Günter knew him well enough by now to know there was more behind the question. He had a look on his face which Günter had come to understand. Something was on his mind.

"Spring is coming," he said, "everything is gearing up."

"What do you do?" Gaetano asked.

"Help them check out the engines that haven't been running for a few weeks," Günter said as he was gathering the eggs. "It helps them, and I get the sense of still being involved. Pays a little too."

"When do the passenger trains start to run on a regular schedule again?" Gaetano asked figuring there was not any reason to hide what he was thinking. Not that it would prevent Günter from figuring it out.

"Any day now," Günter answered, "why?"

Gaetano put the pitchfork against the wall and leaned on the gate. "I've been thinking about what I should do next. It may be time for me to move on," he said.

Günter paused and looked at him, "I see." There was a long silence between them. Gaetano looked out the door and saw Karl's buggy coming up the driveway. Günter heard it too.

Karl came in and talked with Günter for a while. He said hello to Gaetano in German and then a struggling Italian. Gaetano gave him a wave and picked up the pitchfork again to finish up in the stalls. Günter still had some eggs to gather so Karl followed him around making small talk. He put the eggs in his buggy and pulled out some milk to give to Günter. With a few more pleasantries, Karl left, and Günter came back into the barn.

Günter continued to look for eggs because he knew there were more around someplace. After finding four more eggs, he decided to call it quits. Gaetano could tell he was through looking for them, so he said to Günter "Is that all right with you?"

"You moving on?" Günter questioned.

"Yeah, I just figured it may be time with the weather changing," Gaetano said shrugging his shoulders, "I've been a burden on you long enough."

Günter walked up to the stall and leaned on the gate. "Gaetano, you have not been a burden on me. Please don't look at it that way. If you feel it's time for you to make a move, then it's time to make a move," Günter said trying to paste on a smile, "Do you have any plans?"

"Well," Gaetano said.

"Up the top of the hill," Günter said pointing to the spring at the same time Gaetano pointed at the spring. This had become a regular joke with them ever since Günter told Gaetano about the raccoon falling into the tank. Whenever one started a sentence with the word 'Well,' they would both point to the spring and the other would say 'Up the top of the hill.' They both started to laugh.

"Well," Gaetano repeated and pointed, "my original plan was to try to get to a harbor and make my way back home to New Jersey."

"Is that what you plan to do?" Günter said with a tone which made it obvious there was something on his mind.

"I just don't know anymore," Gaetano said dipping his head down. "It all seemed to make sense last year. Seemed like I should just keep running. And now, I'm not so sure."

"You do know running never solves anything?" Günter said sounding very fatherly.

"It gets me away from that awful war," Gaetano replied, "It's not like I'm even an Italian citizen anymore, they just grabbed me and put me in a uniform."

Günter had the look on his face which indicated he had a lot more to say. Gaetano knew that look and figured he had learned it was usually something worth hearing so he asked him, "What do you think I should do?"

"Gaetano," Günter said in a soft voice, "If you continue to run, you will always consider yourself a coward. Is that what you want?"

"I don't feel like a coward," he replied, "I think I'm doing the right thing."

"Now you do," Günter added, "but in several years from now and especially when you get to be my age, you will always wish you had not run. Once you reach that point, you will see yourself as a coward. And then, there won't be any going back to change it." Gaetano listened with some sadness in his heart. It was good advice but not comfortable advice.

"This is the time to change it Gaetano," Günter said firmly, "You don't want to spend your life thinking of yourself that way. I knew a man who did. Two actually. But only one of them well. We worked together on one of the lines I ran regularly. He was a conductor," Günter paused. "He was a broken man at the age of forty, always living with regret. You've got more going for you than that."

Gaetano stayed silent just absorbing what Günter was saying. It was one of the factors he had been struggling with for over two months now. Several times he started to say something but stopped before he spoke and just stood there leaning against the pitchfork. Günter could tell he was pondering the thought but was not at the place to make a decision.

"I have one more thing to add," Günter said, "Right now, you're rationalizing your feelings. Once those feelings go, and they will go. All you will have left is your decision. That is what you will have to live with. Make sure it's a decision you can live with."

Gaetano looked up at him and nodded his head. Günter figured he had said enough and had made his point. Nothing more was said about it the rest of the day. They did the usual things around the house and Günter made a light dinner of chicken lentil soup with some carrots cut up inside. Gaetano had learned how to bake bread and helped him to put two loaves in the oven.

That evening they broke out the cribbage board for their usual game and made some coffee. The conversation stayed light for most of the evening. They had agreed not to stay up too late this evening because Günter had plans to go into town so he could find out when they would need him at the train yard.

"Mind if I go with you tomorrow?" Gaetano asked.

"Not at all," Günter said figuring he had a good idea why, "What did you need to do?"

"I was going to stop by the train station and look into the schedules," he replied.

"Train schedules?" Günter questioned.

"Yeah....................I wanted to see when the next train to Bologna would be," Gaetano said looking up at Günter with his eyes only while his head was dipped down.

"Bologna?" Günter said, "that's south."

"Yeah, I know," Gaetano answered, "I've decided to go back and that's the only Army base I know about."

Günter sat looking at him with a broad smile and a slight tear in his eye, "That is a decision you can live with....... and one you won't regret."

"I already regret it," he said with a chuckle, "I guess I'll have to learn not to regret it."

"Remember what I said about once the feelings go," Günter added.

"And they will go?" Gaetano asked, "you promise?"

"That is entirely up to you," he said.

• • • •

MORNING CAME EARLY for both of them, and they had decided to get some breakfast in town instead of at home. The train station opened early and there was a small bakery just across from there. On the other side of the station was the office where Günter was going to go to talk to his old friends and see how they might need him to help with the spring activities.

They left the wagon at the train station because there was a place for it there and they could leave the horses where someone could keep an eye on them. They each got a pastry and a cup of coffee. Günter offered to go to the station with Gaetano to help him understand the schedules. Gaetano had never booked his own train before, and he was a bit uncertain of what to look for.

After they finished breakfast, they walked over to the ticket booth and of course, the attendant knew Günter very well. The next scheduled train south that would take Gaetano to Bologna was coming through on Monday afternoon at two o'clock.

"I can cover your fare," Günter offered.

"No, I have enough money," Gaetano replied, "Thank you though. I've been doing pretty well at Eber's lately. Maybe I can make a living at barbering someday. It pays well if you work hard."

"Monday?" Günter sighed. That was very soon, and he was not sure he was ready to bid his new friend farewell. These couple of months had been very pleasant for Günter and the thought of not having his cribbage partner anymore was not pleasant.

Gaetano felt it also but chose not to say anything about it. "While you're at the office, I'm going to walk over to see Eber. You know, let him know this week will be my last."

"That's a good idea," Günter replied, "Let's meet back at the wagon when we're done."

Gaetano paid for his ticket after Günter walked out to go over to the office. He put the ticket in his coat pocket and headed over to see Eber. It was after eight o'clock and the shop was just opening.

No one was there when he walked in. Eber was sweeping up and had started a pot of coffee. He kept the coffee in the back room on the weekdays unlike Saturdays when it was open for all.

"Good morning, Eber," Gaetano said as he walked in.

"Ah, Gaetano Buongiorno my friend," Eber replied, "have a cup of coffee. What brings you to town today?"

"Thanks, I just had some, but do I like yours better," he replied as he reached for some coffee. "Günter needed to come in for to talk to people about helping in the train yard."

"Yes, I know he still gets involved," Eber said, "I don't think he'll ever stop. He lives the railroad. How are you today?"

"Doing well," Gaetano said, "There's something I have to tell you."

Eber leaned his arm on the broom handle, "What is it?"

"I have to go back to Italy next week," Gaetano said trying not to get too detailed.

Eber knew some of what had happened with Gaetano coming north but did not know he really was not supposed to be there. He suspected, but figured Gaetano would tell him when he wanted him to know. By now Eber was aware Gaetano had been in the Italian Army but thought maybe he was either let go or on leave. The rest he could always get from Günter if he were willing to divulge any of it.

"Oh?" Eber said with a surprised tone, "Are you coming back?"

"Well," Gaetano paused, "not right away. I have some things I need to take care of and then, who knows. But I can work tomorrow and Saturday like usual."

"That would be good," Eber added, "you know how busy it gets."

"I wish I could have given you more notice," Gaetano said, "This came up and the train leaves on Monday. The next one is not until the next Monday, and I can't wait that long."

"That's fine," Eber said, "You've only been working two days a week. Well, sometimes three. I'll get by, I did before you came."

"I'm glad you're all right with it," Gaetano said with a sigh.

"Of course, I am. Anytime you need a job," Eber said patting him on the shoulder, "you come see me. There's always a place for someone like you in my shop."

Eber finished sweeping and Gaetano sipped on his cup of coffee. The two talked for a while about the usual things and just as Gaetano was finishing his coffee the first customer came in. "I'll let you go, you have work to do," he said.

"See you tomorrow," Eber replied, "Tell Günter I said hello."

"I will," Gaetano said as he left. He decided he would walk around a bit. Günter said he would be over an hour, so he had some time to kill. The weather was cooperating, and he was enjoying walking around with his coat open. The only difficulty was the melting snow running everywhere, and he had to avoid the mud on the side of the road.

After he felt he had walked enough, he went back to the wagon to wait for Günter. It was about nine thirty when he got there. About ten minutes later Günter came out of the office and walked over to where he was.

"Everything go well at Eber's?" Günter asked.

"Yeah, he was good with all of it," Gaetano replied.

"So, you're going to work tomorrow and Saturday?" Günter continued.

"Yes, he said he still needed me to come in," Gaetano said, "it's still busy. He may have to look around for another barber."

"There's bound to be someone who comes in on the train during the warmer months who can help him. Summertime usually brings people for the season," Günter said, "he'll do fine. I was thinking though, I'll come to pick you up tomorrow afternoon and then bring you in on Saturday too. That way you won't have to sleep in that dirty room upstairs."

Gaetano knew Günter just wanted to see him as much as possible before he left on Monday. He felt the same way. They freed up the horses and headed back to Günter's house on the side of the hill.

Once they arrived and put the horses away, Gaetano went into the house and started to prepare his things. He went through his pack and pulled out anything he wanted to wash. Then he went downstairs and started to set up for some laundry. He wanted to wash his uniform properly this time so he could wear it and also wash the blanket before packing it up with his other things.

He did not want to be rushed on Monday and did not want to take the time on Sunday to pack these things. So, he got everything ready on that Thursday. This way he could work at Eber's without worrying about packing.

The weekend seemed to go by in a flash. Gaetano worked the two days and Günter came to get him like he promised. They went to church on Sunday, and the preacher talked with Gaetano for a few minutes afterwards. Gaetano told him a little bit about how he had come to be in Gifbourg and what Günter had told him. The preacher told him he agreed with Günter and going back to face the responsibility of seeing it through was the best decision he could make.

That evening Günter made Sauerbraten and Chnöpfli. He had begun to marinate the meat on Thursday when he realized Gaetano was leaving. He figured since it was the first meal they had together, it should be the last. He was hoping he would one day see his friend again.

Sunday evening was both fun and somber. They made the most of the time they had playing cribbage and sipping coffee. Having coffee was all right because Gaetano's train did not leave until the afternoon. They could sleep in for a bit on Monday morning. Before going to bed, they noticed it was starting to rain, a very chilly rain and probably resulting in the road being icy.

The trip into town on Monday was difficult because it was raining, and the roads were barely passable. The temperature had warmed just enough so it was just raining and no longer ice. At one point, Gaetano offered to go the following week, but Günter said he had driven his team in much worse weather. It was late enough in the morning so the near freezing temperatures the night before were no longer a concern.

It took a bit longer to get into town, but they realized it would and left extra early to make certain. They got into town just before noon and decided to go to the hotel for lunch. The spot by the fire was open so they asked to sit there. Günter enjoyed the chicken soup of the day.

Gaetano had taken out his cleaned uniform on Sunday and was wearing it under his coat. He also took his pack and his rifle. The rifle had not been touched in over two months. It was not pleasant for him to pick it up again nor was it comfortable for him to put on his uniform. The uniform was now a bit tighter on him. He attributed that to Günter's cooking. He was not able to remove all of the stains, however.

The train was a bit late because of the rain and the slick tracks. Günter told him the engineers always slow it down when the tracks get wet because the wheels do slip, and it is more difficult to control.

The train finally arrived heading south at four fifteen in the afternoon. The parting was simple but pleasant. They shook hands and wished each other well. Neither man wanted to make too much of the farewell. Gaetano would always remember his time in Gifbourg and the man he met named Günter.

Chapter 34

The freight train which Gaetano had rode in on took him almost two days to get to Gifbourg from where he hopped on. Bologna was even farther south. He saw the conductor coming to collect his ticket and he asked him how long the trip might be.

"Mi scusi Signor," Gaetano said as the conductor walked by. The conductor stopped to listen to him, "How long to Bologna Signor."

The conductor looked at his pack and his uniform. Gaetano had taken his coat off and put it on the overhead luggage rack. The conductor was aware of the Army base there. "In a hurry to get back to the fighting?" he said with a chuckle.

Gaetano gave the obligatory chuckle back, "I guess I must be."

"Early Wednesday morning," the conductor added, "If all goes well with the weather, you never know if there is a landslide or even an avalanche. It's a bad time of year for the trains. We just started running again last week."

"I've heard," Gaetano said trying to pick up a conversation with him, "A friend of mine is a retired engineer. Maybe you know him."

"Maybe," the conductor answered.

"His name is Günter, Günter Haas. Do you know him?" Gaetano had gotten used to everyone in Gifbourg knowing Günter.

"Hmm. Don't think so," he replied.

"Well, that's all right. I'm sure there are a lot of engineers," Gaetano said a bit embarrassed, "he lives in the town where I got on, in Gifbourg."

"Yes, there are a lot of train people in Gifbourg," the conductor said as he punched Gaetano's ticket.

"Thank you, Signor," he said as he stuffed the ticket back into his shirt pocket.

While they were at lunch Günter had suggested he have the hotel pack some food for his trip. It was something they were used to since the trains would often stop in Gifbourg so the passengers could have a meal. It was past five o'clock by now, but he was not hungry. He put his head back and dozed off for about an hour while the train rumbled along.

He woke up suddenly as the car took a hop from a rough piece of track. This was more common in the spring after the winter weather took its toll on the tracks. Even with the occasional rough spot on the tracks, this was a much more pleasant trip than he had experienced on the way north. A seat with a window and a small coal stove at the end of the car made this much nicer. Even with the stove, it was still a bit chilly. So, he reached up and pulled down his coat to cover himself with it. 'At least I don't have to stuff my coat with hay,' he thought to himself.

The section of track that had the tunnels was close enough to where he had boarded in Gifbourg. He knew they would pass through them during the night in the dark. He could not really see them as they passed through. But the sound in the car was different when they entered. He could feel the change in pressure in his ears. So, he knew when they were in one. The game of holding his breath to see if he could make it all the way through just was not any fun this time. Playing the game on the way north made him feel free and this trip was anything but. However, he realized if he had gone in the other direction, it would have eventually made him feel even less free.

By nine o'clock he decided to eat the packed dinner he had got at the hotel. It was a roll with butter with some type of pressed ham and cheddar cheese. They had included two carrots, sliced, peeled and a small packet of salt. He had filled his canteen at Günter's before he left the house and made a point not to dip into it until he was on the train. He drank only a little bit because Günter had warned him the restroom facilities on passenger trains were unpredictable. Sometimes one would be better off waiting until they had a break stop and use the restroom at the train station. At least those were serviced more often.

Gaetano still was not very hungry, but he decided to eat anyway. He took his time and gazed out the window to see what he could in the moonlight. It was only about a half-moon that night, a waning moon, And it did not offer much help in providing a view. But he made the best of it. The night sky and landscape passing by had a hypnotic effect on him. He was not sure exactly what time he fell asleep, but when he woke up, it was from the sun hitting his face from the east.

His pocket watch was in his pants pocket. So, he took it out and checked to see what time it was. Six thirty in the morning. It was surprising to him he slept as long on the train since he did not even remember laying down across the two seats where he was. There were only about eight people in the same car as him. That was probably due to how early it was in the season. He figured most people would not plan a trip with all the uncertainty which the conductor mentioned.

As he went to put his watch back in his pocket, he realized he would need to hide it in his boot again. So, he bent over a bit and slipped it in the place where he had become used to keeping it the previous year. It provided some protection from water. Probably the only reason his watch still worked.

Each of these little things. His watch in his boot, using his canteen again and having people notice he was a soldier, was bringing him closer to realizing he was indeed going back.

The weather changed quickly once they came out of the Alps. The terrain changed as well. They were in the foothills for a while and then quickly transitioned to open farmland which was not very hilly.

The train arrived in a small town in northern Italy late morning for a break stop and they were told they would have just over an hour to get a meal and use the restroom. Gaetano waited a bit until the conductor came through. "Excuse me Signor," he said to the conductor.

"Yes, young man," the conductor answered.

"Signor, I had planned to get off for a while, but I don't think I should carry my rifle off the train or leave it unattended," he told the conductor, "Is there a safe place to keep it on board? I shouldn't just leave it at my seat."

"It's not loaded, is it?" the conductor asked hoping he would know better.

"No, no Signor," Gaetano shook his head, "I left the ammunition behind in Gifbourg. I figured they had plenty more where I'm going."

"Follow me then," the conductor signaled as he went forward. He took out a key and opened a closet at the end of the car, just opposite the stove. It was usually reserved for the conductors to keep their belongings. "You can keep it in here," he said, "Just see me when you want it back. I'm on through Bologna, so if you would like, you can keep it in here until you arrive."

"You're very kind Signor," Gaetano said as he stashed the rifle in the closet. There were still forty minutes left before the train would leave. Gaetano got off and made a quick stop in the restroom as well as finding a place to fill his canteen. He was not sure if he should eat or just get on the train.

Just like Gifbourg though, there were places nearby to the train station which offered packed meals. He decided to get one and maybe eat a bit later. Then he started to think. 'What will happen when I get there?' After all, he had run away. It was not likely they would have a festival in his honor. Then he thought maybe because he still had his rifle, he could say he got lost after being separated and just held up for the winter at someone's home who was willing to take him in. Most of that was true. He figured he would skip the part about making it all the way to the Swiss Alps.

It was just before five o'clock the next day when the train pulled into the station at Bologna. They had stayed mostly on schedule. He recognized parts of the town as they were coming in from when he was there on furlough. Upon arrival, the conductor let him into the closet so he could retrieve his rifle. Once he had everything that was his, he got off the train and headed for the pickup location for the soldiers who were in town on leave. He hoped it was in the same place.

There was a local mercantile at the corner of the street where the trucks would park. Most of the soldiers would go in there if they were a bit early to poke around. They might buy something for a girlfriend while they were waiting to get on the trucks. Gaetano thought the proprietor would have some idea if they were running the trucks or not that day.

Sure enough, there was a scheduled pick up at ten o'clock that evening. The merchant had seen the men being dropped off that morning and expected the extra traffic in his store. Gaetano knew he had some time to kill so he decided to go to a restaurant he remembered and enjoyed. He still had some money left which he had earned at Eber's and figured he probably would not need it if they sent him back to the fighting, or worse, sent him to jail.

The restaurant was packed but he managed to get a small table in the back. He ordered the meal he remembered getting the last time and even got a glass of wine. This was not exactly a time to celebrate. But it was a transition for him, and he wanted to make it significant with a delicious meal.

He stayed in the restaurant until about eight o'clock. Then headed to the waiting area for the trucks. There were other soldiers waiting there also and they looked at him strangely. Gaetano realized their look was because he still had the coat on which he had found at the farmhouse in early December. It was not the type of coat a soldier would wear. He tried to take it off inconspicuously with some success. Most did not pay any attention. There was a bench on the side of the road, so he laid it over the back as if it were the natural thing to do if he was too warm with it on. After a moment or two, he drifted away and left it to the past.

Ten o'clock eventually came and the first truck rolled around the corner. The driver pulled over and got out. Gaetano walked up to him to find out about getting a ride.

"Can I get on?" Gaetano asked him.

The driver was a corporal, and he looked at Gaetano carrying his pack and rifle. "You're not here on furlough, are you?" he asked.

"I came in on the train earlier," Gaetano answered.

The corporal looked at him again and figured something was out of the ordinary. Even soldiers who were returning from leave did not have their rifle and pack with them. They would just leave with a carry bag of some sort for their clothes. "You got your papers?" he asked Gaetano with a tone of uncertainty.

"Papers?" Gaetano said with a look of fear on his face.

The corporal shook his head. "That's what I thought," he said, "you didn't have leave did you? Everyone who goes on leave has papers."

Gaetano was not sure what to say so a part of the truth would have to do. "I got separated from my outfit and tried to get back. But the weather took a turn for the worse and I got lost. They told me trains wouldn't be running again until early March. So, here I am, reporting for duty."

"I'm not the one you have to convince," the corporal said not really wanting to deal with it anymore, "you'd better hope the captain is in a good mood. Get on."

Gaetano jumped on in back. He was the eighth man on so there was only room for two more. When the second truck pulled around the corner, the corporal decided to head out. There were not too many men left to pick up that night so two trucks were almost too many. Gaetano did not say anything to the other men on the truck, and they did not really pay any mind to him either. The trip was short as he recalled from before. They were at the camp by eleven.

As he got off the back of the truck the corporal was coming around. They looked at each other both knowing the next few minutes would likely be unpleasant for them both. Gaetano because he had to possibly face the music and the corporal because he just did not want to have anything to do with it.

"Where should I go?" Gaetano asked him humbly.

The corporal let out a big sigh and waved him over to follow him. He did not even say anything about following him. They both just knew. The captain's office was not open at that hour so the corporal took him to the military police so they could process him.

As they arrived the corporal told him, "Wait here," pointing to a chair in the waiting area. He walked in the back of the office and two soldiers came out.

"What outfit are you with?" one of them asked bluntly.

"I was with Sergeant Grillo last. Before him it was Sergeant Patrizi," Gaetano said hoping they would know those names.

"Don't know Patrizi, but Grillo, I've heard that name," the soldier said.

"You need me anymore?" the corporal asked.

"No, you can get out of here," the soldier said.

"What are you going to do with him?" the corporal asked.

"He'll have to stay with us tonight," he said, "they'll sort it out in the morning."

After the corporal left the soldier looked at Gaetano, "You'll stay in one of the cells tonight since you don't have barracks assigned. Because you came in on your own, we won't bother to lock you in. That way if you need to go to the restroom, you can without someone having to open your cell."

Gaetano was a bit surprised, but he figured most soldiers who had run away did not just come walking back in on their own. "You're all right," Gaetano said.

"Give me your rifle, they're not allowed past that door," the soldier said.

Gaetano handed him the rifle gladly, "It's not loaded by the way. I had it on the train and I was told they wouldn't mind me carrying it on the train if it wasn't loaded."

"If you say so," the soldier said hoping the night would go back to the normal quiet, "You'll have to explain yourself to the captain in the morning. For now, I don't want to know you're here, got it."

"Got it," Gaetano replied.

The small cell was cold and bare. Gaetano wished he were still at Günter's with a nice bathroom across the hall and a warm quilt to sleep under. This cell had a pillow which looked like it had not been washed since the fighting started. There was a single blanket in a pile that smelled like the previous occupant had been locked up for drunkenness. He wished now he had not left the coat behind.

There was a small window looking out on the compound. Gaetano stood at the window for fifteen or twenty minutes looking out into the dark Army camp. The lights were out, and his door was closed but not locked. He was not sure he wanted to lie down on the cot that was there but figured he had better get used to things being a bit rough again.

He pulled his own blanket out and took some things from his pack so he could place it over the pillow. That way his head would be on the pack instead of the pillow. Difficult as it was, he tried to get comfortable enough to fall asleep. It took some time between the smelly conditions of the cell and the repeated going over in his mind of what he would say to the captain in the morning. Eventually, at some point, he drifted off.

Chapter 35

The all too familiar sounds of morning on an Army base shook Gaetano from an uneven sleep. Sleeping on the train the night before had been a much more comfortable experience. It was six o'clock and still dark outside. The first signs of dawn were peeking in through the window. He could hear the troops already up and about preparing for their morning exercises.

Gaetano wondered if the same soldiers who put him in his cell the night before would still be on duty or would he have to explain things to someone new. He jumped out of the cot and began to gather his things. He put the items back into his pack which he had taken out the night before. Then he rolled up his blanket and got everything ready. Gaetano waited for about an hour looking out the window and wondering how the day was going to unravel. He did not want to wait too long to go to the restroom in case they needed to hurry him along.

They had put him in the first cell. One of twelve in the building. It fortunately was the closest to the restroom. He did not see anybody around when he looked out but when he came back, there was a guard standing at the door of the cell which he had been in.

"You Private Santorini?" the soldier asked.

"Yes Signor," he replied.

"Get your things, come with me," he said with absolutely no enthusiasm.

Gaetano grabbed his pack and hurried after him, "Signor, my rifle?" he said as the soldier reached for the door.

"We'll keep it for now," he replied, "We know it's yours. You can pick it up anytime."

They left the building and went straight for the captain's office. It was quite some distance from the building where he spent the night. He had only been to this location on two other occasions and did not know his way around as well as he thought he might. As they were walking, Gaetano kept looking closely to see if there was anybody he would recognize. There were no familiar faces. Not yet anyway, so he kept looking.

The captain was not in his office, but one of the sergeants assigned to him was. The guard walked in first and gave Gaetano the sign to follow. As he went in, his heart started to pound rapidly. There was no telling what was ahead for him.

"Sergeant?" the guard said as they walked up to his desk, "This man came in last night on one of the trucks from town. Says he got separated from his unit................ last December."

The sergeant looked up at him as if to say, 'Oh please, not this morning!' He paused for a moment presumably hoping the guard would take him back where he had him before and not bother him anymore.

"What's your name?" the sergeant asked.

"Private Gaetano Santorini," he replied.

"Who was your sergeant the last day you were out?" he continued.

"It was Sergeant Grillo," Gaetano answered, "We were up in the Gorizia area back in early December and the enemy cut right through our lines. So, I got separated with two others...........they were killed."

"That was three months ago," he said raising his voice in disbelief.

"Well, I got..." Gaetano started.

"Save it for the captain private," he snapped. "Go sit over there," he said as he pointed to a row of four chairs placed under a double window to his left. "Did he give you any trouble last night? Think I have to worry about him?" the sergeant said to the guard.

"No sergeant, he didn't make a move all night," he responded, "he did come in on his own. If he were looking for trouble, I don't think he would have come in on his own."

The sergeant let out a slow sigh and leaned back in his chair, "Yeah, guess you're right," he said as he nodded his head to Gaetano to go sit where he had told him. Gaetano nodded back acknowledging the command.

It was not until nine o'clock that there was any further activity in the office. The sergeant sat there and did not pay any attention to him. Another sergeant came in and sat at the next desk. It took him some time to get settled and he kept noticing Gaetano sitting there. After about fifteen minutes he looked over to the other sergeant. "What's he doing here?" he said softly but not softly enough for Gaetano not to hear him.

"Came in last night," he replied, "says he got separated from his unit............three months ago."

The other sergeant looked over at Gaetano and chuckled, "Good luck with that one," he said shaking his head. This made Gaetano a bit more nervous.

Gaetano had not eaten since the night before and was not given a chance to go to the mess hall before the military police took him to the captain's office. He thought about mentioning it to one of the sergeants, but he decided not to do anything which would cause them to be upset with him.

An enemy right now would not be a good thing. It would be much better to go a little hungry. After all, he went to a great restaurant the night before and had a minor feast. So, he could afford to skip a meal. However, the smell of the coffee the first sergeant had been brewing all morning was making him very hungry.

Every ten minutes or so, Gaetano would have an inner struggle trying to decide if he should ask one of the sergeants when the captain was expected. The same logic prevailed as for not asking for anything to eat. Patients would be his saving grace this day, hopefully.

Eleven forty-five was the time on the clock over the door. Finally, the second sergeant looked over at him and said, "You hungry?" The instant expression on Gaetano's face answered for him before he could speak it. "That's what I thought," he said and then looked over to the first sergeant, "What are we going to do with him."

"Captain will probably want to see him," he responded.

"But he's got to eat," the second sergeant said.

Gaetano felt like he had a new friend, but he decided not to say anything unless they asked him a direct question. "What are you thinking of?" the first sergeant said. "We can't just let him go all over the camp until we know what the captain wants to do with him."

The second sergeant nodded his head and grunted then sat back down. 'Was that it?' Gaetano thought to himself. 'He's not going to let me eat?' He decided it was best to go back to keeping quiet.

Twenty minutes later, the second sergeant got up and went for the door. "I'll bring something back for the both of you," he said as he was leaving. The other sergeant just grunted his approval.

There was a back door to the office and just as the sergeant was going out the front door for lunch, they heard the back door open. Gaetano could not see who it was but by the change in the sergeant's demeanor it was obvious it was the captain. There was some rustling around in the back where the captain's office was and then they heard footsteps heading over to the door which connected the captain's office with where the sergeants' desks were.

As the captain entered, the sergeant stood to attention and a split second later so did Gaetano. It had been a while since he had to respond to an officer coming into the room. He was glad the sergeant was there and triggered his memory. It would have been a problem if no one were with him and Gaetano just sat still when the captain entered the room. Even worse, if he had just said hello as if the captain was a customer in Eber's barber shop.

The captain entered and without looking up just said, "At ease."

The sergeant sat back down and went about his business as if the captain had not even come in. Gaetano followed and also sat down. The captain walked over to the file cabinets and opened the top one on the far right. The file cabinets were just inside the front door and there were six in the row. At the end of the row were the four chairs where Gaetano was sitting.

After about five minutes of the captain looking through some files he glanced over at Gaetano. He was not sure what to do so he just kept looking forward towards where the sergeant was sitting. The captain seemed oblivious to the fact there was a private sitting in his outer office. He took three file folders over to the sergeant and placed them on his desk. The sergeant picked them up right away and looked to see what they were. Once he knew what was in them, he just placed them on the right side of his desk to deal with later.

"Who is he here to see?" the captain said tilting his head in Gaetano's direction.

"They brought him in this morning from the holding cell," the sergeant said looking over towards Gaetano. "they say he came in on one of the trucks from town. Says he got separated from his outfit and made his way back on his own."

"What was he doing in the holding cell, is his trouble?" the captain asked.

"No captain, he just slept there," he replied, "they didn't know what to do with him."

"Did you pull his records?" the captain asked.

"No Signor, I haven't looked into it," he answered with an element of embarrassment realizing he should have. It would have made it easier for the captain so he would not have to wait. He stood up and went over to the file cabinets the captain had been looking through and gave Gaetano a look which acknowledged he knew he had messed up.

"Bring it into me when you find it," the captain said as he went back into his office.

"Right away," the sergeant said.

It took him about ten minutes to find what appeared to be Gaetano's service record. Gaetano was surprised his records were right there, so close to where he was sitting all that time. Up until that very moment, he had never even thought he even had a service record. Everything he had done in the Army seemed so hands-on. The thought of someone keeping tabs on him as well as what he did and where he was, and then writing it down somewhere, seemed mind boggling.

The sergeant walked into the captain's office to bring the file to him. Just as he left the room, the other sergeant came in and put down a bag which looked like it might have come from the mess hall. Gaetano was really hoping he would get to eat something before going in to see the captain. He figured the captain would need to read through his service record and it would give him enough time for a fast lunch.

The sergeant who came in opened the bag and took out two sandwiches. He left one on the other sergeant's desk, for when he came out of the captain's office. Then he took the other one over to Gaetano. "Salami all right with you?" he said.

Gaetano's eyes lit up, "Yes sergeant, Salami is fine, thank you for thinking of me."

The sergeant handed him the sandwich and just said, "Yeah."

Gaetano did not waste any time getting to it. He had eaten most of the sandwich by the time the sergeant got to his desk and sat down. It did not go unnoticed. The sergeant let out a chuckle when he saw how fast Gaetano was eating.

The other sergeant came back just a moment later and looked at his food then looked over at Gaetano. "Did you forget him?" he asked the other sergeant.

"No, he ate it already," he replied.

"Guess you were hungry," the first sergeant said with a chuckle. Gaetano just nodded his head and smiled.

It took until after one thirty before the captain called for the sergeant to bring Gaetano in. The first sergeant looked over at him and gave him a hand signal to go where he was standing. "Come on," he said.

Gaetano got up and almost tripped on his pack which was still at his feet. He bent down to pick it up, but the sergeant told him to leave it there. It felt good to stand for a change. He had been seated in the same chair for over five hours.

The captain's office was nice. His desk was solid oak, and he had a chair that could swivel and rock. There was one file cabinet in his office which was also made of solid oak. The two were a matched pair. It was dignified but not overdone. 'Is this what you get when you make it to captain?' he thought to himself. He also knew he had no intentions of ever becoming a captain to find out.

Gaetano stood at attention and looked straight forward knowing not to speak unless the captain asked him something directly. He stood there for about three minutes as the captain read from his record.

"Three months huh?" the captain said with almost a mumble not looking up. It was not a direct question, so Gaetano remained silent. "Says here, you punched a lieutenant in the face one night. He filed a complaint but never followed up. It also says what you were doing at the time........................ Seventeen?" Gaetano just looked forward and did not say anything.

The captain kept reading and Gaetano kept standing at attention. It almost seemed like a test to see if he would trip up and say something before being asked to. "The last entry says you were presumed either killed or captured................ It doesn't say presumed a deserter. There was a lot of that last year. Why do you think they didn't think you deserted?"

This was a direct question, so Gaetano decided it was time to speak. But he knew he would have to keep his answers simple and to the point. "I don't know Signor, but my sergeant always treated me well. He must have known I would come back." He figured he might be able to make a good case for himself.

"Three months though. Where were you?" the captain asked sounding confused.

"During the summer, a friend in my outfit got separated," Gaetano said trying to explain, "he told us he circled around to the north to get away from the enemy and got back to us in a few days. I thought I would do the same."

"So, what happened?" the captain said, "It only took your friend a few days."

Gaetano hesitated a bit because his answer seemed foolish, "Well Signor, I, I got lost."

"For three months?" the captain exclaimed.

"Well Signor, then the weather turned," Gaetano said as if he were a kid who forgot to do his chores and needed to make up an excuse. "And I found someone who put me up until I could get a train here?"

The captain shook his head and sighed obviously not wanting to have to deal with this. "We can't just let soldiers disappear for months at a time. Could you imagine how much chaos there would be if we did that private?"

"Yes Signor," Gaetano said knowing he deserved a scolding and hopefully not worse.

"This is going to have to be dealt with," the captain said changing his tone, "there will have to be a court martial and then they will decide what is best to do with you."

'Court martial?' Gaetano thought to himself.

"They're actually in session right now, just two buildings over," the captain said as he stood up, "let's get this thing over with right away. Sergeant!"

The sergeant came in to acknowledge the captain's call, "Take Private Santorini over to the court martial that's under way. Find out if they have an opening this afternoon. They were slow this morning when I walked through. Tell them I'll be over shortly." He reached down and picked up the folder that Gaetano's service record was in and handed it to the sergeant. Gaetano saluted the captain and was sent with the sergeant.

They left through the door the captain had come in that morning and turned right. The sergeant did not say anything, and Gaetano was scared to start a conversation. They approached the building where the court martial was being held and the sergeant opened the door. He held it for Gaetano as he entered and said, "The captain didn't seem too upset with you. That's good."

It was a relief to hear. But he still had to face the court martial, and he had no idea what that would be like. The sergeant stepped up ahead of him as they went down a hallway. As they approached the last door, the sergeant touched Gaetano's arm. "Wait here," he said.

Gaetano stood at the door looking in to see how much he could make out. There were two rows of desks with what appeared to be mostly corporals working. 'These must be the clerks,' he thought. The sergeant walked down to the third desk on the left and handed the folder to the corporal and exchanged a few words. The corporal kept looking over at Gaetano and nodding at what the sergeant was saying. At one point he let out a chuckle and looked over at Gaetano shaking his head. It was a bit embarrassing, but Gaetano just wanted to get this over with, so he did not care.

The sergeant looked back at him and signaled him to come over to where he was. As Gaetano got closer the sergeant said to him softly, "Maybe your lucky day, they're slow and that's always as good sign."

Gaetano gave a half smile but was not so easily convinced. The sergeant took him by the arm and pulled him in the direction of a set of double doors at the end of the room. They looked very official, so Gaetano assumed it was the room where the court martial was being held. They went in and the sergeant pointed to the row of benches on the right side. There were benches on both sides set up like a church. Gaetano had never been in a court building before, so he did not know how things were supposed to be. To him, this still looked like a church.

"Sit there," the sergeant said pointing to the third bench from the front. He sat down and the sergeant leaned over to speak softly into his ear. "Wait here until the captain comes in. He'll do everything." Gaetano just nodded his head. He knew he needed to be silent, and it would also be best not to attract any unintended attention towards him. The sergeant gave him two pats on the shoulder and turned to leave.

It was already after two o'clock, so he figured most of the day was over. This likely would not take forever. He sat and watched as four other cases were heard. The one which was underway when he sat down was for a corporal who fired his pistol in a restaurant in town. It had only scared people. But since he was drunk at the time, he was being prosecuted. He was sentenced to a month in jail.

The next case was also a corporal who hit a lieutenant. This struck a nerve. He remembered the captain had mentioned the time he hit the lieutenant the previous year. This soldier had also been drunk in town and picked a fight with an officer. He did not have a case. They busted him to private, and he got a month in jail as well.

All the men being processed were in uniform except for the next one. He was a deserter and was caught trying to get on a boat to get out of the country. He did not look too good. Someone had given him a severe beating at one point, but Gaetano had no way of knowing who. He remembered the first day at training camp with the one guy who disappeared after getting a beating from the sergeant and figured it had been something like that. This soldier was sentenced to ten years in prison. His trial only took fifteen minutes.

The next soldier was the most despicable of all. He was being charged with raping a young girl in a farmhouse while battles were being fought. This had happened in September of the previous year. The girl managed to get away and call for help. But not before trying several times before and being beaten for her efforts. The soldier was crying and pleading. His defense lawyer, who was a captain seemed only willing to help him through the process and was not trying anything fancy to get his client off.

After they read the charges with all the details stated clearly for all to hear, the soldier's defense lawyer whispered into his ear and the soldier shook his head to say no. After a couple more tries the soldier came to realize he should take the advice, so the lawyer entered a guilty plea and asked for mercy in sentencing. The court martial officers talked amongst themselves for a few minutes seemingly unified. Then sentenced him to forty years hard labor.

Things were getting a lot more intense, and Gaetano was getting a bit nervous. As they were taking the prisoner away crying and shaking, the captain that saw him earlier came in from the side door. He walked right over to the officers and began to speak softly to them. The corporal who had been given his file came in just after the captain. He must have known he was coming because he had Gaetano's file and some other papers with him.

One of the officers looked over at him and it gave him a chill. This was it. He was going to face the music and there was no backing out. The captain walked over to one of the tables and sat down looking over some papers. Then he stood up less than a minute later and signaled Gaetano to come forward. He stood in the same spot the other soldiers had stood in when they got their sentences. There was no one else left in the room. He would be their last case of the day.

The captain began to speak, "This is Private Santorini. He was absent from his duties for three months following the last battle in the Gorizia area. He just came in last night on a truck from town and turned himself in." Gaetano did not like the sound of 'turned himself in.' It sounded too much like he had committed a crime. Not exactly the tone he was hoping to set before these officers.

One of the officers looked directly at him and asked him "What happened? Tell us in your own words."

Gaetano looked at the captain. The captain leaned over to him and said into his ear, "Just tell them what you told me." This helped him to calm down a bit.

"Well Signor," he began cautiously, "we were fighting, and the enemy was on the offensive. We had become used to them holding their positions so when they came at us, it took us by surprise. Somehow, they cut right through our lines. I got separated along with two others. We were in a ditch, and I tried to get the other two men to come with me so we could circle around to the north." He paused and looked at the captain again. The captain nodded to him to continue.

"The others refused to make a run for it. I crawled away to a row of brush and went behind it just as the other two were overrun by the enemy............. They didn't have a chance, Signor. I would have been killed too. There must have been twenty-five of them."

"Did they surrender?" one of the other officers asked.

"One of them tried," Gaetano answered with his voice shaking by this point. "They shot him before he could even stand completely with his hands up. The other one tried to run but they shot him in the back. I thought I did the right thing to try to get back to my unit." The officers seemed to not be moved by the story. They probably heard this type of thing all the time.

"So, did you know where you were and where you needed to go?" the same officer asked.

"I thought I did," Gaetano continued, "Everywhere I turned there were enemy soldiers. I hid best I could and moved only at night. It took me two days to get to a place where I didn't see the enemy everywhere." He paused for a moment to see if they had any more questions. They did not say anything, so he figured they just wanted him to keep telling his story. "I wandered for several days and ran into some enemy positions but managed to stay undetected. I stayed in an abandoned farmhouse for a couple of nights and found some food in a root cellar that was concealed under a carpet in the kitchen. Then I tried to find my way back."

One of the officers interrupted and asked him, "Tell me soldier, did you think of running away and not coming back?"

Gaetano paused for a moment, "Yes Signor, the thought did cross my mind, several times."

"So why did you come back?" he asked.

Gaetano became very somber. "Well Signor, I had jumped a train and went into the mountains. Once I knew I could not stay on the train any more I wandered a bit and found a barn to sleep in. The owner came in and found me. He let me stay for the time I was away." He paused a longer time "It was him, Signor. He convinced me that if I didn't come back, I would spend the rest of my life thinking I was a coward."

"And he would be right," the third officer said, "I think we've heard enough."

The three officers turned to each other and spoke very softly. They had become exceptionally good at speaking so no one would hear what they were saying to each other. Gaetano looked over to the captain, but the captain offered no response.

The officer in the center turned to Gaetano and began to speak again, "You do realize we can't have soldiers disappearing for months at a time?"

"Yes Signor," Gaetano answered.

"We've reviewed your service record briefly. There is a lot to read in here," he said holding up the file folder. "Your sergeant had a lot to say and there are some interesting entries. Did Sergeant Grillo tell you that you were being considered for a promotion to corporal?"

Gaetano looked surprised, "No Signor," he said looking over at the captain again.

"I'm sure you'll understand that can't happen now," he said as Gaetano shook his head in agreement and realized he needed to speak his answers.

"Yes Signor," he said, "I completely understand."

The officer let out a deep sigh. "So, three months? Your sentence for being away three months without leave......................... three days in jail."

The officer signaled to the corporal who had brought in his file to come forward, "You will go with this corporal. He will take you back to the jail."

Gaetano looked over to the captain and with the obvious look on his face was asking 'That's it?'

The captain answered without him asking, "That's it, three days." It was obvious by the captain's response he must have put in a good word for him.

"My pack is back at the captain's office," he told the corporal, "should we go by there to get it?"

The corporal looked to the captain for instructions. "That will be all right," the captain said.

They left through the side exit which led right to the road where the captain's office was. They retrieved his pack before continuing on to the jail. The walk did not seem as long this time as it had in the morning. The guard on duty in the jail was the same one who was there when he came in the night before. The corporal went over to him and explained what was happening. The soldier looked over at Gaetano and nodded his head up and down obviously impressed by the light sentence.

The corporal left and the guard looked at a chart on the wall. He tapped the last cell in the row. It was the farthest one from where he had stayed the night before. This one was not any better, but he figured three days was manageable under any conditions. They took his pack and told him he would get it back when he got out. He settled in and decided to make the best of it. It was still hard for him to believe he got off so easy.

Chapter 36

It was a common occurrence for the men in the brig to eat later than everyone else who went to the mess hall. They would get whatever was left over and not usually the best on the menu. It was past eight o'clock when the tray of food arrived for Gaetano's dinner.

Having spent most of the day seated in the captain's office, and the nervousness of not knowing what was next, his stomach was not in the best shape. He decided he would eat what he could anyway. As the guard came to his cell to deliver his tray, he told Gaetano they would leave the tray for only a half hour. Then he would have to turn it in so it could be sent back in time to be washed with the other dishes in the mess hall before the shift of workers were released for the night.

The food was cold and beyond tasteless. He just nibbled on what was best and left the rest. After the half hour was up, he heard them coming down the hallway. So, he took the tray over to the door to be ready for them when they came. The guard looked surprised he was willing to help because they usually had to go into the cell. Not only to pick up the tray but often order the prisoner to clean up around his tray so it was ready to be moved.

Shortly after they took the leftovers away it was nine o'clock and was time for all the lights to go out. Unlike the previous night when he was simply given a place to sleep, this night he was locked up. Gaetano had been content to stay in the cell the night before, but there was something about having a lock on the door made him want to get out and walk around.

This cot was not much cleaner than the one the night before. But at least the pillowcase appeared to be clean. The blanket had not been soiled by the previous occupant either like the other cell. That guy had obviously been very drunk and had lost control of himself. He covered himself with the blanket then tried to settle down. It must have been after midnight by the time he fell asleep. He spent the entire night dreaming and reliving the previous year of his life. And wondering what lies ahead for him on the battlefield.

Being a prisoner meant he did not have to get up for exercise. He again heard the sounds of the men in the camp doing their early morning workout. Nothing would be said if he wanted to sleep until they came with the morning tray of food. As the night before, it was served after everyone else in camp had eaten. It did not come until after nine o'clock and again, everything was cold and not very tasty. But he ate it anyway. They gave him the usual 'only a half hour to eat' mandate and he chuckled wondering what would happen if one day they forgot, and the prisoner did not eat on time.

There was nothing else to do in his cell but pace around. The guards normally would never come by except when they were delivering the meal and even then, they did not talk to the prisoners. Gaetano figured there must be good reason for this, but it escaped him as to what it might be.

Even though he had slept most of the night, Gaetano found himself dozing off in the late morning. At around eleven o'clock he was abruptly woken up by the sound of a rapping on his door.

"Santorini!" a voice called out.

He shook himself to a seated position, not certain if he actually heard something or was dreaming.

"You have a letter," the guard said.

"A letter," he said with disbelief, "who knows that I'm here?"

"Return address says New Jersey," the guard said, "They brought it by from the captain's office. Someone in the mail room sent it there to put in your file. Guess when you showed up, they realized they had been holding a letter for you since January."

Gaetano stumbled to his feet and walked to the door. The guard put his hand through the slot where they put his tray and gave it to him as he approached.

"Thank you," he said as he turned to go back to his cot. He recognized the writing on the front. It was his Mamma's handwriting. He instantly felt an overwhelming homesickness taking over. 'Mamma,' he thought to himself. The letter was wrinkled and smudged but not damaged. The impulse to tear it open was counteracted by his concerns of what was in it. That and the hurt he knew his Mamma must have been feeling when he had written home. It was back when he was on his furlough the previous year. Now it made sense to him why the letter was at the camp since he mailed his from there.

He sat on his cot and stared at it for almost twenty minutes before opening it. It was two sheets long with writing on both sides of the papers. His Mamma always did a good job of writing letters. He had remembered that from the time he spent with his grandparents while his Mamma and Papà were getting established in America. She would write long letters every month and he would read them over and over again until the next one came. It had been months since he sent his letter and had not received a return. Up until this very moment though, he had never even thought about whether or not he would get one.

The words on the page did not seem real as he gazed at them. He looked at the letter without reading it. Just looking at what he knew to be his Mamma's handwriting held him. This was the first real contact from home he had since leaving the dock in Jersey City on the Hallwick. He savored the moment just because he could. After almost an hour of looking at it and holding it, he began to read.

My Dearest Gaetano,

Your letter got to us in late November and by the date you put on it, it looks to have taken almost three months to arrive. We had heard from Captain Stevens that you were forced into the Army right from his ship. I know how brave you are and believe in you. You will do what you have to in order to survive this terrible war.

We received bad news from Montoro Superiore. The family who was looking in on Nonna wrote to us in late September to tell us she passed away in her sleep late in August. Just about the time you sent your letter. She was very weak, and her strength gave out when she took sick.

When your Papà heard you were taken into the Army, he thought about going in your place to take care of her. But they would not let him travel at that time because they said it was too dangerous with the war on.............

• • • •

GAETANO COULD NOT READ anymore. The thought of his Nonna passing away and not being there made him both sad and angry. 'Who are these people who could just force me to join the Army when I had to take care of my Nonna?' he thought to himself. The tears began to well up in his eyes, but he did not break out into a cry. Instead, he leaned over and put his head down on the pillow and stared at the window until he fell back asleep.

He fully expected his lunch tray would not come until after two o'clock. So, when he heard someone fumbling with his door at one o'clock, he wondered what it was about. The door opened and the guard who gave him his breakfast tray came in. He did not have a tray of food with him for lunch. It seemed a bit confusing.

"Get up soldier," he said, "you're heading up to the front lines."

Gaetano sat there with a very puzzled look on his face, "I thought I had to be here for three days," he said with a bit of a whine.

"Every man needs to head to the front lines," he repeated, "its spring, back to the fighting."

Gaetano stood up and ran his fingers through his hair. He did not dare ask if he could hit the showers before heading out. He had not showered since the morning he left Günter's for the train. "When does the fighting start up again?" he asked.

"Started today, up in Gorizia," the guard answered.

"Gorizia. I know it well," Gaetano said with a sigh.

"Your sergeant got a telegram saying you were back, and he asked for you to be sent up right away," the guard said sounding like he questioned why a sergeant would request a soldier specifically.

"Sergeant Grillo?" Gaetano asked.

"I think so," he answered, "you have to be on a truck in thirty minutes. We have your pack ready at the desk. You have to sign for it."

"They took my rifle yesterday. Do you know where it is?" Gaetano asked.

"I'll check, I think I saw one in the lock up," he said, "it must be yours."

Things moved at a brisk pace as they gave Gaetano his pack and as he was signing for everything the guard came with a rifle in his hands. "This one yours?" he asked.

Gaetano took one glance at the rifle and immediately recognized it by the chips taken out of it from the various battles the year before. He nodded his head and looked back down to finish signing the papers. They hustled him out and took him to the staging area where the trucks were. The guard went to a truck which he must have known in advance would be the one to take Gaetano back to Sergeant Grillo's outfit. The trucks pulled out just before three o'clock.

He thought he was going back to the Gorizia area but the others on the truck said they were going to Trentino instead. There was talk of an enemy offensive starting up there as well. One of the men had been assigned to work under Chief of Staff Cardona for a short time to relieve one of his staff. He heard the people in the office talking about the commander of the Austro-Hungarian Army deploying fifteen divisions to the Trentino area, so they had to go there to be ready.

Gaetano remembered what Sergeant Grillo had told him about spreading the troops too thin. If there were a major offensive by the enemy and the Italians were ill prepared, then they could cut through the lines quickly and easily. It would be a repeat of late fall all over again. This time he would personally be more prepared for that type of thing. Whether or not the rest of the men where, was yet to be seen.

They drove through the night rather than staying at the service point they had stopped at when he was on furlough. They only stopped for refueling and to let the men stretch their legs for twenty minutes before hitting road again. It was still very cold at night, so the men took out their blankets to keep warm. Gaetano pulled his over his head because the wind from driving on an open truck was causing his ears to freeze up. This reminded him of the train ride to Gifbourg when it was snowing in the mountains. This time there were no hay bales to pull from and stuff in his coat.

He was not really sure if he had dozed off during the night. With the blanket covering his head, he thought he might have. They arrived just before dawn at the camp in Asiago. The same one he had been to when this all started almost a year earlier. It looked all too familiar.

The driver had been given instructions as to where Gaetano was to be dropped off. The others went on without him. He did not wave to them or even say good-bye as he got off the truck. Since he did not know any of these men and probably would never see them again. He figured there was not much point to it.

Gaetano walked into the tent the driver had pointed out to him. As he walked in, he instantly recognized the corporal at the desk. "Paulo!" he called out.

Paulo looked up and paused for a moment not sure if he was seeing who he thought he was seeing. "Gaetano?.............. Gaetano!" he screamed then ran over and gave him a hardy hug. "Where have you been? We didn't know if you'd been captured or killed."

"Almost both," Gaetano answered, "they told me the sergeant was expecting me. He got me out of jail."

"Jail?" Paulo asked with a turn of the head. "What did you do, punch another lieutenant in the nose?"

"No, they would have thrown away the key if I'd done that," he chuckled, "I was away too long for their liking."

"How long were you away?" Paulo asked laughing through the words.

Gaetano held up three fingers. "Three weeks?" Paulo said with disbelief.

Gaetano shook his head. "Three months," he said.

Paulo raised his eyebrows all the way and screamed "Three months!!!? Are you kidding me?"

Gaetano could not help but giggle like a schoolboy. He shook his head up and down, acknowledging that Paulo hit the nail on the head.

"Where were you?" he asked.

"Switzerland," Gaetano said with a smirk.

"Switzerland?" Paulo said with even more disbelief, "you were free, why did you come back?"

Gaetano suddenly got serious. "The nicest old man put me up for the winter. He told me that if I didn't come back, I would spend the rest of my life thinking I was a coward."

Paulo also became serious. He looked Gaetano right in the eye and nodded. "He's right. You're not like that. I know you well enough. Hey, you're supposed to be a corporal like me, why the private uniform?"

"That was the price I had to pay for being away without permission," Gaetano said, "That and twenty minutes in jail." Paulo looked confused. "Never mind, I'll explain later. Where's the sergeant?"

"Oh, he'll be back in an hour or so," Paulo said, "he went to the captain's tent to get our orders."

Gaetano nodded his head. "Where do I drop this stuff?" he asked.

"Just leave it in the corner over there," Paulo said.

"Who's left?" Gaetano asked quietly.

Paulo paused for a moment. He had not thought about the Patrizi men for some time and seeing Gaetano was bringing back many memories, some good, but few. "Tomaso and Valentino," he said quickly as if he did not want to talk about how many had been lost. Gaetano nodded again and then things got quiet.

Gaetano put his pack down and walked over to the opening of the tent. "It doesn't look like the weather will hold up if the fighting starts," he said.

"Doesn't matter," Paulo commented, "Rumor has it, Cadorna is going to start the fighting so the Austrians will divert some of their forces away from Verdun."

"I thought we were fighting for Italy, not France," Gaetano said with a tone of sarcasm, "Guess we'll fight whoever is coming at us, don't you think?"

Paulo just grunted with a half agreement. Not that he agreed with the idea but with the observation. "Yeah, the Germans are said to be ready to come at us if the enemy needs help."

"Sounds like they're planning something more than just holding the line," Gaetano added.

"I think so," Paulo said, "rumor has it by launching this attack, the Germans will see the need to move away from Verdon and send them here to support their ally."

• • • •

IT WAS OVER TWO HOURS before Sergeant Grillo returned. He was glad to see Gaetano had made it all right but did not make too much of it since he was still in command of him. They exchanged some greetings and then Gaetano was sent to the tent where the other men under Sergeant Grillo were staying. There he saw Tomaso and Valentino. The three of them sat and talked for a couple of hours about what had happened to each of them since they had last seen each other.

"I got much better at cutting hair while I was gone," Gaetano told them. "There was a barber shop in the town where I was and the old man who I stayed with knew the owner. He set it up, so I got to make some money and learned a thing or two."

"I still don't trust you to cut my hair," Tomaso said laughing. Valentino shook his head back and forth saying the same thing.

The rest of the day did not see much activity. They knew there was fighting back in the Gorizia area but none directly where they were.

The battle, which seemed so important it could not wait, was hampered by harsh weather and an insufficient force. When it started, it started fast. They hit the enemy hard and kept up the pace. However, this battle was to be short lived. By the seventeenth of the month, Chief of Staff Cadorna called for a halt in the assault. Many speculated he had felt his obligation to the French Commander in Chief Joffre was completed and now he would focus on his cause. What goes on in the mind of a commander is rarely known and even more rarely understood. But men such as these do not get to be in those positions unless they truly have something to offer.

The battles were not very inactive during April of nineteen-sixteen, with only minor exceptions. Gaetano and his outfit conducted some reconnaissance missions similar to the one they had engaged in when they first arrived at Asiago. But had limited contact with the enemy.

In late April, the men were approached by the captain overseeing Sergeant Grillo's outfit. He was looking for two volunteers to conduct a reconnaissance mission behind the enemy lines. Any more than two would draw attention. The small number had a better chance of getting in and out without being noticed.

Gaetano remembered the previous December when he had to stay hidden from the enemy behind their lines. He figured he was best suited for the mission since he had some experience avoiding enemy forces. Paulo was watching him out of the corner of his eye afraid he would be the one to volunteer. As Gaetano raised his hand to offer his experience, Paulo raised his hand also. He wanted to look out for his friend and would not have volunteered if anyone other than Gaetano was going with him.

They headed out in the late afternoon before the sun went down. It was still light until well past seven o'clock by this time of year. So, they knew they had a chance to get well into the venture before dark.

Using the same techniques he had used in December and showing Paulo a few tricks about hiding in nearly plain sight, they managed to work their way deep into the enemy territory. What they found was very disturbing. Germans, few, but Germans nonetheless were gathering.

It took them four days to work their way back. The route they had taken to get in was now more heavily populated by the enemy than just days before. They had to revert to Gaetano's technique of traveling only in the dark. During the day, they would hide in the brush and have to be completely still. One morning they were in a similar situation to the time when Gaetano had slept in the overturned truck.

This time, they were lying down behind a wall along the road when a convoy came by. The trucks stopped precisely where they were and parked there for several hours while the soldiers interacted with one another. If only one had looked over the wall, they would have been discovered.

They could not tell how many trucks there were or how many soldiers. It would not be wise for them to raise their heads high enough to see. Their mission was to get back alive with the information about the German involvement. Whether there were fifty soldiers of five hundred on the other side of that wall was not important. Getting back was all that mattered.

The road was on the side of a short hill and the wall was facing downhill. If it had been facing uphill, they would have been trapped there until the trucks left. Several more hours passed by. As darkness came on them, the trucks were still parked, and soldiers were moving about. Gaetano gave a tug to Paulo's leg, which was the only signal he needed to know it was time for them to sneak away.

They moved inch by inch until they made it to a tree line down the hill. It took over an hour for them to move twenty yards. Once they were a couple hundred yards into the woods, they both stopped. Neither of them had been able to pee all day so they took care of that first. It helped since because they were trapped, they also could not drink anything. But holding it all day was not easy.

Afterwards they found a safe place to sit and eat some rations along with taking a drink from their canteens. On a mission like this, they were taught to eat only small amounts so as to avoid being slowed down by the usual bodily functions. They could not risk being detained by nature when the enemy might be upon them at any moment.

Once back, they gave the captain a report. It was not a surprise to him because he had been informed the German Army was soon to be in the area. He just did not think it would be this soon and this close. What was just ahead of them was more than anyone could have predicted.

Chapter 37

On May fifteenth, nineteen-sixteen, the Austro-Hungarian Army launched a major offensive. Their goal was to cut through the Italian lines and isolate their troops along the Isonzo so they could not get reinforcements. They came through the Trentino Mountain pass to take over the northern plains. The plan was, once on level ground they would be able to dig in and hold the line.

Within two weeks they had overrun the camp where Gaetano was stationed. The fight for Asiago was the fiercest they had seen since the start of the war. The trenches which the soldiers had dug around Asiago in the first days of the war were now their stronghold. For three days twenty men held the line. Gaetano and the other three remaining Patrizi men were four of the twenty. They all survived and eventually were given the order to fall back. The Italians retreated from the area on the twenty-ninth of May.

There was one thing missing though, German soldiers. The Germans had elected not to take part due to the heavy fighting at Verdun and redeployed their troops to that front. The plan from the March had worked. It drew the Germans away from Verdun and then back again. It gave both the Italians and the French the edge they needed.

At first it did not deter the Austro-Hungarians. They were well equipped and outnumbered the Italians four to one. The advantage the Italians had was their supply routes were over flat ground, and the Austro-Hungarians had to get their supplies through the mountain passes. This gave Chief of Staff Cadorna enough time to reach out to their allies in Russia to ask for help. Just like Cadorna had done for the French in March, he would now ask the Russians to do for him in order to distract the enemy to a second front. This came to be known as the Russian Brusilov Offensive. It was by this time the Austro-Hungarian Chief of Staff Conrad von Hotzendorf regretted not having aid by his German allies.

While this was being launched, Cadorna used the railroad system which was running very efficiently at this time to bring in reinforcement. With added artillery and his ability to redeploy five hundred thousand men to the area by train, he was able to turn the tides. By the second of June, he pushed back Archduke Eugen and his Army to just five kilometers from where they had first launched the offensive, and with a high price. Each side lost approximately one hundred and fifty thousand in this offensive.

The defeat was a major blow to the Austro-Hungarians and would mark the last offensive they were able to launch without help from their German allies. It also gave a boost to the Italian war effort because there had been some resistance to fighting from many of the pacifists in the northern area who were not convinced the Austro-Hungarian enemy was a real threat to them. But now with a major offensive aimed directly at them and the fear of invasion, those pacifists in power around Trentino were thrown out of office and a new government headed by Paolo Boselli came to rule.

With a couple of months to prepare, Chief Cadorna set up to launch yet another offensive. Sergeant Grillo and his outfit were once again off to the Gorizia area for another shot at taking the area back for Italy. His men arrived by truck on July thirty-first in the late afternoon. Gaetano recognized the terrain. He had fought there the previous year.

On August second, the offensive began. The fighting was determined and focused. A strange thing happened on the third day. Gaetano and the rest of Sergeant Grillo's men stormed one of the enemy positions and took it with heavy fighting. Once they secured the location, Gaetano and Paulo jumped into a shell crater to get away from any fire which might erupt and to plan the next steps. Sergeant Grillo joined them as did ten others. As they were sitting there, Gaetano had a feeling he had been in that exact spot before.

He looked over to his left facing north and saw a line of brush. At that moment he was convinced he was in the same spot he had been in when he was separated from his outfit in December. This was likely the same spot where he and two others had been pinned down. He could not be absolutely certain, but it looked so familiar, it effectively did not matter. The feelings were the same. 'What were their names?' he thought to himself. "Luigi and Vinnie" he said out loud.

Paulo looked at him. "What was that?" he asked.

Gaetano looked at him and shook his head. He did not realize he had said what he was thinking. "Oh, it was the name of the two men I was pinned down with. Remember when I came back, I told you about the day I got separated?" Paulo nodded his head "It was here............or someplace just like here. No..................it was here.......... well, maybe," he said craning his neck to get a better look around.

"Right over there," he said pointed to his left. "I crawled over into that line of brush............or one just like it. That's when the other two got hit." He sat back and stared with a look of disbelief. This was likely the spot, the exact spot where he had been.

Gaetano felt like he was being given a second chance to prove himself. Because he came back, and came back on his own, he felt everything was made right now. From this point forward, he would never feel like a coward. Not ever.

• • • •

BY THE SEVENTEENTH of August, the battle was over, and the taste of victory was ripe for the Italians. They had broken through the enemy lines and taken Gorizia. The seemingly unattainable was now in their hands. This having followed their pushing back the enemy at Asiago boosted the morale of all the Italian soldiers. As a result of the victory, the Italian government was emboldened and just two weeks later declared war on the Austro-Hungarian ally, Germany.

In the months which followed, several more minor offensives were launched to the north of Gorizia with a different technique. This time Chief Cadorna used a more focused attack to accomplish specific goals. However, it was not met with much success. By November little was gained. In each and every battle, Sergeant Grillo's men were right near the front line. Gaetano and his outfit likely saw the most fighting that year of any outfit. And it was taking its toll on all of them.

· · · ·

THE BREAK IN FIGHTING during the winter months was just in time for all the men in their outfit. It was back to the camp outside of Bologna by early December. Unlike the previous year, Gaetano would spend most of his time on the base. He would only go into town on Sundays with some of his friends he could count on not to start any trouble. And just like the winter before, he was back to cutting hair. But this time, he did not get paid for it. He volunteered to work at the base barber shop.

As he would show up each morning for his duties, he would try to see himself in Gifbourg and think about going home to play cribbage with Günter. Unfortunately, none of the other men had even heard of the game and a cribbage board was nowhere to be found. However, the memory of those days was something he could hold onto.

One afternoon, Gaetano was cutting hair, and two pilots came in. They were in the camp for a couple of weeks getting some training in ground reconnaissance techniques and how they could best assist from the air. There was one other barber working with Gaetano that day and about eight soldiers waiting to get their haircut.

On any Army base, things which are out of the ordinary get the most attention. Having two pilots on the base made for a lot of questions aimed at them wherever they were. The barber shop was the ideal setting for conversation. The questions were predictable since most people would ask the same ones. 'Are you scared up there?' 'Did you ever crash?' 'Do you get sick when you're flying?'

Gaetano asked them what turned out to be somewhat of a new question. "Where did you learn to fly?" he asked the first pilot who sat in his chair.

"An American taught me last year at an airfield south of here. I can't tell you exactly where. It's supposed to stay a secret," he replied.

"An American? Really?" Gaetano said, "I used to live in America. Do you know where he was from?"

"No, I don't, not really," he replied, "I never asked him. But you can. He's here on base taking the recon training with us."

Gaetano's eyes lit up and he became curious. He knew he could not get too excited, or this poor pilot would end up without any hair left. "Where can I find him?" he asked with a slight raised pitch to his voice, high enough to crack just a bit. The other barber laughed at how he asked.

"When do you go to the mess hall tonight?" the pilot asked.

"I usually go by six o'clock," Gaetano answered.

"I'll tell you what," the pilot said, "Let's meet outside of the mess hall at seven o'clock and I'll introduce you to him, he usually eats with us. Let's meet by the front entrance."

"Sounds good, does he speak Italian?" Gaetano asked not having any idea who this man was.

"He's from Italy originally and speaks Italian as a first language," he added. "That's probably why they assigned him to train us. What's your name so I can tell him?"

"Gaetano," he answered, "Gaetano Santorini. What's yours?"

"Name's Dino O'Sullivan," he said. There was a long pause, "Yeah, I know. My grandfather was from Ireland. He was a ship's captain Used to travel to the Mediterranean a lot. That's where he met my grandmother. Napoli, they said is how the story goes."

Gaetano chuckled. "Hey, you should hear some of the name combinations in America," he continued, "just in the New York area alone we must have over fifty different nationalities and quite a few marry someone from a different country. I guess that's part of what America is all about."

Just about then, Gaetano had finished cutting his hair. It was after two o'clock and the line was not getting any shorter. The one good thing about not getting paid for cutting hair is you do not have to be as careful. You just have to get the soldier through to the next haircut. Cut it short and on to the next man. He could cut two in the time it would take him to cut one at Eber's shop.

The line did not taper off until after five o'clock. Probably since most men would rather have dinner than get their haircut. Gaetano rushed over to his barracks to clean up. It could spoil his dinner if he had hair all over him while he was trying to eat. Two of his bunkmates were ready to go over a little before six o'clock, so they walked over together. During dinner Gaetano watched the clock on the wall to be sure he did not miss the seven o'clock meeting with this pilot from America.

At six fifty-five he excused himself from the table where his group was seated and returned his dishes to the kitchen. He walked out the front door of the mess hall which was not his usual point of exit since it was on the opposite side of the mess hall from where his barracks were. He waited about seven or eight minutes when he heard his name called. It was the pilot whom he had met that afternoon and there was another man with him.

Immediately Gaetano took note of how short both of them were. Neither man was taller than five foot four inches. Gaetano reached his hand out to shake the man's hand even before Dino could introduce them.

"Gaetano Santorini meet Carmen Galano," he said as the two were shaking hands.

"Carmen. Where are you from?" Gaetano said to him in English.

"The Bronx, in New York," he said back in English with an accent Gaetano fully recognized.

"The Bronx?" he said with his voice almost cracking again from the excitement of meeting someone who was from such a short distance from where he lived. "I lived in Jersey City. Well for a few years until I came back to Italy. Ever been to Jersey City?"

"Yes, I have, a few times," he replied, "the thing I remember most about it was the wind. Knock you right over. And a lot of train tracks."

"That's right," Gaetano chimed in feeling like he was right there. "It's because of the docks. My Papà works on the docks. For over ten years now. The trains bring stuff from all over the country to ship out to other counties through the harbor."

"Docks in Jersey City huh? So, you must have heard about Black Tom," Carmen said.

"Black Tom?" Gaetano looked puzzled.

"I guess not then," Carmen continued, "Black Tom Island is right off Jersey City in the harbor. Back at the end of July there was a huge explosion at the pier there. They said it was German saboteurs. Supposedly arrested a couple of them but no one really knows for certain if they got the right men."

Gaetano stood dumbfounded. He could not believe the war had struck so close to his home in America and that close to his parents. "Did anybody get killed?" he asked.

"Not many," Carmen replied, "all kinds of reports. Can't be sure, maybe seven or eight, a small miracle in and by itself."

Gaetano nodded his head to agree. "Was it an attack or what? What happened?" he asked because he was used to a frontal style of warfare.

"The paper said pencil bombs," Carmen said almost sounding like he did not believe it himself.

"What the heck is a pencil bomb?" Gaetano asked with a snicker.

"The Germans came up with it," he continued, "it's basically a small cylinder with chemicals in it. They do something that mixes the chemicals together and it takes several hours or maybe even days to go off and then Whoosh!!! It catches fire. Really hot fire from what they say. The paper said they think they sunk a few ships after they set out from port because these things were put into the cargo by saboteurs before they even reached the dock. Hard to catch them that way."

"That's amazing," Gaetano said shaking his head in disbelief.

They went inside so they could continue talking out of the cold and shared all they could about the things they had in common. Both had been to Lower Manhattan on Mulberry

Street and over on Bowery. They hoped maybe they both may know somebody in common. But other than having been to the same places, they had to accept the fact New York was a large place, with a lot of people, and a lot of Italians.

They sat and talked laughing about some of the lighter things in New York until well after nine o'clock. They realized it was lights out before long, so they shook hands again and went their separate ways. Carmen was only supposed to be in camp for a couple of days, so they did not see each other again. Gaetano was glad to have met someone from America. This was the only person from there he had met since arriving back in Italy almost two years earlier.

· · · ·

AS THE NINETEEN-SEVENTEEN rolled in, the focus took a different turn. They had done some training early on for mountain climbing, but now it was far more intense. Paulo, having the most experience in that area, was overseer of the outfit. He would help the men along as they were learning how to use the gear.

One evening Gaetano and Paulo were eating together in the mess hall. "What do you make of all this mountain training?" Gaetano asked.

"They never actually tell us," he said, "but I figure we're likely to go deeper into the mountains to flush them out or stop their supply lines. That might give us the edge we need."

"Most of these men are afraid of heights," Gaetano added, "hate to see us up on a ridge and someone freeze."

"Could happen," Paulo said nodding his head.

Later in the spring, about half of the men who were in training for mountain duty were pulled away and sent north to work their way into the various mountain passes. Gaetano and Paulo were not sent since they both were well known for their fighting capability in the more traditional setting. Both had fought in every battle which Italy had engaged in thus far and survived to talk about it. Both men were known and respected amongst the officers. Promotions were unheard of at that time so they both kept their ranks as private and corporal.

The outfit which went into the mountains was attempting to get some light artillery up as high as possible to have a vantage point capable of attack from above to impede the enemy supply lines. The cannons were being pulled by mules into the foothills and up into some of the passes. They reached a point where the incline was too steep for even the mules to pull. For three days in late April, the outfit was held at a standstill.

One of the soldiers said jokingly, "Why don't we just carry these things on our backs." An officer heard this and ordered the cannons to be disassembled and carried by the soldiers. The pieces were divided up and carried by either two men or four depending on the weight and size. Men would scale rock faces and set up pulleys and manual winches.

Other soldiers would carry the shells with them strapped to their backs. Then they would return to repeat the process. Once the munitions were up to the desired locations, they would return to gather their own gear such as their rifles and packs. Some men also were assigned to carry loads which were even more precious, the food. With the added workload lifting and climbing, as well as the higher elevations, men became very hungry and thirsty. Fortunately, mountain streams and springs were plentiful.

By the end of April, they had found positions to set up the guns. Some were precariously placed on rock ledges, Some needed to be strapped down. Anyplace they could get a foothold for a firing position, they took. They could now send down fire on the enemy which they could not send before. It was hoped this would give them the edge they were looking for.

Chapter 38

That year saw fewer battles but equal casualties. The efforts would be more extreme, and the consequences equaled the degree of effort. A campaign to recruit more soldiers was underway and it had some success, The seasoned soldiers still made the difference when it came to holding positions or taking on an assault.

The first offensive began in May on the twelfth. Sergeant Grillo's outfit was of course among the first to go into battle. Chief of Staff Cadorna conceived the battle along with the French to coordinate this plan. It was to coincide with an attack at Aisne which was an exceptionally large offensive.

The Italians still needed to gain ground east of Gorizia. They made significant advances closing in on Trieste only to be pushed back by the end of May. On June eighth, a cease fire was called. It would be several weeks until the fighting resumed. The return to battle in nineteen-seventeen was beginning to take its toll on everyone and Gaetano was no exception. It would have been better to just keep fighting rather than to have long breaks in between.

Sergeant Grillo's men did not go on any furloughs that summer. They stayed at the front. This added to the fatigue and depression felt by the men. A solid victory would help to boost morale. But the constant waiting was more taxing than the actual battles. Men were becoming sick more regularly and food was not as plentiful as the year before.

Like most times of waiting, it had to come to an end. On August nineteenth, the fighting once again resumed. The goal was to take as much land east of Gorizia as possible. The main focus was the Carso and around the bridgehead at Gorizia. This would bring about the morale boost they needed so badly.

At one point, Gaetano, and the rest of Sergeant Grillo's outfit had been so successful in their advances they were ahead of the supply lines and even more, the artillery. On the first of September, a Saturday, a battle broke out along what used to be Austro-Hungarian trenches. These had been in place since the beginning of the war and were dug deeper each year. In places the only way to get over the edge of the trench was to climb a ladder. Several were in place along the front.

That day saw the fiercest fighting of the year thus far. It carried into the night and had a lull for about three hours just before dawn. The fighting resumed on Sunday the second and ran until early afternoon. Each side would attack and be pushed back. Then the other would attack. The area between the two lines was riddled with casualties.

With the fighting ceased for a time in the afternoon, there was a shortage of cooks that day. Most had been redeployed to other areas. The supply officer requisitioned volunteers to assist in preparing a meal for the soldiers. The first they had other than rations in a week. Gaetano was 'selected' to volunteer from his outfit along with two others.

None of the men were in any mood to do volunteer work in the mess tent but the prospects of having a warm meal took over and they reluctantly accepted. They gave the men each a long apron to wear. They were new, they were white, and they were clean. As Gaetano put it on, he looked at his uniform. It was the same uniform he was issued when he first joined the Army. Not only was it filthy but it was torn, and blood stained.

Some of the stains went back as far as the first battles. He could no longer make out which stain was which. Though faint, they were all still there. For the longest time he had known which stains were Augustino's, but not any longer, there were just too many.

He had not spent any time thinking about his friend for a while and that bothered him. A man should be remembered, even if he lived a short time. Who would be the one to remember Augustino other than him? But how to remember without the pain of seeing him killed that way.

Without having slept for several days and with the last two days of battle still pumping through his bloodstream, Gaetano found himself having little patience with anyone. This was not a good day for him. It was the first time in over a year he had taken the time to remember Augustino and it was just the wrong combination of emotions.

The past was with him on this day. He sat on a stool in the mess tent and was peeling potatoes and carrots. There was a large pot in front of him in which he would throw them in once peeled. It could hold over ten gallons, so it took some time to fill. They put water in to keep the potatoes fresh until they could put them on the fire. Gaetano would peel the potatoes and then toss them in. Inevitably splashing water out every time. Each time seemed to get him more angry.

The mess tent was at the base of one of the deeper trenches near an opening to a clearing. It was completely out of the line of fire and that is why they chose that spot to set up. From where he was sitting and peeling. He could hear the familiar sounds of the battlefield just after a fierce battle. It was nothing new to him. But this time it was just too much for him to take.

The cries of dying men begging to have someone finish them off were agonizing. This went on all the time he was peeling the potatoes. 'How can we eat when they're dying out there?' he thought to himself. As he would toss the peeled potato in and get splashed again, he would pulse deeper with anger.

The other men in the tent with him were seemingly deaf to the cries of the wounded. He remembered that rainy night in nineteen-fifteen when he heard these cries for the first time. How could he have grown callused to them? These were men who he may have known. They had families and friends and would be missed.

The breaking point finally came. Gaetano cried out "Somebody do something!" Everyone just looked at him without making a sound as if there was something wrong with him. He looked back and forth at them and then kicked the pot he was working on dumping all the potatoes and water on the ground. The nearest ladder was just twenty feet from the opening of the mess tent. Gaetano stormed over to it and started to climb. Two sergeants reached out to stop him, but he pushed one away and kicked the other in the chin from the fifth rung of the ladder.

The enemy must have been just as fatigued as the Italians because no one seemed to notice at first. But no one could miss this thin soldier wearing a white apron which went from his chest to below his knees walking across the battlefield without a rifle and without a helmet. He grabbed the first soldier he found who was wounded and lifted him up onto his shoulder.

Two soldiers had climbed up ladders to see what was going on. Once they realized there was someone pulling the wounded off the battlefield, they pulled three ladders together so they could hand down the wounded. The ladders were eight feet high, so they set up two soldiers at the top and two mid-ways down. Gaetano handed off the first wounded soldier and then turned back to get another.

There were two German soldiers looking over their trench and saw this man in an apron just walking out on the battlefield. They started to call out "du must dir das ansenhen" to the others in their line to come observe this spectacle. Gaetano could hear them laughing. Some of them would take shots at him but none seemed to be able to hit him. No one was sure if they were missing intentionally or if they were tired from all the fighting themselves and could not take good aim.

This went on for over two hours. Gaetano would pull someone off the field and then return for more. The enemy fire increased, and Gaetano found he needed to take cover and crawl in order to get to the wounded. No one else came to help him. Neither the Italians nor the Germans or the Austro-Hungarians could believe what they were seeing.

As he brought in the wounded to hand them off, sometimes there were applause................ from both sides. That did not stop the enemy from taking shots at him though. A couple came so close he thought he was done for. The commotion was spreading throughout the trench on the Italian side. Paulo was wondering what was happening, so he asked someone who was passing by.

"Some crazy man is out there pulling the wounded off the battlefield," the soldier told him.

He immediately knew it had to be Gaetano. He ran over to where the commotion seemed to be originating from and climbed up on the side of the trench to see what was going on. Sure enough, it was Gaetano. He was pulling in his twenty-fourth wounded soldier. When it started to become dark, they could not hear anymore cries from the wounded.

No one was really sure why he stopped. But at one point, Gaetano brought a wounded soldier in and just came down the ladder. That last soldier had been handed off. Then he simply walked away. He did not go back to the mess tent. He just disappeared.

Paulo saw him and followed. After they got to a place where no one else was around, Gaetano stopped and fell to his knees. He looked up and saw Paulo standing beside him and he began to weep like he had never done before. Paulo put his hand on his shoulder and stayed with him.

Word spread around for weeks about this crazy man who went out on the battlefield with a long white apron and pulled over thirty-five wounded soldiers to safety. Some said they knew who he was. Some said he was wounded trying. Some even claimed to know him personally. Some said he was killed at one point. Some said the whole thing was made up. Those who knew Gaetano, knew the truth because they knew the man.

• • • •

LESS THAN TWO WEEKS later, another ceasefire was called. It was now the twelfth of September. This battle had seen some involvement by German soldiers but not a full commitment to engage their forces against the Italians. It was mostly to give their ally as much boost as needed to keep them stable. That was soon to change.

A few weeks had gone by, and the Italian troops were just waiting with seemingly no plan to launch an assault. The cooler weather was beginning to settle in, and the evenings were foggy and rainy. The men would settle into wherever they could keep dry and try to get some sleep. The evening of October twenty-third was no exception.

At two o'clock in the morning at Caporetto the enemy began to launch one of the most extensive artillery attacks to date. With six German divisions and nine Austro-Hungarian divisions they initiated the most aggressive assault since Asiago. The main difference this time was it was planned and executed by the Germans. Their commanders were far more experienced in aggressive warfare and their first efforts proved it.

Gaetano and the rest of Sergeant Grillo's outfit were a bit north of the main offensive. They positioned themselves to hold their line. By the late afternoon on the twenty-fourth, the enemy had pushed their way twenty-five kilometers south. The main offensive was decisive and unstoppable. However, the secondary offensives which were run mostly by the Austro-Hungarians were not as effective. But they were still more aggressive than any other they had launched before. The position Sergeant Grillo's outfit held stood firm as a result of the indefatigable efforts of his men. Most looked to Gaetano for the inspiration they needed. He seemed to be the most resolved to hold the line. Anytime others would waver, he would encourage them not to retreat but to stand and fight.

The Germans used heavy artillery, smoke, flamethrowers, and something the Italians had not seen very much of, gas. This had a demoralizing effect on the Italians who up until now fought with more traditional methods. The Italians still had the numbers on their side. They were able to outflank the enemy on some fronts but were not able to stop them where it mattered most.

Chief of Staff Cadorna believed he could turn things around and push back the enemy just as they had done earlier in the year. But on October thirtieth the order was given to retreat across the Isonzo to reestablish a position in a more secure location. Once established, a cease fire was called on November seventh. Some fighting continued sporadically in the following weeks.

The defeat at Caporetto had one major casualty. Chief of Staff Cadorna was relieved of his authority by a new government which was formed soon after the battle. The remaining pacifist movement was no longer able to keep a position of influence. Vittorio Orlando as named Prime Minister to run the new government and Chief of Staff Cadorna was replaced with Armando Diaz.

The other major change which occurred because of the defeat was a new policy that was invoked. Prior to this, the policy had been the Italians would cover the front in their own country without direct help from their allies. The assistance thus far was restricted to diversionary attacks on other fronts. But now they would enlist the support of French and the British.

• • • •

WINTER WAS SOON UPON them and the usual stance of holding positions was set. Fighting continued in small pockets well into December, but the major offensives were held off. This was partly due to the coming winter. But mostly it was to give the Italians a chance to reestablish themselves with the new leadership and policies.

Sergeant Grillo's outfit did not return to the camp outside of Bologna until after the New Year. It proved devastating to these seasoned soldiers. With health problems and food shortages, the morale of the soldiers suffered greatly. During the first week of January, the decision was made to relieve the men and send them to the camp. It was not a moment too soon for Gaetano who had developed a chronic cough and would wake up at night with chills and shaking. He lost even more weight and was consistently pale.

Once the transfer was ordered and they were returned to the camp, Gaetano spent three weeks in the infirmary. He would sleep twelve hours a day and try to drink and eat as much as possible. The doctor's orders were that he build up his strength. It was not so much the fact he was sick, but mostly exhausted and malnourished. Though it took some time, by the end of February he felt as if he was back on his feet.

When Gaetano returned to his regular barracks, he noticed there were a large number of new recruits. Most of them were under twenty years old. One morning he was at breakfast with Paulo and three other men from his outfit along with Tomaso and Valentino. Across from them was a table filled with new recruits who were getting very loud.

"They barely look old enough to shave," Paulo said.

"It wasn't all that long ago we were their age and looked as young," Gaetano chimed in.

"Hey," Paulo responded, "Don't forget, I've got at least ten years on some of you."

"Yeah, and my Papà looks younger than you," Tomaso jabbed. The problem was, he was probably right. Nearly three years of fighting a war will put the years on.

"Maybe we should call you Papà from now on," Valentino laughed.

Paulo gave him a look that said, 'Don't even start.'

"Look at their uniforms," Gaetano said, "we never had uniforms like that."

"The people believe more in the war effort now," Paulo responded, "The uniform you got back in fifteen was leftover stock from eleven. That was the last time we fought with this enemy. These are the latest model."

"They look warmer," Gaetano said.

"That's their winter uniform," Paulo said, "they get a lighter one for summertime."

Gaetano turned his head to look directly at Paulo seated next to him on his left. "And why don't they give us new uniforms?" he asked with a sneer.

Paulo just shrugged his shoulders. Tomaso jumped in, "Hey, everyone knows we're the ones who held up all this time. It's like the older the uniform, the more experience you have. They look up to us just because we have these old beat-up and blood-stained uniforms. Don't knock it."

They all nodded their heads in agreement, realizing Tomaso had hit the nail on the head. After a long pause Gaetano said, "Still though, I wouldn't mind having one of those."

Chapter 39

New soldiers with new uniforms and new equipment all led to an inspiration to achieve like the Italian Army had not seen in many years. With a new leader and a fresh desire on the part of the Italian people to see victory, the spring of nineteen-eighteen brought a vibrancy that was quite overdue.

The recently appointed Chief of Staff Armando Diaz wasted no time in deploying the appropriate forces in key locations from the Alps to the Adriatic Sea. He had carefully studied the tactics of the enemy and anticipated their next likely move.

In contrast to the new Italian exuberance, the Austro-Hungarian Army was now demoralized and ill equipped. The Russians had withdrawn from the war which would seem like a boost. But the Germans were applying pressure on them to achieve the goals they were setting before them. This further reduced the confidence of the Austro-Hungarians.

They too had a new Chief of Staff. Arz von Staussenberg had taken over and was faced with several unpleasant obstacles besides the Italian Army. There was a rivalry between two commanders who were more interested in their own achievements than victory for the country. Knowing this and trying to appease them both, von Staussenberg divided the troops into two equal groups. This added to the demoralization of the Army. It also weakened them as a total force. When your enemy engages in divide and conquer, that is one thing. When you divide yourselves, you defeat yourselves.

Sergeant Grillo's outfit was of course among the first to be deployed once the weather broke. They were positioned along the Piave River in what was supposed to be only a precautionary move. Armando Diaz had watched the troop activity of the enemy and was able to get some solid intelligence on where things might next escalate. His anticipations proved to be correct. On June fifteenth, the enemy launched what was to be their last consolidated effort in the war. The fighting was significant, but the Austro-Hungarian Army was still outnumbered by the Italians.

The battles were widespread. Too widespread to be effective. Holding the line was not easy but not as difficult as battles in the past. Many of the soldiers on the Italian side were the new recruits. Sergeant Grillo's men were assigned to a line of trenches they had used over a year before.

During a lull in the fighting Gaetano, Paulo, Tomaso, and Valentino were laying low in one of the trenches. The new recruits were inexperienced in this setting. They did not understand when the seasoned soldiers would tell them how important it was to keep down. The older soldiers would try to teach them to never look over the top of the trench unless you were directed to and ready to fight the enemy.

It was early afternoon on the seventeenth of June. The fighting had been going on for a couple of days but only in spurts. Three young soldiers came walking by. They were not hunching over so as not to be seen. One of them sat down next to Gaetano and asked him for a smoke.

"All out," Gaetano said rather than say he did not smoke, "you'd better keep your head down."

"What do you mean?" the young soldier said, "the fighting has been on hold for over three hours. I'll bet you they're sleeping over there."

Gaetano and the rest of the older soldiers just shook their heads in disbelief. The young soldier turned and looked up over the edge of the trench and then sat back down. "See, I told you, they're asleep."

Paulo chimed in, "They don't sleep, just like we don't sleep."

"No, I mean it," he repeated, "they're asleep."

With that he turned and looked up again. A single shot rang out and the young soldier fell back to the other side of the trench. Paulo and Gaetano looked at each other and shook their heads some more. "Damn fool," Tomaso said.

"That guy had good aim," Valentino added, "caught him right in the forehead," referring to the enemy soldier who had shot him. The other two young soldiers began to shake uncontrollably. They lunged forward as if to take a battle position. The rest just laughed.

The young soldier had received a single bullet right in the center of his forehead. As he was lying on his back with his eyes still wide-open Gaetano said, "How old do you think he was............eighteen?" After seeing so many be killed over the past three years, it was hard for them to feel pity for one who had brought it on himself. It was not that they were not caring for another soldier. It was more like they knew everyone had to be smart in order to survive. And that day, a foolish eighteen-year-old was not.

"A strange thing about someone being shot in the head like that," Paulo said, "there's almost no bleeding. Why is that I wonder?"

"The heart stops beating immediately," Gaetano replied, "the instant death along with the gravity of lying on his back. The bleeding is all internal. It's that simple."

The others then got up hunched over and moved away to go further to the left. They did not want to be anywhere near where this obviously fine marksman was stationed directly across from them in the opposing trench. However, Gaetano stayed. He sat across from the dead soldier for several minutes.

'He looks to be about my size,' he thought to himself. A thought he did not want to admit he was having. But after so long and seeing so much, this almost did nothing to his feelings. Feeling was something he could no longer afford to do.

After another twenty minutes of pondering went by, he figured 'why not.' Looking both ways to see if anyone was around, he took off his uniform, down to his skivvies and proceeded to swap uniforms with the dead soldier. 'He's not gonna need it anymore' he thought to himself.

Knowing he could not leave a fellow soldier without any clothes on, he put his old, stained, torn uniform on the young soldier who never had a chance to taste a victory on the battlefield.

As he put on the jacket, Gaetano looked at the inner lapel. "Santino Carvelli?" he said in a soft voice, "Thanks for the uniform." In the Italian Army during that time, the soldiers did not have identification tags or bracelets. They would have their name monogrammed into the inner lapel of their uniforms. The same was the case for his old uniform.

Gaetano crouched down and walked away making some adjustments to his new uniform. Any remorse he might feel from taking a dead soldier's uniform was far outweighed by his need to shed the uniform which held the blood stains of his former comrades, enemies and yes, Augustino.

He made his way back to where his outfit was. Paulo took one look at him and shook his head. "You didn't," he said with a sadness in his voice. Gaetano just shrugged his shoulders and kept walking.

• • • •

THIS BATTLE WAS ONLY two days old but not by any means over. The men barely had time to force down some rations before the shooting started again. They all sprang into action without needing to be ordered. By now, these men were a well-adjusted machine who could work together in harmony. One looking out for the other.

By the nineteenth of June, the battle was nearly over. The Austro-Hungarian Armies who were once almost impossible to get past and feared when on the attack were now in full retreat across the Piave River. The large numbers and strong rapids made it difficult for them to have a speedy retreat. This gave the Italians a chance to flank the enemy and attack even more severely. By the twenty second of June, the Austro-Hungarians were completely across the river and fully humiliated. It was now just a matter of time when the Italians would be able to end this conflict decisively.

During the following months, through the summer of nineteen-eighteen, many wanted Chief of Staff Diaz to attack and put an end to it. Knowing how things were progressing on the Western front in France, he hesitated. It was possible the Germans would focus all their attention there and completely leave the Austro-Hungarians to themselves. This gradually came to pass, and the Austro-Hungarians were increasingly on their own. There were minor assaults which he would launch locally but no efforts at a great offensive. Not yet anyway.

During that summer, Gaetano went on many missions with the rest of Sergeant Grillo's outfit. During late August, Valentino was killed when they went out on one. They went to destroy some munitions they were told the enemy was stockpiling in a town just ten kilometers away. The mission was a success, but several enemy soldiers gave chase to them as they tried to flee the scene. There were three men on the mission. Gaetano was the only one to return alive.

There were other assignments Gaetano took on. He became known as the first one to go to if you needed a volunteer. And he always got the job done. By mid-September, the missions stopped. There was a plan afoot and all the experienced soldiers were kept close by in order to help the younger ones along so they would be ready.

A final offensive was being planned. Chief of Staff Diaz had been carefully studying the best way for cutting off the enemy. The intent was to divide their forces by attacking them at the Piave River. That would separate the enemy forces on the plains from the forces in the mountains. Then separate Armies would attack each remaining division. A classic case of divide and conquer done the right way.

On the twenty-third of October, he launched simultaneous attacks on both the Lower Piave and Upper Piave. The enemy knew they would have to reinforce either location should an attack come but were unable to do so since both were attacked at the same time. This was the key to an Italian victory and Diaz knew it. This was known as The Battle of Vittorio. The name Veneto was added later, and the name of the battle was then changed to The Battle of Vittorio Veneto.

During the first day of the assault, Gaetano and his outfit were pinned down for several hours before they could completely leave the riverbank area. Gaetano's new uniform got soaked from lying in the riverbed to stay under cover. The newer material held moisture longer and with the chilly autumn air he developed a case of hypothermia. By nightfall, the first day he could not stop shivering. Sergeant Grillo ordered him to fall back and get dry by a fire that was going near a temporary mess tent.

As he stood there trying to warm himself and get dry, he noticed a lieutenant walking in his direction. The lieutenant stopped to get warm for a bit also. After a moment or two the lieutenant looked at Gaetano and pointed. "I know you.........Santorini, right?"

Gaetano stared at him for a bit to try to figure where he would know him from and then it came to him. 'The lunatic lieutenant,' he thought. This was the officer who had shot Augustino so long ago. Gaetano thought for a second and shook his head. "No Signor, Carvelli," he said as he pulled back his lapel to show the name.

"Hmmm," he muttered as he shook his head, "you look just like him...... older though. Did you join late? Your uniform is from this year. I know because I picked the uniforms for this year."

"Yeah, this year," Gaetano mumbled.

"Why did you wait so long to come fight for your country?" the lieutenant demanded.

Gaetano did not answer him right away. He pretended to be shivering too much to speak. "No reason," he finally said.

The lieutenant was becoming furious by now. "I never forget a face. You are him. You and the others disappeared after our mission and I thought you all ran away like cowards," he began to sputter.

Gaetano leaned away wishing he were still in the icy river rather than standing next to this madman.

"Where did you go, where did you get that uniform. You are him I know because I put you in my report that day and came looking for you because the captain wanted to meet you. But you and the others were gone. I looked like a fool in front of the captain," he continued to rant. Gaetano just kept silent and rolled his eyes wishing he were somewhere else or better yet, someone else.

The lieutenant grabbed Gaetano by the collar and pulled him into an adjacent tent. He continued to grill him about how he had a new uniform on. And that he had obviously been in the Army for years now. No one else was in the tent with them so after several more minutes of being scolded and tormented, Gaetano took one swing at him and punched him square in the nose knocking him out cold. Now he had some fresh blood on his uniform. He looked down at him for a moment and then walked out.

He made his way back to where Sergeant Grillo was holding out with the men and told him what had just happened and who had confronted him. "Can't go around punching lieutenants all the time," the sergeant said to him remembering the other time he had punched a lieutenant.

"Go wrap yourself up in a blanket and get warm," he said, "you're starting to look like you did last January again." Gaetano was definitely feeling the weather. His cough was slowly coming back, and he just could not warm himself.

• • • •

ONCE THEY STARTED FIGHTING again and even with his diminished capacity, Gaetano still fought harder than most and was usually the first to get to the enemy line when they attacked. While fighting, one could not tell he was struggling with illness. At night he would run a fever, and it would take almost an hour for him to stop coughing when he woke up. But he insisted on continuing to fight with his outfit. They all knew the end was near and he wanted to be there for the final victory.

This man who was reluctantly drawn into the Army and then voluntarily came back when most would have kept running was now determined to see this through to the end. Even if it meant his end. The fight was in him. And it had to come out if he were to ever get past this period of his life. Nothing was to be left unfinished.

Like most of the major battles of the Great War in Italy, this one was over within two weeks. The cease fire was called on November second and the official end to all hostilities was declared on November fourth. This marked the end of the Austro-Hungarian Empire and the beginning of the circumstances which would return them to battle within two decades.

• • • •

GAETANO AND THE REST of Sergeant Grillo's outfit were sent back to the camp near Bologna for discharge. The official ceremony was to be held on November twentieth but as they arrived at the base on the eighteenth, Gaetano was terribly ill with a fever that would not break.

Sergeant Grillo and Paulo both insisted he go to the infirmary first thing. He resisted because he wanted to be there for the official discharge. But he was in no condition to even stand for the half hour it would take. They each took one of his arms and started to escort him down the road which led to the infirmary. Sergeant Grillo purposely avoided telling him where they were taking him in order for him to go. He viewed him now not as a private under his command, but as a close friend whom he was simply helping.

Gaetano's fever grew extremely high. For three days he was delirious. They fed him fluids and gave him aspirin. There was not much else they could do. He stayed in the infirmary until the November thirtieth. By then all his friends from his outfit had been discharged. Sergeant Grillo, Paulo, and Tomaso had come to see him on the day they were released, but he was not aware they were even there. One of the nurses told him the following week they had come by on their way out of camp.

Now that he was more alert, he noticed his uniform was gone. He began to panic as to where it had gone.

"Nurse?" he said softly as she walked by, "My uniform, what did they do with my uniform, and my boots?"

"They burned them," she replied.

"Burned them?" he sighed in disbelief, "Everything?"

"Yes, everything," she said, "with the influenza everywhere, they can't be too careful."

Gaetano fell back into his pillow and sighed like he had just lost a best friend. "I'll be right back," the nurse said as she scurried away. About five minutes later she returned.

"I think this belongs to you," she whispered to him so that no one else would hear. She grabbed his right hand and pulled it towards her, She put something in it. It was his pocket watch.

Gaetano's eyes filled with tears. "I thought it was gone forever," he cried.

"The day you came in we had you put right to bed," she continued, "within the hour your fever shot up so high you were delirious before we could take off your uniform. When we did, this fell out of your boot. I grabbed it before anybody saw it. It's not regulation you know."

"I know," he said, "that's why I've always kept it in my boot. It was a gift from my friends in America just before I came to Italy way back in the spring of fifteen."

"Did you come to join the Army?" she asked.

"I came to take care of my Nonna," he replied.

"Oh, where does she live?" the nurse asked.

"She passed away that summer," he sighed, "I never got to see her. They recruited me from my ship, practically at gunpoint."

"That's so sad," she said trying to console him, "you must have been very close to her."

"My Mamma and Papà moved to America before me. I stayed with her for almost five years," Gaetano said almost not wanting to remember this part. "We got word she was getting weak so we decided I would come back to care for her in her last days. Papà couldn't afford to lose his job on the docks........................ I never made it................ Then she died."

"Well, you have good friends in America to give you such a nice watch," she said shaking his right hand which was still closed over it, "I figured it was special, so I hid it in my locker until you came to."

"Well, thank you," he said not knowing what else to say. He looked at it and listened to it. It was ticking.

"It's working!" he exclaimed, "It started working again."

"It wasn't wound up when I found it," she added, "and I didn't want to wind it up because someone might hear it ticking and take it."

"It hasn't worked for over a year," he said, "I was afraid it was broken."

She smiled and looked around just to make sure no one was looking. "I took it home last week to try to wind it up, but it didn't work," she began, "so, I took it to my father's shop, and he offered to look at it when I told him it belonged to a soldier who I was caring for. I thought maybe it was just wet or dirty," she added. "My father is a watchmaker, and he showed me how they work on the inside. Just a little dirt and they stop. He said it was the least he could do for one of our fighting men."

"He cleaned it?" Gaetano said with the most excitement he had shown in over two years. "He cleaned and polished it. It's like new. Thank you so much. And thank you for keeping it quiet." She gave him a pat on the arm and then she walked out of the room. He pulled it close to his chest and fell asleep.

· · · ·

A COUPLE OF DAYS LATER, Gaetano was released from the hospital. He was not certain what to do next. The camp was beginning to look deserted. As he left the infirmary that morning he went by the captain's office where he had gone when he returned from Switzerland nearly three years earlier. There was no one in the office and the name on the door was not the same captain as before. He was still weak from his stay in the infirmary.

They had given him civilian clothing. On the day he was supposed to be discharged with the others in his outfit, all his paperwork was set aside. His pay along with a packet of documents was brought to the infirmary for safekeeping. Everything he needed for discharge was there. Gaetano gathered all of his papers but never really went through an official process or signed any of the papers. It was not a definitive discharge from the Army.

After trying the captain's office and a couple of other places to see what he should do, he started wandering about on the base. By now, Gaetano knew his way around and went over to the spot where the trucks would come and bring soldiers into town. He was carrying the small pack that they gave him to take with him. It held one change of clothing and some needed hygiene items as well as medication to help his lungs clear. He asked one of the drivers and found out there was a truck scheduled to leave within the hour, so he jumped on to get a ride into Bologna.

He arrived by five o'clock and decided to go to one of the good restaurants so he could celebrate, albeit by himself. This was the end of a very trying period in his life. They had given him his soldier's pay at the infirmary. It was more than he could have imagined. It was enough for him to buy train fare and a ticket to New York on a liner. The pay was significant because he had not been taking any furloughs over the past year. It all added up to be a significant amount. He knew he did not have to worry about his next meal for a while.

After ordering the best meal he had eaten in more than two years, he went over to the train station to look at the schedules. The ticket office was closed so he walked to the hotel, which was about two blocks away and took a room for the night.

He slept well in the warm bed of the hotel and left early to get to the train station. There was a rack of schedules written on the wall. He had walked right past them when he arrived back early in nineteen-sixteen and had not paid any attention.

There was a train to Marseille, and a train to Napoli. Both of which would have ships bound for New York. He walked up to the ticket agent and put a down some Lira. "Gifbourg please, one way to Gifbourg."

Chapter 40

The train which would go through Gifbourg left in the mid-afternoon. Gaetano got lunch and ordered some carry out food for the train. Most of the restaurants around the train station would do this just as they did in Gifbourg. It was reaching the end of November so Gaetano was confident the trains would get through. Sometimes the weather would stop the train lines as early as this but not most years. At least the portion of the trip through northern Italy would be clear.

Once on the train, Gaetano asked the conductor when they would arrive in Gifbourg. According to what he said, they would pull into the station at midday on the second of December. Hopefully just around the noon hour.

Gaetano settled into his seat. The car he was in was quite full. The seat he was in was empty except for him. Before long he noticed the seat in front of him was empty as well. He figured out it was likely because he still had a harsh cough and did not look healthy. The influenza season was in full swing, and everyone was afraid of someone who was coughing every three minutes.

The Army had let him keep some souvenirs from his pack. He had his canteen, which he made certain was full before he left the station. His mess kit which he vowed never to eat from, ever again and of course, his barber tools. Even though he had not cut any hair in nearly a year, he still knew how. And these were a part of the Army he did not mind keeping for the memory.

There was some cough medicine in the pack they had given to him at the infirmary. He did not want anyone to see him take it since they already seemed to be squeamish about his cough. Once it turned dark in the train car, he opened the pack and took a nip of the cough medicine. He knew he should measure it properly, but that might give him away.

He took the watch out of his pocket which he no longer had to keep hidden and checked the time. It was seven thirty. The train car was warm enough, but the nighttime air still made him chilly. He took out his extra shirt and put it on. Then he put his coat back on over everything. They had also given him a bottle of aspirin. He took some and tried to find a comfortable position. Seeing how the seat next to him was still empty, he put his pack on the seat to use as a pillow and lay down on his left side. Once the aspirin took effect, he fell sound asleep and did not move from that spot until the sun started shining through the window on his face the next morning.

It was Sunday the first day of December, and he was feeling much better than the day before, which was surprising to him. He did not think he would get much rest on the train, but he slept very soundly. His back was cramped and sore and his feet were chilly, but overall, he felt good.

The train stopped for a meal break at around eleven, so he got off and went into the station to use the restroom and fill his canteen. They had two hours to wait until they left again so he decided to get something to eat. This restaurant also offered a lunch sack for the train, so he had them make two. The doctors at the infirmary told him to eat as much as he could to build his strength. That day he wanted to eat like he had not been for a long time. He was more than happy to accommodate them.

That afternoon as they left the station, they began to enter the mountains which meant they would soon be going through the tunnels. The first one was rather short, so Gaetano played the game of holding his breath. It was easy to do but as the tunnels got longer, it was much more difficult for him to hold his breath. His lungs were still recovering and very weak.

One time he took a very deep breath to hold in as much air as he could, but it caused him to start coughing and he could not stop. He decided to take out his cough medicine even though people could see him. The game was fun, but he could not afford to start coughing again so he stopped and instead would see how far he could count to himself before they got through the tunnel. It was almost as much fun and helped him to feel free.

There was snow on the mountain sides and some right along the tracks. He was not sure how long the trains would be running for if he decided to try to get back to a harbor in order to board a liner to New York. It was still early enough in December, and he was confident he could pay a visit to Günter and still make it back before the trains were snowbound.

As he went to sleep that night in a similar position to the night before, he spent a lot of time thinking about the winter he spent with Günter and all that they talked about while playing their evening cribbage game. He remembered talking about things which were really important in life. If it had not been for this kind old man, he might have made a foolish mistake and rather than feeling a sense of completion as he did at this moment. He would be living with guilt and regret. The main reason for this trip was to make certain Günter knew how much he appreciated what he had done for him in the brief time they were together. And to thank him once more.

When he woke up, it was snowing rather hard. Not enough to stop the train. But it was piling up on the sides of the track. He was now familiar enough with the terrain to know this would not be a severe snowstorm but rather just an introduction to the winter which was soon to come.

The conductor came by at around seven thirty. Gaetano stopped him to ask "Signor, will we making a breakfast stop or continuing right through to Gifbourg?"

"We stop in twenty minutes," he replied.

Gaetano was relieved. He had eaten well the day before and he was even more hungry now. He started thinking about some of the great breakfasts he and Günter would prepare with fresh eggs Günter had just retrieved from the barn. Sometimes they would have ham, sausages, or bacon. Then there would always be the muffins Günter made fresh before Gaetano would get up. And the coffee. What he would pay for a cup of Günter's coffee right now.

Twenty minutes seemed like two hours with Gaetano's stomach reminding him how hungry he was. As they stopped the conductor told them it would be a short stop this time. Only forty-five minutes because of the snow falling. He wasted no time jumping off the train and heading for the restaurant in the station. It was very crowded, and he was concerned about the service, so he went to the counter and ordered a double order of eggs to take out. He asked if they would fill his canteen with coffee. They were willing to fill it from the pot directly. That way he would be able to keep it warm by putting the cap on. The canteen held the same as three cups served in the restaurant. He did not mind the extra boost one bit.

Gaetano went back to his seat on the train and started to eat before it showed any sign of leaving the station. It was much easier to eat when the train was not rolling and bumping along the tracks. The eggs made his stomach feel good and the hot coffee made his lungs feel even better.

It had stopped snowing by the time they left the station and now it was only five hours until they reached Gifbourg. Gaetano had thought several times over the last couple of days about how he would surprise Günter by showing up unannounced. He had been tempted to send him a telegram letting him know he was coming but he liked the idea of surprising him. And he suspected Günter might actually enjoy that as well.

The terrain looked familiar with the mountains in the close distance and the rolling hills with the farms nestled in the valleys. He took out his watch and looked to see what time it was. It was eleven thirty-five, very soon now. His trip this time was under quite different circumstances. He would not have to worry about getting chased off the train by the freight conductor or have to hide when someone came by. The fare was paid, and he had a legitimate ticket for the seat he had been in now for almost two days.

As the train slowed to enter Gifbourg, he could see the train yard where Günter would work even past his retirement. It was not busy since most trains were preparing for the winter slowdown. They seemed to inch along. He just wanted to be there. Plus, he was dying to get off and get walking. Most of his things fit nicely into the pack he had. He gave a careful look around and under the seat to make certain he was not leaving anything behind. The pack was buttoned up and he was ready to get off. If only the train would reach the station.

Many thoughts can go through a person's mind while waiting for things to occur. The fact he was not carrying a rifle this time crossed his mind. Back in nineteen-sixteen he had the rifle with him coming up and going back, but no more. The only rifle he ever wanted to see ever again would be for hunting, if he decided he wanted to. He did not really know what had happened to his rifle. It was with him when he took the truck back to the camp just outside of Bologna. Since he was so ill when they arrived and the rifles were not loaded anyway, he figured they just stayed on the truck, and someone eventually picked it up and put it back into the armory. Or possibly even threw it away.

Finally, the train stopped. By then, Gaetano had already been standing for ten minutes. He dipped his head to read the sign as they pulled in and he started looking around as if someone might be waiting for him to give him a ride. But he knew that was not possible since he had not told anyone he was coming. The feeling was there, nonetheless. That morning, he had decided to stop at Eber's barber shop first just to say hello and possibly find someone who could give him a ride out to Günter's since he was still weak.

The shop was about a ten-minute walk from the train station. Fortunately, his pack was not loaded down with too much, so it was light to carry. There was still quite a bit of room in it if he needed to carry more, but he was glad he did not. Carrying a heavy pack around for the past three years had made him glad to be traveling light. As he approached, he saw from across the street that Eber was there and had just finished cutting a customer's hair. The customer was handing him some money, and they were talking. Eber was the only barber working.

The sound of a familiar door opening will bring back many memories and this door did exactly that. The bell on the top and the creaking of the hinge were familiar. Every time a customer came in, it would make the same sound. It came to mean making money. He was looking forward to making money again, but likely not until he returned to New Jersey. With his Army pay, which was back pay for almost two years, he had enough to get by with for some time.

As the door creaked closed and snapped on the latch, Eber looked up casually as he would each time a customer came in. Most times he would give a nod or a soft hello to whoever it was and maybe a bit more if it were a regular. He looked up and gave the grunting hello and then caught himself. "Gaetano? Is that you?" he said to him in Italian.

A huge smile came over Gaetano's face as he walked over to where Eber was standing equaled only by the size smile on Eber's face. Gaetano had to hold back the glassy eyes as they both gave an embrace. "When did you get back?" Eber asked.

"I just got off the train," Gaetano responded, "Just ten minutes ago. I thought I would come over and say hello before going out to see Günter."

Eber's face dropped, "Gaetano," he said solemnly, "come sit down." Gaetano looked puzzled and was a bit afraid of what he might be about to hear. "I have something to tell you," Eber continued. They sat in the chairs where the customers would sit while waiting their turn just as the door was closing for the last customer who was leaving.

"What is it?" Gaetano asked almost knowing already.

"It's about Günter," he continued, "he passed away about three months ago."

Gaetano was upset by this revelation but deep down it came as no surprise. He had wondered even before buying his ticket if this might be possible. But he also knew he would want to know for certain. And also, he would want to find out this way rather than in an unreturned telegram.

"How? What happened?" he asked.

"He was getting very weak this past year," Eber said, "the doctor says it was his heart just getting old. He was always in good spirits and even joked about not having as much strength as he once had."

"Was he in a hospital?" Gaetano asked with concern on what might have happened, "How did they know? Was anybody with him?"

"We all took turns going out to check up on him," Eber said somberly, "Near the end, we would make certain someone stopped in each day to see how he was holding up. He stayed downstairs on the first floor mostly by then. The stairs were too much for him. Karl found him one morning sitting in his chair with a book on his lap. Karl said he looked very peaceful. I hope I get to go like that."

Gaetano was trying to see in his mind the image of Günter sitting in his favorite chair that evening reading and at one point just lowering the book. And then gone.

"He always said you would return though," Eber continued, "he always talked about you and how you made him proud when you decided to go back to the fighting on your own. I think he saw you as the son he never had."

That was more than Gaetano could hear without breaking down. His tears were gentle but full. He took a couple of choppy breaths and shook off the cry. "What about his home?" Gaetano asked, "What will happen to it? It was so beautiful."

"Günter gave all of his property to the church since he didn't have any family," Eber said sounding a bit lighter now that the heavy news was out there. "He did leave you a couple of things though and the pastor asked me to hang onto them just in case you should ever come back." Eber stood up and went for the back stairs which led to the room where Gaetano used to stay on Friday nights.

"I'll be right back," he said as he turned the corner. Gaetano was baffled by this. Eber's footsteps could be heard throughout the barbershop especially since no one else was in the building. They were very distinctive directly overhead, and Gaetano realized that everybody probably could hear him walking about when he stayed up there. The steps moved back towards the stairs and down came Eber with a box in his hands.

"It wasn't until middle of October when they read his will," he said, "I was there along with everyone who had been looking in on him. The pastor, Karl, a couple of men from the train yard, we all looked in on him. Günter had a lot of friends in this town."

He handed the box to Gaetano, and he opened it. It was not sealed up, just folded over. Gaetano looked in and stared for a moment and then let out something that sounded like a cross between a laugh and a cry. "I don't believe it," he said.

In the box were only two items, Günter's æbleskiver pan and a cribbage board. The same cribbage board they had used when playing all those evenings. He took out the cribbage board and showed it to Eber. "Many evenings we played this," he said. Eber knew it well. He would play with Günter on the days he was assigned to look in on him. He knew exactly what it meant to Gaetano to get this.

"Günter spoke of you just last summer, now that I think of it," Eber said, "we read in a newspaper from Rome that someone brought on the train, the war was soon to be over. But no one could say exactly when. The paper said the battle in June was decisive, but it wasn't over until the Austro-Hungarians actually surrendered and ceased hostilities."

"That's right, just like it said," Gaetano quipped, "guess they needed one more whipping."

"Günter hoped he might see you again and hoped you might come up after the war was over," Eber said sadly. "But he didn't make it that far."

"I wish I could see the house one more time?" Gaetano said pessimistically, "I'm sure someone is living there by now though, right?"

"Funny you should say that," Eber said with curious tone, "Pastor Goehner was just in here two days ago talking about how he can't figure out that contraption Günter had set up in the basement. He was concerned no one would want to buy the house with such an elaborate set up. They haven't sold it yet and they probably won't until spring arrives now. He was concerned about the pipes freezing and everything getting ruined from the water. So, he very much wants to figure out how it all works."

"I know how to work it," Gaetano jumped in.

"Do you think you still remember?" Eber asked as he looked at the clock. Gaetano just nodded.

"I'll tell you what. It's been slow this morning. I'll put up the sign that I'll be back in an hour, and we'll go over to the parsonage and see if the pastor is home. Maybe you can go out to see the house and show him how the thing works."

Gaetano sat back and nodded his head. "Sure," he said, "that will be good. That way I'll get to see the place again." Eber suggested Gaetano leave all his things at the shop. They walked out and went the eight-blocks to the church.

"Sometimes he has to look in on someone who's sick. He may not be there," Eber said trying to make sure Gaetano's hopes would not be dashed if the pastor was not home. The wondering was soon over when they found the pastor in his office. The door to the parsonage was slightly open so they walked in.

Once Pastor Goehner saw Gaetano was back, he did not even have to ask. He knew why they had come. "Gaetano, schön, dich wieder zu sehen," he said to him in German and then realized by the look on his face that he did not understand him. So, he repeated himself in Italian "Bello vederti di nuovo Gaetano."

Gaetano chuckled. He had to because this was the first time in two years, he heard German spoken by someone who was not trying to kill him. "Come stai Pastore?" he said with a smile.

After some discussion about Günter and his house, they decided the pastor would take Gaetano out to Günter's house at around four o'clock. He had to give some marriage counseling to a young couple who were going through some growing pains.

That was to be over by three thirty and he would then hitch up a team and come by Eber's to pick him up.

Gaetano and Eber left and headed back to the shop. "Have you eaten yet?" Gaetano asked with his hunger now completely taking over.

"Not yet," Eber said, glad he asked. If Gaetano had not come in when he did, he would have been closing for lunch anyway. He decided to take the extra hour off and have a late lunch with his old friend and employee. They stopped at a small place where they served food all day. Most restaurants in town stopped serving lunch by two o'clock and started up again at five o'clock for the dinner customers. But because this restaurant was set up mostly for light meals, they knew they could get something to eat mid-afternoon.

"I would imagine his house is all cleared out by now," Gaetano said wondering how things had developed since Günter's passing.

"Actually, that's one of the things we discussed a couple of days ago when I first talked with the pastor about the house," Eber added, "I'm surprised he didn't bring it up. He probably will when you go out there. His furniture is all there and most of his canned goods are still there as well. And they're still good. He didn't do any canning this year but there was quite a bit left from the year before. And the chickens are still there too. Karl goes three times a week to feed them and gather up whatever eggs he can find. Then brings what he can't use to town when he comes. He has over twenty chickens now. But the horses are gone. He sold them over a year ago when he realized his strength was leaving him. Too much to take care of you know. The chickens were not so much work. They'll probably stay for the next owners. It's best for them also if they don't get moved."

Gaetano nodded his head knowing full well how much work caring for those two horses had been. They got the food to go and went back to the barber shop and stayed together for the afternoon.

"After I get back," Gaetano said, "I will need to get a room at the hotel."

"You can stay in the room upstairs if you like," Eber replied, "It's a bit messy," but it would save you getting a room."

"Maybe, that could work," he responded. Gaetano could afford a room in the hotel and preferred a clean place. But an offer like that seemed to be the right thing.

Just as Pastor Goehner had promised, he came by to pick Gaetano up at Eber's just after four o'clock. They headed out right away. "How have you been Gaetano?" the pastor asked as they rode along.

"Just getting over a bad case of something," he replied.

"We lost ten people in the congregation this year from illness," the pastor added, "It is a miracle you survived it. It's a bad one this year."

"I'm just glad to be getting over it," Gaetano said, "I still have a bad cough at night, but they gave me some medicine for it."

"So, you saw a great deal of fighting?" Pastor Goehner asked.

"That's in the past now," Gaetano said as politely as he could.

"And that's where it belongs," Pastor Goehner said as he patted Gaetano's knee.

Chapter 41

The snow which had recently fallen did not have any effect on the horses or the carriage. It was too early in the year to put on the sleds. The few centimeters of snow did not slow them down in the least. Gaetano felt like he was going home. He recognized the various points in the road and the houses they passed. He could see Karl's house as they rode by but there was no sign of Karl. Understandably since it was getting rather cold now December was upon them. He was likely inside keeping warm.

The path up to Günter house had no tracks cut into it yet. It was obvious they were the first to come here since the fresh snowfall. The snow on the ground reminded Gaetano of that first night when he saw the barn from the road and decided to circle around in order to not leave any marks in the snow. As he remembered, he chuckled inside at the fact he had not realized it was actually Christmas Eve that night. 'How can someone not know that it's Christmas Eve' he thought? It was a time of confusion for him. But now he felt he was right on track.

There was enough daylight left for them to look at the boiler and still have time to get back to town, but not much. Gaetano figured they would have to spend just a brief time going over how the boiler worked so the pastor could understand its nuances. He knew exactly where to go and how to turn on the gas lights. It surprised him when he walked in and realized Günter had converted over to electricity and all he had to do was flip a switch and on came the lights.

They went in the basement and walked over to the back section where the boiler was. Gaetano looked at the burner section hoping did not use electricity also. "Do you want me to stoke up a fire?" he asked Pastor Goehner.

"Well," he started.

Gaetano interrupted him, pointed to the back of the property, and said, "Top of the hill!" Pastor Goehner looked at him most confused as to what that meant. "Old joke between me and Günter," Gaetano said with a grin.

The pastor nodded his head still not certain what Gaetano was talking about. "Yes, of course. Like I was saying, it's not going to be easy to keep this place in good condition for the winter. Karl checks in when he comes for the eggs. But it's not the same as someone living here."

"Maybe someone from the congregation can stay here for some time and care for the place," Gaetano suggested, "Or maybe someone different each week."

"Or maybe you," the pastor said which brought an instant silence to the room.

"Me?" Gaetano replied, "I just got here."

"That may be the hand of the Lord," Pastor Goehner said in his preacher's voice. "Just as the cold weather comes, so does the only other person who knows how this crazy thing works."

Gaetano stood for a moment and pondered the thought. He had not even considered staying in Gifbourg for more than a few days at best. Now he faced the prospect of spending the winter. And staying in Günter's house. But without Günter. The thought just astounded him. All the thoughts that can go through a man's mind when contemplating something so new and interesting led him to think about the possibilities.

Did he have enough money to buy food for the winter? He could always work at Eber's for extra money. It would only be for three months or so. He did not care for the idea of going home while he was still so ill and looking so tired. It was not the way he wanted his Mamma to see him after three years.

Then some of the more difficult questions came to mind. How would he get to and from town if he did work at Eber's or needed to get supplies? Maybe he could work something out with Karl to bring him in when he was going to town for his supplies. Or maybe someone had a pair of horses he could take care of and use to get into town. So many questions. The idea was all so new.

"I.........I............I don't know," he stammered, "it sounds inviting, very inviting. You don't have anyone else?"

"No," Pastor Goehner said, "no one else. I think this is the right thing. Do you?"

Gaetano pondered some more, "I.... I guess so. It would give me a chance to rest up before going home."

"To America?" Pastor Goehner said.

"Yes," Gaetano replied, "to America where my family is. My Nonna passed away a couple of years ago now. She was back in our hometown. So, all of my family is in America now."

"That settles it?" Pastor Goehner said, "you can stay. I'll have to have some firewood brought out from town. Since the church owns the property, we're responsible for providing the upkeep. So, we'll bring out some firewood. Günter didn't have time to arrange for it this autumn. There is about a month's worth in the shed which should be enough for now."

Gaetano suspected maybe the pastor had considered making this offer earlier in the day when he first found out he was back. It does not seem like something one thinks of at a moment's notice. He was touched the pastor would trust him to take care of the place.

"I left my things at Eber's," he said remembering he planned on staying in town that night. Once Eber told him about Günter, the idea was to take a train in a day or two to Marseille or Napoli.

"I think I can get by tonight. But I will have to get into town tomorrow to get them," he continued, "Actually, that's one thing I was wondering, how I would get back and forth to town now the horses are gone?"

"Have just the thing in mind," Pastor Goehner added, "one other thing Günter left the church. He brought it at the end of seventeen rather than continuing to hitch up the horses."

They went out back to the barn and Pastor Goehner opened the barn doors. Sitting there was an automobile. A real beauty of an automobile. "What is it?" Gaetano asked, "I've seen the trucks we used in the Army and some officers had automobiles which were pretty beat up, but this..............this is beautiful."

"It's a Martini," he said proudly, "they make them about two hundred kilometers from here. You should have seen Günter try to drive this thing the first time. He could engineer huge locomotives, but an automobile frightened him."

"Frightens me too," Gaetano added, "I've never learned how to run one of these."

"Drive one, they call it driving. Karl can teach you," Pastor Goehner added with a smile, "I plan to stop in on him on the way back to tell him you'll be watching the place. He can show you how. Maybe tomorrow he can take you into town in it. Günter has some petrol in the woodshed and there is a place near the train station where you can buy some also."

"Now that you mention it, I remember walking by that place this afternoon when I was going to Eber's. It looked new," Gaetano exclaimed.

There were suddenly a lot of new and exciting things happening to him. To be at Günter's and have the opportunity to stay. Possibly learning to drive an automobile for the first time and being in Gifbourg again was more than he could absorb. As each minute went by, Gaetano was more convinced staying was the right thing to do.

"Let's go back inside and see to that boiler," the pastor said, "it's getting pretty cold, and I've been worrying about freezing those pipes."

They went down to the basement, and it only took Gaetano a few minutes to start up a good fire. Quite the contrast to the night he had spent in the hunting cabin back in December of nineteen-fifteen.

"You should have enough to eat with all of Günter's canned goods," Pastor Goehner said as they were going back upstairs after the steam came up.

"I think I'll go back to the barn and see if I can find any eggs," Gaetano said, "I'm in the mood for some eggs. Real eggs not the yellow soup they called eggs in the Army."

Pastor Goehner chuckled, "I can only imagine. I was never in the Army. I can't see myself ever doing that."

"Four years ago, I would have said the same thing," Gaetano said with a deep sigh.

Before leaving, the pastor asked to say a prayer with Gaetano to bring happiness and rest to him and make his stay more joyful than he could hope for. They shook hands and gave each other an embrace. Gaetano walked him out and when Pastor Goehner left, he walked out to the barn to look for some eggs. He found several without even trying. It was getting dark and hard to see so he figured he had enough to fix a good meal and went back inside.

The kitchen was starting to warm up, so he decided to go upstairs and see how things were up there. It was obvious no one had been living there for some time. The house was in need of a good cleaning. He noticed that right away. Eber had mentioned the several people who would check in on Günter would spend some time with him and do some basic housework. But it was obvious with Günter's failing health, the place was neglected compared to the way he kept it that winter he spent with him.

The room where he had stayed was exactly the same. Even the same quilt was on the bed. This was indeed like coming home. He opened the drawer of the dresser and much of the clothing he used when he spent the winter were still there. The bathroom also needed a good cleaning. He knew he had his work cut out for him. If the church were to put the house up for sale in the spring, he knew it would be important that it be in the same shape which he was used to from his previous stay and not its current condition.

The faucet in the bathroom sink had not been turned on in several months and the water was discolored. Gaetano remembered the story about the Raccoon falling into the well and hoped something like that did not happen again. Like Günter told him to do, he turned on the faucet in the sink and the tub to let the water run through the system. Then he flushed the toilet to put fresh water in the tank. He repeated the effort several times to be certain.

He also ran downstairs to the kitchen to turn on the faucets there, both the hot and cold sides in all sinks. The water was not very hot at that point, so it was good to flush out the system including the water heater section of the boiler. To make certain the entire system would be flushed out, he went down to the boiler and opened the faucet at the sink with the large basin for washing clothes.

After about an hour, he tasted the water to see how fresh it was. 'That should do it,' he thought to himself. He checked his watch to see what time it was. Six thirty, it was definitely time to eat. As he went down to the basement to turn off the last faucet, he went into the pantry area where Günter had set up for all his canned goods.

There was quite a bit of his apple cider and apple sauce. He found some potatoes which were in decent shape, so he decided to fry some up with the eggs. The boiler was in full operation now and the clanging of the pipes was mostly over. The house was starting to get a homey feeling to it. It made for a much better environment for eating.

Taking his time with dinner, Gaetano did not get done with eating and cleaning up until almost nine o'clock. As nice as the eggs with potatoes and apple sauce were, he wished the meal had been Sauerbraten with red cabbage and Chnöpfli. And he was wishing he would have had the pleasure of Günter's company. Then afterwards maybe play a game of cribbage with coffee.

Gaetano went downstairs to stoke the fire just the way Günter had shown him so the heat would last the night. Then he went upstairs to the bathroom and decided to take a hot bath. There was enough hot water by now and he knew it would help him sleep. He had not taken a shower since he was at the infirmary the day before he left, so he was looking forward to getting clean before he went to sleep in the bed. A bath was much more appealing than a shower.

As the water was filling up the tub, he went to the linen closet and took out a fresh set of sheets. The bed only had the quilt he used to sleep with since no one had been sleeping in that room. Even Günter's bed was not made up because he had been sleeping downstairs and using the small half bathroom down there. The upstairs really had not seen much activity for almost a year, best he could figure.

He knew he had quite a bit of work to do the next day, so he soaked in the tub to warm himself up and loosen his lungs. The warmth and moisture helped his cough. He still coughed quite a bit. But it was better than past evenings when it would hit him just about bedtime. He got out of the tub and got ready for bed. He was happy he carried his cough medicine and aspirin with him in his coat pocket instead of keeping it in his bag. It was still necessary. He knew if he could get enough rest and take a hot bath each night, it would help him heal up in no time.

He pulled out a set of cotton pajamas from the dresser and put them on. Considering all the activities of the day and having slept on a train for the past two nights, hitting a soft pillow with sheets and a quilt was all it took. Gaetano was asleep in seconds. He did not budge until nine o'clock in the morning. Even the sun shining in on his face did not wake him. He tried repeatedly to open his eyes but would keep drifting back off. At eleven o'clock, he heard the door open from the back of the house, and it startled him.

"Gaetano?" he heard from downstairs. Best he could figure it was Karl. It had been quite some time since they had seen each other, and Gaetano was not sure if it was his voice he was hearing.

"Karl?" he responded as he hopped out of bed.

Karl was heading over to the stairs and as Gaetano got to the top. He could see Karl at the bottom. "Guten Morgen Gaetano," Karl said with grin.

"Guten Morgen Karl," he replied, "How have you been?"

"Oh, doing well and getting older too," he said in English with a thick Swiss accent, "Pastor Goehner stopped by last evening just before supper and told me you were back."

"Can you believe it?" Gaetano said looking back at his bedroom, "I just woke up."

"Pastor Goehner told me you've been ill," Karl said sounding a bit concerned, "Are you on the mend?"

"I must be," Gaetano continued, "Two weeks ago I couldn't get out of bed."

"A lot of people sick this year?" Karl exclaimed, "It's bad everywhere."

"So, the pastor stopped in to see you," Gaetano said changing the subject.

"Yes, yes," Karl answered, "I asked him to stay for the meal, but he said he needed to get back for a meeting at church............. So, he showed you the Martini?"

"That is some automobile!" Gaetano exclaimed as he started down the stairs, "Pastor Goehner said you know how to run it."

"Drive it," Karl said gently correcting him, "they call it driving and yes, I do know how and yes, I will teach you. But you have to get dressed first."

Gaetano looked down at his long pajamas and nodded his head realizing he had not thought to put on a pair of trousers before running to the stairs. "I'll be right back," he said, "Do you want some coffee?" he asked Karl.

"I've been up for hours," he replied, "So no thank you. But I'll make some up for you while you dress."

"Sounds good," he said as he turned to go back upstairs to his room. After throwing on his clothes, he made a stop in the bathroom and then headed down. The coffee was just starting to brew so he knew it would be a few minutes. Gaetano ran downstairs quickly to add to the fire since he had slept in for so long. It did not take long for the pipes to start to clang.

"Pastor Goehner said you'll need to go into town today to get your things?" Karl asked.

"Left everything at Eber's," he said, "didn't think I would be staying here last night."

"I've been checking in three or four times a week to make sure everything is all right," Karl continued, "and to get the eggs. Guess you'll be keeping most of them now."

"Not sure how many I'll need Karl," Gaetano said, "We'll make sure you have what you need also. There's a lot more chickens out there from the last time I was here."

"You'll be needing some milk I suppose," Karl said, "I can bring some by and trade you for eggs, just like I did with Günter."

Karl paused for a moment realizing Gaetano was still not used to the fact Günter had passed away. It was old news to the people of Gifbourg, but for Gaetano, this was still fresh. "Sorry you missed him," Karl said.

"So am I," Gaetano sighed, "I wanted to thank him for all he did for me."

"He would speak of you often you know," Karl said in a more somber tone, "He wondered how you were making out, whether or not you were even still alive. So many died in that war."

"I thought of writing to him, but," Gaetano hesitated, "I don't even write home to my Mamma. Only the one time, and then she only sent one back." He leaned on the side of the sink, "That's understandable though since the letter she sent was nearly lost. Who knows, maybe she did write more." Gaetano shook his head back and forth showing he held some regret that he never wrote letters. "I don't even know if they're all right. Who knows what I'll find when I go back."

"You'll be going back then?" Karl asked having had the question ready but had not asked it, "When do you plan to go?"

"Based on the conversation I had with Pastor Goehner last night," Gaetano said raising his eyebrow, "not until the spring. I guess I'm the new caretaker of the Haas estate."

Karl chuckled, "I guess so. That coffee smells too good not to have some. I think I changed my mind."

Gaetano looked into the pot and saw there was plenty, "Looks like you planned that all along Karl."

They sat and had some coffee, and Gaetano went downstairs to get a jar of applesauce. He dished some up for both of them and they continued to talk about Günter, Gifbourg, the war and what lay ahead for Gaetano in America. Shortly after twelve o'clock, they decided to go out to the barn and look into getting the Martini running. The afternoons were short now and if they wanted to get things done in town, they would have to move.

They agreed Karl would just drive and show Gaetano how to another day. They unhitched Karl's team and put them in the barn to get some hay and a bit of leftover oats that were still around for Günter's horses. Before leaving, Gaetano stoked up the fire in the boiler so the house would stay warm for the evening. He planned to get some food at the market and maybe even some meat for dinner. Günter had bought an electric icebox that kept food cool and had a small area where could freeze meat. So, he planned to get enough to freeze some along with what he could eat that night.

The errands took until after four o'clock. While in the meat market, Gaetano inquired of the butcher as to how to make Sauerbraten. He showed him a cookbook that was at the front of the store. It not only had Sauerbraten but also the recipe for Chnöpfli. The only problem was it was written in German. He figured Karl could help with the translation. Red cabbage was still available at the produce market so he decided he would try to make some Sauerbraten first chance. The butcher reminded him it sometimes takes several days to prepare with the marinating of the meat. So, he bought the vinegar, not certain if there was any at Günter's.......... Or from now on should he just call it home.

Last thing, they stopped at Eber's to get his bag, and the box of things Günter left him. "So how did you sleep in your old bed?" Eber asked.

"I slept for over twelve hours," Gaetano chuckled, "Karl woke me up when he came in."

"You looked tired yesterday when I first saw you," Eber said.

"Of course," Gaetano said, "I spent two days on a train and had just been released from the infirmary. I would say I had good reason to look tired." he grinned and chuckled knowing his friend cared.

"Once you get rested up a bit," Eber said, "remember, I could always use some help around here."

"You can count on it. I think it may be a few days though. That house needs some big cleaning. I thought you told me you and the others were taking care of the old man," he said jabbing his finger into Eber's side, "That place is filthy."

"Hey," Eber said with shake of his head, "It has been over three months you know. And besides, it bothered Günter when we did too much cleaning for him. He would say he should be able to do that. There was one time he started to cry a bit about it. He was troubled by aging. So, we would straighten up and clean the kitchen since we would fix a meal for him. He didn't mind us doing those things. But I'm not surprised the house needs work."

"I looked around and found enough cleaning supplies," Gaetano said, "but I picked up some other things I saw at the market which are supposed to be for house cleaning. Some new liquid that smells like lemons or something. Don't know how lemons will make it cleaner, but the lady at the market says it's the latest thing."

They headed back to Günter's house and unloaded the supplies he had bought. Karl left him off and hitched his horses after gathering some eggs for home. They said their goodbyes and Karl was off.

The added activity that day made Gaetano very tired, and his cough was coming back. He took some cough medicine right away before preparing a meal and put the things in the new icebox which needed to stay cool. He put the meat in the freezer in smaller portions so he could take out only what he would need per meal. They had some bratwurst at the market also. So, he got some for that night and froze the rest for having with well anticipated breakfasts.

It was too late to start doing housework that evening, so Gaetano fixed his meal and warmed up some tea to drink during the evening. He was finished earlier than the night before, so he decided to look for something to do before going to bed. He looked at the box Eber had given him and saw the cribbage board. 'Too bad there isn't someone to play with,' he thought.

There was a small room near the front of the house where Gaetano had rarely gone into while he was there before. It was Günter's study, and he kept all his books there. Gaetano went in and started to look through the books on the shelf. Most of them were in German but not all. Some were in Italian and several in English. One caught his eye, so he settled into the chair which had been his favorite when he was there before and began to read.

Gaetano jolted awake and looked around. He checked his watch and saw it was two o'clock in the morning. The house was getting chilly and that is likely what woke him. He went down to the basement to stoke up the fire and then went straight to bed. The book would have to wait until the next night.

Chapter 42

The first light came at around seven o'clock, but it was not enough to wake Gaetano from a sound sleep. At five o'clock he had woken up with a bad cough and went downstairs to get some water and take two aspirins. After another dose of the cough medicine, he went back up to bed. The aspirin kept him asleep through nine o'clock when he woke up and noticed the sun was shining in through the window.

He could have decided to stay right there for two more hours, but he had promised himself he would not put off getting the house in order. It was a bit chilly, and he did not really want to get out from under the quilt. But nearly four years in the Army had broken him from giving in to these types of temptations. The robe he used to wear when he stayed with Günter was still in his closet, so he put it on to go downstairs.

Coffee was high on the list of first things to do so he started up the gas on the stove and got the percolator going before going down to the furnace. The wood supply was rather low in the basement, but he had enough for the day and decided he would go to the shed and bring some in that afternoon. It would likely not warm up very much that day so he figured he would keep a close eye on the furnace. A quick breakfast would be in order and then the next thing was to tackle the house cleaning.

Karl stopped in briefly at around twelve o'clock, but Gaetano declined the driving lesson for the day. He wanted to get most of the house done on the first day, at least enough so it would look presentable. While Karl was there, he helped him to translate some of the cookbook. Just enough so he could get the Sauerbraten started in the marinade. Karl would give the Italian word for the main ingredients and explain the procedure as Gaetano took notes. Between his notes and what he could understand of his improving but still limited German, he felt comfortable enough to try it.

Karl left some milk behind, so he was able to do some baking. That evening he made muffins, just like Günter had shown him. He had hardly made a dent in the cleaning and felt a bit disappointed. Then he had to remind himself he had been sick and did not have his usual energy to get things done. There was always tomorrow.

Friday afternoon, Karl came by to show Gaetano how to drive the Martini. They spent about two hours with Gaetano stalling out the engine four or five times and grinding the gears while he was trying to understand what the clutch was for. By supper time he was an old pro at it. He could even start on a hill without stalling.

Before Karl left, Gaetano asked him if he and his wife Emily would join him for supper on Saturday. The Sauerbraten would be ready, and he did not want to eat that meal alone. Besides the recipe was portioned for four. Karl accepted and they agreed they would come over at five o'clock and Emily would bring a pie for after supper.

By noon on Saturday the house cleaning was starting to take shape and the bathrooms looked like new. They were just the way Gaetano remembered them when he first saw them back in nineteen-fifteen. It would make Günter happy if he could see his house coming back to its right form. With guests coming over that evening Gaetano was motivated to get more done. He still had to watch himself though, because if he became too tired, that awful cough of his would start up and it was the last thing he wanted with visitors.

Gaetano stopped working on the house at around two o'clock to make certain he had enough time to take a bath and put on some clean clothes for the evening. He was nervous because having guests and cooking for them was not something he had ever done before. 'What if the meal is terrible?' he thought. Not only was this his first effort at cooking for someone, other than the kitchen duty in the Army. But he was trying to cook something he had only eaten twice in his life and had not had a hand in cooking either time.

Karl and Emily came by right on time and Emily could tell Gaetano was in over his head. She gently offered to assist, and he was smart enough to accept. The oven needed a slight adjustment to make it warmer and the Chnöpfli was a bit overcooked. But not ruined. They sat down for the meal at six thirty and Gaetano could not believe he had pulled it off. The Sauerbraten was a bit different than what he had remembered but it was still quite tasty. The cabbage turned out well thanks to Emily's help.

It was not until after the meal was over that Gaetano took the time to think about how everything went. He sat back in his chair and grinned with satisfaction. "I'm going to have to do this more often," he said to his guests, "This is a lot of fun. I didn't think I knew how to cook, other than boiling potatoes."

They all laughed at the thought of a twenty-five-year-old young man fixing a meal for guests and not ruining everything. Gaetano put some water on the stove for tea and then they had Emily's pie. Karl and Emily told him earlier they needed to leave rather early and would not be spending the evening. They left just before eight o'clock and that was just fine with Gaetano because he was exhausted from the day's work and the nervousness of fixing the meal. He cleaned up the kitchen and sat for a short while reading the book he had started earlier in the week.

• • • •

THE NEXT MORNING WAS Sunday and Gaetano wanted to make it into town to attend church. He had not seen Pastor Goehner all week but that was all right since he had everything he needed. The only thing Gaetano wanted to talk to him about was the firewood supply. He had enough for a while, but he did not want to go more than a couple of more weeks without replenishing the supply.

Even if they had delivered the wood that week, Gaetano was far too tired and had not recovered enough to take on doing work like that outside. Just going out to the barn to gather eggs was enough to start him coughing. If he had tried to pile wood in the shed, his cough would have forced him to stop and go inside. So, it would be fine if the wood had not been dropped off yet.

First thing Sunday morning Gaetano got up and took a hot shower to loosen up his lungs. He shaved and put on a nice pair of trousers which he had worn back when he stayed while Günter was alive. It was almost as if time had stood still in Gifbourg. Things he had left behind were still there waiting for him as if it were always understood he would one day return. The only difference was, no Günter.

Gaetano went out to the barn to get the Martini started and let it run for the five minutes Karl had instructed him to do. If he tried to drive it in the chilly air without the engine being warmed up first, he could have stalled it and flooded the engine. It would have made it almost impossible to start up again for quite a while. The thought of being stranded on the road with an automobile would not run while people passed by on horse and buggy was also a motivation.

He bundled up and wrapped a scarf around his neck. The scarf used to be Günter's. He felt a bit awkward using it, but he figured Günter would have given it to him to keep warm anyway if he felt he needed it.

Sunday service started at ten thirty. Gaetano was able to get there just a bit early. He was not sure how long he should plan for getting there since he was used to going to town with two horses drawing a carriage. Using an automobile was much faster. There was a place on the street across from the church where he could leave the car. There were not very many cars in Gifbourg, and everyone knew this was Günter's car. Not everybody knew Gaetano would be driving it tough. It caused a bit of a stir at first.

During the service Pastor Goehner mentioned to the congregation that a young man who used to attend there three years earlier had returned from the war and was taking care of Günter's house and of course driving his car. He did not make too much of Gaetano's time at war because some of these people had relatives who had been in the war as well. They would have more than likely fought on the other side though. This was a subject Pastor Goehner knew better than to broach.

He openly thanked Gaetano for being willing to change his plans and stay long enough to care for the property which now belonged to the church. This, he told everyone, would ensure the house would be cared for and made ready to sell in the spring. After service, Gaetano stayed around so he could meet with the pastor. They discussed the wood supply briefly and Pastor Goehner assured him he would come out with two other men to stack the wood in the shed. He knew full well Gaetano was in no shape to take on that kind of work.

After he left, Gaetano was tempted to go to the hotel and order some soup but decided not to in order to save his money. He would still need enough to get back to New York in the spring. There was enough for now. But in order to have what he needed to live on during the winter he would probably have to start cutting hair again at Eber's. He planned to come into town by mid-week to see when he might be able to start at the shop.

All he could think of at that moment was getting back home. Fatigue was already setting in, and he had decided since it was Sunday, he would not do any housework and just rest.

He put the Martini in the barn and took a few minutes to gather some eggs. Once he got inside, he placed the eggs in the icebox and went downstairs to stoke up the fire. It would be enough to carry the heat through until late evening. Gaetano's watch said it was one o'clock. He was trying to decide if he was hungry or too tired to eat. The latter prevailed so he went upstairs and lay down on his bed with the just quilt covering him. Within two minutes he was sound asleep.

It was six o'clock before he opened his eyes. His room was dark, and he could not tell if it was the middle of the night. After a couple of minutes, he realized he had been asleep all afternoon, and it was evening and not nighttime. He managed to get up and sat on the side of the bed for several minutes.

Making his way down to the kitchen, he turned on a light so he could see where he was going. He was not really hungry, but he knew he should eat something. Breakfast that morning was the last he had eaten and skipped lunch in order to sleep. He looked in the ice box and saw there was just a little Sauerbraten left so he decided to try to warm that up. It was best to eat it soon so it would not spoil. He placed it in a pan and put it on a low fire, adding some water to keep it moist. After eating he did not feel like doing anything but sit and read. With his long sleep that afternoon, it did not seem likely he would be able to go back to sleep at his regular time. But by the time eleven o'clock came around, he was more than ready to go back to bed.

His cough had not started all evening, which he saw as a good sign. He thought maybe he should just sleep for two weeks and then he would be all better. Another hot bath before going to bed sounded appealing. He put the book down and went downstairs to set the furnace for the night.

A tub filled with hot water was just the thing for his lungs at that moment. The steamy heat rising up into his nostrils loosened him up and he started to cough but not an annoying cough. It was one which brought up a great deal of moisture from his lungs. This helped him since he had been struggling with not being able to cough up anything definitive for weeks. He took some cough medicine and aspirin and went to bed. Falling asleep was no problem. It only took a few minutes, and he was out.

Tuesday morning, he took the Martini into town to go to Eber's. He arrived at the barber shop at around eleven thirty.

"You look much better!" Eber said to him as he walked in.

"I've been doing nothing but sleeping," Gaetano said, "and cleaning. The place is starting to look the way it did when Günter took me in."

"I was worried about you," Eber continued, "If you didn't look better by now, I was going to have you see the doctor in town."

"Actually, I may go see him anyway," Gaetano said, "they told me when I left the infirmary to find a doctor when I got settled. I think I'll need some more cough medicine soon and I sure don't want to run out of that if I need it. Sometimes it's the only thing that helps me when the coughing starts."

"Well, I'll pay for it," Eber offered, "You probably don't have a lot of money to throw around. By the way, when do you want to start?"

Gaetano knew what that meant. "Anytime you need me," he said.

"How about starting this Friday?" Eber asked, "You can start off just like you left off working for me on Friday and Saturday. Or is that too much?"

"Not too much," Gaetano said with his head nodding showing his approval, "Friday it is."

Eber walked over to the cash register and reached underneath. He pulled out a piece of paper and began to draw a map of the town. "Go right over and see Doctor Hilgenbecker," Eber said, "tell him you work for me and to put it on my bill. I'm sure he knows about you from when you were here before. He'll remember you. You should recognize him because he came in for his haircut every two weeks by the clock. Doctors have to look the part as you can imagine. So, he keeps his hair and his beard very well trimmed. You go see him. He'll take good care of you." Eber handed the piece of paper to him, and he looked it over.

"I can take care of the bill," Gaetano said as he was studying the hand drawn map, "They gave me some combat pay, and I should be all right."

"Not a chance," Eber rebuked him, "you work for me, and I take care of my people. You just get better, understand?"

Gaetano grinned and chuckled as he nodded his head like a child how had just been corrected, "I will," he said.

The doctor's office was easy to find by the directions Eber gave him. He went into the office and asked the nurse if the doctor could see him.

"Doctor Hilgenbecker is at the hospital on the other side of town and won't be back until three o'clock," she told him.

"Would I be able to see him then?" Gaetano asked.

"He has two other patients to see when he gets in," she continued, "Could you come in at four o'clock?"

"Four o'clock?" he said looking at his pocket watch, "Sure, I'll be back at four o'clock, thank you." He gave her a polite nod and left.

'What to do for three hours,' he thought to himself. He did not want to spend any money shopping, and he did not have a great deal of energy for walking around. A short walk through the grocery store to pick up a couple of things and then back to Eber's to sip on some coffee would fill his time nicely. That was the plan. Besides, Eber would want to know if he made it to the doctor's office and what happened. He cranked up the engine on the Martini after a short walk around the park which was right across the street from Doctor Hilgenbecker's office. Then he headed off to the store and back to Eber's.

Three hours went by fast. He realized it was getting on four o'clock, so he said his goodbyes to Eber and went back to the doctor's office. Coming in a bit after four o'clock was not a problem since Doctor Hilgenbecker had been delayed himself. As it was, Gaetano did not get to see him until after five o'clock. He was concerned about finding his way back to the house in the dark. Horses could find their own way home, but an automobile had no mind of its own and Gaetano would have to be certain he did not take any wrong turns. His familiarity with Gifbourg was still fairly limited. Even when he was there years earlier, he did not venture out very much because it was winter.

Doctor Hilgenbecker listened to Gaetano's lungs with his stethoscope as he took several deep breaths. "You just came back from the war, did you?" he asked.

"The fighting stopped about a month ago," Gaetano answered him, "I spent the next two weeks in the infirmary."

"That doesn't surprise me," he continued, "with the sounds I hear in your lungs, you must have been really sick."

"That's what they told me," Gaetano said, "I was unaware of what was happening for about a week according to the nurse who took care of me. She was really nice, took my watch to her father to get it fixed for me, see?" He pulled his watch out and showed him.

"Very nice," he said, "Was she married?"

Gaetano chuckled, "I don't think so, why?"

"A good lady is hard to find," he said, "when you find one who is that nice to you, you find a way to keep her."

"I think she was just being a good nurse," Gaetano added, "besides, I had no interest in staying around there. I wanted to go home."

"Here to Gifbourg?" the doctor asked.

"America," Gaetano said with pride, "I'm actually from America now."

"So how did you end up here in Gifbourg?" he asked.

Gaetano looked up and thought for a moment. "Fate?" he said with a slight tearing up which only he could tell was happening.

"It must have been fate as well that you survived your illness," he said, "your lungs have been through a tough time. I can hear where it is healing but you still need to take it easy for a while. Try not to go out at night with the cold damp air and only for short periods during the day."

"So, I guess it's a good thing that I came to see you," Gaetano said, "I was starting to feel better, but I still don't have the strength I used to have. That should come back, right?"

"At your age, of course," he said, "but you may always have some weakness in your lungs. You don't smoke do you?"

"Well, some in the Army if they were passing them around," he said, "but I never really cared for it and definitely not before I went into the Army."

"No more," Doctor Hilgenbecker said sternly, "smoking with your lungs will stop them from healing. No smoking and you'll probably be as good as new in a few months. Do you still have fever at night?"

"Sometimes," he answered, "but not always. The aspirin helps. I start to sweat after about twenty minutes."

"That's fever," he said, "Keep taking the aspirin and I'll give you a prescription you'll need to get filled before you run out of your cough medicine."

"Is it for the same cough medicine?" Gaetano asked, realizing Doctor Hilgenbecker was really trying to help him much more than the doctors at the infirmary.

"What I'm prescribing is much stronger, and it will help you cough up what you can't cough up now," he continued, "that's the only way you'll shake this."

Gaetano took the prescription and put his shirt back on as the doctor left to get something. When he came back in the room, he gave Gaetano a bottle. "This is a small sample of the cough medicine I prescribed. You can still use what you have during the day, but I want you to take this at bedtime."

Gaetano opened the bottle and sniffed it. It seemed much stronger, "How does it taste?" he asked.

"Don't think about how it tastes," the doctor said, "Just tell yourself it will make you better."

"Tastes that bad huh?" Gaetano chuckled.

"Yes," he replied, "It tastes that bad. And don't drink any water after. It has to coat your throat."

Gaetano rolled his eyes, "If you say so."

"I say so. Go home and get well," he said patting him on the shoulder, "You're staying out at Günter's house I hear. You're the young man the pastor mentioned on Sunday?"

"That's me," Gaetano said with a smile.

"Günter was a good man," Doctor Hilgenbecker said with a sigh, "I took care of him in his last days. He was a fighter. Most men don't last as long as he did with his condition. Sad to see him go."

Gaetano nodded his head in agreement and then he left to go home. He was able to find his way without any problem. Horses may be able to find their way home in the dark, but automobiles have lights on the front to show you where you are going. Gaetano drove slowly so as not to miss any turns and pulled into the barn just after seven o'clock.

He picked up some eggs in the barn using the lights from the car to see where he was going and then headed into the house. The furnace was not too hot at that point and the house felt it. The first thing was to go down and stoke up the fire. Then he went back up to fix himself something to eat.

He had some ham in the icebox which he bought the day Karl took him to town, so he diced it up. The pipes were clanging a bit, so he ran downstairs to make a couple of adjustments to the system. He grabbed a potato while he was down there so he could have that also. With the potato diced and the ham diced, he fried them for a while and then broke three eggs to scramble with them and stirred it all up. It was breakfast for dinner, and it hit the spot for him. There was a muffin left over from Saturday, and he ate it with some tea as he relaxed with his book late into the evening.

The decision was made after the visit to the doctor that he needed the extra rest. He would not get up early unless it was absolutely necessary. The housework was coming along nicely and after all, he had all winter to fix up the place.

He took two aspirins and some of the new cough medicine about fifteen minutes before going upstairs. A hot bath and a long night's sleep were just what he needed. He was going to enjoy every minute.

The cough medicine Doctor Hilgenbecker gave him started to work while he was in the tub. The coughing kicked up, but it was controllable. He was coughing up fluid just as the doctor said he would so he figured it would be best to get out and deal with that standing up. It took about twenty-five minutes for the cough to stop, but it was a productive cough. That was the term the doctor used, productive.

Once the cough settled down, he brushed his teeth and went to bed. Just as with most nights since he came to stay at Günter's, he fell sound asleep and did not budge until morning. With his lungs more opened, he slept much better and felt more rested when he got up. It was Wednesday and he decided to take it easy and rest since he had been out and about most of the day before. If he felt up to it in the afternoon, he would try to do some light housework. But rest was more important to him at this point.

Later that morning Karl came by to trade some milk for eggs. He offered to stay for a while and play some cribbage with Gaetano. He took him up on it and they sat and drank coffee while playing several hands. It was not quite as much fun as the times he played with Günter. On those occasions it was more about the conversations than the cards. How he missed those times.

Chapter 43

The next couple of weeks went by like a vacation retreat. Gaetano slept in every morning and took a nap each afternoon when he did not work at Eber's. They agreed two days a week was enough for the time being while Gaetano was getting his strength back. Eber would even let him go home early on Saturday if things slowed down after two o'clock. The money was not the real motivation for Gaetano. To be working again was. It was also about keeping connected with people and feeling a part of something.

That next Tuesday evening just before supper, around four o'clock, Gaetano walked out to the barn. He stood in the barn remembering it had been the same night three years earlier when he was just a scared kid trying to find a place to stay warm and sleep the night. On that night, Christmas Eve nineteen-fifteen, he met a kind old man who took him in and showed him something which is likely one of the most important things a person needs to know about themselves. How you see yourself is more important than how others see you.

He stood in the same spot he stood that night and tried to imagine the scene when Günter came in through the barn door. Gaetano choked up a bit thinking about that time. He thought long and hard about what that moment meant to him. He stood there for quite a while contemplating how life would have been vastly different if he had not come into this very barn on that very night. "Thank you, Günter," he said out loud. After standing there for a few minutes more, he shook off the emotions and went back inside to eat his Christmas Eve dinner.

It was not going to be Sauerbraten this time, but instead it was going to be a Santorini tradition, Lasagna. The grocery store had the necessary ingredients, for the most part. He was able to adjust for the rest. He decided to make it for his special Christmas Eve meal because he knew a bit more about how it was made, compared to Sauerbraten. Besides, it would mean leftovers for the few days. That would work since there was now an electric icebox to keep it in. 'Leftover lasagna is always better' he thought to himself.

There was no shortage of invitations extended to him for Christmas dinner. Eber invited him to join his family. Next was Karl and Emily, and the Sunday before Christmas Pastor Goehner invited him. He felt he should accept the first invitation. That was the proper thing to do. The invitation from Eber was the one to prevail. The others asked him to come on the following weekend.

His calendar was booked solid for that week. Eber's on Wednesday evening Christmas day, Friday at Pastor Goehner's parsonage with his wife and children and then Sunday at Karl and Emily's. Gaetano could easily get used to this.

Eber and Pastor Goehner both lived in town. Karl and Emily lived just down the road about a half kilometer west. With the Martini to get him where he needed to go, it was easy to get back and forth. No horses to feed or unhitch. Just crank up the engine and off he would go. He did, however, obey the doctor and left early to limit the time he would be out in the damp air at night.

The memories of the war were gradually losing out to the new life he was beginning to embrace. But deep down, he knew this too was temporary. The house was to go up for sale in the spring and then he would have to establish himself. Günter's house was available now, but it would not be for long. This was his chance to recover and get his life back. From then he would have to decide what he wanted for his own future. Should he go back home to America or find a way to settle in and continue the life he was finding in Gifbourg?

• • • •

THE WEEKS WHICH FOLLOWED found Gaetano slowly regaining his strength. He would go for walks around town after church each Sunday and he increased the chores he could do outside. By late January he would spend an hour or two each day in the barn cleaning up and caring for the chickens. He was glad not to have to take care of the two horses anymore like he did back in fifteen. But he did miss having them around because they had taken a liking to him.

The house was clean and in order now. All he had to do was the standard cleaning each week. In early February he started to work three or four days a week at Eber's barber shop depending on how busy they were. The barber tools they had given him back when he first entered the Army were still the tools he used each day. His hands were used to their feel, and he did not have to think about what he was doing. It just came, naturally.

This winter was considered mild though Gifbourg did see some major snowstorms. It was much lighter than the other winter Gaetano had spent there in nineteen-fifteen to sixteen. That winter had almost set some snowfall records for the region. It was one of the reasons he was not able to return to his unit until spring that year. The extra time helped him to make the right decision.

The light snowfalls helped him to get back and forth with the Martini. If there was a heavy snowstorm, he pretty much was housebound. There was one snowstorm in particular on February tenth which was very heavy. Almost a meter of snow fell in two days. Fortunately, it started on a Monday. He was stuck in the house until late Thursday when Karl came by and showed him how to put chains on the tires of the automobile.

Karl had picked up a set while in town that day knowing the Martini should have some anyway. Pastor Goehner and Karl had discussed it the week before and decided it would also be a good selling point for the car if it came with snow chains. Since the Martini belonged to the church and would be sold around the same time as the house Pastor Goehner decided to have Karl buy them.

One advantage about the horses though, was they could pull the sled through a significant amount of snow. With the automobile, Gaetano had to put the chains on the tires to get any traction. This was a very new concept for the people of Gifbourg. The sound of Gaetano coming down the street with the jingling of chains wrapped around his wheels caused everybody to turn and look as he drove by. He even received some dirty looks from people who would say the chains caused damage to the roads and scared their horses since they were not used to the noise. There was not much he could do about their discontent.

Evenings in late February were starting to get repetitive and Gaetano found himself looking for things to keep him busy. He had more energy to burn than he had had in many months and was at a loss as to how to expel it all. During the daytime he would spend more time in the barn rearranging things and cleaning the inside of the Martini. He polished the steering wheel almost daily. One Monday afternoon he was pulling out some old tools from behind the workbench and he found the pair of snowshoes Günter used to use to walk around the property.

That Wednesday morning, February twenty-sixth he bundled up and decided to venture up to see the well house. He had been up there only once with Günter but knew exactly where to go. The snow was packed down enough and with the snowshoes, he figured he should be able to make it up and back by lunchtime. He broke out his canteen and filled it with hot coffee. Then he wrapped it up in a towel to keep the coffee warm and put it in his pack. He also brought along some dried beef just in case he could not be back until afternoon.

The uphill walk was slow and tedious. He followed the opening in the tree line for over an hour. It was uphill all the way. The view from the hillside of the house was quite spectacular. The snow on the roof of the house and the barn with the glimmer of the sun through the clear winter sky was one of the most peaceful scenes he had ever beheld. If only this image could be with him forever.

The well house was covered with about a meter of snow, and he could barely see it. He knew it was there though. And he knew he had made it all the way up there to see it. His strength was finally back. "Well," he said to himself as he stood there and then started to laugh. "Well............ top of the hill............... right here at the top of the hill.............It's still here Günter," he shouted as loudly as he could.

At that moment he knew what he was going to do. His time there was over. Günter was gone and all he could think about was going home to his family in America. It had been long enough. The trains were still not running, but it was time to start the process of finding his way home.

That Saturday was the first of March. He worked at Eber's in the morning but told Eber he was going to take a walk over to the train station. Eber knew what that meant but did not say anything about it. "See if they have the paper," he said to Gaetano as he left. The train station would get papers from several regions, but it was rare that any trains would make it through at this time of year. Due to the light snowfall that year, some freight trains would try to get through, and he thought he might get lucky and get his favorite newspaper from Rome.

The train station also had ticket and schedule information about the ocean liners for people who would want to travel.

It was pretty much the only travel information center in town. There were no travel agents to help people plan trips. Most people did not go far especially for pleasure. He took some extra time just after lunch to walk over and see what he could find out. The attendant that day was an old friend of Günter's named Hansli. He did not have much to do since the passenger trains were still not running. Being he had been a good friend of Günter's, he wanted to help Gaetano anyway he could.

"So, you're leaving us?" Hansli asked trying to make small talk.

"Not right away," Gaetano replied, "I figured it was time to start looking into it though. I'll need to know what's available in the spring headed to New York."

"New York huh?" he said with bit of a teasing in his voice, "Don't want to settle down here in Gifbourg?"

"I thought about it," Gaetano said, "I really thought about it. I have a job here, a place to stay for at least a while longer."

"Nice house that Günter built, isn't it?" Hansli said.

"I sure do wish I could buy the place," Gaetano added, "But not on a part time barber's wage. Maybe if I owned my own place......Hmmm................ I can't see myself ever owning my own barber shop though," he said shaking his head.

"Have some faith," Hansli said patting him on the shoulder, "Didn't Günter teach you that?"

"He taught me a lot," Gaetano said with a smile, "But I've been thinking everyday now about going home. I miss my Mamma and Papà. I don't even know how they're doing."

"And why don't you write?" he said with an affectionate rebuke.

Gaetano shook his head knowing full well he had been neglectful in that regard. "Funny you should mention it," he said, "Pastor Goehner was by the house just yesterday and we talked about it. He says it's my way of dealing with being away from them. He said if I write to them, I'll have to admit I'm not there and, he also says it is why I have not written. Guess that means I really want to go home."

"Well then, home is where you will be if I can help," Hansli said trying to show his reassurance to what Pastor Goehner had told him.

He took quite a bit of time with Gaetano looking at the schedules. Most were tentative at that point since they relied on the weather. There was one which caught his eye. The Duca Degli Abruzzi was scheduled to set out on April tenth from Genoa. "It leaves late in the afternoon and makes stops at Napoli and Messina and then off to New York."

"Napoli?" Gaetano said with some surprise, "I usually go through Napoli. That's where my Nonna brought me when I went to be with my Mamma and Papà and that's where I was headed when the Army got their hands on me. They took me right off the ship."

Hansli did not want to continue the conversation about the Army. He knew enough men who had been to war and knew it was a subject that was to come and go quickly. "I'll send a telegram to the Navigazione Generale Italiana offices in Genoa and find out the exact schedule. Do you want me to book it if it's open?"

"No, I'll come back next week and then we'll decide," Gaetano added, "I've had some thoughts about heading west on the train and taking a liner from France. But it might cost too much."

"That it would," Hansli said, "everything in France is expensive these days. They have to pay for rebuilding after the war somehow."

Gaetano went back to Eber's and spent a couple more hours cutting some customers' hair. It was slow but enough men came in to make it worthwhile. Eber did not ask him how he made out. He figured Gaetano would tell him at the right time. There was no paper though. The trains had not been through from the south for a while.

The next Wednesday Gaetano made a special trip into town to go back to the train station. He knew Hansli would be working that day. Hanlsi's work schedule was uncertain at that time of year, but he had told Gaetano he would be there on Wednesday.

"Did you hear anything?" Gaetano asked him regarding the telegram to Navigazione Generale Italiana.

"It came in yesterday while I was not here," Hansli answered, "Christoph was working yesterday. He took the message."

"What'd they say?" Gaetano continued.

"The only openings they have are third class," he continued, "This is a strange ocean liner. It only has eighty first class cabins and sixteen second class. Sixteen? Why bother? Over seventeen hundred can go third class though. Guess they know who wants to go to America. Poor people getting away from the aftermath of the war."

Gaetano looked over the telegram. It had the rates for third class. It was quite a bit more than he thought it might be. He had never paid for a ticket before since the only other times he took a ship were when his Nonna paid for him to get on the Saint Paul. For the trip back he had worked his way across on the Hallwick. Paying for his ticket this time brought him to the realization that he most certainly was now a man and not a boy. Even at twenty-five, one sometimes still feels like a child. He had enough money, and it helped him to feel grown up as well. Still though, the thought of somehow finding where the Hallwick might be was very tempting. But even Hansli did not know where to start for that information.

"So, should I wire them the money?" Hansli asked.

"Do I have to secure the date now?" Gaetano answered with another question.

"I'm sure," Hansli replied, "That's the only way they can hold the ticket."

Gaetano had figured he may be buying the ticket that day. So, he brought his money with him. "All right then, I guess so," he said as he took out his bill fold, "Easy come, easy go."

"Easy come?" Hansli chuckled, "I know how you made that money, and it wasn't cutting hair." Hansli was aware of his Army pay, which had not come easy.

• • • •

THE SECOND SUNDAY IN March was especially cold in the morning. Gaetano had a hard time getting the Martini started. He poured a little gasoline directly into the carburetor to get it to turn over. Once he got it going, he let it run for ten minutes before heading out to church.

Pastor Goehner saw him come in and asked him to stay after service. Once it was over, he sat in the front row and waited while the pastor talked with an elderly couple for a few minutes. "Thank you for staying late," Pastor Goehner said as he walked up to the front. He sat down next to Gaetano, and they shook hands. "We started to advertise the property like we discussed last month."

"How is that going so far?" Gaetano asked with mixed emotions. He knew it was eventually going to happen. Part of him though had hoped the day would never come.

"We've had some interest," Pastor Goehner said, "One family in Gifbourg was interested. But they don't seem to be able to afford a property that size and then there was a telegram from a couple from Schaffhausen. They're looking to retire. He's a banker and he grew up not far from here. They are hoping to move back and should be able to afford the place."

"I would think so," Gaetano chuckled.

"They said they were coming in two weeks," he continued, "They will be here on Friday of that week. I figured you would be working that day so I would take them out to see the place."

"That sounds like it would be best if I wasn't there," Gaetano said, "I'll make sure everything is made up and looking its best."

"I had one other idea," he said sounding a bit hesitant to ask. Gaetano was not sure what he was going to say, but it sounded ominous. "Would it be all right if I brought them out to see the property in the Martini? I would like to see if we could include it in the overall sale of the property."

Gaetano looked at the pastor with a grin not sure how to state the obvious. "It's not my automobile," he said with a slight giggle, "It's yours."

They both started to laugh. Pastor Goehner nodded his head realizing Gaetano's logic was inescapable. "That's true," he chuckled, "but I thought I'd ask."

"Of course," he said, "I'll come by in the morning that day and you can bring me to Eber's. Then if they don't buy it on the spot, you can pick me up in the afternoon." Gaetano was enjoying the little teasing he was able to get away with. Pastor Goehner had a good sense of humor and liked it when someone got him with a good line.

"You said something about having your tickets already?" Pastor Goehner asked.

"I sent the money to the liner company," Gaetano answered, "Hansli helped me." The tickets will come by train in plenty of time. Some of the trains are starting to run now. Eber is even getting his paper again."

"We are going to miss you," Pastor Goehner said, "Even more than the last time. Once you get back to America, I would image that you won't be back for quite a while...............if ever."

Three months earlier Gaetano would have reacted emotionally at this. But he knew it was the right time to go home. "Maybe someday," he said, "What happens if they don't buy the property?

"There will be someone else," Pastor Goehner said, "It's a beautiful place. Someone will buy it."

"I leave on the seventh in the morning to make it to Genoa on time for the ship's departure," Gaetano added.

"That's only three weeks away," Pastor Goehner said with disbelief, "It's going to come fast."

"You may still need to heat the place," Gaetano said, "Are you sure you're comfortable working the contraption, as you called it."

"I'm an old pro by now," the pastor chuckled, "thanks to you. You taught me well............Top of the hill," he said remembering the joke. "Besides, the weather will start to warm up enough, so the pipes won't freeze. Even if the house is cold, just so long as the pipes don't freeze, we'll be all right."

Gaetano went for his usual Sunday afternoon walk around town and decided to stop at the hotel for some of their famous soup. He had avoided doing that too often in order to save his money. But now, the ticket was paid for, and he had enough for the train fare. There would even be a bit left over for when he got home.

He began to wonder if Rocco would still have a job for him when he got there. Maybe his Papà would want him to work on the docks. 'I could always cut hair,' he thought to himself as he was walking out of the hotel restaurant. Up until now, he had made a conscious effort not to think about home. But now it felt right. It helped him to plan.

• • • •

FRIDAY APRIL FOURTH was Gaetano's last day to work at the barber shop. Eber had made no secret of the fact he wanted to put together a little going away party for him at the shop that evening. So, Gaetano stayed late. Pastor Goehner came with his wife. Karl and Emily came and several of the regular customers as well as some of the people he had come to know at church. Everybody brought a dish to share, and Emily had made another pie.

Once they had something to eat, Eber took the stool he used to help young children to get onto the chair and stood on it. "Hello everyone," he called out to the guests. They all turned to look, and the room became comfortably quiet. "We will all miss you Gaetano," he said as he put his hand on his shoulder, "Pastor Goehner, would you like to say something and maybe lead in a prayer for safe travel?"

Pastor Goehner raised his head and nodded in agreement. "Of course, yes," he replied and came up to where Gaetano and Eber were standing. He put his hand on Gaetano's shoulder and said, "Lord please help Gaetano to find his way home safely and find his way in life going forward. Help him to get resettled in America and to enjoy being back with his family again. We're all going to miss him. But we will keep him in our prayers knowing that You are watching over him. Amen."

Eber reached under the counter and pulled out a box. "We all decided to pitch in together for this. This is from all of us," he said.

Gaetano had been in this setting before, but it still touched him that friends could be so gracious. He took the box and looked around. "Thank you................ thank you everyone. You really didn't..............."

"Quit talking and open it," Karl yelled from the other side of the room. They all laughed at how he cut Gaetano off to get him to stop.

Gaetano nodded his head realizing he was outnumbered. He pulled the ribbon off and slid the paper from the box. The box was wooden with a lid. There was a clasp in the front and his initials were on it. He opened the lid and just stared for a minute then looked up at everyone.

"I don't believe this," he said with a quiver in his voice.

"They aren't the best out there, but good for every day," Eber said.

Gaetano reached into the box and pulled out a new pair of cutting sheers. Along with them in the box was a pair of thinning sheers, two combs, a brush and a razor, a complete set. "They are the best, the best I've ever touched," he said with a nervous giggle. Everyone was looking at him as he took each item out of the box and showed them around. He walked around and thanked each and every person there with an embrace.

Some of the people needed to leave right away after the gift but about six of them stayed around for about another hour. Eber was in no hurry to go home so they just sat around and asked Gaetano about America.

About an hour later Pastor Goehner walked up to Gaetano to tell him he needed to go as well. "We'll see you Sunday, right?" he said while patting him on the shoulder.

"Of course," he replied, "I don't have all that much to pack. I can finish when I get home after service. Home............. that's funny. It's not really home, is it?"

"It was for the time you needed it," Pastor Goehner said.

"So, did you hear from the couple from Schaffhausen?" Gaetano asked.

"They'll be here at the end of next week to sign the papers," he answered and then it's theirs.

"Did they take the Martini too?" Gaetano asked with a slight tilt to his head hoping for a positive response.

"No. They decided since they never owned an automobile," he replied, "they didn't want to learn how to drive it at this age."

"So?" Gaetano said leaning forward.

"No, I'll find a buyer for it," the pastor said knowing what Gaetano wanted to see happen. He wanted Pastor Goehner to keep the Martini. "It wouldn't be right to have such an automobile as the pastor while some people in the congregation are in need."

"Speaking of the Martini," Gaetano said looking at his pocket watch, "I need to get her home."

"Her?" Eber interjected, "you called it her."

"Hey," Gaetano responded, "she gets me where I need to go."

"Her?" Eber repeated.

"Yes.......... her," he repeated then they both started to laugh. "I need to go. There are quite a few things I'll have to do around the house tomorrow. I have to wash my clothes for the trip and pack up some things to take."

"We'll see you Sunday," Eber said as Gaetano was grabbing his coat.

"Don't forget," Karl said, "I'll drive you in on Monday to get the train. Eight o'clock, right? You've got your tickets?"

"Yes, they came in on Monday. Eight o'clock it is," Gaetano said, "That'll give us enough time for some coffee before we go."

"We could get coffee in town if you like," Karl said, "That way you won't have to clean up after."

Gaetano nodded, "Sounds good. Let's do that instead."

Everybody gave farewell embraces, and Eber started to close up the shop. Gaetano went out to the Martini and cranked it up. The engine was a bit cold because Gaetano had worked all day and the going-away party went later than expected. He let the engine warm up for five minutes and then headed out to the house.

• • • •

THE NEXT DAY HE DECIDED to sleep in since it would be his only chance to get some rest until he got back home to America. The likelihood he would be able to rest on the ocean liner was slim at best. The seas might be rough, and it was probably going to be very crowded. He remembered the trip to America ten years earlier when he was in a cabin with five other men. Space was very tight, and he did not sleep well for most of the voyage.

He spent the day Saturday washing his clothes and figuring out the best way to pack his bags. There were some things he would make certain not to leave behind. The new hair cutting set he just received for a going away present and his original set of tools as well. His canteen, which he had with him the entire time he was in the Army, was a must. The mess kit was too big, so he decided to leave it behind. The canteen could hold the water he needed to drink on the train and even on the boat.

He had some clothes that fit him which had belonged to Günter. Pastor Goehner told him to take whatever clothing he thought he could use. The rest were going to be packed up and sent to charity. He wrapped the new haircutting tools in some of the clothing to keep the box safe.

Then he took a couple of towels to pack things. He wrapped the æbleskiver pan in one towel and then of course the most important keepsake of all, the cribbage board. He knew he would need more than his pack to carry things in. Pastor Goehner also told him to take one of the suitcases that had belonged to Günter. It was not a large one, but he needed to have it in order to pack everything he decided to take.

He had been putting things to the side he thought he might want to keep for about the past month. Most of it he was not able to fit so he selected a few things and left the rest. His bag was not very large, and neither was the suitcase. He remembered what his Papà had taught him about traveling light so he tried to keep it simple. He took only what he could actually carry by himself.

Once he had packed up everything he could, he had kept out some things he would need on Sunday. His dress outfit for church and the clothes he would travel in were all he needed. The dress clothes could go in last thing when he got back on Sunday.

He was finished packing by four o'clock and looked through the icebox to see what he could fix for supper. There was a small ham steak left so he took it out to dice it up with some potatoes and went out to the barn to gather eggs. Karl would have to get them from now on. Or at least until the retiring couple from Schaffhausen moved in. They would need to use the barn for horses again like when Günter was alive. Gaetano had cleaned out the barn and the stalls were more than ready for new horses to move in.

He fixed his ham and eggs supper with fried potatoes along with some tea. The book he had started to read when he first came back was long since finished. Gaetano had read four books and had just started a fifth. Pastor Goehner told him to take whatever books he wanted as well. The one he was reading was the only one he decided to take with him so he could finish it on the ship. Books were heavy and easy to come by in America.

Gaetano had a library card when he was in his late teens and used it often. So, he figured he could always get something to read. Even if he could not afford to buy the books.

It was after nine o'clock when he stopped reading so he could get to bed. He had to get up for church in the morning. Several of the people he had come to know there could not make it to the going away party, so he wanted to see them before he left on Monday. He stayed around the church for over an hour talking to friends. When it became obvious Pastor Goehner needed to close the church for the afternoon, they all said their good-byes and headed home.

Chapter 44

The alarm clock rang in Gaetano's room at five thirty on Monday morning. He wanted to shower and shave before leaving. The bathroom was spotless from his last steps of cleaning, so he tried not to leave any evidence he had used it. After he was done cleaning up, he put the towels he used downstairs near the basin along with the linens from the bed. Pastor Goehner had told him they were going to come through and take everything out which needed to go before the new owners came.

Then he went back upstairs to straighten up his room. As he spread the quilt over the bed, he thought how much he wanted to have this quilt for all time. His pack was full and so was the suitcase he was taking from Günter's things. He tried folding it several ways to minimize its size. But it was far too big and heavy for him to carry. 'I'll just have to remember it,' he thought to himself, 'just like the rest of Günter's place.'

His bags were all sitting at the back door by seven thirty. Gaetano took one more walk around the entire house to have a last look. It surprised him he was not saddened by leaving. This trip had served its purpose and staying any longer would simply be the wrong thing for him. Maybe if Günter was still there, he might feel sad about leaving. But where he was going was where he belonged. There was no doubt now.

Karl came up the drive while Gaetano was looking at Günter's old room. He could hear him driving up. Karl had taken the Martini with him on Sunday afternoon once Gaetano returned from visiting his friends after church. It was definitely noisier than the horse drawn carriage he was used to hearing when Karl came by.

Gaetano went right downstairs when he saw him coming. As Karl came around the back, Gaetano was already outside with one of his bags. "You look like you're in a hurry," Karl said rolling down the window on the driver's side, "Got someplace to go?"

"Just going into town for some shopping," Gaetano joked.

"Need any help?" Karl asked.

"No thank you," he answered, "Trying to travel light."

"Tell that to my wife," Karl chuckled.

They both went inside to do a walk through just to make certain Gaetano did not forget anything. If he left something behind it would stay. There was no sending it to him in America. This was the first time since Karl had shown him how to drive the Martini that Gaetano sat in the passenger seat. "I'm sure gonna miss her," he said looking out the window.

"Miss her?" Karl said with a shock to his voice, "Did you have a lady friend here? I didn't know that. Someone from the church? Why would you leave if you have a lady friend?"

Gaetano looked over at Karl with a grin. "The Martini," he said, "I'm going to miss the Martini."

"Oh, that's right," Karl said, "you call the Martini her. I remember now from Friday night................ I guess she is a good old girl, isn't she?" Gaetano gave him another smile because he could tell he understood.

They did not talk much going into town. Neither one of them wanted to say anything about this being a final goodbye. The hotel across from the train station was open for breakfast so they went there for coffee and a pastry. The train was scheduled to leave at eleven thirty, so they had plenty of time. It was already in the station and was on a two-hour meal break. Gaetano decided he would get on the train by ten o'clock and let Karl head back home. He would be keeping the Martini at his house until the church could find a buyer. Karl joked about wishing he could afford it. But he knew he could not.

"I guess this is it," Karl said, "it's been an honor to know you, young man. You have a good life and a lot of children."

"I will," Gaetano said, "the good life part, the children talk scares me a bit."

"Well, enjoy your trip," Karl added as he shook Gaetano's hand for the last time.

"Thank you for bringing me down," he said referring to the ride to the train station. Karl left and drove off in the Martini. Gaetano watched until he was out of sight around a building two blocks away.

Gaetano took a seat in the third car. He put his bags up overhead and sat by the window. The conductor told him there were only four other passengers riding in the car, so he had his pick. Knowing he would be sitting for quite a while, he walked over to the door of the car and stood at the top of the stairs to take in the brisk spring air.

He was standing there for about fifteen minutes when he heard someone calling him, "Gaetano!" the voice said.

"Eber?" he called back. Eber was coming across the platform. "I had a feeling I'd see you."

"I couldn't let you go without saying one more good-bye," Eber said as Gaetano hopped off the train. They stood and talked for ten minutes or so about Günter's house and how it would be someone else's by the end of the week. They also talked about how long it would take Gaetano to get to New York.

"Aren't you supposed to be open?" Gaetano asked.

"I put a sign out," Eber said, "gone to say good-bye to a friend."

Gaetano was moved by his gesture and nodded his head along with a slight laugh. "You have been a good friend. I'll miss you. I'll miss everyone here," he sighed.

Eber nodded his head and did not say anything more. He was choking up at the thought of not seeing young Gaetano again. If he were just moving back to Italy, there might be a chance they could see each other again. But America was just too far, and they both knew it.

"All right then, you take good care of your Mamma," Eber said as he gave Gaetano one last embrace. He turned and walked back to the way he had come headed to his shop. Gaetano stepped back on the train and went to his seat.

The train left right on time and as the conductor came by to get Gaetano's ticket, Gaetano asked him the usual question, "When will we be in Genoa?"

"Mid-afternoon tomorrow," he answered.

Gaetano knew it would be a long trip. Not as long as coming from Bologna when he left the camp though, partly because much of this trip would be downhill. He settled in and thought to himself he was glad he did not have to take that awful cough medicine anymore like he did on the trip to Gifbourg.

• • • •

GENOA HAD BEEN A COMMERCE center for centuries but with shifting attention to the new world it became less significant to international trade. It did, however, maintain itself as a major seaport and between squabbles with various factions over the years it had managed to keep an identity of its own.

Unlike Napoli, Genoa had some French influence having been a French protectorate for a number of years. But now, it was back under Italian control. It was the best location for Gaetano to get passage to America from Switzerland.

The train ran a bit late, so they did not get in until early evening on the eighth of April. It was Tuesday evening and there were plenty of rooms available in the hotels which surrounded the port. The conductor had recommended one in particular, so Gaetano headed over there to book a room.

The Hotel was just under a kilometer away from the train station, so Gaetano was glad he had once again taken his Papà's advice and packed light. His bags were still quite full, but it was nothing he could not handle. And nothing compared to the pack he had to carry at times in the Army.

He did not venture out far from the hotel under the advisement of the desk clerk. With the war over and things just starting to get reestablished, there were a large number of criminals around the docks who were looking for travelers as their next victims. He was told to only go out between seven o'clock in the morning and early afternoon. That seemed to be the safest time. The clerk said it was the time the crooks were probably sleeping since they would prowl all night long.

The morning of the tenth was warm for early spring. Gaetano left his room and checked out of the hotel. The tickets came with instructions for when passengers were to report. Any time after nine o'clock in the morning would be allowed so he decided to get there first thing and try to have his pick of a bunk. The upper bunk was his first choice. He had the upper bunk when he went to New York ten years earlier and was glad he did since the man next to him got very seasick and hit the man below him as he was vomiting. It was not one of his most fond memories. He could still remember the smell and the fury of the man who was in the lower bunk.

They took his ticket and pointed him to the stairs where his cabin would be. He was the first to get into the cabin as he had hoped. There were three sets of bunks and a set of shelves for the bags where a fourth set of bunks could be. It was almost identical to the cabin he stayed in on his first voyage. Gaetano put some items on the bunk he preferred, which was the one closest to the door. That way the air from the hallway could come in if they left the door open.

His cabin was below the water line, so he decided to venture out to see which parts of the ship he was allowed to go. As expected, there were restrictions. But since there were very few first and second-class cabins, he was able to get to more decks.

The ship set out on time at three o'clock in the afternoon and headed south for Napoli. That leg of the voyage would take just over a day. They would be pulling into port late in the evening the next day. He checked out the dining accommodations and then went back to his cabin. Three other men had moved in by then and none of them had taken any issue with Gaetano's choice of bunk. They all accepted the first come first served rule. It was obvious they all needed to get along for the next week and a half. Four to a cabin was much better than six.

Traveling on the Mediterranean while the sea is calm can be very peaceful. That night Gaetano did not sleep very well though, mostly because of the other men snoring and turning about. The crowded conditions had been something he was used to in the Army. But it had been over four months since he got out, and he wished he could have a cabin to himself. However, being he was still a third-class passenger, he accepted things for what they were. He was glad to have a place to sleep where no one was shooting at him. And likely never again.

After dinner, the next day he heard the engines slowing down to enter port. He wanted to find a porthole to look out to see if he recognized where he was since he had been to this harbor twice already. He went up three decks to a promenade which was above the water line but still not open to the air. There was a series of portholes from which to choose. It would still take about an hour for the ship to line up to the dock and secure.

He peered out one of the portholes as they entered the harbor. It all looked somewhat familiar, but he could not identify any specific landmarks. It was impossible to tell where the Saint Paul departed with all the crowds waving goodbye to their loved ones. They did not go near to where the Hallwick docked. Still, it was nice to watch the process of the ship pulling into dock and the tugboats helping.

Each ship he saw moving in the harbor made him wonder if the Hallwick was anywhere nearby. There was no one to ask who would know that sort of thing. He thought about leaving the ship to ask around, but he remembered what he was told about people getting left behind in South Hampton back when he met Niles. 'I wonder what ever happened to him?' he thought.

They would be in Napoli for twelve hours to pick up more passengers and then depart for Messina. Messina would be an entire day layover to load not only passengers but some basic cargo such as mail and specialty shipments. After that, it was off to America.

The first night they were in the Atlantic was the night of the fifteenth, a Tuesday night. Gaetano made a point to get out of the dining cabin early. He wanted to get up high enough to look out through one of the portholes and watch the sunset. Each and every night onboard the Hallwick the sun was not visible due to the harsh weather. He never saw the sunset on that trip. He wanted to be certain he would see it this time.

He got there around six o'clock and grabbed the best porthole he could find and stayed in place so no one would be able to prevent him from seeing what he had come to see. It must have been no one else had ever seen this because he was the only one positioned to watch from any of the portholes. People would walk by, but none looked out to see what he had come for. He came to see where Heaven meets Earth. Since the time he had first seen it and now, he had seen where Hell meets Earth.

As he had done years before, he stood and gazed out. First to see when the sun would touch the horizon and then once you could not see the sun anymore. That split second from when you see the sun, and then you do not. This was a private treat in which he would indulge in every night of the trip. The evening sky was clear for all the days of the crossing.

• • • •

THE MORNING OF APRIL twenty-third the Duca Degli Abruzzi entered New York Harbor. Gaetano went up to the porthole to see what he could. He was on the side of the Statue of Liberty so he could not see New York directly. As they passed Governor's Island, Gaetano went back to his cabin to gather his belongings. The stewards were in the corridor with the manifest documents needed to allow these immigrants to enter the country. Gaetano however was not an immigrant. He once lived here with his family and was returning to America.

The steward told him he still had to get processed through Ellis Island. All Gaetano could think of was the doctor who turned his eyelids inside out ten years earlier to see if he had a disease. He hoped he would not have to go through that again. It was at that moment he realized why he needed to spend the winter in Gifbourg. If he had come to America in December, they may have turned him away because he was still extremely ill and barely recovering from his cough. The officials at Ellis Island would certainly be reluctant to let someone into the country who showed signs of carrying anything.

The Duca Degli Abruzzi pulled into dock on the west side of New York at around nine o'clock in the morning. Shuttle boats were already standing by to bring the immigrants to Ellis Island. Gaetano was not able to get on the first shuttles, so he had to wait until almost eleven o'clock to get on one of the next waves. Once they arrived, he got on board and stood along the railing of the shuttle as they crossed the Hudson for Ellis Island.

During his time in the Army, he had lost all of his paperwork which showed he had lived in America from nineteen-oh-nine through nineteen-fifteen and that he had worked for more than two of those years at a restaurant in Hoboken. Some of these documents had been left behind on the Hallwick with his belongings so he could not have saved them if he tried. He waited his turn like everyone else and fought the urge to try to find someone who would listen to him and possibly let him out earlier without all the standard examinations.

As Gaetano was standing in the line outside of the main building, a man came up to his group who had just come off the shuttle boat. He was one of the officials there and he had a clipboard with him. "Has anyone here already been to America?" he shouted.

Gaetano raised his hand along with two other passengers. The official pointed to the three of them and said, "you three, come with me. Do you all speak English?" The other two acknowledged they did as well as Gaetano.

They were escorted in through a secondary door which was around the side of the building. Each of the three was brought to a counter where there was another official waiting. Gaetano went to the closest one. There was a woman in her late fifties working there and she had obviously been doing this job for a long time. These positions were likely the most sought after because they were set up to process returning immigrants who had left the country for a time and were now returning.

"Do you speak English?" the official behind the counter asked.

"Yes, I do," he answered.

"Name?" she curtly continued,

"Gaetano Santorini," he replied, "Oh I guess it should be Tom, Thomas Santorini. That's the name they told me to use here in America the last time I came through here."

"And you're all right with that?" she continued to speak bluntly.

"All my friends here call me Tom," he said trying to convince her to just let him go home.

"What year did you come in the first time?" she asked slightly more pleasantly.

"Nineteen-oh-nine," he replied, "I left to go take care of my grandmother and ended up in the Italian Army."

She looked up at him showing some interest, "Did you join the Army when you got there?"

Tom leaned his head to the right and nodded, "They told me to join..................I didn't really have a choice."

She paused for a moment trying to comprehend what that would be like. "Where did you live when you were here from nineteen-oh-nine to nineteen-fifteen?" she asked with a much more pleasant tone in her voice.

"Jersey City," he answered, "I used to work in Hoboken at Rocco's restaurant. Have you ever eaten at Rocco's?"

She shook her head, "I don't believe so." She looked over his papers and asked him some other questions. Based on what she was asking, it became clear he would not have to go through the same rigorous examinations he had gone through the first time. The interview took about twenty minutes and then Tom was told to go sit on a bench against the wall to his right.

It was almost one o'clock and Tom was hoping he would be on his way shortly. The official who had called out the three men in the front of the building came up to him.

"Come with me," he said.

"Can I go home now?" Tom asked.

"Yes, you'll be released right away. We'll put you on the next shuttle back across the river," he said nicely.

"Would it be possible to get a shuttle to Jersey City instead?" Tom continued, "When I came to America ten years ago, there was a shuttle to Jersey City."

"Only if you want to wait for three hours," he told him.

"No," Tom said shaking his head, "Not for three hours. I can get over to New Jersey easy enough, right?"

"Yes, you can," he said taking out a sheet of paper with a small map of Manhattan on it. "The shuttle will drop you off at this dock," he said as he pointed, "you can walk over to Hudson Terminal and can get on the Hudson and Manhattan Railroad. That will take you to Jersey City and then you can catch the trolley."

Tom liked what he heard. This official was treating him like a citizen without all the talk about coming to America and what it would mean to be an American citizen. It was like talking to a neighbor or a local merchant. Tom felt right at home. "How can I exchange my currency to American?" Tom asked.

"That's easy," he replied, "once you get to the dock in Manhattan there are signs for the currency exchange in the building. Get it exchanged there and not at any of the shops around the docks. They'll rob you and give you less than your money is worth."

"Thanks for the advice," Tom said as he picked up his bags to get to the shuttle boat.

He had to rush to make it. The boat was about to leave. They held the gate for him as he ran down the walkway from the building lugging his bags. Again, it was wise to have listened to his Papà and pack light.

Crossing New York harbor in the middle of the afternoon in late April was a refreshing treat. There was a mixture of sea air with the wind from the west coming across New Jersey. Tom held onto the railing and took it all in.

Once back in Manhattan, Tom stopped to exchange his Italian and Swiss currency and then walked the several blocks it took to get to Hudson Terminal. He studied the map to see where the train let him off in Jersey City. It seemed easy enough, so he walked over to the agent and bought a fare.

By the time he made it over to Jersey City it was going on four o'clock. The trolley line would start to get busy when the dock workers got off work. So, he was hoping he could miss the rush. It was as if he had never left. He knew exactly which trolley to get on and how to switch lines at the proper intersection.

Tom sat by the window taking in the view of his hometown and did not take the time to look around him in the trolley. He sat looking out with his bags in the seat next to him. Across from him was a woman with her ten-year-old son. She looked over at him and then away. After a moment, she looked back again.

"Tom?" The woman called out to him over the trolley noise.

Tom looked over and noticed her and her son. He thought he might recognize her but was not sure. "Sophia?" he answered.

"Tom," she continued, "is that really you?"

"In the flesh," he said.

"I just don't believe it," Sophia said, "We thought you were dead."

"I know, I should have written," Tom said sheepishly, "There's no excuse. I'm really sorry about......."

"No Tom," she cut him off with a sense of urgency, "you don't understand. We really thought you were dead. We were told you had been killed last year."

"Why, I don't understand," Tom said looking puzzled.

"Your Mamma," Sophia said, "she came into the restaurant sobbing uncontrollably one day last autumn. I forget exactly what day it was. They sent her a letter saying you were killed in battle and buried in your hometown."

"My Mamma thinks I'm dead?" Tom said, sounding shocked.

"Yes Tom. She does," Sophia said with sadness to her voice, "Are you on your way home now?"

"Yes, I was going to surprise her," Tom said hesitantly.

"That might do more than surprise her," she continued, "she'll think she's seeing a ghost."

"What should I do?" Tom asked. He was very concerned for his Mamma at this point.

"Tell you what. I'll go with you. You wait around the corner," Sophia suggested, "I'll take Anthony and go in first. That way I can break it too her and she won't be frightened."

"Do you think that will help?" Tom said, realizing it would be best.

"I'm sure it will," Sophia said, "she is going to be so happy you're all right."

Chapter 45

> > >

The interrogation room had two overhead lights most would normally not notice during the day. They were not very bright and with the sun shining in the window, having them on was nearly useless. But now it was past ten thirty in the evening and rapidly approaching midnight, so they brightly lit the tabletop between Tom and Signor Marcellino.

Remnants of the evening meal were still strewn across the table with two coffee cups and a water pitcher. Tom had been talking all afternoon and evening while Signor Marcellino just sat and listened. Both men were exhausted, but each knew there must be a reason for Tom to tell his story after all these years.

Tom reached for the pitcher and poured some water into his coffee cup. He paused for a moment and took a sip. Signor Marcellino continued to stare at him and by now Tom was so used to it that it did not faze him. "Was your Mother all right?" he asked.

"When I went home after the war?" Tom asked back to clarify. Signor Marcellino nodded. "It took a few days for her to feel like it was all real. But looking back, I'm very glad Sophia and Tony were on that trolley."

Signor Marcellino stared some more. Tom took another sip of his water. The two men just sat there as if there was nothing left to say. After about seven or eight minutes, Signor Marcellino started to speak, but then hesitated. "You know," he started "I was in the war."

Tom lifted his head looking surprised. "You were?" he asked.

"Yes. But not for long," he said quietly, "You see like you, I too was recruited into the Army, but not at the harbor. They came to my town and recruited most of the men my age."

"So, you were there," Tom said solemnly.

"Only for a short time," he said, "just a few months at the beginning."

"What happened?" Tom asked reluctantly.

"I was wounded in battle," he continued, "I hadn't seen much action up until that point. It was a gruesome battle. Men shot to pieces right in front of me."

Tom nodded his head, "I saw too much of that myself."

Tom looked at the cane which was leaning against the table. Signor Marcellino had held it close to him the whole time. He would use it to help him get up with quite a bit of difficulty and leaned heavily on it while moving about. Tom nodded upward as if to point to it with his eyes.

"Yes," Signor Marcellino said quietly, "I've walked with a cane ever since. I spent six months in the infirmary and had several operations to try to help me walk again. It took over a year before I could stand on my own. And another year before I could walk with just a cane."

"I'm glad you were able to walk though," Tom said, "So many never made it."

Signor Marcellino dipped his head forward. He sat looking down at the floor. Then he lifted it up halfway and said, "I was left to die on the battlefield. I was there for hours. The enemy would shoot at the men who cried out the loudest. So, I tried to be silent. It got very, very dark, and then started to rain. I prayed I would die so the pain would stop. Then I heard a sound nearby and suddenly.................. suddenly............I felt a tug. I thought God was reaching down to lift me up to heaven. But instead, I felt someone grab my collar. He didn't say anything. He just grabbed my collar and started to pull me across the field. I thought my legs would fall off. The pain was so terrible. It was much worse than when both of my legs got shot up by the machine gun. Part of me wanted him to stop and let me die. But I knew........................I just knew I had to hang on for a while longer." His voice was starting to quiver.

Tom put his cup down and Signor Marcellino continued. "We got to the trench where our side was, and he looked over to see who was right there so he could hand me down. Then he turned round to see me. It was the first time I looked at him. All I could see up until then was the rain falling on my face. The strangest thing though. He didn't say a word." By now a tear was coming down his face. "I looked into his eyes and saw the eyes of a man filled with kindness. I will never forget that moment. It was a look I have not seen since."

Tom watched on not wanting to interrupt.

"This day," he continued, "for the first time in over forty years I can once again look into those eyes at the man who saved my life. You are a hero signor. You are Gaetano Santorini, the man who pulled me off that battlefield in the pouring rain when no one else would come."

There was a brief silence at that point. Signor Marcellino shifted in his chair and then struggled to get to his feet. He put both hands on the table but would not reach for his cane. It was obvious without the cane it was near to impossible for him to stand up on his own. But he was determined to stand on his own power. As he continued to struggle, Tom considered getting up to help him but realized this was something he wanted to be able to do on his own.

He straightened up as well as he could trying to keep his balance. His lower lip was quivering as though he was trying not to begin to cry. It looked like he might stumble, but he caught himself on the table and attempted to come to attention. Once he was as tall as he could be, he snapped his right hand to his forehead and saluted.

Tom slowly stood to his feet and returned the salute. They looked into each other's eyes for quite some time. The three people who had been watching through the one-way glass sat speechless. What they had assumed was an interrogation of a suspected fraudster was actually a reunion between two men who had not seen one another in over forty-four years. Two lives which were brought together for just a brief moment so long ago with a chance encounter that had an everlasting effect on both of them.

The woman who had been bringing in the meals was in the booth. She was the first to start to cry. Within moments they all had tears in their eyes. The technician who was recording the entire day reached over and turned off the tape machine.

• • • •

AFTER RECEIVING SOME disappointing news from Tony in New Jersey, Maria tried to keep her hopes up. 'Maybe I'll take another bath tonight,' she thought, 'It's getting late, maybe I shouldn't.' She did not want to start getting nervous again like she had the first night Tom had been arrested. 'Maybe a shower,' she thought some more.

She looked at the clock in the room as she went to turn on the radio to the classical station for some help in getting back to a relaxed mood. It was just after eleven o'clock, but she did not feel the least bit like sleeping. With all the walking and shopping that day along with the underlying anxiety of wondering what would come of everything, she felt like she must be tired. But she was not.

The idea of the shower stayed with her so she decided it would be the best way to relax. With the lights turned down to their lowest setting and the soft music in the background, she went into the bathroom to start her shower. In the evening, the water pressure was always better than in the morning. Fewer people were using the showers to lower the overall pressure. The water was hitting her back like sharp needles of heat. It was like getting a massage.

Fifteen minutes into her shower the phone rang in the room. 'Tony must have forgotten something,' she thought. Maria stopped the shower and grabbed a towel to wrap herself. "Please don't hang up," she shouted as if the operator could hear her. "Hello?" she said, picking up the phone and nearly out of breath.

With her hair dripping onto the carpet, she listened to hear "Honey? It's me." It felt like a dream. This was Tom on the phone, not Tony.

"Tom?" she barely answered, "where are you? Are you all right? Where are you?"

"I'm fine," Tom said trying to reassure her, "Everything is fine now."

"What happened?" she began to cry, "I've been so worried. What did they do to you? Who are those people anyway? I talked to Tony back home he tried to get help from there and his lawyer has a sister here and she took me to see a lawyer today......"

"Don't worry Maria," he said trying even harder to set her mind at ease, "everything is fine now. It's all taken care of."

"What?" she continued crying, "What is this all about?"

"There arranging for a car now to bring me back," Tom said, "I should be there within the hour. Please don't worry."

"I don't understand," she said trying to calm down, "who is arranging a car?"

"It's probably best if I explain it all when I get there," Tom continued, "I'll tell you everything when I get there. He's giving me the sign from the door. The car is here."

"Who's giving you the sign?" Maria said befuddled.

"It's all right. Please don't be upset," Tom said trying again to console her. He knew the only way was to actually be there with her. "We're leaving now. I'll be there soon."

"Well. All right, I'll wait here," she said, "Hurry, I miss you."

"Me too," he said, "I have to go. I love you very much."

"And I love you," Maria said though the shaky tears of joy and confusion.

She put the phone down and stood there thinking of all that must have been happening to Tom since she last saw him. After a few minutes she realized she was standing there wrapped in a towel and her hair was still dripping wet. She walked into the bathroom to dry off and get dressed again.

It seemed like several hours while she waited for Tom to come through the door. She paced the floor and kept going into the bathroom and then back to the window. She kept that up and occasionally looked through the peep hole in the door to see if she could see Tom coming down the hall.

Her feet were tired from all the walking all day so at one point she just stayed looking out the window. She was there for about ten minutes when Tom came in. The front desk clerk gave him an extra key since he did not have one with him. Maria started walking slowly towards him and sped up her pace with every step until she was almost running.

She wrapped her arms around him and held him as if to never let him go again. "Oh. I've missed you," Maria said though all of her tears, "Please don't every leave me again." The room was silent as they embraced to make up for lost time.

Tom had released some deeply buried feelings he thought could never be healed. To know that one of the men he pulled off of the battlefield had mended enough to have a productive live was a blessing to him and it lifted a burden from him he had carried for decades. There had been a purpose for all of it. There was a reason he was there all those years ago. Back then he could not figure out why all of it was happening to him. But now he understood.

Maria finally stopped shaking and crying but still would not let Tom go. "So, did they finally realize you weren't the man they were accusing you of being?" she asked.

Tom pulled back just enough to look at her directly, "Actually................"

• • • •

THEY SAT AT THE EDGE of the bed for an hour while Tom explained the goings on for the past couple of days. Then suddenly Maria asked what seemed to be an irrelevant question "Who drove you back?" she asked.

Tom was surprised by the question. It did not seem important considering everything else. "Oh uh, Signor Marcellino has a brother with a car service," he told her, "he called him because he always drives him everywhere and is always standing by. He told me ever since he got out of the Army, his brother always had to drive him everywhere. It was because, with his legs being so severely injured, Signor Marcellino could never drive a car. So, his brother always felt obligated."

"Oh," she said seeming to be satisfied with the answer. She still could not believe all of it though. It seemed so hopeless just hours before and then suddenly it was all over, and Tom was back. But it was not as if he had never left. There was something different about him. He seemed to be free like she had never known him to be. "So, what do we do next?" she asked.

"Signor Marcellino wants us to come by in the afternoon tomorrow," Tom said, "He told me he has to check on some records from the old days. He wouldn't say exactly what, but he sure seemed excited about it whatever it was."

"Tony!" Maria said, "We need to call Tony, Richard, and Linda! They've all been worried sick!" She walked over to the phone and picked it up. "Operator? I would like to make a person-to-person call.................."

. . . .

THEY WERE NOT ABLE to settle down after getting off the phone with Tony. It was after one o'clock in the morning before they fell asleep. They finally relaxed and snuggled up to each other like they used to over thirty years earlier.

Their vacation having been shaken up still had over a week left for them to enjoy the sights. They woke up at nine o'clock and decided to hurry down to one of the sidewalk cafés which Maria had become familiar with. The sun was shining but the air was cool. There was a nice breeze coming from the north which kept things comfortable and dry.

During breakfast Maria told Tom about Anna and how she had helped so much. She said they would have to call her first thing after breakfast so she would not worry if she tried to call the room and Maria did not answer. Once they got back to the room, Maria called Anna. She asked if she could come by later and meet Tom since so much had happened in the previous couple of days. Maria said they would arrange something once they got back from the appointment Tom said they had back at the government office.

Tom and Maria discussed what to do with the rest of the vacation. Tom knew he still had to arrange for the pension fund. The office manager, who had seemed so angry with him when he first went in, made a point of it before he left the night before. This office manager had been one of the people in the booth behind the one-way glass. When Tom came out of the interrogation room, he made every effort to show Tom how ashamed he was for the way he had treated him. After all Tom was one of the war heroes whom he was committed to protect. No matter how much Tom tried to assure him he had no hard feelings, the man was nearly inconsolable and wanted to be sure everything about the pension was in order.

They went for a walk around the hotel area for a couple of hours to see some of the local sights. It was not too far of a venture, but it helped them to feel like they were actually on a vacation again. It was just before noon when returned to the hotel. As they walked up the driveway towards the front door, Tom noticed Signor Marcellino brother was standing next to his car. He had been there for over an hour and once he realized Tom and Maria were not in their room, he stayed and waited for them to return.

"Signor Santorini?" he said as they walked up.

"Victor. How are you?" Tom said, "Maria, this is Victor. Signor Marcellino's brother. He's the kind man who brought me back last night. Is everything all right? We were planning on calling for a taxi when we got back."

"Signor," Victor said speaking in English, "My brother and I would like you to know, our car service is available to you at no charge for the rest of your stay." He spoke English to them since he felt they would be more comfortable. His English was quite good being he often used it when driving American tourists around Rome.

Maria was taken aback. Tom was also surprised. "I don't understand," Tom said.

"My brother told me of the way you were arrested for the wrong reason," he continued, "we want only the best for our nation's finest fighting men. I will drive you where you want to go and if I get tired of driving, one of my other drivers will drive you. When you are ready to go back to your ship in Napoli, we will drive you. You won't need to take the train."

"That's very kind of you, but......" Tom began to say.

"No signor," Victor interrupted, "Nothing is too good for the man who saved my brother's life."

Tom just stood there dumbfounded and shook his head, "Well, I guess so, if you insist."

"I insist signor. I insist," Victor said as he opened the door to the car. "I can show you some terrific places where the tourists never go. Where would you like to go first?"

Maria still did not know the whole story. She did not really know what he meant when Victor said Tom had saved his brother's life. Only that they had met before.

Tom and Maria told him they needed to stop in the room to get the camera and some other things for the day and also Signor Marcellino had mentioned he would need to see them later. Victor said he would call his brother while they were getting their things to see what time would be best for them to meet. They went up to the room and were back down within fifteen minutes.

They could not think of where they wanted to go first because there was just so much to see. They decided to let Victor choose for them. Tom and Maria got in the back of the car, and they headed out for a full afternoon of sightseeing throughout Rome. Victor knew all the best places to go.

Signor Marcellino had told Victor to bring them by the office at the end of the day. After spending half a day stopping at several sites in Rome, they went to the office. It was close to five o'clock when they went up the elevator to the sixth floor where Signor Marcellino's office was. He was still there waiting for them. Most of his staff had just left and there were only two other people in the office as they walked in.

"Signor Santorini," Signor Marcellino said grabbing his cane to get up from behind his desk, "and Signora Santorini."

He walked up to Maria first, "Signora, I must tell you how sorry I am for what you have been through. Please accept my humble apology for this misunderstanding," he said taking her hand.

"Tom told me everything," she said being a bit embarrassed at the attention, "he says you met many years ago, but you were not certain it was him. So, you had to find out if he was really the same man."

"Did he tell you how we met?" he asked, looking over at Tom.

Maria looked at Tom also with a confused look. "No," she said, "just that you met." Tom shook his head to signal Signor Marcellino, he need not tell her the details. Signor Marcellino nodded back to acknowledge his request.

"Ah," he said turning back to look at Maria, "Not important. Someday maybe he will."

"You had some records you were going to look up," Tom asked trying to move the conversation along. He figured they must have something to do with the long-awaited pension fund he had come for in the first place.

Signor Marcellino released Maria's hand and turned to go back to his desk. He picked up a small stack of papers he had set to the side earlier anticipating Tom's arrival. "There is more to research and other places to look Signor," he said, "But from what I have found so far, you have something coming to you."

Tom figured this was old news since the night before the office manager had told him to come back for the pension fund paperwork to be completed. "Yes," Tom acknowledged, "I spoke with the gentleman last night before I left. I plan to go back on Monday to finish the papers."

"Oh.................no signor," Signor Marcellino said sounding embarrassed, "You don't understand. After you went back to America, they awarded all of the metals. It was years later. Since they thought you were killed, they put them in a storage vault for soldiers whose families did not claim them."

"Metals?" Maria said, "What metals?" Tom looked just as confused.

"Signora," he said with his eyes opening brightly, "Do you not know your husband is one of the most decorated war heroes in our nation's history? They teach of him in our schools. Every child in Italy knows the name Gaetano Santorini."

Tom and Maria turned to each other and did not say a word. They just tried to see if the other's reaction would bring some reality to what they were hearing. Then they both turned back to Signor Marcellino, and both said at the same moment, "What?"

Chapter 46

The next day was Saturday. Tom and Maria had been in Italy now for nearly a week. This would be only the second day they could simply see the sights and do nothing but enjoy the day. Victor arrived at eight o'clock to take them wherever they wanted to go. They had discussed the night before what time he would arrive. Tom and Maria got up early to get ready and have time for some breakfast at the café. They were back at the hotel by the time he arrived.

"Where would you like to go today?" Victor asked as they approached the car. Maria looked at Tom with some hesitation and Victor could tell they had something in mind but did not want to say.

"You look as if you would like to go someplace but are afraid to ask. Am I right?" Victor said.

"Well," Maria said, "We talked about it last night, but...."

"Where Signora? Just tell me. Anywhere you want," Victor insisted.

"Tom............. well, both of us actually," she hesitated more, "we............we were thinking we would like to go to Tom's hometown."

Tom stood looking a bit sheepish. He was not used to asking for things that other people would have to do for him. "Montoro Superiore. The town is called Montoro Superiore. I'm sure it's too far to drive," Tom said apologetically feeling this would be far too much to ask.

"I have a map signor," Victor said walking to the back to open the trunk, "I can tell you exactly how far." He put the key in the lock and swung it open. There was a satchel strapped to the left side of the trunk which he used to keep his documents such as his license to operate the car service and his insurance papers. He also had several maps of the region and a national map.

"Do you know where it is on the map signor?" Victor asked.

Tom looked over the map. "It's south of here and east of Napoli." he said moving his finger back and forth, "There, in Avellino." He tapped his finger on the spot.

Victor looked and said, "It would only take us three and a half hours to get there. Maybe four if we stop. I would say it's just over two hundred-fifty kilometers from here."

Tom and Maria looked at each other and shook their heads, "Oh, it's too far," Maria said.

"That would be too much driving for you Victor," Tom said, "Back and forth on the same day. That would be seven or eight hours behind the wheel."

"You give the word signor," Victor said with confidence, "and we will go." They continued to look hesitant. "You can rest on the drive," Victor added. They still looked hesitant. "I can rest while you are visiting your hometown, so I'll be rested for the drive back." Tom and Maria continued to look at each other, seeming conflicted. "I often drive farther Signor."

"I'll tell you what," Tom said, "we'll buy you a nice lunch in Montoro Superiore. You pick the restaurant."

"Lunch it is," Victor said sounding happy he had convinced them. He opened the door so they could get in the back. "I will make one stop just outside of the city," he added.

• • • •

THEY HEADED OUT AND got on the main road leaving Rome going south. Victor knew exactly where he had planned to stop. Shortly after leaving Rome, he stopped at a small market and went in by himself. He came out with some fruit and three bottles of juice and a jug of water. "For the ride down," he said handing it in through the back window.

Tom took it in and looked at the bundle. "Grazie Victor," he said gazing at it with disbelief of the treatment they were getting.

Victor got back in and continued on his way. They sat back and looked out the window admiring the countryside. It was pretty much the same route the train had taken up from Napoli but being in a car helped them to feel more connected with the terrain. Occasionally Victor would point things out and explain what they were. Each hour they stopped for a bathroom break and a brief walk to stretch their legs.

About three hours later they saw a sign that Avelino was just ahead so they decided to stop for lunch before entering Montoro Superiore. They found a quaint little spot along the roadside and decided this would be the best place to eat. It was just before twelve o'clock and it was beginning to get very warm. Tom and Maria were glad they were drinking enough juice and water along with making their brief stops. It helped them to stay cool in the car with the windows open just a bit to keep the air flowing.

Tom had a handkerchief he would wet with water from the jug. He would shake it about in front of the window to cool it off then place it on his neck. The heat did not bother either of them though. The adventure was well worth it.

After lunch, they made a bathroom stop and then got back in the car. "I wonder if Signor Rizzi's vineyard is still there," Tom asked, "maybe one of his sons has taken over the business."

"I'm sure someone will remember," Maria said, "It's a small town from what you said. I'm sure a lot of people will know the history."

"Maybe," Tom said, "I'm actually getting a bit nervous. I haven't been here since nineteen-oh-nine. That was fifty years ago. The place must have changed a lot. It must be more modern."

"Signor," Victor injected from the front seat, "Many of these towns have not changed very much since the two wars."

"How much is there to see in Montoro Superiore?" Maria asked Tom.

"I'd like to go to Chiesa alla fraz Banzani," Tom said, "If I remember right, it's up on a hilltop. An old building, I'm not sure it's still standing. Who knows like Victor said with two wars? The first was far away but the second one may have been closer. That part I do know."

"I looked at the booklet I have for the region just after we stopped for lunch," Victor said, "There are castle ruins you may want to see. Rovine del Castello Longobardo I think the name was."

"Really, I lived there for fifteen years and never knew that. If we take the time to see everything, we could spend our entire vacation here," Tom said regretting they only had a short stay planned. "I think we'll just go into the center of town and walk around a bit. That'll bring back memories I hope."

"Who knows," Maria said, "maybe we can come back someday and just visit here for the entire two weeks."

"I would if I still had family here," Tom said.

Victor pulled the car into the center of town and drove around a bit. People stared at the car as they passed by. "They must think we're a couple of rich people in a chauffeur driven limousine," Maria said. Tom just chuckled at the idea.

They parked in what appeared to be a central shopping area with a nice walkway which had some benches for people to sit on underneath the trees. "This looks like a good place to get out," Tom said.

Victor told them he would park in a shady spot and close his eyes for a bit while they walked around. Tom and Maria got out and started to stroll up and down the streets. Much of it was new indeed but there were still some of the older structures. "It seems familiar, but it's been so long.......... I don't know," Tom said.

Tom thought he recognized one of the churches. "I think I used to go there with my Mamma and Papà before they moved to America. That might be the one. I just don't remember."

Maria saw some shops she wanted to go into for a quick look around. "You go ahead," Tom said, "I think I'll just sit out here on the bench and try to remember."

She went across the street and went into the first shop. It was a ladies clothing store. After a brief walk around to see the styles, she left and went into a general store which was right next door. It was similar to some of the five and dime stores back home. However, this was a bit more interesting. Much of the merchandise was older and seemed to have been on the shelves longer than most stores would keep it. 'This store was likely around back when Tom lived here,' she thought.

The people in the store looked at Maria a bit strangely but not in an unfriendly way. It was obvious they realized she was not from their town. This store was quite interesting. She thought Tom might like to come in and look around because some things hanging on the wall looked like they could have been there for fifty years.

Maria walked up to the front counter where the owner was standing by the cash register. She gave him a smile and a nod. He returned the gesture. As she walked by him, she noticed a photograph hanging directly behind him of a soldier. At first, she figured it was either the owner or maybe his father since the owner did not appear to be older than forty-five or so.

She looked closer at the picture and thought she recognized the soldier. With a double take she realized who she was looking at. "Mi Scusi Signor," she said to him, "But who is that soldier in the photograph behind you.

He had noticed her looking at it closely. "That is our war hero Signora," he said with pride, "he lived in this town and was one of our nation's greatest heroes."

"Do you know his name by any chance?" she asked anticipating the answer.

"Yes of course Signora," he said again with even more pride, "That is Signor Santorini. He was killed near the end of the war but not before he accomplished many heroic acts."

"Signor Santorini, you say?" Maria clarified, "Signor Gaetano Santorini?"

The owner looked shocked that she would know his first name. "Yes. Yes, Signora that's right, Gaetano Santorini. His family was from here even though they moved to America at some point."

"Signor," Maria said cautiously, "This man in the photograph, Gaetano Santorini, you say he was killed in the war."

"Yes Signora," he answered seeming to be perturbed at her continued questioning about a photograph which had hung in that very spot his whole life. The store had been in his family for many years, and he had taken over when his father retired.

"Signor," Maria added, "That man is not dead. He didn't die in the war." The owner looked very confused and almost angry. "That man is my husband," she continued, "you see, my name is Maria Santorini, and my husband is sitting right across the street on that bench over there. Do you see him?" She pointed out the window. They could both see Tom sitting with his back to them.

"That is impossible Signora," the owner said abruptly, "they taught us Signor Santorini was killed in the war."

"Well, it's true, he's alive," she said, "We actually just found out this past week. They told us in the government office Tom.... well Gaetano was a war hero. We never knew."

The owner pulled the photograph off the wall and walked towards the front door. "I'm going to see for myself," he said in a bit of a huff. Maria was concerned Tom might have a repeat of the events on Tuesday of the previous week where people were accusing him of being an imposter. She followed him out but had a tough time keeping up.

Victor was watching from the car and felt something was not right. He stepped out and started to walk towards them. He was about twenty meters from them when the owner reached Tom.

"Signor!" the owner said abruptly, "Can I speak with you?"

Tom seemed a bit confused by the way he was asking. He nodded and stood to greet him. "Yes, what can I do for you?" he asked.

The owner showed him the photograph and Tom took it to get a better look. "Is this you Signor?" the owner asked.

"Oh, my goodness," Tom said, "Where did you get this? I remember taking this photograph back in nineteen-fifteen. I never actually saw it though. They took this just before we were sent to the front lines. Right at the training camp if I recall."

The owner looked closely at Tom and then back at the photograph and then back and forth. "This can't be," he said, "This man in the photograph is Signor Santorini our town's war hero. Everyone in town knows of him."

Just then Maria and Victor caught up with him. "I told you," Maria said, "This is my husband. Signor Santorini. Tom, he had this hanging on the wall in his shop."

Tom looked surprised but based on what he had just been through that week, none of it was unthinkable. After all, he had just found out he was considered a national figure. Victor looked at the photograph and nodded. "It does look like you signor. You were very handsome when you were young."

The owner took the photograph back and stared at it with a great deal of confusion. Occasionally he looked up at Tom. "I must tell the Mayor," he said, "Oh no, it's Saturday he's not in his office. I have to tell someone." He started walking back to the shop and stopped once he reached the other side of the street to turn one more time. It was hard for him to tell if it was all real.

When he went back into his shop, Tom, Maria, and Victor all looked at each other and began to laugh. "Maybe we should just walk around outside," Maria suggested, "It might be easier that way." Tom nodded in agreement.

"I'll go back to the car," Victor said, "Just come by when you want to move on."

Tom and Maria agreed and started to walk around the vicinity. They headed up to the hillside south of town. Once they reached the end of where the houses were built, the hill looked too steep for them to have a comfortable walk. Things had changed significantly enough so Tom was not certain where anything was. It was nice to think he was in his hometown. But he truthfully could not remember many details. After all, he was only fifteen years old when he left.

They took their time walking back because the late afternoon sun was a bit strong. It made sense for them to walk slowly so they would not get overheated. The water jug was in the car and there were not any stores on their path to get something to drink. It was not far, but with the heat, they did not take any chances. There was a short rock wall under the shade of a large tree, so they decided to sit for a while and enjoy the peacefulness of the town. It was relaxing and quiet.

By four o'clock they were coming back to where Victor was parked. As they came around the corner, they noticed several people standing around Victor's car. They were about four blocks away when one of the people noticed them walking towards them. It was the shop owner who had the photograph of Tom when he was young. He tapped one of the other men there and pointed towards them as they approached. He said something to him which perked his attention.

The two men started walking towards Tom and Maria as they got closer to the car. "Signor and Signora," the shop owner said with a nervous tone in his voice, "This is Signor De Franco, the mayor of our town." Tom and Maria put their hands out to shake his.

"Good day Signor and Signora," the mayor said cordially, "Vincenzo tells me you say you are this man in the photograph. Is this true Signor?" He was holding the photograph in his hands.

Tom looked at the photograph again to make sure it was the same one he had seen earlier. "Yes, that's me," Tom said, "When I was much younger indeed."

Victor stepped out of the car and walked over to them knowing what their concern was. "I explained to them everything my brother investigated this week Signor," he said, "they are having a hard time believing it though." the mayor nodded his head in agreement.

"Well," Tom said, "that is most definitely me in the picture. I actually remember the day it was taken in May of nineteen-fifteen."

"If you are from this town, what can you tell me that would verify who you are?" Mayor De Franco asked.

Tom thought for a moment and then perked his eyes up and said, "Umm.......... does anyone remember the vineyard that was owned by a Signor Rizzi? It would have been around that time. He took me to Napoli in nineteen-oh-nine with my Nonna so I could get on a ship to join my Mamma and Papà in America. Does anybody know if the vineyard is still in business?"

"Rizzi? Vineyard?" Vincenzo asked, "Yes, I think so, but not for many years. There was a family on the west side who had a vineyard. I am pretty sure the name was Rizzi. My father would remember if he were still with us, rest his soul."

"Did you know them at all?" Tom asked.

"Not very well," Vincenzo answered, "If I recall, there was the old man, around the second war. His son was killed in the war, and he left to live with his other son in Napoli. He was quite old and did not take the death of his son very well. The vineyard? I don't think anyone continued the vineyard. There are some in the area, but not that one, not anymore."

"I used to work for Signor Rizzi, the father, when I was a young boy," Tom said, "he was like an uncle to me. I'm sorry to hear about his son. I recall he was just a baby when I left."

The mayor looked confused because he wanted to believe Tom and Maria, but it was hard to get used to the idea that the town war hero who they all thought had died over forty years earlier was standing right before them. Tom took out his American driver's license and his passport to show them. He explained the Ellis Island rename from Gaetano to Tom in order to make him seem more American. The mayor understood since he too had relatives who moved to America and had a similar experience.

"So," Mayor De Franco asked, "if you are Gaetano Santorini, who is it that is buried in the grave with your name on it?"

Tom paused for a long moment. He did not want to have to admit he had changed uniforms with a young soldier who got himself killed by being careless. It was not one of the things he was proud of. Plus, he was not really sure it would be him. "I don't know," he said, "there must have been some kind of mix up. Victor's brother Signor Marcellino asked me the same thing."

Within fifteen minutes there were over fifty people gathered around. As a new person would come up curious as to what was drawing a crowd, someone would tell them that this was Signor Gaetano Santorini. The reaction was always the same. At first disbelief, then they would come up to Tom and Maria and want to shake their hand.

Mayor De Franco asked Tom and Maria to give him their address in America so he could correspond with them in the future. Tom and Maria asked for his address as well to return the gesture as the crowd slowly dissipated. Everyone said their farewell to Tom and Maria at around six o'clock, then Victor opened the car door for them. They got into the back seat of the car. As they drove off, Mayor De Franco and Vincenzo the store owner waved good-bye to them.

• • • •

THE ENTIRE DRIVE BACK to Rome consisted of them recounting all the things the town's people said to them. It was a shock and a joy to think in some way Tom had left an impression on the people of his hometown. His only regret was he did not go to the cemetery and see if his grandparents' graves were somewhere he could find. They just figured that would be one of the things they would have to do then next time they came to visit Montoro Superiore. Tom suggested they ask the mayor in one of their letters to help verify things. The visit was more than they had hoped it would be.

They arrived at their hotel shortly before ten o'clock and decided to enjoy the local tradition of a late dinner. They invited Victor to join them, but he declined saying he needed to get home to rest up for tomorrow's adventures with the Santorinis. Tom and Maria laughed at the idea that being with them as an adventure.

Chapter 47

Victor had arranged with Tom and Maria to come just after lunch on Sunday. This gave them a chance to rest up and all have a leisurely breakfast. They slept in until nine o'clock and took their time getting out for coffee and a bite to eat. They were not very hungry since they had eaten so late and had a rather large meal.

It seemed best to stay close by to the hotel all day, but they did go out for two junkets in Rome to see some things Victor suggested. With anticipating the need to take care of several business items on Monday, they wanted to keep things light so as not to be too tired for the next day. Victor left at around five o'clock, so Tom and Maria decided to have a light dinner and then go to the movie theater for another film. They had seen the preview the week before and hoped to see this film while they were there. It was not likely to be showing at any theaters back home in its original language and they felt it would be more enjoyable to see it with the original Italian and no subtitles.

After they came out of the theater, they both realized how tired they were. So, they went back to the hotel room and Maria took a bath while Tom read by the window. She showed him the light classical station on the radio and they both enjoyed the peace and quiet. By the time they went to sleep, they were both very relaxed and slept soundly all night.

• • • •

THE ARRANGEMENT FOR Monday was for Victor to pick up the Santorinis at eleven o'clock from the hotel and take them to the government office where Signor Marcellino's office was located. They were told to dress nicely. Their Sunday best as Tom would call it. They were not sure why, but they figured in Italy, business was to be conducted with dignity, thus the nice clothes.

Victor seemed excited for some reason but would not say why. He just kept telling them, "This is going to be a good day." Each time he said it, Tom and Maria looked at each other and shrugged their shoulders. The drive was the normally long struggle through the heavy Rome traffic.

It was one week ago they had first come here. Things were quite different now though. One week ago, no one knew who Tom and Maria Santorini from America were. Now they were being chauffeur driven to what seemed like a standard business meeting. The process of filling out some pension forms. They arrived just after twelve o'clock and went right upstairs to the office.

"Ah, Signor and Signora Santorini," Signor Marcellino said with his hand stretched out to greet them, "This is going to be a good day." Tom and Maria looked at each other surprised he said the same thing Victor had been saying all the way over. This made them even more confused. It did not seem like getting his pension fund straightened out was so significant to warrant such a comment.

"Come in and sit please," Signor Marcellino said almost out of breath from his excitement. They sat on the couch in his office. "Today, at three o'clock," he began, "there will be a ceremony. General Patrizi, ah," he paused to look at Tom, "No relationship to the sergeant you spoke of I'm afraid. I asked him if he had any relatives killed in that war. Well, like I began to say, he will be here."

"General?" Tom said confused.

"Yes," Signor Marcellino said even more excitedly, "I called him on Friday to discuss your case, and he suggested it."

"Suggested what?" Maria chimed in.

"They are going to give Gaetano oh, Tom, is it? I guess it doesn't matter," he stumbled a bit as he spoke, "They're going to give him his medals.......................all of them."

Tom and Maria looked at each other, still not used to this idea of Tom being some sort of war hero. To them, he was simply Tom the barber from Jersey City who could make a fabulous meatball parm when he went to Tony's pizzeria for his second job. All this hero talk was almost too much for them. But they understood by now how important it was to these people who they had recently come to know. Partly, they were going along with it because it seemed so important to everyone around them.

The office manager who they had met the week before came in with all the paperwork for the pension fund. He had prepared everything, so all Tom had to do was sign in five places. His continuous apologies started to get on Tom's nerves. But he understood this too because all of this was just so important to them. That along with the fact he was still a bit embarrassed by the way they had treated Tom when he had him arrested.

Signor Marcellino had sent out for lunch, and it was set up in the interrogation room where they had spent two days reliving Tom's past. He escorted them in and recommended they take some time and eat lunch. Tom and Maria were not very hungry but figured they might not get to eat until later in the evening, so they each took a plate of food.

On the ground floor of the government building was a small auditorium which was often used for civic events. It seated about two hundred people according to Signor Marcellino. He had described the plan for the ceremony but had not elaborated much. Tom and Maria pictured themselves on the stage with the General, Signor Marcellino, Victor, and a few of the office staff who they had come to know.

They went down at one thirty to do a walkthrough of the ceremony with Signor Marcellino. The auditorium was larger than they expected and had somewhat of an echo due to the empty house. They were told where they would sit and then where they would stand when Tom was being given the medals. It was a new experience for them and though it was a bit unnerving, they were enjoying the excitement just the same.

Tom was not used to being the center of attention and would always shy away from it. Even on their wedding day many years before, he did not care for all the focus on him. But this was a once in a lifetime event and he decided to just take it in and enjoy himself.

After the rehearsal, they were escorted back upstairs to rest until the ceremony an hour later. Tom dozed off for a bit when he leaned his head back on the couch. Maria was too excited to nap so she read some articles she found in a magazine. Signor Marcellino came in and whispered to Maria that the ceremony was going to be delayed half an hour because the General was running late. She nodded quietly and thanked him.

Tom did not open his eyes until three ten and shook his head. He looked at the clock on the wall. "Are we late?" he asked Maria.

"No Tom," she answered softly, "They pushed it back a half hour."

Tom shook his head more to wake up, "Oh," he said then got up and went to the restroom since he did not know how long the ceremony would be.

Signor Marcellino peeked in the door to see if Tom was still asleep. Maria signaled to him Tom had gone to the restroom. "We will go downstairs in five minutes," he said and then closed the door. Maria nodded her head to acknowledge she heard him.

When Tom returned Maria told him they would be going right away. "Well," Tom said, "I guess this is it. Are you nervous?"

"Sort of," she replied as she stood up to join him.

Signor Marcellino was waiting outside of the room and showed considerable excitement when they came out. "We must go, they are here. This is going to be a good day," he said. Tom and Maria just looked at each other and did not even bother to shrug their shoulders this time. They were beginning to get used to things.

The elevator ride down seemed to take longer for some reason. They had been on this elevator several times before now, but it seemed to take forever to reach the ground floor where the auditorium was.

As the elevator door opened, they noticed the hallway was very busy with people. More than they had ever seen there before. They were not sure what to make of it. The walk to the stage door was about fifty meters with one turn to the left. They walked slowly because Signor Marcellino was escorting them all the way. The stage door was open, and Signor Marcellino had them stand backstage behind a curtain and said, "Please wait right here until you hear me announce your names. Then you will go and sit where we showed you earlier."

The auditorium was rather loud compared to when they had left an hour and a half earlier. It was quite a buzz, and it made them very curious because they could not see out front. They could only see the stage and a very small part of the front row on the other side. There were three men with cameras. They were the only people Tom and Maria could see.

Signor Marcellino walked to the lectern and began to speak. As he spoke the audience became quiet. He began, "Signore e Signori, today we come to honor one of our nation's finest soldiers. A man whose name most of us equate with heroism and bravery. A man who for most of us had believed we would never meet. This is a man who God has brought back to us so we can pay him the respect and the honors he deserves. Might I add up until recently, he knew nothing about any of what we have known for all of our lives." The audience began to applaud and cheer.

Tom looked at Maria in disbelief and leaned to speak into her ear. "Is there someone else coming?" he asked.

Maria poked him "Don't be silly," she said, "he's talking about you."

Signor Marcellino continued, "Signore e Signori, please help me to welcome Signor Gaetano Santorini and his lovely wife Maria." He turned to them and gave them the signal to come.

Tom and Maria walked out onto the stage and could not believe what they saw and heard. The house was completely full. People were standing on the side isles and in the back. The roar of applause and cheers was deafening. Flash bulbs from all the cameras in the front row were going off and making it difficult for them to find their way to the seats which Signor Marcellino had instructed them to go to. Halfway there they were met by Signor Marcellino who helped them find their way.

They stood for a moment while the applause continued. Signor Marcellino gave the audience a sign they should conclude the applause and then gave Tom and Maria the sign to sit down. Their chairs were stage right of the lectern and across on the other side of the lectern were four other chairs. One was for Signor Marcellino and the others were taken by three soldiers in dress uniform.

One of the soldiers was obviously an officer and the other two were honor guards. They rightfully assumed it was General Patrizi as Signor Marcellino had told them.

Signor Marcellino began to tell of the stories which many in the audience had been taught in school about this famous war hero. The tale of how he had single handedly taken out a machine gun pill box and how on at least two occasions he had gone out onto the battlefield to rescue many wounded soldiers who had been left for dead including himself. Maria had never heard any of this because when Tom returned home to America and by the time they met and got married, he had put these things far behind him. Even the night the week before when he returned to the hotel, he had not given any of these details.

Signor Marcellino continued to tell of the missions which Gaetano Santorini would go on behind the enemy lines and on at least one occasion would be the only one to return with his life. There was no mention of the winter of nineteen-fifteen when he went to Switzerland to return on his own conscience. There was no mention of the two times Gaetano had punched lieutenants in the nose. This was a time to honor him for what he had done for his country.

He concluded his speech and then introduced General Patrizi. The general spoke from records since he had never met Gaetano Santorini personally. Like most people there, he had only learned of him from the history books. His comments were just as honoring as Signor Marcellino's had been. It was almost as if he had indeed met him. Strange, Tom thought, this General had the same last name as his first sergeant.

Once the general had concluded his comments, Signor Marcellino asked Tom and Maria to stand in their predetermined spots. The flash bulbs again began to go off uncontrollably. It was almost too much for them to stand. The strobe of the flashes had a certain hypnotic effect on everyone who was standing on the stage. It was as if an hour had passed while they waited to hear General Patrizi begin to speak again.

The General read off each of the awards, what they were for and the name of the medal as he pinned them on Tom's jacket. The list seemed to be endless. Each time General Patrizi pinned on another medal, the audience would cheer and applaud again. The flash bulbs would resume as well with varying intensity.

The medals and honors segment of the ceremony took nearly forty-five minutes. At the last medal, General Patrizi gave another invitation for applause. He then turned to Tom and offered him a salute. This was never initiated by a higher-ranking officer and certainly never from a General to a private. Tom graciously returned the salute, and the audience began to roar louder than any other time before. With a few more handshakes from all the people on the stage the ceremony was brought to a conclusion.

Tom and Maria were escorted off the stage through the door they had entered and back to the elevator to go once again upstairs where Signor Marcellino's office was before any of the reporters could get to the backstage area. They got in the elevator and Maria kept staring at Tom. He noticed and felt a bit uncomfortable. "What?" he said.

"You took out a machine gun nest on your own?" Maria said with a look of amazement on her face.

Tom shrugged his shoulders being a bit embarrassed. "Believe me when I tell you," he said, "I was more afraid of the lunatic lieutenant with the pistol than I was the enemy machine gun."

Maria's face asked the question without her having to speak. Tom realized she did not understand. "The way I saw it, I stood a better chance with the enemy who was nearly fifty meters away than the lieutenant who had already proven he would put a bullet through your head if you didn't obey." Maria did not want to ask any further about that day. She could tell by the look on his face this was not one of his fondest memories. It was one of the things she knew must have existed in his mind, but he had succeeded in stifling. Maria reached over and took Tom's hand and held it like when they were out on a date before they married. Tom gave her hand a gentle squeeze.

It was now after five o'clock and most of the office staff were beginning to leave for the day. Signor Marcellino invited them into his office where he had one more thing to show them.

"I found this over the weekend and thought you may want it," he said as he reached to the side of his desk. It was a case which was for Tom to carry the medals. It was lined with red velvet and had padding where he could pin them onto. "It is my gift to you Signor."

Tom was still in a state of shock over the ceremony and would have normally been embarrassed by such a gift. He realized how much it meant to Signor Marcellino to give this to him. He took it graciously and thanked him.

"Take a few moments Signor and place your medals in the case," he continued, "then Victor will take you back to your hotel."

Tom nodded and thanked him again for the case. Maria helped him to take the medals off his jacket and place them into the case one by one. As they were mounting the fifth medal Signor Marcellino came in again and handed them the stack of documents that went along with the medals explaining what each one was for. This process took nearly half an hour to take off the medals, put them in the case and sort out the documents. Signor Marcellino also gave them a satchel which held the documents and then helped them to put all of them in.

It was now time to go downstairs to where Victor had parked the car. When they came to where the car was, they tapped on the window to let Victor know they had arrived. He had gone down there to wait for them knowing they would not be long. He got out and opened the door for them. "I told you it was going to be a good day," he said to them as he got back into the driver's seat and closed his door.

"That you did," Tom replied, "that you did."

• • • •

TRAFFIC WAS AS HEAVY as expected. They just sat and did not say much. Tom and Maria were out of words because the day had been filled with excitement such as they had never experienced before. Occasionally they would look at each other and the look spoke clearly. They both understood what the other was thinking.

It was evening by now and they were anxious to get up to their room and relax. Absorbing this day would take more than the usual effort. Victor pulled up into the driveway of the hotel and stopped at the bottom of the ramp. "Signor," he said, "I don't think it's over yet."

Tom was not sure what he meant so he leaned forward to see what he was talking about. There were about a dozen reporters with cameras and a film crew who seemed to be from the local news program. "My goodness," Tom said as he sat back.

"What do you want me to do Signor?" he asked.

"I guess there's only one thing we can do," Tom said, "greet them."

"All right Signor," Victor said. He pulled up closer to where the reporters were but stayed back a bit, so they were not right up to them. "I'll open the door," he said as he got out.

One of the reporters saw Victor going around to open the door and tapping the other while pointing in the direction of the car. The two began to walk over as Tom and Maria were getting out. The rest realized they had arrived and followed the other two reporters.

Again, the flash bulbs began to go off. This time was a bit different because someone turned on two very bright television lights which practically blinded both of them. The questions started to bombard them quickly. They asked questions such as, "When did you move to America?" "Didn't you know you were a hero?" "Do you have any children?" "How do you feel about all the starving people in the world?" That one caught Tom off guard. 'What did that have to do with him being in the Army?' he thought.

Some of the questions were good but most were silly. Finally, one reporter said to him, "Most people assumed you were no longer alive. Our history books said you were killed near the end of the war."

Tom thought for a moment and said, "Well, in the words of the American author Mark Twain, the report of my death was greatly exaggerated." This brought a round of laughter which lightened up the rest of the interview. They stood out in front of the hotel for almost thirty minutes talking with the reporters and then excused themselves to go to their room.

Victor walked them into the lobby to make sure they were well on the way to their room without further interruption. "May I suggest you order room service," he said. "There may be more reporters wanting to talk to you. They'll keep you up all night asking questions. And I suggest you tell the front desk not to send any calls to your room tonight."

"We were expecting our daughter to call tonight," Maria said.

"Well Signora," Victor continued, "Maybe tell them long distance only from America. That will help."

Tom and Maria thanked Victor for everything and told him they did not really need him to drive them around tomorrow, but he insisted whenever they needed him, he or one of his other drivers would be there. They agreed Tom and Maria would call him in the morning and discuss it further.

Victor left to go home then Tom and Maria went into the elevator to go up to their room. As they came out of the elevator Tom handed Maria the case with the medals so he could undo his tie and take out the key. Then he took it back so she would not have to carry it down the long corridor. As they approached the room, he had the key in his left hand and the case in his right. Maria offered to take the case again so he could open the door.

They went inside and locked the door behind them. Tom put the key down on the dresser and Maria placed the case right next to it. She turned and looked at him and they just stared for a moment. Then she said, "Unbelievable."

Chapter 48

They took some time to settle down and each had a turn in the bathroom. They wanted to go to one of the nearby restaurants they had come to love but Victor's warning held some gravity. Since they had never experienced anything like this before.

"Maybe if we change our clothes to something very casual, they won't recognize us," Maria suggested.

"That might work, even better," Tom added, "maybe we should go out separately and meet up at the corner." This seemed to be the right plan, so they changed. Tom decided to go down first to scope it out. It felt to them like they were in an action movie about spies and needed to keep a low profile. It was a bit humorous since this was so out of place for them.

"If anybody approaches me, I'll come right back. Then we'll take Victor's advice," Tom said as he left. "See you in a few minutes."

Ten minutes later, Maria came down and met him at the agreed upon location. There were no reporters nearby. They walked the four blocks to the restaurant they had hoped to go to and asked the host to seat them towards the back in a quiet booth. They got to the restaurant at around eight thirty.

The dinner was relaxing and everything they had hoped for. By the time they were finished, it was well after ten o'clock. Even for a Monday evening, the restaurant was full. They walked out without anyone noticing. "Maybe it is over," Tom said, "You know............ the publicity. How big of a story can some old guy getting a few medals be anyway?" Maria nodded, seeming to agree.

After returning to their room at around eleven thirty, the phone rang with the expected long-distance call from America.

"Person to person call for either Tom or Maria Santorini please," the operator said. Linda had gone to Richard's house in anticipation of calling their parents in Rome. Maria took the phone first. It was as if she held in all her excitement from the day and let it out at this very moment.

"You wouldn't believe what happened today," she started, "I am so proud of this man standing in front of me."

She went on and on about the awards, the medals, the ceremony itself and of course, the reporters. "Those flash bulbs were blinding," she continued, "and the applause, well they were just so loud."

Tom was beginning to get a bit embarrassed by it all. "Do I get a turn?" he said, tapping Maria on the right arm.

"Well," she said with a silly grin, "I have to brag about everything they said about you. These are your children after all. They should know what the people here think of you."

"You'll have plenty of time to brag when we get home," Tom said showing his embarrassment.

They each took turns talking to both Richard and Linda but also tried to keep it short. Long distance calling from New Jersey to Rome was an expensive pastime.

It was getting late, and it was after midnight by the time they got off the phone. Maria still wanted to take her lovely evening bath she had become spoiled with. Tom figured it was good to sit up for a while and let the meal digest. They stayed up until almost two thirty in the morning. It took that long for them to both wind down.

• • • •

THE NEXT MORNING WAS another one of those 'wake up when you feel like it' mornings. It was almost eleven o'clock when they finally got up and about. Breakfast was far past in all the bistros. There was a café nearby which served muffins and coffee anytime. They had gone to this one on the first morning they were in Rome. That was the morning they had originally gone to the government building to fill out the pension papers.

As they walked through the lobby of the hotel, the desk clerk stepped out from behind the front desk and excused himself.

"Pardon me Signor and Signora," he said, "are you the couple who were interviewed for the news last evening just outside of our lobby?"

Tom hesitated some and then nodded they were. "Did you see yourselves on the news last night?" he asked.

"No, we didn't," Maria chimed in, "We went out for a late dinner and then spoke with our children in New Jersey. Why? Were we on Television?"

"Oh yes," he said with exhilaration, "and in all of the newspapers this morning. Everyone on the hotel staff has been talking about it all morning." He looked at Tom. "You're Signor Gaetano Santorini is that correct, the man we learned so much about in school?"

"That's what they tell me," Tom admitted, "It's still all too new for me."

"I won't keep you Signor," he continued, "I just wanted to say how proud we are to have you staying here with us in our hotel. If there is anything you need, please don't hesitate to ask."

"Thank you," Tom said politely. He looked at Maria with the look that said, 'Let's go.' It was still all too embarrassing for him to absorb.

They went to the café and sat down outside. Both ordered the same thing, a muffin with their coffee and tea just as they had planned. When their coffee came, someone walked up to their table and placed a pad of paper and a pencil in front of

Tom. "Signor, please excuse me, but could you give me your autograph?"

Tom looked up startled. "I've................... never done this before," he replied, "I'm not sure what to do, just sign my name?"

"Please sign it to Deborah," the stranger said, "It is for my wife. We saw you on the news last night and I told her I could tell which hotel you were staying in from seeing the interview. I work in this café and was hoping I would see you today, since it is so close by."

"Oh," Tom said a bit taken by it all, "to Deborah?"

"Yes Signor. It would mean so much to her," he repeated.

Tom signed it 'To Deborah, best wishes, Tom Santorini.' He handed it back to the man and he looked quickly at it. A look of shock came over him. "Signor?" he said, "I thought you were the famous Gaetano Santorini. Are you someone else?" the man looked thoroughly embarrassed at asking what seemed to be a total stranger for his autograph. Only to find out he signed a different name than he was expecting.

Tom looked at it and chuckled. "Oh, I am so sorry," he said sheepishly, "Tom is my name in America. I've grown used to it and rarely use Gaetano these days. Please allow me to do this again."

The man turned the page and handed the pad back to Tom. This time he signed it Gaetano Santorini then handed it back. The man had a big smile on his face as he left their table. "I suppose I need to remember that just in case this happens again," he said to Maria after the man was far enough away so he would not hear. They started to look around and noticed most of the people in the café were staring at them.

"Maybe we should call Victor," Maria said, "It might be better if we had someone who could whisk us away if we need to."

Tom agreed. They hurried to finish their light breakfast and returned to their room to call Victor. It was obvious they were not going to be able to continue as typical tourists since they had been on the evening news and in all the papers.

On the way to the room, Maria stopped and noticed some of the papers on the news stand just outside of the hotel. She picked up the first two she could grab and paid the attendant. He took the money without much acknowledgement. But then did a double take when he saw Tom standing next to her. "You're the man with the medals!" he exclaimed.

Tom nodded his head reluctantly and they both wasted no time making a beeline to their room. It was midday Tuesday, and their ship was not due to depart from Napoli until Friday morning. The thought of being trapped in their room for the next two days did not appeal to them at all, so they called Victor to see if he could offer any alternatives.

"Victor?" Maria said, "It's Maria."

"Good afternoon, Signora," he replied, "I was wondering why I hadn't heard from you this morning."

"We slept in," she said, "sorry to say we didn't take your advice last night and went out for dinner."

"Was everything all right?" he asked, "no reporters."

"No reporters," she said, "But that was nothing compared to this morning. Did you know Tom and I were on the news?"

"Oh yes," he said, "I saw it for myself. My car was on the news too. But no one cares about my car." He began to chuckle trying to make the situation more lighthearted.

"Here, let me have you talk to Tom," she said handing Tom the phone.

"Good morning, Signor," Victor said cheerfully, "I hear you have had some excitement this morning."

"Not too bad," Tom said, "The desk clerk came up to us. There was a man at the café who wanted me to sign my autograph. That was very strange. People were staring at us. And then there was the newspaper attendant. So yeah, we came right back to our room."

"I see Signor," Victor added, "What do you wish to do?"

"Well," Tom continued, "It's obvious we won't be able just walk around like we've done before all of this. So, we were wondering if maybe you might have some suggestions. You've steered us right so far."

"When did you say you needed to get back to Napoli?" Victor asked.

"The original plan was we would check out of this hotel on Thursday morning and take the train back to Napoli picking up a room there so we could get to our ship early," Tom explained.

"Let me call you right back Signor," Victor said, "Oh, on second thought, you did tell them not to put any local calls through to your room, right?"

"Yes, we did," Tom replied.

"So, call me back in a half hour," Victor continued, "I'll make some phone calls. I have an idea that might work."

Tom agreed and hung up. They wondered what to do for half an hour while Victor made his calls. Maria remembered Anna would likely try to call and not get through. She called her to fill her in on what had been happening.

"We've never had anything like this happen," Maria said.

"You sure have had an exciting week, haven't you?" Anna added, "so what do you think you will do?"

"Hard to say," she continued, "Victor, the nice man who has been driving us around is supposed to look into some options. We'll call him back in a little bit. I'll let you know what the plans are when I find out. I still want you to meet Tom."

She hung up the phone and Tom laid down on the bed and kicked off his shoes. Maria went into the bathroom to freshen up. When she came back, Tom had dozed off. She did not want to lie down herself, because she figured she would do the same thing, so she grabbed her book and sat by the window to read.

About forty-five minutes later she noticed the time. "Tom!" she whispered, "It's time to call Victor back."

Tom lifted his head since he was not sound asleep and then sat up. He looked at the clock next to the bed. "Oh, right," he said and picked up the phone.

Maria got up and came to sit next to Tom on the bed. "Victor?" Tom said, "you told us half an hour, but I fell asleep. Sorry for the delay."

"That's all right Signor," Victor said, "I just got off the phone myself."

"What did you find out?" Tom asked.

"Well, I called my cousin," he continued, "what would you say if you spend your last two days here in Italy at a villa on the Mediterranean?"

"A villa?" Tom said, surprised.

Maria looked at him, "A villa?" she repeated.

"Where?" Tom asked as if he would know where it was.

"My cousin owns a villa near San Fabiana Circeo," he said.

Tom realized he had no idea where it was. "Is it nice there?" he asked, "And how much would it be?"

Victor started to laugh over the phone. "No, no Signor. You don't understand. Once I told my cousin Fredo you were the famous Gaetano Santorini, he insisted you be his guests."

"Victor, not you too," Tom said, "Please, don't say famous, I still can't get used to it."

Victor laughed even harder knowing Tom was such a shy man and not used to all the attention. "Of course, Signor, what you say," he continued to laugh. Tom rolled his eyes at Maria since she could tell what the conversation was about and could hear Victor laughing.

"When?" Tom asked.

"Today if you like?" Victor responded. I can pick you up in two or three hours and then drive you down. We could be there late evening. And then you could stay until early Friday morning. Then I will bring you directly to your ship."

"What do you think?" Tom said to Maria, "A villa on the Mediterranean to ourselves for a whole two days?"

"Well Signor," Victor chimed in, "I would be in the guest quarters."

"Oh," Tom said, "Of course you would."

Tom and Maria looked at each other for a moment then Maria started to giggle nervously. "A villa? Overlooking the Mediterranean? Oh boy. Can we?" she said like a schoolgirl.

"Yeah," Tom said just as excitedly.

"So, it's done," Victor said able to hear them discuss it. "I'll be there at five o'clock to pick you up. You will have to check out of your room."

"That's right. And pack too," Tom added as he said good-bye to Victor.

"I'll call the front desk. It's too late to check out today, they'll probably charge us for tonight as well," he said looking at Maria as he hung up the phone.

"So, what," Maria said, "the villa is free. And we'll be checking out early which saves Tony two nights from his offer to pay for the room while we're here."

Tom called down immediately to give them time to calculate the bill. "I understand it is too late to check out for today," he said to the clerk, "this just came up. We understand if you have to charge us for tonight as well."

The desk clerk was very cordial as would be expected. But he did not commit to what the charges for that day would be.

Tom hung up and then they started to pack. It seemed to take much longer than they had expected. The original plan was to start packing on Wednesday evening and take their time. It was around three thirty when they finally got things ready to go so Tom decided to go downstairs to settle the charges and check out. Maria stayed upstairs in the room since she had some items which still needed to be packed properly.

"Why don't you call Anna back," Tom said, "It doesn't look like I'm going to be able to meet her after all."

"Oh, she'll be show disappointed," Maria pined, "she helped me so much."

"Make sure you exchange addresses with her," Tom added, "that way we can keep in touch. If we come back, we can meet up with her then."

Maria nodded, understanding full well this was just the way it was. Tom gave her a kiss and went to the elevators. The elevator door opened in the lobby and Tom hesitated. He did not want to venture out and come across people who had seen him on television or in the papers. The lobby was slow at that hour, so he tried to walk as inconspicuously as possible.

"Excuse me," he said to the desk clerk, "I called down a couple of hours ago. We were going to check out today."

The clerk looked up at him and his eyes lit up, "Oh, of course Signor Santorini, right away." he said and turned nervously. He signaled the head clerk who came right over.

"Yes Signor," he said to Tom, "You wish to check out late today."

"Yes," Tom said feeling a bit embarrassed, "Someone made us an offer to stay at a villa, and we couldn't pass it up."

"Of course, Signor," the head clerk said, "We understand but as you would imagine we will be sad to see you leave."

"You are very kind," Tom replied, "I came down to check out and pay the bill."

The clerk grinned and lowered his head briefly, "Signor, your bill has already been taken care of."

Tom paused for a moment, not certain what he meant. Maybe Tony had already paid it by sending a check from New Jersey or maybe he was simply mistaken. "I don't understand. What did you mean 'taken care of'?" he asked.

"Most certainly Signor," the head clerk said with a broad smile, "the management has insisted you and lovely wife be our guests at no charge."

Tom stared at him without saying anything since this was not something he had expected. "I.......I don't understand," he repeated.

The head clerk was clearly enjoying this opportunity, "You are one of our nation's heroes Signor. It would only be right for us to have your stay here as our guest. It will be on the house."

Tom was taken aback at his offer. He did not know how to respond other than to stammer a few times "Uh and oh."

"Please let us know when you need the bell captain to come for your bags. We will be glad to accommodate you. And please come visit us again Signor," the head clerk said.

Tom reached out to shake his hand and thanked them over and over again. He was obviously embarrassed by the gesture. As he walked back to the elevator, he tried to figure out how he would explain it to Maria. This was a real shock to him.

He walked into the room while Maria was coming out of the bathroom with the last of her things from in there. "Everything all right Tom?" she asked, "did they charge us for tonight?"

Tom stood there not saying anything with a confused look on his face. "What?" she asked. Tom continued to say nothing even thought his mouth started to move as if to speak.

He shook his head and looked at her. "You're not going to belief this," he said.

"Believe what?" Maria asked, puzzled.

"Our stay here," he stammered, "our entire stay here was free."

Maria paused not certain if she heard him correctly. She shook her head and like Tom began to mouth the words without saying them.

Tom nodded his head up and down and repeated himself, "That's right. Free. They said our stay was on the house."

"That's impossible," Maria exclaimed, "This is not a cheap hotel...... ....how can they do that?"

"Probably easier than we can," Tom chuckled, "Like you said, they're not a cheap hotel."

They were pretty much speechless for the next hour until Victor came. He called up from the lobby to let them know he had arrived. Tom called the front desk and asked the bell captain to send someone for their bags. Victor had the car waiting at the front door and the bellhop brought their bags right to him. He placed all their belongings in the trunk of the car and then Tom gave the bellhop a sizable tip especially considering the generosity of the management.

They noticed some people looking at them and pointing, but nobody approached them. Tom and Maria got into the car and Victor started up the engine. As they left the hotel driveway, both Tom and Maria turned to look out the back window. When they turned back around Tom looked at Maria and said, "We have to come back here someday."

Chapter 49

Victor took the route just inland from the coast. It was the best way to avoid the summer traffic of people going to their vacation spots. The road took them through Pomezia and Aprilia. Just after they passed Latina they discussed stopping for dinner. It was approaching eight o'clock and they were all rather hungry.

Tom and Maria had gone for coffee and a pastry at around eleven o'clock and realized they did not take time for lunch. Victor had eaten lunch but was more than ready for a good meal as well. They stopped to get petrol for the car. While there, Victor asked the attendant if he could recommend a good place to stop.

His recommendation turned out to be a little bit of a disappointment compared to the restaurants they had become used to in Rome, but it was acceptable for eating on the road. Victor guaranteed them San Fabiana Circeo would have several good restaurants for them to eat the next two nights.

They arrived at San Fabiana Circeo just after ten o'clock and Fredo was there to greet them and give them a tour of the place to help them settle in.

Victor walked up to him at the front door while Tom and Maria were getting out of the car. "Victor," Fredo said as he gave him an embrace.

"Fredo," Victor responded, "It's been too long."

These two cousins had grown up close to one another and were like brothers. So naturally if Victor would ask, Fredo would deliver.

"Fredo," Victor continued as he turned to look back at the car "I would like you to meet two of the nicest people I have met for a long time. From America, the Santorinis."

Tom looked at Victor hoping Fredo would not do the famous hero line but to no avail. "Ah Signor and Signora, it is my humble pleasure to meet you both. And what an honor to meet such a notable person. None other than the famous Gaetano Santorini." Tom smiled politely and gave Victor a nudge.

"Fredo?" Victor added, "you remember what we talked about right?" Fredo nodded knowing full well what he was referring to. "You promised not to tell anyone they are here until after they leave, right...Right?"

"Yes, I promised," he said, "And I'll keep my word. But after they leave, I get to tell everyone Gaetano Santorini stayed at my villa."

"Of course," Victor responded like the big brother.

"Humph," Fredo grunted then looked back at Tom and Maria, "Please, let me show you around."

"Grazie," Tom said.

"I'll get your bags," Victor said as Tom and Maria went into the house.

It was too late for them to get a good look at the surroundings, but they could see the Mediterranean from the terrace just outside of the bedroom. The moon lit up the water exactly right, so they could see how far away it was from the villa. They were only three hundred meters from the beach. The Villa was on a small hill. There were no other homes between them and the water.

"The property between here and the beach is ours, so you won't have to be bothered by anyone when you want to go down for a walk," Fredo said proudly, "Victor knows his way around. He can show you. I will have to be at my shop all day tomorrow."

After showing them the layout of the villa Fredo excused himself and left for the night. He had promised to take them out for dinner on Thursday evening to his favorite place.

"My room is downstairs if you need me," Victor said, "what time would you like to have breakfast in the morning? I will fix you a something nice."

"Oh, Victor," Maria said, "you don't have to fix us breakfast. We can just get something at a café or something."

Victor chuckled, "Ah, Signora, I'm afraid there are no cafés nearby. The nearest place would be quite a drive. We are in the county here. You wouldn't be able to walk anyplace other than places on the beach. They are a bit of a walk."

"All right then," she responded, "breakfast it is."

"Nine o'clock?" Tom chimed in.

Victor nodded his head. "Nine o'clock. Good night then."

Tom and Maria went into the bedroom and opened the bag they had packed which had only the essentials for a short stay. They figured they would be getting in late, so they prepared what they needed in one bag. Off the bedroom was a terrace. It was too inviting to just go to bed. So, they walked out and leaned on the railing.

There was a warm breeze coming off the water. They could smell the sea air. There was not much to say to each other. The experience said it all. This was quite different from looking out their back porch in Jersey City. Even their vacations at the Jersey shore did not come close to this. They just stood there leaning on the railing and gazed out at the sea for over an hour before going to bed.

They left the doors open to the terrace so they could feel the breeze all night. The air was warm at first but by two o'clock in the morning it began to get chilly in the room. Neither of them wanted to get up to shut the door, so they rolled close to each other and helped one another keep warm. They were both very content with the arrangement.

Eight o'clock came fast and the breeze was still chilly in the room. Neither of them really wanted to stay in bed. But the fresh air blowing in and the nip in the air made it very tempting. It set the stage for the day with all the peace and quiet they had hoped for.

• • • •

VICTOR HAD BREAKFAST ready when they came down. He had made muffins and was ready to scramble the eggs once they had sat down to their morning coffee and tea.

"So, Signor and Signora," Victor asked, "I hope you slept well."

"The air is so fresh here," Maria said, "We left the door open all night."

Victor smiled. He was happy they were enjoying themselves. "I would do that whenever I came here as a boy as well," he said, "this is a special place for my family."

"What will you do today?" Tom asked.

Victor thought for a bit. "I will drive you wherever you want to go," he replied.

"Not today, Victor," Tom said, "We don't plan to go anywhere but right here and maybe walk along the shore."

"Shore?" Victor asked, "The beach, you mean the beach."

"In New Jersey we call it the shore," Tom chuckled realizing most people did not. Being they had been talking to Victor in English, the American terms were coming out.

"Ah, shore it is," Victor said and then realized what he had said, "Shore it is............ sure, it is.......... that's funny."

Maria had heard that one far too many times to laugh but she chuckled a bit because Victor was enjoying himself so much.

"I don't know if I'll go to the shore as you say, but I will go for a nice walk," Victor added, "I have friends in the area. I'll see if any of them are home today."

"You promise not to.........." Tom started.

"I promise not to tell anyone the famous Gaetano Santorini is staying at our family villa. I promise," Victor said with a smirk.

"Stop with the famous stuff already," Tom quipped. They smiled at one another and sat down for breakfast as the eggs were now ready.

• • • •

TOM AND MARIA WASTED no time heading down the path to the shore. It was the most inviting thing so far on the trip. Being it was during the middle of the week, and these were mostly private beaches, they only saw a few people on their walk. Not one of them gave any indication they recognized them. It was all they could hope for.

There is no getting lost when you are walking along the beach. The land was almost straight east to west where they were. Most of the coastline runs north to south. But at this point the land turns to the east. So, the villa faced directly south looking over the sea. Ships could be seen further out as well as many pleasure boats closer to shore.

Overall, it was a day filled with soft warm breezes and the sounds of sea birds and gentle waves. Most of the businesses down on the beach were closed, but there was a small snack shop open. They stopped in to get something to drink. Tom had remembered to bring some money just in case they needed something or possibly came across a place where they could buy a souvenir.

There was some seating outside under an awning. They were the only two people there. The breeze continued to blow which helped them to stay cool. They sat for an hour before deciding to head back. As they were about to leave, Maria noticed someone had left a newspaper on one of the other tables. When she walked by, she glanced at it. On the front page was their picture standing on the stage at the government building from Monday. She calmly turned it over and kept walking. As they left, she told Tom what she had seen. "Glad the person who bought the paper had already left," he said. Neither of them wanted any more publicity for a while.

That evening Victor drove them to a restaurant he was familiar with. He had made arrangements for a secluded area near the back. He did not tell the owner who was coming. All he said was they were special friends from America, and they preferred a quiet spot. That along with a sizable tip guaranteed a choice table, and silence if he figured out who they were.

The meal was heavenly. One of the best they had on the trip. Which was significant considering some of the fabulous restaurants they had gone to in Rome. They stayed out until midnight. Both Tom and Maria looked forward to spending some more time on the terrace outside of the bedroom. Rarely do you get to repeat such an enjoyable experience. But this was an exception. The second night was as pleasant as the first. As was the cool breeze which blew in all night.

"Our last day," Maria said as they woke up. There was a sadness to the sound of her voice. Tom did not say anything, but it was obvious he felt the same. They had agreed with Victor the night before on a light breakfast with just some pastry they had brought home with them the night before. That would suffice along with coffee and tea.

There was a bit of a cloud mix early morning. The previous day saw a clear blue sky. The clouds were not enough to bring rain, but it did change the feel of the day. Victor sensed the change in demeanor. "May I suggest............. a drive through the park," he said.

"Park?" Maria asked.

"Yes," Victor continued, "There's a national park nearby. It has many wonderful things to see. You can see dunes and marshes and a forest area too." He was trying to convince them. It would not be too difficult to do. Both of them were open for some excitement since they were not able to be typical tourists anymore.

"We can go in about an hour and be back in plenty of time for dinner with Fredo," he added.

"That's right," Tom said, "dinner with Fredo tonight...looking forward to it," Tom was hoping Fredo would keep his word and not tell anyone about who was staying at his villa.

They took their time getting ready. They were still out the door within the hour. Victor knew exactly where he was going. The Parco Nazionale del Circeo had been one of his favorite places to go when he was a teenager. There was a view of the sea which was more than beautiful.

As they were leaving, Victor put a basket into the front seat next to him. "A picnic lunch," he said.

"Victor," Maria said, "you think of everything." Tom and Maria had become very fond of this very generous man. They had only known him for a few days but felt very close to him as if they had been friends their whole lives.

The afternoon was filled with fantastic sights and new things. This was the first time either of them had seen a strawberry tree complete with fruit. "Where we come from, Strawberries grow close to the ground and not on trees," Maria said.

"They aren't actually Strawberries," Victor said, "They just call them that since their fruit looks like a strawberry."

"I suppose they only grow in the Mediterranean area?" Tom asked.

"Believe it or not, they grow in Ireland too," Victor added, "my Papà taught me that years ago."

"Look!" Maria said pointing up at a tree nearby, "Is that what I think it is?"

Victor looked up and smiled, "a Falcon?" he said.

"We usually only see those in captivity," Maria said, "I saw one in the zoo in New York once. She's beautiful."

"He," Victor said trying not to correct her, "the small ones are the males. This one is quite small. Maybe a young one."

They got back in the car and headed down the hill towards the dunes. The roads were narrow and not really suited for Victor's car. But he took it slowly and they were able to get to most of the places they wanted to see. By six o'clock they were all very tired.

"Victor," Tom said, "We should head back so we can get some rest and shower for dinner. Fredo would appreciate it if we look fresh for dinner, I'm sure."

"You mean you're shore?" Victor chuckled amused by his newfound humor. Maria just shook her head.

They headed back and got to the villa by seven. The plan was to go out around nine o'clock for dinner, so this gave them time to all shower and even rest for a bit. Tom napped for about twenty minutes while Maria got ready.

Fredo was right on time as he promised. He left his car at the villa and Victor drove since he had the larger car and knew exactly where they were going. This was the family's favorite restaurant and everyone in the family knew how to get there.

Victor and Fredo were in the front seat talking. They seemed to have some disagreement about something. Victor turned to him and said, "you tell them."

Fredo was a bit embarrassed but turned around nonetheless and said to them, "I really hope you won't mind, but I asked my daughter and her husband to join us tonight."

"We don't mind," Maria said, "You invited us if you recall. You can invite anyone you wish." Tom nodded his head to agree politely. He was, however, concerned about whether it would turn into a spectacle about what had occurred on Monday.

"I told them you were friends of Victor's from America, but didn't tell them anymore," Fredo said trying to calm any concerns they may have. "My daughter Andrea knows the story of how you saved Victor's brother many years ago. I would like to tell her after you leave that it was you, she had dinner with."

Tom was moved by his sincerity. "Fredo," he said quietly, "you can tell her while we are together. It's all right. It would be for the right reasons. It is about family after all."

Fredo's eyes began to tear up. "Grazie Signor," he said with a shaky voice, "It would mean a lot to us."

Tom nodded his head and turned to look out the window afraid he may tear up as well. The rest of the way to the restaurant, no one said anything.

Chapter 50

The plan for the morning was that Tom and Maria would get up at around six o'clock to get ready. They would stop close by for a nice breakfast and then head to Napoli to board the ship bound for New York. They hoped to arrive by ten o'clock in order to keep with their original intentions of getting on board early.

The restaurant experiences the night before had been very moving for Tom. As Fredo told his daughter she was having dinner with the man who saved the life of one of her dearest family members she reached out to touch Tom's hand. "Signor," she said, "Our world does not have enough men like you." Tom's eyes became glazed with tears as he just nodded and thanked her. But she insisted it was her who must thank him.

This memory stayed with him on this morning as he began the trip back home. From here on in, things would be different. Maria now knew everything. Most of these stories had stayed with him for decades with minor exceptions. It was necessary for Tom so he could move on with his life. His inner struggles were just that, his. He saw no reason to cause his darling wife to relive these things with him. After all, when they met, Tom had already been home for over a year. Why bring up the past when it was not her past.

In the car, they spoke about their trip. When they arrived in Rome, they did not know what to expect. Looking back, they had hoped to have seen more of it. The unforeseen events of the first week put a quick stop to that. The conversation then turned to Tom's hometown of Montoro Superiore. Tom had not felt as connected to it as he had thought he might have been. However, they still decided on the next trip, if there ever was one, would include going back to Montoro Superiore and spending more time there looking for whatever memories Tom could find and share.

The ceremony for the medals and awards still seemed like a dream to them. They were not quite sure how they would be able to tell their friends about it without sounding like they were making the whole thing up. Then there where the reporters. They found it interesting to be on the other side of the microphone and cameras. Usually, they would watch other people in that predicament. They would never watch a news interview the same again.

By the time they were approaching Napoli they were talking about the Parco Nazionale del Circeo and all the beautiful sights there. The recap of their trip helped them to see a completion of their time in Italy. They kept promising Victor they would come back and when they did, they would definitely visit him. They felt they needed to reassure him since he kept bringing it up. It was obvious he did not want to see them go.

"Parking will be very difficult at the docks," Victor said, "It may be best if I just drop you off and leave right away. I have to drive back home by evening."

None of them wanted this moment to come. Victor had become a very dear friend. "Maybe you can come visit us in America," Maria said trying to reassure him.

"I would like that," Victor said nodding his head, "I will look into it." He knew it would not likely happen though. He did not have much saved up and his car was going to need to be replaced before long. Still though, offering it helped them with parting.

Tom had the directions to which dock the Christoforo Columbo was set to leave. This was the same ship they had arrived on less than two weeks earlier. The ship had not returned to America but had made a short trip to Greece while they were in Rome. So much had happened in such a short time.

Even though Tom had been to this harbor three times now, he did not really know his way around. Victor had to ask for directions as he got close to the docks. It all looked so confusing. His mind was more on having to say good-bye than finding his way. But his instincts guided him, so he did not get lost.

Victor pulled up to the passenger unloading area just after ten thirty. He sat in the driver's seat for a moment before getting out just looking down. Maria figured he was composing himself. "Well, this is it," he said trying to convince himself, "We're finally here...............Time to get out." He paused for a moment more then opened the door abruptly as if he were fighting the effort.

The unloading area was not too busy yet since they were early. Tom had checked before leaving the boat upon their arrival as to whether it would be all right to board early. The steward assured him any time in the morning of the departure would be acceptable.

All their bags were out of Victor's trunk. He stood there again wishing this moment had not arrived. Maria walked over to him and gave him a hug. "We'll write once we get home," she said.

Victor nodded his head having trouble saying anything. Finally, he said, "I will too."

Tom reached out his hand and shook Victor's. "you've been very good to us Victor," Tom said, "you're a good man. I'm proud to say I know you."

Victor nodded his head rapidly trying not to start sobbing. "I will miss you both," he said, "now you need to get on your ship and find that cabin with your name on it before they give it to someone else." He began to chuckle while wiping his eyes.

"Maybe if we're lucky they will give it to someone else," Tom quipped.

Maria looked at him. "Tom?" she said.

"It is a pretty small cabin after all," he responded, "besides, then we will have to stay. Maria grinned knowing he was trying to make up for what he said.

Tom and Maria had discussed earlier whether they should offer Victor some money for driving them. His brother had insisted early on they were not to pay for the car service. It was to be all covered by him. Considering the circumstances, they did not want to insult Victor by giving him a tip. After all, there was not enough money in either of their wallets to properly compensate Victor for all he had done for them.

A ship steward saw them at the end of the gangway and came to help them with their bags. Victor would not be able to come aboard since he did not have a ticket. They hugged again and shook hands again then realized this was indeed farewell. Victor walked around to the driver's door and stood watching as they walked onto the ship. As they reached the top of the gangway, they turned and waved to him. He got in the car and drove away.

"Signor and Signora Santorini?" the steward said while examining their tickets. "Ah, I can show you to your cabin." Then he whispered to them, "We really are not supposed to escort people in the tourist class section, but you seem like such nice people and it's early." He gave them a wink.

Tom and Maria were glad to have some help. They had become somewhat familiar with the ship on the trip over and could have found their own way. But the steward was helping them with their bags, so it was appreciated.

The cabin on the return trip was closer to the stairway than the cabin on the way over. Tom was concerned to think it might be noisier than before. But they were on their way home and it was all that mattered at this point. The steward placed the bags in the cabin and began to leave. Tom gave him a tip as he passed him in the doorway.

"This cabin looks exactly like the other one," Maria said hoping this would make up for the potential noise from the stairway. Tom just nodded his head. It did not really matter to him.

"Let's go for a walk around," Tom suggested as they put their bags away.

"Great idea," Maria replied, "Maybe we can find something to drink. I'm thirsty all of a sudden."

They started up the stairway to find out if things on the ship were open already or if they were closed waiting until the ship was underway. The ship was not bustling yet, but they could tell it would not last for long. They remembered the trip coming over, and how crowded things could get with more than a thousand people on board. Still, they were headed home.

The first lounge they came across was closed but one of the other lounges was open on the next deck. It was not tourist class, but they were allowed up until the ship was underway and then they would have to use the other lounge designated for tourist class passengers.

The lounge overlooked the harbor rather than the dock. It was a relaxing view for them as they drank their lemonade. The conversation had shifted from the things they had done while in Italy to what they would need to do when they got home. There was still almost a week of vacation left considering the trip back, but this felt like the end of it for them.

Overall, it was over an hour before they returned to their cabin. As they went down the stairway, they noticed two men were standing by their cabin door. It was the steward who had escorted them and what appeared to be the head steward with him.

They did not think much of it since there was likely a great deal of work needed to be done by all of the stewards. And it was just a coincidence they were talking near their cabin.

The steward who escorted them noticed them coming down the stairs and tapped his superior on the shoulder nodding in their direction. The chief steward turned around and suddenly became extremely nervous. Tom figured they had made a mistake on their cabin assignment and were afraid to tell them. That would likely explain the nervous reaction.

"Ah, Signor," the chief steward said as they approached, "Signor and Signora Santorini? Is that correct?" This further confirmed Tom's suspicions.

"Yes, that's us," Tom replied.

He hesitated for a moment and then said, "The captain would like to see you at your convenience Signor."

Tom looked at Maria and shrugged his shoulders, "We need to stop in the cabin for a moment, if that's all right?" he replied.

"Certainly, Signor," the chief steward said, "steward Barnes here will be just outside the door to escort you to see Captain Fanucci when you're ready."

Tom nodded his agreement, and they went inside. Both wanted to use the bathroom and freshen up a bit. They closed the door and Tom whispered to Maria. "Imagine that Maria, the captain wants to see us."

It only took about five minutes for them to get ready. They opened the door and sure enough, the steward was there waiting and still acting nervously. "Please follow me," he said politely.

They followed him up the stairs and walked for quite a while. This part of the ship was unfamiliar to them since they had stayed mostly in the tourist class section on the way over to Italy. The steward walked them into a room which looked more like it belonged in an office building than a ship. It was the captain's office along with several other members of the crew.

"Please have a seat," the steward said pointing to the couch against the wall, "the captain will be back in just a minute."

"Thank you," Tom replied and then sat down signaling Maria.

They sat in the room for only a minute or so when the captain came in. He immediately acknowledged them. "Ah, Signor and Signora Santorini," he said as Tom and Maria stood up to greet him. They both put out their hands to shake his. "Are you the same people we heard about this week in the papers and on the news?"

They knew what he was referring to even though it had been a couple of days which they had been free of the notoriety. "You are the man they gave the medals to in Rome? The famous Gaetano Santorini?"

Tom knew his reluctance to accept this newfound status was something he needed to keep to himself. "Yes, indeed, it was a real surprise to us both," he said reaching out to Maria to take her hand, "I had no idea." Tom was trying to play it down somewhat.

"Well then," Captain Fanucci continued, "they tell me you're booked with us to New York." Tom acknowledged with a nod.

The captain nearly stood at attention and said, "Well Signor, no war hero rides in tourist class on my ship. We will adjust your accommodations accordingly." The only thing missing was a salute.

Tom and Maria slowly turned to look at one another. Not certain of what he had just said or what it meant, Maria asked, "What do you mean, adjust?" She figured they would get a nicer cabin with a porthole which they could look out and see the sunset. She knew how much Tom liked looking at the sunset on the ocean.

"We will provide you with first class accommodations immediately," he said proudly, "Nothing is too good for such a man as Gaetano Santorini."

Tom was thoroughly embarrassed by this point. Being called famous was one thing. Being treated to a first-class accommodation was another. "Why thank you sir," Tom said quietly not certain how to react. He put out his hand again to shake the captain's one more time.

"You will also be guests at my table for dinner tomorrow night." Captain Fanucci said, "tonight will not work since my duties on the night we set out are always full. Steward Barnes will show you to your new quarters and then retrieve your bags from the other cabin." The captain signaled steward Barnes to show them the way.

They left the captain's office and followed him back down the hallway which they had come in from. "So, steward Barnes," Maria said striking up a conversation "We will have a nicer cabin then."

Steward Barnes looked at her. "Oh Ma'am, maybe you haven't ever seen one. You have been given a suite. We call it the Apartment Deluxe. They are usually full, but the captain held it for you once he knew you were coming on board. There was a cancellation day before yesterday, and three other parties were in line for it. The captain insisted they reserve it for you."

Maria looked at Tom. He had a look of continued disbelief. "How 'bout that?" he said quietly.

The steward took them to the port side of the ship at the highest level where all the finest cabins were located one level below the bridge. They entered their new accommodations and just stood at the doorway looking around. Neither of them had ever seen anything like this. The only thing they felt could be better was there were two twin beds separated by a nightstand.

It would have been preferable to have a double bed, but such was not common on cruise ships even in first class cabins.

This was still better than the cabin they had been in which was originally set up for two sets of bunk beds, each a twin size. The upper bunks had been converted into baggage storage in a few cabins. Most of the other tourist cabins were set up with four beds so families could stay together.

"You have access to the first-class lounge and the first-class pool if you like," steward Barnes added, "your apartment is close to the main promenade. But not so close that you'll be disturbed by others. The first-class dining room will have two sittings for each night. Your table assignments will be posted at the entrance each night. With of course the exception of tomorrow evening when you will be guests of the captain at his table."

This was all too much for them to absorb. Tom and Maria continued to gaze at the beauty of the apartment. "We'd better not get too used to this," Tom said quietly to Maria.

"I will return with your bags shortly," the steward said as he headed for the door.

"Oh, thank you," Maria said as he left. It only took about ten minutes for him to return with their bags. Fortunately, they had not begun to unpack. They had planned to do so after returning from the lounge.

"I can put these in the closet for you," the steward said as he opened a door next to the right bed. Then he pointed to some drawers at the end of the bed, "You have these dressers to use as well."

Tom reached into his pocket to get him a tip for bringing the bags. "Oh no Sir," he said politely holding his hand up, "you already gave me something today. It would not be right," Tom tried anyway but to no avail, "I insist sir."

"Well, okay then," Tom said as he put his hand back in his pocket. He was not sure what the proper protocol was for being in a first-class cabin so he figured he would just have to go with the flow.

As steward Barnes left, he said, "If you need anything, just dial zero on the phone and someone will assist you right away."

This was like the hotel they stayed at in Rome. Tom and Maria spent the rest of the afternoon wandering about the first-class section of the ship. The lounge was finished in maple and walnut panels. The chairs were leather and the one thing missing was the crowds. Much more room was set aside for the first-class accommodations.

The ship was about to set out from the dock, so Tom and Maria went to the main promenade to watch. It was quite different seeing it from such an angle. Neither of them had ever been this high on a ship before. The experience was a special treat for both of them. It took over an hour for them to head out of harbor and they watched every move the ship made treasuring the moment. It was a far cry from Tom's experience leaving this harbor when he was a boy.

The dock was far behind them by now. The wind was picking up and the ship was gaining speed slowly. They decided to go to the dining room to see if they were scheduled in the first or second seating. It was close by the lounge, so it only took a moment to check. Their names were not on the list. "You think they forgot about us?" Maria asked.

"They probably didn't have enough time to add our names," Tom replied, "After all, we've only been in first class for about four hours. I guess we'll have to give them some time."

"We should call like steward Barnes suggested," Maria added, "Based on the way they've treated us so far, I'm sure they wouldn't want to forget us for dinner."

"Good point," Tom said. They headed back to their room to call because it was only an hour away from the first seating. Within ten minutes of Maria calling, steward Barnes came and knocked on their door. Tom was closest so he went over to open it.

"They told me you were not on the list," he said, "I've seen to it you will be in the second seating. That will give you enough time to get ready."

"Why thank you," Tom said and closed the door as he left, "They sure do know how to treat you around here."

Maria chuckled, "I think you are getting used to this."

Tom chuckled too, "Sure am," he said.

Dinner and the evening at the lounge were so much fun, they did not want to go back to their 'Apartment Deluxe.' The sunset had already come and gone, but they were still in the Mediterranean. It was different from viewing it on the Atlantic. Tom was not as intrigued by this one. They got back to their room after ten o'clock and were both so exhausted they decided to go right to bed.

Chapter 51

Waking up on a ship at sea was something which Tom had some minor experience doing. It was certainly not something he was used to though. This time, being higher on the ship caused them to feel the motion of the ship more than at the lower level he was more familiar with. The seas were calm enough due to the time of year. But being on a ship has an unmistakable feeling.

There was a schedule of meals posted in their cabin, so they knew what time they needed to be at breakfast. It was served as a buffet and was set out for about an hour and a half between eight o'clock and nine thirty. Neither of them was especially hungry but they wanted to get up and about. They went to the dining room to sit with their coffee and tea. Once Tom saw the spread, he decided to fill a plate with scrambled eggs, breakfast sausage, and just a little bacon. He topped it off with some pancakes and syrup. Maria took a blueberry muffin.

"I thought you weren't hungry," she poked. Tom grinned and nodded.

An empty table by the window gave them the opportunity to just look out and enjoy the view of the sea. They were just about to pass the Rock of Gibraltar as they sat down, so they picked a table on the starboard side to get the best view. It was a beautiful morning. The sun was bright and there was not a cloud in the sky. They relaxed and watched the spectacle from a vantage point Tom had never been to before.

They had to look at the Rock from the portholes on the way over. Back when he came over on the Hallwick, he was more concerned about the U-boats than looking at the scenery. He practically ignored it on that trip. At that time, his eyes were glued to the sea looking for periscopes and torpedoes. But on this trip he sat with his wife and sipped their coffee and tea for quite some time watching as the ship passed and entered the Atlantic.

"I want to go swimming," Maria said as they were finishing.

"Did you pack a suit?" Tom asked. They had not used the pool at the hotel in Rome, so he did not know if they were prepared. Even though they had access to the tourist class pool on the way over, they had not taken advantage of it.

"Yes, I did," she replied, "and I even packed one for you."

"You did?" Tom said surprised, "Where was it. I didn't see it when I unpacked last week."

"It's in my suitcase Tom," she continued, "I washed them both the night before we left so I just put them both in mine. But after that breakfast, you have to wait an hour before going in the water."

Tom nodded his head showing his reluctant approval and confidence Maria would always take care of him. They headed back to their cabin to change and get ready for the pool. First class accommodations on an ocean liner lacked nothing. The morning was as relaxing as they had hoped. Maria and Tom sat back practically laying down on the deck chairs. "Not a care in the world," Maria said.

"Ain't that the truth," Tom said softly.

Extended time at the pool and a light lunch made Tom ready for a nap. They both agreed to lie down for about an hour in their 'Apartment Deluxe' and take a short snooze. Maria set the alarm so they would not waste the entire afternoon away.

It was two o'clock when they got up and went for another walk around the promenade. Before long they were back at the pool where they had spent the morning. The deck chairs looked just as inviting as before, so they took two which were together and facing out. The late afternoon breeze was warm and pleasant.

They did not want to stay out and about for too long. This was the night they would be guests of the captain at dinner.

The plan was to head back to the cabin and clean up for dinner around four o'clock or so. They got back just before four thirty. Tom took a shower while Maria got her clothes ready. She wanted to be presentable for the captain. It was after all a very prestigious thing to dine with the ship's captain. Only a few people on each voyage would get the honor.

Tom was ready long before Maria but that was not anything new. He stepped out and walked over to the promenade to watch the sea a little bit more. It was only about twenty minutes later Maria came out to let him know she was ready. Dinner was not for nearly an hour yet but as Tom always said, 'If you can't be there on time, be early.'

The lounge was bustling for an hour before. It became obvious most people in first class dressed for dinner. The first night was not so much of a formal event, but once out to sea, it was customary to dress for dinner. Tom and Maria were not aware of this, so it was a good thing they dressed for the occasion of eating with the captain. They would remember this for the rest of the journey home and agreed it would be a clever idea to follow suit.

They came into the lounge at about five thirty. Their seating with the captain was scheduled for six fifteen. Diner would be served at seven with the first forty-five minutes dedicated to conversation and appetizers.

Maria was starting to get a bit nervous at the prospect of having dinner with the captain. "He seems like a nice man," she said quietly into Tom's ear so no one would hear her, "I hope I don't say anything embarrassing."

Tom knew Maria tended to worry more before an event than during, so he was not concerned. "If he's anything like the captain I had the honor of working with years ago, you'll be fine." He was referring to Captain Stevens of the Hallwick. Even though it had been many years since he had seen him, the memory of that journey from New York to Napoli was still rich in his memory. It was probably the strongest memory from that season of his life.

They walked over to the captain's table at ten after six. One other family was already seated, and they looked even more nervous than Maria. It was a family of four, one son and one daughter. Tom and Maria introduced themselves as they approached.

"Good evening, we're Mr. and Mrs. Santorini," Maria said. She used their last name initially for the sake of the two children.

The husband stood to greet them. "Hi, we're the Arnolds," he said with a quivering voice reaching out his hand to shake Tom's, "I'm Jack, this is my wife Beth, that's short for Elizabeth............Ah.........but then again you probably knew that."

Tom nodded, he understood. "I'm Tom and this is my wife, Maria. That's not short for anything," he quipped trying to lighten Jack's awkwardness. They both laughed realizing everyone was anxious about dining with the captain.

"And these two are our children," Beth jumped in because moms usually introduce the children, "Sandy who's eleven, she's the oldest and Jack Jr., he just turned nine, yesterday as a matter of fact."

"Oh, Happy Birthday," Maria said. Having a son of her own she knew children loved birthdays at that age. "What grade are you going into when you get home?"

"Fourth?" young Jack said sheepishly.

"I have a granddaughter who is going into the fourth grade too," Maria said, "You look much older than her though." Jack Jr.

smiled. Every nine-year-old boy wants to be told he looks older than he actually is.

Tom and Maria took the seats which had their names on them. "Where are you from?" Maria asked.

"Philadelphia area," Jack replied, "Just north in Bucks County."

"Oh," Maria said, "I've never been to Pennsylvania, but I hear it's beautiful. What do you do there?"

"I work in the Steel industry," Jack answered.

"Jack just landed a big contract to supply all of the girders for the bridges on Interstate eighty. All the way from Pittsburg to Cleveland," Beth said proudly. Jack was a bit embarrassed and gave her the look. It did not faze her. "We decided to take a vacation to Europe so we could celebrate."

"And what do you do Tom?" Jack said, trying to get the subject off from him.

Tom hesitated for a moment "I'm a barber," he answered.

Jack tried hard not to look surprised. "Oh, we need barbers," he said realizing immediately how that sounded. He was not expecting someone else in first class to be a barber. "I mean it's a good line of work. I have a barber who I use all the time. Great guy, Bernie's his name. Maybe you know him." By now it was obvious Jack did not know how to get out of this.

"He lives in Pennsylvania as well?" Tom asked. Jack nodded his head with a look on his face which was just begging for forgiveness for saying the wrong thing. "Then I probably don't know him, sorry."

"Where do you live?" Beth asked trying to get Jack off the hook.

"Jersey City," Maria answered, "That's where Tom's barber shop is, in Jersey City."

Jack saw an opportunity and tried to redeem himself. "You own your own barber shop?" he asked hopeful this would work.

"Yes, I do," Tom said politely.

"A business owner," Jack jumped at the newfound chance to fix things, "I wish I owned my own business. I just work for someone else. Sales, you know, always with the quotas."

Tom knew Jack had not meant anything by the 'we need barbers' comment, so he decided to help him a bit. "Well someday you may own your own business," Tom said, "Who knows, the steel industry may not last forever."

"Oh, American steel?" Jack said surprised, "It's a sure thing for all of my life and probably Jack Junior's as well. I hope he follows in the old man's footsteps someday."

"Sounds good to me," Tom said just as another couple came to the table. They were all very relieved the focus could now be shifted to the new guests.

Both Tom and Jack stood up to greet them. "Good evening," Jack said extending his hand since they were seated right next to him, "Jack Arnold and this is Beth, Sandy and Jack Jr."

Tom also reached out his hand, "Tom...............Tom and Maria Santorini."

"Ben and Martha Anderson," the husband said, "Good evening. So, it looks like this is it for the table tonight?"

"Looks like it," Jack said, "Don't see any empty chairs except where the captain sits."

"How are you enjoying your trip so far?" Maria chimed in.

"It took me a while to calm down," Martha said, "I still get nervous whenever I'm at sea."

"Is it the motion?" Maria asked.

"No, not really," Martha said cautiously, "I think it's not being able to see what's below us. You know, in the water. How deep is it? What really holds us up at the top? I worry about that type of thing for about a day or so. Then I'm usually all right."

"Do you travel by ship often?" Beth joined in.

"Usually once or twice a year. Mostly when I go with Benjamin on his business trips," she replied.

"What line of work are you in?" Tom asked Ben.

"Banking," he answered, "I'm a commercial real estate mortgage banker. We mortgage large office buildings all over the US and Europe."

"How many trips do you take per year?" Jack asked.

"I'm good for at least six," Ben answered again.

"So, where's your office?" Tom asked.

"In New York," he replied simply, "our building is on Park Avenue, not far from the Pan Am building. You know the one where they land helicopters on the roof."

"Really?" Jack Jr. exclaimed, "They can land a helicopter on the roof of a building. I want to see that."

"Someday you may," Ben said, "And what line are you gentlemen in?"

A chill ran down Jack's back at the prospect of repeating the last conversation. "I'm in steel production," he said and finally learned to stop while ahead.

"And you Tom?" Ben asked, turning to Tom.

"I'm a barber," he said without hesitation this time.

"Tom has his own barber shop," Beth inserted.

Ben gave Tom a huge smile. "I don't believe it," he said, "my father's a barber. Still cuts hair to this day. He's in his seventies. Can't get him to retire, says he loves the people too much."

"Please don't give Tom any ideas," Maria said with a chuckle, "We're all trying to get him to retire."

Just then, the captain came to the table. The men stood up as he approached. "Please be seated, you are acting like members of my crew," he said with a hardy laugh, "Please, you're my guests."

"I want to first thank you sir for inviting us to join you for dinner," Ben said.

"Yes," Jack said, "It's a real honor."

"And a pleasant surprise," Tom added.

"Well, I find it to be the most pleasurable part of my job," Captain Fanucci said.

Tom and Maria sat quietly trying to get a feel for how things were going to develop. Captain Fanucci and Ben struck up a conversation about the last trip Ben had taken and how the weather had not cooperated. "I'm just glad Martha didn't come with me on that one," he said.

Maria and Beth started to talk about Tom and Maria's grandchildren and how it was much nicer to have grandchildren because you could always hand them back to their parents when you got too tired. "Can't imagine that," Beth said laughing. The two children sat as still as they could, having nothing to say and no one their age to talk to other than each other.

The appetizers came and the waiter offered them all wine, the adults that is. Captain Fanucci passed on the wine. "While at sea the captain of any ship should never touch a drop," he said confidently, "Even if you are off duty, an emergency could arise. You have to be ready."

"That's very respectable," Ben said, "It takes a good man to say that."

"Probably the best man at this table," Jack said laughing meaning mostly he did not feel like the best man himself. But as usual it did not come out that way.

The captain looked at him and paused for a moment then said, "I would love to own that title sir. But I cannot. That honor goes to the man who is sitting to my left. Signor Santorini. He's the best man at this table."

There was a brief silence as Jack and Ben looked over at this humble barber and tried to size up why Captain Fanucci would say that. Tom shyly nodded his head and said, "Thank you Sir. That was very kind." Maria reached and took Tom's hand then gave it a squeeze showing her agreement with what the captain had just said.

The table went back to conversation and then the dinner arrived. Tom and Maria had ordered the prime rib. There was a selection of either a chicken or fish dinner as well. Tom was never big on fish and chicken was a common meal at home, so the prime rib won out.

As they were all finishing with the meal and the waiters were taking away the plates Captain Fanucci looked over at Ben and Jack and asked them, "Did either of you watch any news this past week, maybe in your hotel rooms?"

Tom had a feeling he knew what he was referring to. "I did," Jack piped up. "Why?"

"Did you see anything about a man being awarded some medals?" he continued.

Jack thought for a moment and Beth chimed in. "Remember Jack. I think it was Monday night, something from Rome?"

Jack perked up, "Oh yeah. Some old guy. The news said something about them thinking he was dead. What about it?"

Captain Fanucci paused for a moment not sure what to make of the last thing said. "Well, that 'old guy' is sitting right there," he said pointing to Tom.

At least Jack knew when he had put his foot in his mouth. "I'm sorry about the old guy comment Tom, really," he said quietly.

"I think I read something in one of the papers," Martha said, "We get the paper delivered to our room in English and it's sometimes all I have to read in the morning if Ben is out on business. From World War one, wasn't it?"

"That's right," Captain Fanucci said, "Tom here has always been a well-known person to the Italian people. But what a surprise to everyone this week when we came to find out he has been alive all these years and living in America."

"Amazing," Ben said with his eyes opened widely, "A true war hero, right here at our table."

Tom was clearly embarrassed by the attention. "It's been an interesting week, to say the least," he said, "I still have a hard time with the hero part."

Young Jack Jr. was dying to jump in and ask all kinds of questions. Soldiers were his favorite people and having a soldier who was a hero right there where he could see him was exciting. But he had a hard time understanding how this gentle older man could be a soldier let alone a hero. Soldiers to him were young and tough.

"What did you get the medals for?" Beth asked.

Maria did not want to leave Tom to fend for himself, so she answered, "The list is rather long."

"It's actually too much for me to comprehend," Tom said trying to stifle the attention, "In ways, I wish I hadn't found out. The instant fame was a bit much."

"We actually left Rome and stayed at a private Villa a couple of hours from Napoli for the last two days," Maria added, "Tom's a private man and not used to attention."

"You seem troubled by the adulation," Captain Fanucci said.

"Some," Tom answered, "some."

"Well, I wish I had medals," Jack Jr. said finally having an opportunity to say something, "I think that's amazing." Beth tapped him on the knee to remind him he was not a grown-up and had to watch what he said.

"It was a very long time ago and....... quite frankly," Tom said, "I could do without the attention."

Captain Fanucci looked at him and said, "Sir, I don't think you understand. Those medals are just as much for the people of Italy as they are for you." Tom was taken aback not knowing exactly what he meant by that.

Seeing Tom was uncertain, he continued by addressing the entire table. "You see wars are a terrible thing and often we don't even know why we're fighting them. Some would say we should not fight at all. But we do."

Ben nodded his head because he understood what the captain was trying to say.

"When we are called to fight," the captain continued, "only a few really come through. I have read up on you, Signor. I first learned of you as a boy. They teach about Signor Gaetano Santorini in schools if you live in Italy you know." Everyone at the table had a look of astonishment on their faces. "Oh yes, this man right here is indeed famous in our country."

Tom was starting to feel a bit put out by the attention. "Well, where I come from, I'm just a barber," he said trying to maintain a certain politeness.

Captain Fanucci felt like he needed to reassure Tom as to his intentions. "The reason I mention all of this is to say, it isn't just the medals you received. It is what it all means to the rest of us as well. You see Signor, the first war we won, and the second was quite a different story. We all needed to remember there had been a time of heroes. I fought in the forties. I was in the Italian Navy. We entered the war thinking we were going to all be men like you. But we lost. This country needs its heroes, even if we have to go back forty years to find them."

Tom looked at Captain Fanucci and slowly nodded his head. "So, all the attention somehow helps the people of our county?" Tom asked.

"Very much so," Captain Fanucci answered, "Finding out you were actually alive brought a renewed feeling of national pride. So, all this attention which is being bestowed is not just for you. This means a great deal to all of us."

Maria gave Tom's hand another squeeze. He sat there silently pondering what Captain Fanucci had just said. It took all the events of the past two weeks into another realm. Tom realized this whole episode was not just about him and what he had done, but about how he and his fellow soldiers had effected a nation.

"The pride of a people is what holds them together," the captain said, "You Signor, make us proud........................and you deserve those medals." Captain Fanucci stood to his feet and put out his hand, "Allow me the honor to thank you personally and publicly for all you have done." Tom stood up slowly and reached his hand out to shake the captain's. "On behalf of the people of Italy Signor, I thank you for all you did for our country."

"Here, here." Ben said standing to his feet. He reached out his hand as well. Then Jack stood up awkwardly and shook his hand also. Jack Jr. had a smile on his face like his mother had never seen before. This was all too exciting for him.

Tom sat down trying to hold back the tears. This was the first time since everything had unfolded where he truly understood what it was all about. Heroism is a complicated thing. Because the actions of a single person have such an effect on so many others.

Chapter 52

C aptain Fanucci had duties which required him to return to the bridge following dinner. The work assignments for the night still needed to be completed due to the illness of one of his crew. He excused himself just before eight o'clock. Jack, Beth, and the children excused themselves right after he left. Ben and Martha sat for about ten minutes talking with Tom and Maria about their plans once they got home. Ben offered to take Tom out to lunch if he could make his way into the city. Tom agreed but knew it would likely never happen.

Maria tapped Tom on the knee. "Tom," she whispered, "we wanted to catch the sunset." This would be the first night they could watch the sunset over the Atlantic now they were clear of the Mediterranean.

"Well," Tom said, "Ben, Martha, we'll be seeing you on the rest of the trip, I'm sure."

"That you will," Ben said as he stood to shake Tom's hand again, "Maybe we can meet for drinks one evening."

"Sounds good," Tom said.

Tom and Maria left heading towards the port side of the ship. Being the ship was headed northwest, the sunset would be best viewed from the port bow. It was still thirty minutes until the sun set completely, but Tom wanted to take it all in.

This would be the very first time he would get to watch the sunset without looking through a porthole. While he had been on the Hallwick, even though he could have watched the sunset from on deck, every evening was cloudy or even stormy. On the stormy nights they had been ordered to stay below. So, this was going to be a special occasion for both of them.

"Look Tom," Maria said, "there's practically no one here watching. It looks like we have the whole place to ourselves."

"Everyone else is probably at the bar getting an early start," Tom said sarcastically, "they don't know what they're missing."

Tom could not take his eyes off the horizon. He stared as if every second was a day added to his life. Maria looked out as well. Occasionally she would turn to look at the expression on Tom's face. After about ten minutes she noticed Tom had a tear in his eye.

"You okay?" she said softly.

Tom stood there staring out. He started to speak a couple of times and would stop before saying anything. Finally, he said with a quiver in his voice, "they said I was a hero.......... How 'bout that? Me.......... a hero."

Maria could tell this was touching him much deeper than he would let on. "Tom," Maria said softly reaching out to put her hand on his arm. She had been married to this gentle man for long enough to know she needed to make certain she completely had his attention before continuing.

"Tom," she repeated. Tom slowly turned his head looking away from the horizon. "I've always known that about you."

Tom had a surprised look on his face. From his perspective he thought he had always kept his war experiences to himself. How could she possibly have known? His eyes asked the question, and she already knew the answer. "You've always been a hero, Tom. In everything that you do. You're always there for people when they need someone and no one else steps up. And you never back down when most people do."

"That's different," Tom said.

"Is it?" she asked, "Is it really? Most people turn and run from the hard things of life. You've always worked hard and put yourself last."

"It's really not the same thing," he replied,

"Okay then," Maria continued, "Remember the time back around what was it, fifty-three? Or maybe fifty-two. A young boy was hit by a car right outside of your shop. Remember?"

"Yeah," Tom said hesitantly, "Timmy something."

"Timmy, I think that's right," she added, "Do you remember what you did?"

Tom paused then nodded his head acknowledging he remembered. "You ran right out there, left a customer in the chair if I recall," she chuckled.

"Yeah," Tom smiled, "good thing I had two other barbers working with me at the time.

"You ran out there and went right to the boy. Remember?" Maria said with her voice up a notch. "Everyone else just stood there on the side of the road. You were the only one who rushed out to help."

"They just gawked," Tom said.

"That's right, they just gawked. But you acted," she said, "that's what heroes do."

"Well," Tom hesitated.

"Well, nothing," Maria said firmly, "Not only did you go help him, but you stayed with him, right next to him. You laid down on the pavement right next to him and looked him in the face to reassure him that help was on the way and he was going to be all right. Because he couldn't lift his head to see you, so you got on the ground to help him be brave."

Tom nodded again. "And then," Maria continued, "you rode with him in the ambulance because he was scared, and his parents hadn't been reached yet. Then you stayed with him at the hospital until his parents arrived."

"Like I said," Tom interrupted with a bit of a chuckle, "Good thing I had other barbers working. I just left that customer..................one of the other guys had to finish him up."

"Obviously, he didn't mind if I recall," Maria said, "wasn't he a regular for years after that."

"Yeah," Tom said, "he kept telling people about that day. It got to be a bit embarrassing."

"Like the captain said," Maria continued, "it's not just for you, it's for all of the people inspired by your actions."

"All right," Tom said, "But that was just the one time.

"Really?" Maria said lifting her eyebrows not ready to give up, "What about the time just after the second war when those two thugs came in and tried to get protection money."

"Oh them?" Tom said, "they were just kids."

"Kids with a knife," Maria said sharply, "and willing to use it."

"I don't know," Tom hesitated again, "one of them maybe but not Mark. Besides, it's not like they were the Black Hand or anything, they were just kids trying to act tough."

"You," Maria said tapping him on his arm with her index finger, "you stood up to them and look what happened."

"Yeah, I remember," Tom said reluctantly realizing where she was going with it. "One of them ran away and the other just stood there scared to death I was going to finish him off."

"I would be too," Maria said, "I've seen that look on your face. Probably the look you had when you were earning all those medals I would think."

Tom chuckled, "Poor kid practically wet himself."

"But then what did you do?" she asked and then paused............ "That's the hero part. You sat him down and talked with him for hours about how he could either do something with his life or waste away in prison, remember that?"

"Yeah," Tom said quietly, "he actually was a good kid."

"But if not for you and your willingness to stand up to them," she continued quite excitedly, "he would have ended up in prison. Instead............ remember.........instead?" Tom was starting to get the point by now. "Instead, you took him under your wing and got him back into school and even gave him a summer job when you couldn't afford it sweeping up the hair in the shop."

Tom realized he was out gunned. Maria continued, "Then you remember what happened... Mark went to college, and now.................. he has a respectable job............. on Wall Street."

Maria kept tapping him on the arm. Tom looked down at his arm as she continued to tap it harder and harder. She realized what she was doing and the both of them started to laugh. "Oh, sorry," she said, "but he's doing really well now, thanks to you."

"Yeah, makes more than I ever made," Tom quipped.

"That has never been what motivates you Tom," she said, "you always accepted what was before you. You worked two jobs your whole life to make sure your family was provided for."

"That's what a man is supposed to do," Tom added, "it's how I was raised. I don't know any other way."

"But how many live it?" she said firmly, "men like you are not as common as most would think. Just walk by any bar on payday and you'll see what I mean."

Tom tilted his head in a hesitant agreement. He understood what she meant and was glad she understood these kinds of things. "You've always covered for me," he said, "you didn't complain when I had to work extra."

"It's what you're made of," she added, "that's what I saw in you the day we met, remember?"

"July fourth, nineteen-twenty," he said, "how could I forget.............at the fireworks."

She paused for a moment. "Of course," she said, "fireworks. Now I understand why you never liked fireworks. I never put it together. That was only two years after the war. No wonder. I could tell you hated them that night and wondered why. I had never met someone who didn't like fireworks."

Tom slowly nodded his head, "It took me until the thirties to learn to tolerate them."

"See," she added tapping his arm again, "that's another example. We took the kids to Fourth of July fireworks every year and you never complained. I always figure you'd rather do something else.............now I get it."

"You know," Tom said slightly changing the subject, "once we get back, I really don't want anything to be different. I mean, I don't want to talk about this with everyone............... you know, the medals."

Maria looked at him somewhat confused. "Don't you want everyone to know what happened these last two weeks?" she asked.

Tom gazed back at her and shook his head, "No............not really."

"Why not?" she asked.

"It was better the other way," he answered, "I'd like it to be like it was."

"Well, the kids already know," she continued, "Tony and Dottie know. By now, they've probably told a lot of people who know us."

"I'm aware," Tom said hesitantly, "I just don't want to make a big deal of it. You know what I mean."

She paused for a moment and then realized he was indeed the same man she had always loved. "That's my husband," Maria said with the biggest smile of the night.

The sunset was just about to happen. The bottom of the sun had just touched the line of the ocean. There were no portholes to obstruct their view this time. It was wide open for them to see. Maria leaned closer to Tom and put her arm inside of his and held his hand. The breeze was gentle but consistent. She squeezed his hand again. Together they gazed forward looking directly towards where Heaven meets Earth.

About the Author

A storyteller at heart, Conrad Pelletier, is a delightful writer who helps bring words to life through his wonderful stories in a tangible way. He was a hobby writer for 15 years while working as a systems engineer in the Audio-visual business. It is now time to make these stories come to life for all readers. Conrad currently lives in Florida with his wonderful wife Lisa, and they enjoy spending their time being involved in their local church where he is able to assist in their Audio-visual needs. His books will have you looping back to read them again and again.

www.ingramcontent.com/pod-product-compliance
Lightning Source LLC
Chambersburg PA
CBHW032251020726
47495CB00001B/63

*9 7 9 8 9 9 3 1 2 4 5 1 3 *